SHE ONCE VANISHED

SHE ONCE VANISHED

ZACHARY GOLDMAN MYSTERIES
BOOK NINETEEN

P.D. WORKMAN

ISBN: 9781774687345 (KDP Paperback)
ISBN: 9781774687352 (KDP Hardcover)
ISBN: 9781774687369 (Large Print)
ISBN: 9781774687376 (Lulu Paperback)
ISBN: 9781774687383 (ePub)
ISBN: 9781774687390 (Accessible Audio)

ALSO BY P.D. WORKMAN

FIND MORE BOOKS AT PDWORKMAN.COM

MYSTERY/SUSPENSE:

Zachary Goldman Mysteries

Private Investigator

She Wore Mourning

His Hands Were Quiet

She Was Dying Anyway

He Was Walking Alone

They Thought He was Safe

He Was Not There

Her Work Was Everything

She Told a Lie

He Never Forgot

She Was At Risk

He Drowned in Memory

Their Walls Were Empty

They Came for Him

They Sought Vengeance

She Was Their Target

His Fear Was Real

She Was Out of Reach

He Was Deceived

She Once Vanished (Coming Soon)

AND MORE AT PDWORKMAN.COM

*To those trying to start their lives
again*

1

Although Zachary was a private investigator, there wasn't usually any cloak-and-dagger involved. That was for spies, not private investigators, and even the spies he knew didn't use that sort of thing. But his new client had insisted on absolute privacy, and Zachary understood why.

His client had checked in at a motel under a name that was not his own, probably paying cash. Even so, the motel manager had probably taken down his license plate number so he would have a way to trace him if he trashed the room or ran up long-distance charges. If the car was a rental, that was one more hurdle to overcome to find out who the man who had asked to meet Zachary really was.

Zachary knew who he was supposed to meet. They exchanged several emails before graduating to a phone call so that Zachary could talk to him in real-time and try to get his questions answered.

But Zachary would not take on the case until he knew for sure that the man was who he purported to be. It would not do for a private investigator to be hoodwinked by accepting a retainer from someone who was not who he said he was. A public scandal would not be good for business. People liked to think the person they were hiring knew what he was talking about.

Zachary parked down the street from the motel and walked in. If the new client had any shadows—reporters, law enforcement types, or rabid fans—Zachary did not want his car to be identified or targeted.

No one seeing Zachary would give him a second look. In fact, most would avoid taking even a first look. He was on the short side and skinny, having to work to keep his weight up to the low-healthy zone. His hair was dark and buzz-cut short, the epitome of easy to care for. He usually had several days' growth of beard, making him look scruffy and unkempt.

People did not like being approached by a scruffy, possibly homeless man. They would cross to the other side of the street to avoid him. They would not look at him very closely and if asked to describe him, they probably wouldn't be able to. That was how he kept his anonymity. Not with dark glasses, a hat, and a trench coat. Just social stigma.

He watched for anyone suspicious on the street. People hanging around who didn't belong. Sitting in their cars for more than a minute or two. Anyone who was obviously watching the motel.

Everyone seemed to be minding their own business. No one watched Zachary's progress as he made his way down the street, pausing occasionally by garbage cans as if he might be looking for bottles or discarded food.

Eventually, he had reached the motel. He looked at each car in the parking lot. No one was sitting in any of them. No one smoking and studiously looking in the other direction. Nothing of any note.

Zachary knocked on the door he had been told to, though there was no car in the parking spot assigned to that room. He'd been told to knock loudly, which seemed to contradict the client's wish to remain unnoticed, but Zachary followed his instructions anyway.

A curtain twitched two motel rooms down. Zachary stood still, watching it, waiting for the door in front of him to open. Instead, the door two rooms down opened, and a young man stuck his head out the door.

"Mr. Goldman. Come down here."

Zachary joined him. The man shut, locked, and chained the door. He closed the blinds and pulled the curtain straight so that there was no way for anyone outside to see in. The stale air inside the motel room was tinged with a faint scent of bleach and cigarette smoke.

The man turned to look at Zachary. He removed dark glasses, which had probably made him half-blind in the dim motel room.

"Well, you wanted to see me face-to-face," he told Zachary. "Are you satisfied?"

Zachary was mildly surprised that the man *was* who he said he was. That he had told the truth about moving to Vermont and wanting to hire an obscure private investigator and have him investigate a case that, as far as the police were concerned, was not a crime. The file had been closed and life went on for the rest of the world. For everyone except Dain Porter and Elysse Allan.

Zachary held his hand out to Dain Porter to shake.

"Good to meet you, Mr. Porter."

"Dain. And may I call you Zachary?"

He nodded. He always preferred that his clients call him by his first name. Mr. Goldman was just too formal.

"Have a seat."

The motel room was provisioned with a small table and two straight wooden chairs, and Dain and Zachary both sat down. Dain stood again to fill a cup of coffee from the small motel room carafe. "Can I get you one?"

"Sure." Zachary could always use another cup of coffee.

Dain brought both cups over to the table and sat down again. He looked around as if he thought he might have forgotten to do something else. Traffic hummed in the distance and there were occasional voices or the sounds of footsteps from the other motel rooms. Then he brought his gaze back to Zachary, studying him for a moment as if he weren't sure he could trust him.

"I'm not much to look at," Zachary told him. "But you wouldn't want me attracting attention."

"No," Dain agreed. He looked at the window, confirming that

3

no one could look in at them. This was what he had become. Someone who was hunted everywhere he went. He always had to be on the alert. Always looking over his shoulder, and in front of him, and on his flanks. He could never be sure that he hadn't been seen and recognized.

"I didn't see anyone suspicious," Zachary confirmed. "I don't think you were followed."

"No. Of course not. That's good."

"I appreciate you meeting with me in person. I know this is probably not what you had in mind when you first emailed me."

"No, that's true. I figured I'd just be able to email you, and you would take the case." He gave a crooked smile. "But I appreciate that you didn't. I appreciate that you respected my privacy enough to ensure that it was actually me and not someone else using my name."

"I suppose I could just have verified it was you via a video chat, but with all of the technology available these days… it wouldn't be that hard to fake a video."

Dain nodded. "I've seen some pretty convincing deepfakes. I appreciate your caution."

"Good. Now that I know it is you, and you know my rates…"

Dain pulled out his phone. He tapped the screen a few times, and then Zachary's vibrated in his pocket. He pulled it out to see the notification that the e-transfer from Dain had been auto-deposited into his account.

That was the second matter taken care of.

"Thank you. So… why don't you tell me exactly what you hope to get from this investigation?"

Dain rolled his eyes. He had, of course, already told Zachary what he wanted him to investigate. He didn't see why he should go through it all again. But Zachary wanted to be clear on exactly what Dain wanted him to find out. What he wanted Zachary to do was no small undertaking. Zachary needed to know the exact parameters and when Dain would consider the job complete. What if what Zachary discovered *wasn't* what Dain had hoped to find? What if the truth were something quite different?

"I want you to find out what happened to Elysse when she disappeared," Dain said firmly. "What *really* happened, not the story she told the world."

"What do you think happened?"

Dain looked away. "I don't know. I wish I did. But the story Elysse told when she got back didn't make any sense. It didn't fit. She would never do something like that."

Zachary nodded slowly. It was easy for one partner in a relationship to be wrong about who their partner was. It happened all the time. People who thought they knew each other found themselves incompatible. Or they discovered that their partner had been pretending and wasn't who they said they were. People kept secrets, some of them buried deep until, one day, they wouldn't stay buried any longer.

"Why don't you tell me what you know?" he told Dain. "The full story from your point of view."

"You already know my story; it was all over the media."

"The media adds or omits things, gets things wrong. I want to hear it directly from you. Everything."

2

"It's not that complicated," Dain sighed, raking a hand through his hair as frustration flickered across his face. "We had an argument. Elysse stomped off. It wasn't the first time she'd done that. I knew that she would cool down, and then she would come back, we would make up, and… happily ever after."

"Or at least until the next fight."

Dain shrugged. "No relationship is perfect. People argue. Couples have different opinions. Personalities. Elysse and I are both… passionate people. We love each other. We have arguments. Sometimes yell at each other. And then it blows over. We make up… just as passionately."

He actually blushed.

Zachary chuckled. "So that's the summary, the short story. I'd like to hear more. If you want me to be able to figure out what happened, I need all the nuances, the little things that happened along the way. More about your relationship, your plans, and how they went off the rails."

Dain rubbed a hand over his face. "That seems like a waste of time. I know what happened when we were together; I want to know what happened when she left."

"How far have you gotten on that in the last six months?"

"*I'm* not a private investigator," Dain snapped. "If I was, I wouldn't have needed to hire you. I would have just figured it all out on my own."

"Well, I *am* a private investigator and I need more information than you have given me. How did the two of you meet?"

"Why do we need to go back that far?"

"I need background. I need more details about your relationship. I need to start building a profile of Elysse that is not just based on her Instagram feed."

Dain sighed. "Remember before Instagram was a big thing? We knew each other in school. Grew up together. Small community in Oregon. She was this cute girl who attended some of the same classes as me. Back when we were both awkward and gawky, before she was a social media influencer."

"And you liked each other back then?"

"Sometimes yes and sometimes no." Dane laughed. "You know kids… boys and girls fight, don't want anything to do with each other in the younger grades. And then you start to grow up and the hormones and social pressure take over. Then suddenly, you're looking at each other in a totally different light."

"And eventually, the two of you got together."

Dain nodded. "We started going out together… getting more serious… going steady… then her Instagrammer life took over. Suddenly, she's one of the most recognizable people on the planet. She has millions of followers. Everything she posts is an instant hit. What started out as being something fun ended up taking over her life. She spent every waking minute planning her next post, getting it just right, obsessively monitoring her views."

"That must have been hard on the relationship."

"It took over the relationship. Instagram became her boyfriend. I was just this guy who showed up in some of the shots. But people loved the relationship stuff. She had to post about us some of the time if she wanted to keep her views up."

Zachary nodded encouragingly.

"I just... sometimes I wished we could go back to the way it was. To be able just to be boyfriend and girlfriend in a small town, this little rural place... like it was idyllic. Of course, it wasn't really; there are always challenges. You want to do different things and have to consider each other's feelings, and their backgrounds, and their families. But it seemed like it was a lot simpler before she became a famous influencer.'"

"I have heard that it can be very stressful."

Zachary didn't know a lot of famous social media figures, but he did know one, Brittany "the bombshell" Blake. He had misjudged her initially, thinking that she had it all made. He thought she had a life of leisure, with everyone worshiping her, and all she had to do was post a few pictures. He hadn't realized how hard she had to work to look good, stay healthy, and make all the appearances that her fans expected. He had thought she was snobby and stuck up when she was really down to earth, thoughtful, and cared about other people. Her fans had rescued them from a dire situation, and she had also helped Zachary on another case since then.

He wouldn't ever judge someone by their popularity again. Being famous did not equate with a life of leisure and luxury.

"It was incredibly stressful," Dain agreed. "You don't know how many times I thought about leaving. Just let Elysse live her life online, being the darling of social media, and live my life outside the spotlight, without all those expectations. Only... I love her. How could I leave her because she's too popular? It sounds... ridiculous and shallow."

"I'm sure that wasn't the reason you thought about leaving."

"No. Not exactly, but that was what it would look like. For the rest of my life, I would be the guy who left Elysse Allan. I would be the villain. The jerk who broke Elysse Allan's heart." He grimaced and looked away.

"And what you got instead was..."

"For five days, I was the guy who murdered Elysse Allan."

Dain swallowed hard. He stared at the window as if he could see it all playing out before him.

"Everyone was so sure of themselves. I was the one who reported her missing! I was the one looking for her, insisting that the police follow up on her disappearance. But the police and everyone else made me the prime suspect. They decided that I had murdered her and dumped her body somewhere it might never be discovered."

3

Everyone had been sure that Dain had killed his girlfriend. It had been all over social media and the TV. Everyone knew who Elysse Allan was and everyone knew that she had disappeared, had stopped posting, and had *obviously* been killed by her abusive boyfriend.

Kenzie, Zachary's girlfriend and the assistant medical examiner, had even been called out to a body dump scene that was believed to contain Elysse Allan's remains. But it had turned out the remains were not new and had not belonged to Elysse Allan. Instead, Elysse showed up several days later alive and well as a tourist in the Grand Canyon. That was what Dain wanted investigated. How had she gotten from Vermont to the Grand Canyon? Why had Elysse gone back there when she and Dain had already toured the canyon together? Why had she disappeared from view, not posting to any of her social media sites? None of these questions had been answered satisfactorily when Elysse had reappeared.

"Whose idea was it to go on vacation?" Zachary asked, trying to stay on track with the interview.

"It wasn't much of a vacation," Dain muttered.

"Because the two of you were fighting?"

"Because it was no vacation. You take a vacation to get away from your work. To relax and take a breather. Reconnect with each other. This was... a tour—a production. There was nothing unscripted. No fun, no impulsive choices. She had to keep up her posting schedule. She had locations already scouted ahead of time with her social media consultant, Kristy Echols, ready for her to drop in, set up her shots, make her posts, and move on. I couldn't stand living like that. So frenzied... no time for us. For breaks. For intimacy. It wasn't healthy."

Zachary nodded. "You had already completed most of your tour. You'd started in California, gone through the Grand Canyon, toured through a lot of historic and park sites. You had a few places to see in Vermont and then were going on to New York."

"Yeah. Then, flying back to Oregon. We were exhausted. It had been weeks, and I gotta say, I'm just not big on road trips. Not being able to sleep soundly in hotels, trying to find clean, healthy food, the frenetic pace. I was looking forward to finishing our vacation and being able to relax. Maybe we could actually enjoy some time together. Shut off the phones for a few hours and let the world do whatever they wanted without us."

"What was the fight about?"

"What they were all about. Getting off the merry-go-round. Making time for each other."

"It got heated?"

Dain looked at Zachary for a moment. He was looking for a way to smooth it over, to make it look like it had just been one of those things that happens when people step on each other's toes or are cooped up together too long. Vacations were notorious for causing bickering. People had to live too close together. It wasn't natural not to have any space or alone time.

But there had been cameras. Zachary had studied whatever footage he could get his hands on. He wouldn't believe Dain if he said that it was nothing.

"It got heated," Dain agreed. "It had been a long trip. She was being unreasonable. Maybe I was being unreasonable in demanding that she make some time for me. We both had... tempers."

"Was there abuse?"

Dain swallowed. "Verbal abuse, maybe," he admitted. "Neither of us was being particularly nice. Things had just gone on for too long. Maybe some names were called. Swearing."

"Threats?" Zachary asked.

"I would never do anything to hurt her."

"Were there threats made?"

Dain tilted his head back, staring up at the ceiling. "Not serious threats."

Zachary waited. The smell of the coffee hung in the air.

"Was there physical abuse?"

"No."

"No one was hit?"

"No."

The way Dain's face twitched, it was clearly a lie. No need for any polygraph here. Zachary took out his phone and started tapping the screen. He glanced up at Dain, who was watching him uncertainly.

"What are you doing?" Dain asked.

"I'm going to return your retainer."

"What? No! You said you would take on the case."

"I should have said that we had no agreement if you lied to me. If you want me to find out what happened, you have to tell me the truth. You're not."

"I didn't hit Elysse."

"Did she hit you?"

Zachary didn't need to ask; he already knew the answer. Dain's face was pale in the dimness of the room. He shook his head. Zachary swiped on his phone.

"No," Dain protested. "Don't return it. I'll tell you the truth."

"I can't take a case where the client won't tell me the truth."

Of course he'd had clients lie to him. It wasn't unusual. People didn't want to reveal everything. They wanted things to go a certain way and tried to manipulate the investigation. They wanted him to see them in a positive light. Or people didn't tell him the truth because they didn't know what it was.

But he had to impress upon Dain the importance of telling him the truth. It was obvious he was prone to fabrication. Zachary was only getting one side of the story. If that side was a lie, there was no point in even investigating. He wasn't going to get anywhere.

"Okay, yes," Dain said. "She hit me." He swallowed. "It was just a slap. I got over it."

"She'd hit you before."

Dain looked for a way to deny it. "She was… a physical person," he said delicately.

Growing up in foster care, Zachary had heard a lot of excuses for abuse. It wasn't the first time he'd heard something like that.

"And had you hit her?"

"No."

Zachary raised his brows and waited. Dain fiddled with his coffee cup, turning it in circles.

"I think you have both hit each other on occasion," Zachary suggested. He had seen enough of the red flags in the social media videos.

He could see Dain considering using the "we're both passionate people" line again. It was on his lips. Then he looked down, avoiding Zachary's gaze.

Shame.

"It has happened a couple of times," he admitted finally. Passive language, still avoiding taking responsibility for his actions. "It has happened," rather than, "I hit her."

"Did you hit her that day? At any time during the day, not just during that argument?"

"No."

"Not at all?"

"No."

"But she hit you."

Dain shrugged. "Like I said, a slap. It wasn't a closed fist. Just… for emphasis."

Zachary barely managed to stop himself from laughing at that. The slap was just to emphasize her point. Like an exclamation mark.

"Okay." Zachary decided to leave the discussion of the argument alone for now. He would come back to it again later in the investigation as the verifiable facts were established and the points that Dain had lied about or attempted to obscure became more obvious. "So the two of you had this argument and she took off. Where did she go? Which of you was driving on this vacation?"

"It was… kind of a caravan. We were both driving and sometimes joined by cameramen, tech guys, her publicist, or whatever."

"You and Elysse had separate cars."

Dain nodded.

That cleared up one point that had bothered Zachary from the time he had first heard the story. How had they become separated in the first place? Which one of them had driven the car and which had been stranded? He'd heard that Elysse had abandoned Dain at the gas station. But as it turned out, they had both had transportation after the fight.

"We had a lot of equipment," Dain explained. "And a lot of times, we needed to be in separate places. Elysse had me picking up supplies, or I had to talk to someone or set something up for her. She would be taking pictures or videos at another location. All so we could get to as many different places as possible in a short period of time."

Zachary could see Dain's point about their not having any intimate time together, about it not being a vacation. It sounded like it had been planned with military precision. It had not been about the two of them having a nice time together or taking time to relax. It was just a production for Elysse's fans. And it had been wearing.

"So how soon after she took off was it when you started to worry about her?"

"She missed the next three stops on her itinerary. I was concerned after the first one. It wasn't unusual for us to argue or for her to end it by walking off. But she was always at the next location. She might not wait for me, but she would be there."

"So you were worried right away, with the first one she missed."

"Yeah. There was this maple tree farm we were supposed to go to. Maple *bush*. It was summer, so it wasn't like we would see them tapping the trees, but she still wanted to see the trees and the equipment, get some pictures of the taps and the boilers and everything."

"That was the first place she didn't show up?"

"Yes. I was calling her, apologizing to the people who had been expecting her, trying to figure out where she was and why she hadn't shown up. I never thought... I knew that she was mad at me. Figured that's all it was. That she would show up again once she was settled down. I didn't think..."

"You thought she would be at the next place."

"Yeah, of course I did. She should have been. I couldn't understand why she wasn't. It didn't usually take her that long to cool off. But there had been a couple of times before... when she was upset with me or told me that she just needed space and would go off on her own for a day or two. So it wasn't beyond the bounds of belief..."

"How long was it before you reported her missing?" Zachary had a pretty good idea of the timeline, but wanted Dain to confirm it, to nail down anything that was vague or where there were multiple stories to sort out.

"That night. When she wasn't at the campsite where we had planned to meet..."

"Even though she had taken a day or two off before."

"Yeah—but she wasn't posting! That didn't make any sense. Before... she always kept posting. She wouldn't just *stop*. It was her livelihood. She knew that neglecting her socials could be disastrous. She hadn't posted a thing since she had left me after the fi— after the argument."

And that was one of the reasons that the police and everybody else had been sure that Dain had killed her. Nothing but death would stop Elysse from posting, and Dain had been the last one to see Elysse alive. The last one who had been with her before she disappeared. People had seen them together and knew that they had been fighting. As such "passionate" people, they were well-known for barn-blowing arguments.

The fight had been the last thing anyone saw of her. So of course they had assumed that Dain had been behind her disappearance. She had never reached the maple bush. Everyone *knew* that something had happened to her on the way there.

And then Elysse had reappeared five days later in the Grand Canyon. According to what she had told the reporters after her return, she had simply decided that she needed some time to herself. She and Dain had broken up before but, this time, she knew it was for good. She had apparently doubled back on their trail, going back over country they had already covered to return to the Grand Canyon. She didn't have any good explanation as to why.

Nothing she said made any sense.

So why was she lying?

To begin with, Zachary had thought that it was something Dain and Elysse had concocted together to make her even more popular. A publicity stunt. He would report her missing, and she would stretch it out for as long as she felt like she could, and then she would return, tell her story, and get twice the followers. But it appeared that she had been discovered before she had intended to be. Her eagle-eyed followers had spotted her in the Grand Canyon even though there was no reason for them to look for her there. Her face was too well-known for her to hide, even in a place as packed with tourists as the Grand Canyon.

"Did the police do anything the day she disappeared? I wouldn't think they would want to waste the resources, considering she was an adult and had only been 'missing' for a few hours."

"Yeah, they didn't want to. They said she was voluntarily missing. Most adults reappear within forty-eight hours. They are almost always close by, within a few miles from where they disappeared. They said she would just show up again." Dain shook his head. "And I was sure something terrible had happened. That if they didn't go out and find her, she would be dead. That she might already be."

"So you talked them into it?" Zachary asked, impressed.

"No." Dain shook his head.

4

Zachary cocked his head to the side.

Dain stood up and began pacing the cramped motel room. Zachary took it as his signal to stretch out his legs and get rid of a few fidgets as well. Zachary had jotted down some notes in his notebook but was already familiar with most of Dain's story. Even with how little writing he had done, his fingers were cramped. He interlaced them and stretched them out, palms forward. He had a few more swallows of the coffee, which was starting to get too cold. Dain started another pot on the in-room coffee maker.

Eventually, Dain returned to his seat.

"The police wouldn't listen to me. They thought I was just over-reacting to her being gone and she had just taken off because she felt like it." Dain paused, frowning, and then said as if the thought had occurred to him for the first time, "I guess they were right about that. If you believe her story."

"But you don't."

"No. Anyway," Dain flicked his fingers as if shaking water droplets from them. "Forget that. That was just a random thought. They wouldn't believe me. I knew they had to open a case and start searching for her. They wouldn't find her without a full-scale search, and they didn't want to do that because of the cost and the fact that they didn't believe she was really missing. Or thought that she was voluntarily missing, which is the same thing."

Zachary nodded, waiting for Dain to go on and finish his thought.

"So I went to the fans," Dain explained. "They were already all panic-posting asking what had happened to her. I told them she was missing, but the local police wouldn't do anything about it. Told them they should start calling and emailing the police department if they wanted them to act."

Zachary chuckled. "And with her millions of fans, I imagine a few responded."

"They crashed the police department's phone system. Locked up the exchange; no one else could get through in the entire area. Crashed their email server. People showed up at the police department in person, dozens of them, demanding that they take Elysse's disappearance seriously. The police were begging me to make it stop. Said to let the fans know they would open an investigation immediately and to please stop calling."

"I'll bet they just loved you."

Dain grinned, shaking his head. "I never felt so good about myself before. Never accomplished anything like that. It was incredible to see what effect posting a few words could have. So the police began the investigation. The mainstream media camped out on their doorstep. And plenty of fellow Instagrammers and other social celebs were either there or posting about it."

"Amazing. Did you sleep that night?"

"No, not a chance. I was too hyped up and worried, and there was no way the cops would have let me rest after all that. To start with, I think they were only interviewing me because they wanted to show the fans that they were doing something about the case, and maybe also retaliation against me for causing them trouble... you know, taking turns interrogating me so I wouldn't get a break. It was grueling."

"It sounds like it. And then, at some point, the police decided you were the primary suspect."

"Yeah. Probably that night. It's always the boyfriend, right? And I was the last one to see her, and I was the one making trouble for them, trying to get attention. All suspicious activities, apparently."

"Did they find anything out the first day? The police didn't release anything to the media to begin with."

"They didn't tell me much about what they were doing, but they were looking for her car the first day. Calling her phone. Trying to track its location. But the GPS was disabled. They don't have license plate scanners everywhere, especially in a place like Vermont. It's not like New York City."

Dain rubbed his face, fatigued. Maybe tired from the strain of recounting the emotional experience. Maybe remembering how exhausted he had been that first night when they grilled him all through the night.

"They were looking in New York," Dain went on. "That's where we were supposed to go to finish our trip, and everybody kind of figured that if she was okay, she would be moving ahead with that plan. Even if she wasn't posting her trip anymore, she would still go on to New York because that was where we had booked our trip home from. Police were all over the place waiting to see if she checked in at the airport in New York. And keeping the crowds down, because everybody figured that was where she would go. There were thousands of fans there to catch sight of her, to be the first ones to say that yes, she was okay, and had shown up for her flight. Everything would go back to normal again."

"But she didn't continue to go east. Why do you think she doubled back? Why head back to the Grand Canyon? You'd already been there, and it would have been much faster to go to New York and fly home, even if she didn't catch the flight she had already booked."

Dain shook his head. "It doesn't make any sense. I've looked at it every way possible. But it just doesn't fit. We already went through the Grand Canyon and she didn't even like it very much. She got some nice pictures, and the fans loved them, but Elysse didn't like it. It was hot and dry, and it's not a venue where you can just pop in and out. The trail rides and everything take a lot of time. Sitting on a mule for hours in the sun… she wasn't really impressed with it."

"She said on her TV appearance that she'd wanted to see more than she did when she was with you. That you wanted to look at different things."

Dain shook his head irritably. "She made all the plans. There was no discussion about where I wanted to go or how I wanted to do things. It was *her* itinerary. I didn't take her to a bunch of places she didn't want to go in the Grand Canyon."

"So she'd already seen everything she wanted to there."

"I don't know. Maybe Elysse wanted to go on a helicopter tour or a picnic or something she read about in the brochures while we were there. But I can't believe she really wanted to go back there. Unless…" He trailed off.

Zachary got up and refilled his coffee cup and refreshed Dain's as well. He let the silence work on Dain.

"Unless she wanted to hide," Dain said. "That's the only thing I can think of. No one would be looking for her because we'd already been there. And when we went through together, they talked about the number of people who get lost in the Grand Canyon. Some who never turned up again. But thousands disappear and then are found again. If she really wanted to stay out of sight… well, it would be one of the most likely places to try. She only resurfaced because a fan saw her and wouldn't let it go."

If that hadn't happened, how long would it have been before Elysse had reappeared?

5

Zachary thought about his closing conversation with Dain as he drove back home, taking a circuitous route to watch for any tails.

"So you don't believe the story Elysse gave the media on her return. What do you think really happened?"

Dain shook his head. "I've thought about it, come up with all kinds of scenarios, but I don't know if any of them make sense. I haven't come up with anything that fits... I just know it didn't happen the way that she said. She wouldn't just leave and never come back. That's not in Elysse's makeup. I've known her since we were kids, and I *know*."

"You don't think she just needed a few days to get her head on straight? Like she had done before?"

"No. Elysse had never cut off all communication. She might not want to talk to me if we'd had a fight, but she would still talk to her family and friends and post on social media. I knew something was wrong."

"You think something happened to her, but she won't discuss it."

Dain shook his head, lips pressed together tightly. "I just don't know. Since she came back... she's not the same person."

"In what way?"

"It's hard to put into words. I mean, she's not talking to me, so I only know what I can get from mutual acquaintances. Her family or friends who will talk to me. They say she is just trying to stay out of public scrutiny. But I know that isn't all that is going on. Something is really wrong. I wouldn't hire a private investigator just out of ego because she won't talk to me anymore or to prove that I was right to report her missing in the first place. I really think something happened to her... and the story isn't over."

His words echoed around Zachary's head. *Something happened to her... and the story isn't over.*

Could Dain be right? When Elysse had returned, everyone thought that was the end of it. Elysse would go back to her regular activities. Everything was resolved and back to normal. But what if it wasn't?

Zachary checked the time as he approached the house. The streetlights cast long shadows across the pavement. He hadn't been sure how long he would be in the interview with Dain, so he had warned Kenzie that he might not be home when she returned from the medical examiner's office. Unless she had ended up with a last-minute autopsy that had kept her at the office, she had probably beaten him home. But she had enough control over her schedule that she normally wouldn't start one that late.

He drove up in front of the house and saw that there were more lights on than he had left turned on. So Kenzie was home. Zachary looked up and down the street before getting out of the car, alert for anyone who might be watching from another vehicle. Anyone who was there that shouldn't be.

He was usually careful. But taking on the Elysse Allan case, he knew he had to be more cautious than ever. She had millions of fans. There was no way to keep track of them or know if people around him, even those he knew well, were followers. Would they object to him taking on the case? Would it be seen as an attack on Elysse? Not taking her at her word?

Or would they believe that he was doing something to help her? That maybe he could bring the old Elysse back again?

He was anxious about having taken Dain's case. What if it led to more violence? He didn't want to make a target of himself or those close to him.

There didn't seem to be anyone suspicious on the street, so Zachary eventually got out of the car, carefully locked it, armed the security system, and checked everything again.

He looked at the house and saw Kenzie in the doorway watching him. He tore his gaze from the car and walked up the sidewalk toward her.

"Everything is fine," he assured her.

Kenzie accepted a brief hug and kiss and didn't say anything to him about his being paranoid. Most of the cuts and gouges he had sustained from a package bomb left on his doorstep were healed now, but there were still a few marks on his face, neck, and arms. They had not been caused by an overactive imagination.

They stepped inside and Zachary re-armed the security system from the keypad at the door.

"How was your day?" Zachary asked, keeping his tone light.

"Pretty good. Things have slowed down, and we are getting caught up. Nothing new today."

"Good." He didn't imagine Kenzie would like it if they stopped getting bodies to process and there was nothing to do, but slowing down after the post-Christmas and New Year's Eve rush was good.

Kenzie had apparently just finished preparing dinner. The comforting aroma of chicken wafted through the air, mingling with toasted bread. She motioned to the table, which she had already set. Usually, that was Zachary's job. But she hadn't known when he would be home and had done it herself. "Good timing," Kenzie observed. "I'm glad you got home when you did."

"Is this what it would be like every day if I worked an office job?" Zachary teased. "I kind of like the service."

"Definitely not. You would still have to help."

"Oh, well. That's another dream crushed."

They both chuckled at this. Zachary would never have survived an office job. Having to be in an office or cubicle from nine to five every day sounded like torture. He needed the freedom to move around, to keep his own schedule and work whatever time of day he liked, to have interesting puzzles to solve, and to work with a variety of people. Working in an office environment would have him climbing the walls within days.

"So, did you take it on?" Kenzie asked as she sat down and started dishing up green salad onto her plate. "The Elysse Allan case?"

Zachary let out a long, slow breath. He knew she probably wouldn't like it. He smiled and kept his voice casual and calm, trying to give her the impression that it would be an easy, routine investigation. "Yes. It shouldn't take too long, I don't think, and it will be profitable." He had charged Dain his highest rate and gotten a sizable retainer. "It's an interesting case."

"I'll give you that," Kenzie agreed. "People are wondering what actually happened to Elysse while she was missing."

"I'm thinking alien abduction."

Zachary said it with a straight face and no hint of humor in his voice. He thought he had done an outstanding job at sounding serious.

Kenzie looked at him, startled, and shook her head. "You don't really think that." Her tone indicated that she was ninety percent sure that he was joking. Maybe eighty percent. Sure, but not sure. He could be experiencing new symptoms from his medications. Hallucinations. An extension of his security compulsions. A psychotic break.

He grinned at her. "No, I'm just pulling your leg."

"Thank goodness for that." Kenzie blew out her breath.

"Everyone knows that the high concentration of quartz crystals in the Grand Canyon's rocks creates an energy field that repels UFOs."

Kenzie laughed, buttering a piece of crusty bread. "You are the weirdest guy sometimes."

"I aim to please."

"I'm just not sure about you taking on the Elysse Allan case. With her being such a prominent figure in social media... trying to disprove her story is asking for trouble, isn't it?"

"The whole point is to help Elysse, not to vilify her on social media. I'm sure it won't be a problem."

He knew he was overstating his position. He was also concerned about the potential blowback but thought it would be manageable.

"Besides, no one will know I'm looking into it. I will keep my inquiries discreet. It isn't like Elysse's millions of fans are going to know I'm looking into it."

"You have to talk to people. It will get out."

"No one will be interested in some small-town private eye in Vermont investigating what really happened to Elysse Allan. I'll be right up there with the UFO conspiracy kooks." He smiled again, though it felt as unnatural as if he were wearing a mask. "No one is going to think anything of it. Just another Elysse Allan fan trying to get the scoop. I'm sure people are always asking questions, wanting the inside story."

"Then how are you going to make any inroads?"

"I have charm." This time, the smile came more naturally.

Kenzie shook her head. "I don't know how far that will get you."

"It got me *here*, didn't it?"

Kenzie nodded slowly. "True… although part of it was just, you know, you needing a place to sleep after a psychotic killer kicked your door in."

"The killer used a bump key. It was the cops who kicked the door in."

"Right. I wonder who you paid off to do that."

Zachary laughed. "It always pays for a PI to have friends in the police force."

6

The next day was Saturday, which was normally a short day for Kenzie, so Zachary tried to arrange his schedule so that he would be able to get something constructive done on his case in the morning and then spend time with Kenzie on whatever she wanted to do in the afternoon. Then, they planned a visit to the home of Lorne Peterson and Patrick Parker on Sunday.

Lorne was an old foster father of Zachary's. Though he had only lived in the Peterson home for a few weeks, Lorne had given Zachary the photography bug. They had kept in touch over the years, often poring over photographs each of them had taken, enjoying Pat's culinary accomplishments, and developing a friendship—a family relationship—stronger than any other in Zachary's life. His chosen family.

Zachary decided to begin his investigation with the present and move back in time. Where was Elysse now, and what was she doing? Despite what Dain had said about Elysse having changed, he suspected she would be doing exactly what she had before the period during which she had been missing. He had a feeling that maybe it was all a PR stunt. She had wanted more visibility, and she had certainly gotten it. She had been at the center of the media storm for five days. People had been sure she was dead, and there were memorial posts and lamentations everywhere.

Dain was probably lucky he hadn't been killed by a mob over what they thought he had done. Social media fans could be bloodthirsty and easily developed tunnel vision.

But when he searched for Elysse Allan's social media posts, he was surprised to find nothing recent. Other people had posted comments on her various accounts, some of them angry and some of them pleading for her to post an update, but she had posted nothing since she had disappeared from Vermont.

Nothing during the time she had been missing. Nothing when she had reappeared in the Grand Canyon and made her TV appearance, and nothing in the months since then.

What was she doing, then? What happened to a social media influencer when she stopped posting?

He widened his searches to look at other social media accounts and blog platforms, and then just some general web searches to see what she was doing and what people were saying about her. The furnace hummed quietly and the TV he had left on to prevent the house from becoming too quiet droned on in the background.

Elysse didn't appear to be posting anywhere. Not on any of her old social media platforms. No new accounts he could find. There were some spoof accounts, but it became clear on opening them that they were not the real Elysse Allan, but someone simply posting in her name. All the verified, authentic accounts were silent.

Posts about Elysse were varied and wide-ranging. People who claimed to know her. People with news about her, though it was unclear what was true and what was just made up. Most of it, Zachary expected, was simply made up. Anyone with actual knowledge would have posted backup. Pictures, evidence, names, something to show they knew what they were talking about.

Where was she now? There was plenty of speculation. There were those who, despite what Zachary had said about the quartz crystal in the Grand Canyon, declared that she had, in fact, been abducted by aliens. Some believed that the Elysse who had spoken to the media was an alien or pod person herself, or that her memory had been wiped or she had been programmed to give the statement she had to the media.

But she hadn't made any public appearances since the press release immediately after she was discovered.

There were suggestions that she was living with her parents again. Or that she was living with Dain or another boyfriend. The luxury home she had lived in prior to the fiasco had apparently been sold.

Zachary remembered family members who had spoken to the media while she had been missing. Most of them, he suspected, had not been in touch with Elysse for some time. Even those whom she was supposedly close to didn't seem to be as worried about her being missing as getting their time in the spotlight. They wiped their eyes and speculated with ghoulish glee about what might have happened to her.

Poor Elysse. Poor, misguided, out-of-her-element, too-big-for-her-britches Elysse. It was truly tragic. But she should have known when she got involved with *that* element that things would not end well.

Zachary wasn't sure whether *that element* meant Dain or the Instagrammers or if there had been something truly shady going on. Maybe her family had been referring to drugs, exotic dancing, or some other slander carefully trimmed from the published footage to keep the network from being sued.

Zachary did some general searches and started assembling a background portfolio for Elysse. He should have gotten some of this information from Dain, but perhaps it was better that he dug it out and consulted other sources and didn't rely on Dain too much anyway. He was young and unreliable and had already shown that he would lie if confronted with something he would rather not reveal.

Zachary had assumed by all the sun-kissed pictures of Elysse, Dain, or Elysse and Dain together that they had come from California. Instead, they were apparently from Oregon, which didn't get nearly the same number of hours of sunshine as the California coast.

And not just Oregon, but a small town near Grand Rapids that showed up on a Google search as being one of the poorest zip codes in the state. Elysse had grown up in poverty. The rise to being one of the most famous social media influencers in the country would have been twice the shock. How would someone who had grown up in that kind of squalor feel when sudden success had lifted her out of obscurity?

Had it been too much for her? Had the money and fame been too much for her to handle? Even without the stresses of a "passionate" relationship, she had been turned into something that must have been totally foreign to her.

Was that what she had been running away from six months ago?

And what she was running away from now?

7

Even though Kenzie's house had become Zachary's permanent residence, visiting the Petersons always felt like going home. Zachary had never lived with the two of them. He had lived with Mr. Peterson and his former wife for only a few weeks around his eleventh birthday. He had kept returning there for visits or to develop his latest pictures in Mr. Peterson's darkroom until Lorne and Lilith had eventually separated and divorced. It had not been an amicable breakup. Mrs. Peterson's discovery of her husband's preferences had apparently been quite a shock.

After the breakup, Mr. Peterson had lived on his own for some time before he and Pat had gotten a place of their own. The "roommates" had kept their relationship low-key and even now were not demonstrative in public. They had been together more than twenty years and Pat had become a fixture in Zachary's life as well; a broad-shouldered, nurturing man who seemed to succeed at whatever new projects he tackled.

Zachary stepped into the warm, fragrant house, a smile coming to his face, genuinely happy to be there. He and Kenzie hugged Lorne and sat down in the living room to chat while Pat put the finishing touches on something cheesy and comforting in the oven.

Zachary's nose twitched like a rabbit's at the smell of garlic and toasting bread. He drank in the scent and sighed.

"So what are you working on?" Lorne asked Zachary, switching from his shallow discussion with Kenzie about her work in the medical examiner's office to Zachary. He didn't have the same appreciation for autopsy talk as Zachary.

"You remember Elysse Allan?" Zachary asked, "The young woman who disappeared for a week and showed up later in the Grand Canyon?"

"Sure, of course," Mr. Peterson nodded. His round face was wreathed in smiles, fringed with short, white hair. Somehow, he kept getting older when Zachary wasn't looking. "What about her?" His face grew serious. "She hasn't been hurt, has she?"

"No. No, nothing like that. But Elysse's boyfriend—her ex-boyfriend—doesn't believe her story about what happened while she was missing, and he wants me to see what I can find out about what really happened to her."

"He doesn't believe what, exactly?"

"He doesn't believe she just decided to go back to the Grand Canyon. Which, you must admit, was a pretty bizarre thing to do. He thinks something else was going on, and he wants to know what that was."

"Something else like what?"

"He hasn't put it into so many words, But I think he suspects that she was coerced into doing what she did. Someone forced her or maybe even kidnapped her."

"What evidence does he have of that?" Kenzie demanded, her voice rising as if outraged by the thought.

Zachary hesitated, considering her reaction. Was Kenzie angry because a woman's story had been deemed untrustworthy by a man? Or was it the idea of an abduction? Kenzie was struggling with the trauma caused by her own abduction a year earlier. Zachary knew it colored the way she thought about other crimes, the way she had felt about Christmas this year, and the way she interacted with her father and even Zachary.

"I think it is more Dain's gut feeling than anything concrete," he told Kenzie slowly, feeling his way through the explanation. "I think that the way she changed following her disappearance worries him and has him convinced that it was not as simple as her just driving back to the Grand Canyon for some sightseeing. Sightseeing at a venue they had been to just a week or two before."

"Well, that's strange behavior, but it isn't proof that she was lying about what happened to her."

"No," Zachary agreed. "Dain doesn't have proof of anything. That's why he asked me if I would investigate it. He is looking for some evidence of what happened to her. He's worried about her."

"Then he should focus on his relationship with her, rather than assuming she is lying and hiring someone else to prove it."

Zachary nodded slightly. "Of course. But he can't work on his relationship with her. She broke up with him before disappearing. She won't answer phone calls, texts, or messages. She's completely cut him off."

Kenzie nodded knowingly. "And you don't wonder what he might have done to deserve that kind of treatment? Why is she treating him like a stalker? Why is he acting like one?"

Zachary shifted uncomfortably. "I can't answer any of those questions yet. I need to talk to Elysse. If she tells me that he's stalking her and harassing her—that will change the way I deal with this case."

"How you'll deal with it?" Kenzie echoed, "You wouldn't just drop it?"

"I don't know yet. Maybe getting Dain the information he is looking for will ease his anxiety, and he will back off. Maybe he needs professional help. I don't know."

"It would be one thing if she was the one who hired you to find out what happened to her," Kenzie said, "but the boyfriend hiring you? The *ex*-boyfriend? I just don't trust him. He should leave her alone. It doesn't have anything to do with him."

"It has everything to do with him," Zachary countered. "It affected him too. People thought that he had killed her. He was branded a murderer, and the people who don't believe she is really alive *still* think that. He can't just go about his business as usual. He is recognizable. People are following him, attacking him, harassing him. Her story doesn't clear him from wrongdoing. The people who think this was all just a PR stunt believe he was in on it. They think he whipped the fans into a frenzy just to get a good media storm. A lot of people still don't believe that he is innocent."

Kenzie sat back, thinking about that.

"Well, it sounds like he's in a difficult situation," Mr. Peterson offered.

"Yeah, he is. He's a pariah now because of something that wasn't his fault. He's trying to rebuild his life, but… it's difficult. Nearly impossible. Wherever he goes, people are going to recognize him. And think that he's some kind of showman or media hog. He can't go back to the house they lived in together in Oregon. He's bought a house in Vermont, isolated so he won't run into fans."

"If he hired you because of that, because he wanted to clear his name and get back on his feet again, I could understand that," Kenzie said slowly. "I couldn't fault him for that. But that isn't what he's doing. He's hiring you because of her, because he wants to… be her hero or get back together with her. And what happened is really none of his business. Or yours."

Kenzie had used this line before. That something he was investigating was none of his business. Zachary didn't want to argue with her in front of the Petersons, but he didn't like being called out as someone who just stuck his nose into other people's business for the heck of it.

"I was hired to do this, so it is my business." He scratched his chin and wondered whether he had remembered to shave before leaving the house that morning. "I try not to take cases that are… unethical in any way. Taking pictures of adulterous partners meeting someone else, but no skin, and not just stalking random women. Helping corporations with security leaks, but not helping them to get private employee information or to conduct industrial espionage. Catching fraudulent insurance claimants, but not helping people fool their insurance companies."

"And what is your justification for finding out whether Elysse told the truth? How does that do anything but blacken her name?

She didn't do anything illegal. Stalking her just because her ex thinks she is lying and wants to catch her…"

"I'm not stalking her. Investigating, interviewing, and surveilling are not stalking."

Kenzie shrugged, indicating she didn't think there was much difference.

"Everyone ready for dinner?" Pat asked, coming out of the kitchen with a towel draped over his shoulder. He had probably heard the discussion and was hoping to break it up before things got too heated. Zachary was happy to drop the discussion. He suspected Kenzie's objection had more to do with her level of anxiety being high due to the memory of her own abduction than with Zachary actually doing anything unethical, harmful, or dangerous.

"It smells heavenly," Kenzie told Pat with a genuine smile. "I don't know how much longer I can sit here smelling it and not eating. My stomach is going to digest itself."

"Well, that doesn't sound very pleasant," Pat told her with a laugh. "Why don't we do something about that? Come on over to the table. Everyone. I'll bring in the soup to start."

Zachary hoped the garlic bread would be brought out with the soup. In fact, he didn't care about the soup, as long as he got the garlic bread.

8

During the meal, Lorne's phone vibrated, prompting him to take it out to check the screen. Then he slid it back into his pocket, making apologetic noises.

"Sorry about that. I'm determined not to let the things run our lives, but it seems like there is no way to keep up in the modern world without one, and the more you use it, the more attention it demands."

Kenzie and Zachary nodded. Zachary was used to the rule about no phones at the dinner table, a prohibition that he and Kenzie tried to follow as well, despite demanding jobs that could result in either being called away during a meal.

"You can't even seem to be able to do things like setting up a doctor's appointment without one," Kenzie agreed. "It's gotten to the point where anyone without a phone is considered an old fogy or anti-technology. Everyone assumes you will have one in your pocket and are open to being contacted any time, night or day."

The others nodded ruefully.

"It's a tool," Mr. Peterson said, "but sometimes it feels like they are running us rather than the other way around. And those social influencers… I'm just learning about this; I guess it has been a big thing for a while, and I never knew about it. People who are paid to talk about brand names or who have millions of views when they post a picture of their lunch. I guess the rock stars of yesterday are now the TikTok or Instagram influencers. Each generation has its heroes."

Kenzie looked at Zachary, but he didn't say anything about Elysse, so she left it alone.

"Can you imagine trying to raise kids now?" Pat asked Lorne. "When you had foster kids, it was just a matter of keeping them from monopolizing the landline or wanting to watch TV at bedtime. Now... they all have their own phones, which double as entertainment boxes. You can't separate them; they're practically surgically attached."

"A lot of foster kids won't have them," Mr. Peterson said, dabbing his mouth with a satiny cloth napkin. "Parents can't afford them, kids are cycling in and out of the home, and who will pay for or keep track of their phone plans? Some will buy their own if they have after-school jobs, or social workers might give them a prepaid phone to keep in touch, but many foster kids won't have them, especially if they are moved around a lot."

There were a lot of things that Zachary had lacked as a foster child, constantly being moved from one home to another. He could just imagine how isolating it would be if all the kids at school had phones of their own and he did not. It had been hard enough making friends when he got moved so often. Not being a part of their communication channels would make it impossible. Those who didn't have phones of their own would be permanent outsiders.

"Glad I didn't have that to deal with on top of everything else."

They had an enjoyable evening, despite any anxiety or opinions about Zachary's ethics in accepting Dain's money to try to find out what had really happened to Elysse when she had disappeared.

Zachary spent some one-on-one time with Mr. Peterson, showing him his new digital camera with all its fancy new features, including the ability to share or post photos using a Wi-Fi connection with his phone.

After Lorne and Pat retired to bed, Kenzie and Zachary sat up for a while using their phones or computers until Kenzie started yawning, and they both agreed it was time to try to get some sleep. Cuddling Kenzie in his arms, Zachary nuzzled her curly hair, inhaling the scent of lavender shampoo, sweat, and everything else that combined to form a scent that was uniquely Kenzie in his mind.

"How are you doing?" he asked softly, in case she were already falling asleep. "Is everything okay?"

Kenzie shifted, snuggling more deeply into his embrace, and sighed, letting out a long breath.

"I'm sorry for being so grumpy lately. I know it must seem like I can't even have a civil conversation these days."

"No," Zachary assured her. "That's fine. You're stressed, that's all. I just want to know if *you're* okay."

"I'm just fine. Really. I'll get over whatever this is. Get some more sleep or exercise and it will all smooth out... I'll be back to the usual chill and fun Kenzie..."

"Dr. Boyle was going to give you some recommendations for therapists. Did you ever follow up with any of them?"

"No. I still have them. I just... don't feel like therapy is the solution to my mood. It isn't like I don't understand why I feel the way I do. It's just not something that talking about is going to change."

"It can still help just to get it out in the open, even if there isn't anything you can do to change anything. Dr. B can suggest a psychiatrist who could prescribe meds for you if there is something that will help you. A mild antidepressant or antianxiety prescription. Or sleep aid if you think you're still not getting enough sleep."

"Look who's talking," Kenzie mumbled.

She was the one who always told Zachary to take his prescribed meds or sleep aid, and he had a hard time accepting when he needed to. She had preached the miracles of modern medicine, but now that she might need to take something, she was fighting it.

"Taking a prescription doesn't mean you'll be on it for the rest of your life," he reminded her. "Some people only need to take them for a little while to get through a rough patch. There's nothing wrong with needing to take a prescription."

He kissed the top of her head. She was the one who had told him all those things. She probably didn't appreciate having them preached back at her.

Kenzie snorted, signaling that she did, in fact, recognize her own words.

"Here I thought you were not listening," she told him.

"I always listen. Well, if I'm not distracted by something else. I just don't always... follow directions well."

"No. I can see Joss's point when she complains that you go to her for advice, listen to what she has to say, then completely disregard it and do whatever you want."

"Well, I..."

He knew it was true. He caught himself doing it sometimes, even when Joss didn't point it out. He would go to other people for advice or feedback and then decide based on his instincts together with what he had learned, but that frequently meant going off on his own path rather than following any of the suggestions that had been given to him. Joss, his oldest sister, was the one most likely to call him out on it, while everyone else tried to be tactful and patient and not point out this flaw.

"I know..." Kenzie said, "You gotta be you."

"Well, yeah. I couldn't be anyone else," Zachary agreed.

"I would have thought that you would have learned how to follow instructions in foster care," Kenzie murmured. "Didn't your families have strict rules and lines of authority? And the institutions you lived at must have been pretty strict."

"I told you from the start that I was incorrigible," Zachary reminded her. Though he said it jokingly, the word his mother had branded him with still hurt. *You are incorrigible. You will never do what you're told. You will never change.* "I think having different rules at different homes just encouraged me to make up my own and not worry about what anyone else said. There obviously wasn't just one way to do things. And if I learned one system, I would just have to unlearn it at the next place I went to."

"Mmm-hmm."

She sounded close to sleep. Zachary didn't think he'd be able to carry on the conversation much longer.

"What about you?" he asked. "Did you always follow Lisa's and Walter's rules?"

He didn't think that her parents had been big disciplinarians. They hadn't been abusive. But Kenzie and her late sister Amanda had probably had a long list of rules they were expected to follow. Walter and Lisa were loving parents, but they were also very aware of society's expectations of them and the rules that the people of their class had to follow.

"I was a pretty good kid," Kenzie admitted. "Tried to follow all the rules. I helped take care of Amanda when she was sick and didn't hit my rebellious phase until later in life because of that."

It had been during her twenties as she tried to find her place in her socialite mother's world, not in her teens when they had all been consumed with keeping Amanda healthy. After Amanda's death, Kenzie had really rebelled against her father—who she partly blamed for Amanda's death—and had gone to medical school and become a pathologist. Working with dead bodies was not exactly considered proper in Lisa Cole Kirsch's social circles.

"How is Walter doing?"

"Mmm..." Kenzie didn't rouse to put her thoughts into a coherent explanation, shaking her head slightly and again trying to nestle deeper into Zachary's arms, when she was already cuddled as close as she could go.

Walter was doing fine, Zachary was sure. His recent retirement from a career as a lobbyist was widely purported to be due to a stroke. But Kenzie and Zachary knew his health was just fine. The charade would hopefully keep the thugs who had been pressuring him to push particular bills forward to leave him alone. If he physically couldn't do his job, no amount of threatening would make him. They would need to find another lobbyist they could get some leverage on and forget about Walter Kirsch.

But the fact that Walter was actually healthy meant that he still had the energy to do the job he loved but couldn't. He was probably bored out of his mind and driving Lisa up the walls. Because he was supposed to be sick, Lisa couldn't even suggest that he do more work for the family foundation or make appearances at fundraisers. He couldn't go out golfing with his buddies.

Maybe he could take up gardening or another hobby he could do at home. Cooking, maybe, or one of Pat's other pursuits.

"Are we going to visit them soon?" Zachary asked.

Kenzie snored lightly.

9

Long after Kenzie fell asleep, Zachary lay with her in his arms, his brain repeating the conversations of the evening over and over again, looking for ways he could have handled things better.

He knew that Kenzie was having problems coping with the memories of her abduction. Speculating about the possibility that Elysse had been abducted during the missing time had been a mistake. Zachary was only looking for a scenario that would account for Dain's worries about Elysse and her abrupt disappearance. Elysse had said that she just decided to go off on her own and, until he had evidence to the contrary, that was the story he was going with.

He shouldn't have disagreed with Kenzie in front of the Petersons. Even if he didn't agree with her opinion, he didn't want to embarrass her in front of their friends. That would only make her dig in her heels more. He could have handled things better.

He shifted again, looking for a more comfortable position. Though he had been comfy and cozy when they had settled in, his body wanted to move around now. His right arm had fallen asleep while he held Kenzie. His brain wouldn't stop its constantly repeating soundtrack, reviewing the case and his conversations with Kenzie on an endless loop.

He considered getting up. If he got out of bed, walked around a bit, found something to do that distracted him from the dual ruts his brain kept running along, and then stretched out on the couch for a few minutes, he might be able to fall asleep for a couple of hours.

Kenzie started to move around in her sleep. She pushed him away, and he separated from her, getting some relief from having remained in the same position for too long. He rolled his shoulders and shifted his position, closing his eyes and seeking the relief of unconsciousness.

"No."

Kenzie flailed, hitting Zachary a couple of times with weak, unaimed blows.

"Shh," Zachary whispered. "It's okay. Everything is okay."

He reached out and put his hand on her upper arm, resting it lightly. Letting her know he was there and trying to comfort her without waking her up.

Kenzie sniffled and struggled with her nightmare, making incoherent noises. He wondered whether she was reliving the kidnapping. Had his discussion of what might have happened to Elysse triggered a nightmare repetition of that night? He could kick himself for his thoughtlessness.

"Kenzie. Kenzie, it's okay. Everything is going to be all right," he assured her. "You're safe. You're with me. It's just a dream."

"No, no…"

"Kenzie." He stroked her hair. He didn't want to grab her arm or shoulder or shake her, moves that might be perceived as being aggressive and feed into the nightmare instead of helping her to escape it. "Kenzie, wake up now. It's just a dream."

She growled and flailed some more, and then her breathing changed and she stopped struggling blindly.

"It's okay," he whispered again. "You just had a dream."

She breathed shakily in and out, trying to draw out her breaths and calm her body's panic reaction. "A dream," she echoed.

"Yeah. It's over now. Do you want me to hold you?"

"No." She turned over, facing away from him, and curled up into herself. "Sorry I woke you up."

"It's okay." He rubbed her back, but she stiffened and pulled away from him. "Okay," Zachary said softly. He withdrew his hand and did not touch her. She needed space. That suited him fine; he was stiff from staying in the same position to hold her anyway. He could use some space, too.

He lay for a long time listening to her, analyzing every movement and breath until he was sure she was asleep again.

Zachary awoke in the morning to movement in the kitchen. It took him a few minutes to realize he was not at home and was not in the Petersons' guest room, but on their couch. He opened his eyes and stretched, squinting toward the kitchen. He couldn't see into the kitchen from the couch, but Pat stepped out a minute later as he went through his morning routine and saw that Zachary was awake.

"Rough night?" he asked sympathetically.

"A bit," Zachary admitted. "Sorry to take over your living room."

Pat just smiled. "Our home is your home, you know that. Make yourself comfortable."

Zachary sat up and rubbed his eyes. He stayed in that position for a few minutes, waiting for his body to wake up.

"How are you doing?" Pat asked. "Recovering from the explosion, I mean. It looks like everything is healing up…"

The injuries Zachary had received from the package bomb were fairly minor. Superficial injuries from the shrapnel. The black powder had been old or damp and had not caused the level of damage that had been intended. Zachary's minor concussion had abated quickly, so he was almost back to normal.

Other than his compulsive brain now focusing on the danger of packages. Any packages. Mail that arrived in the community mailbox or envelopes left in the mailbox attached to the house. Online deliveries. Food deliveries. He checked and rechecked the front step to ensure nothing had been left there. And near the front step, in case something had been left just out of sight.

Sometimes, he even checked the neighbors' porches or just sat and watched a courier make his way down the street, leaving deliveries at several houses along the way.

The idea of buying an electronic explosives sniffer had started out as a joke, but he had quickly broken down and purchased one so that he could check packages when they arrived. Just to be sure. He was sure no one would ever send him a letter bomb again, but...

"Yeah, I'm good," he told Pat, who was still waiting for an answer. "No lasting effects."

"Good. You had us all pretty scared."

"You guys were such a help. I appreciated everything you did for Kenzie and me. You went above and beyond."

They had repaired and repainted the kitchen so that there was no trace of the blood, shrapnel, or scorch marks that had been left there after the bomb had exploded. They had fed and cared for Zachary and Kenzie for a couple of days and left them with a fridge and freezer filled with premade meals so they didn't have to do anything but warm them up as they recovered from the experience.

While Kenzie hadn't been hurt, she had seen Zachary bloody and in the middle of a flashback to the fire that had destroyed his childhood home, screaming and thrashing so much that the firefighters thought he was having a seizure. Her house had been damaged, and her peaceful, safe space had invaded. It had been just as traumatic for her as for Zachary.

"We're family. We take care of each other," Pat assured him.

10

The medical examiner's office was in the basement below the police station, so Zachary and Kenzie went in together. They didn't use Kenzie's little red sports convertible when the weather and roads were bad, so it stayed snugly tucked in the garage while Zachary drove his white compact. He parked in Kenzie's reserved spot in the parking garage and they parted at the elevator, Kenzie going down to the morgue and Zachary to the public information desk of the police station.

He didn't know the young officer acting as officer of the day at the desk, so he introduced himself and explained he was there to see Detective Edwards, who was expecting him.

"Have a seat, sir, and I'll let him know you're here."

Zachary paced across the reception area a couple of times and then sat down in one of the uncomfortable plastic chairs. The cold weather was making his joints and tailbone hurt.

Edwards was not long. He was a broad-shouldered, black-haired cop who looked like he'd been on the job for a good number of years. He had probably earned out his pension or was close to being able to do so. But he had kept up his physical condition and not gone to seed. Maybe a bit of extra weight around the waist, but it didn't strain against his shirt.

"Mr. Goldman?" he asked briskly.

"Yes," Zachary stood up. "Thank you for agreeing to see me."

Edwards escorted him back to his office, which it appeared he shared with at least one other person, stopping along the way for cups of coffee. Edwards gave Zachary a speculative look as they sat down. Zachary rubbed his chin, unsure of the reason for the scrutiny. The stubble hid the worst of the damage from the letter bomb, but maybe Edwards thought he should have cleaned himself up better before showing up at the police station for an interview.

"You're Dr. Kirsch's significant other?" Edwards responded to Zachary's questioning look.

"Oh, yeah. I just dropped her off. Convenient that we were both going to the same building."

"She's good at what she does. An asset to our team. And you can tell she cares about her work."

Zachary smiled. His cheeks warmed and he wasn't sure why he was blushing when the praise was for Kenzie rather than him. "She loves her work," he told Edwards. "She loves being able to make a difference in homicide cases, helping to bring the victims some justice."

"I worked with her on the Sharon Briggs case, which started out as the Elysse Allan case, as you know."

The remains that had been discovered during the search for Elysse Allan and had initially been assumed to be hers had turned out to be the much older remains of another woman, Sharon Briggs. It had been a challenging case for Kenzie and the detectives on the case to sort out.

"That was a weird case," Zachary provided.

Edwards nodded his agreement. "It was. So, if I understood the message I got correctly, you wanted to talk about Elysse Allan."

Zachary nodded. "Yes. Since it is a closed case, I hoped to be able to talk about it."

"You can request copies of documents under the *Public Records Act*. As long as there isn't anything that needs to be kept confidential, I'm sure you'll be given what you need."

"Eventually," Zachary said.

Edwards smiled. "You sound like someone who has made Public Records requests before. Yes, sometimes it can take a while for the request to be processed and to actually get the information you have asked for."

"That has been my experience," Zachary agreed.

Edwards chuckled. "Sometimes members of the police department aren't eager to release information, even though they are required to by law."

Zachary nodded. "I wondered if you could walk me through the case, from the time Elysse was reported missing until she was confirmed to have been found in the Grand Canyon."

"I'm sure you can get most of it from the media. It was a big circus at the time. I hope to heaven that I never get another case that is so public. There is enough to do in an investigation without having to field questions from several thousand concerned citizens and the media. Every step you take, you're afraid you're going to put your foot in something. Be photographed doing something that looks stupid or is just plain unflattering. Getting even five minutes' rest to close your eyes and think about something other than the case…"

"Sounds exhausting."

"It was. Of course, the department did what it could to keep the crazies on the other side of the rope, but there were just *so many* of them that it was impossible to keep up with them, and a few were bound to be able to squeeze through." He shook his head.

Zachary nodded. "I remember Kenzie having problems, too. People getting into the parking garage or mobbing her when she drove out of the building. I know there was increased security presence, but it's not like the Secret Service protecting the President. They're spread so thin and trying to protect so many people and guard all access points…"

Edwards grunted his acknowledgment.

"I'm sure Dr. Kirsch was not happy to be targeted like she was. When people thought we'd found Elysse Allan's remains… don't ask me what gets into people's heads. They thought that they could get into the morgue to see her? They wanted to take selfies with her? To take something of hers or touch her clothes? I just don't know where their heads were, but keeping them all out of the building... it was crazy."

"Selfies with dead celebrities. Now there's a niche market."

Edwards made a face and took a sip of his coffee. He shrugged. "So what do you want to know? Like I said... the media was pretty up on every step we took. You can watch all the coverage online."

"Yeah. I'm looking for the insider's view, I guess. Were you on the case right from the beginning, when Dain first reported her as a missing person?"

"Pretty much, yeah. Of course, Vermont BCI gets involved once a missing person file is open, so we coordinated with them. And getting Search and Rescue from Vermont State Police involved. Lots of communication channels to keep open in a case like this. Needs a lot of administration."

"You were one of the LEOs who interviewed Dain?"

"Yeah, one of them. We took it in rotation to keep it going. You're not a cop, so I wouldn't expect you to understand how exhausting it can be to interview someone for hours. You reach a point when you just can't do it anymore and just want to slam the guy's head into the table. It's best to get someone to spell you off before it reaches that point." He took a few swallows of coffee.

"I would guess so," Zachary agreed with a chuckle. He could only imagine what it must be like to keep pushing someone for that long. He knew such an arduous interrogation could result in a false confession when the interviewee reached the end of his rope and would do anything to stop it. Zachary had been on the receiving end of an interrogation more than once, but nothing that had lasted that long. Usually, he was just dealing with a cop who wanted him out of the way because he didn't like private investigators sniffing around his case. It wasn't because they actually thought him guilty of a serious crime. The few times he had been a suspect, there had been other directions to be investigated at the same time, so they couldn't focus all their resources on him, so interviews were kept short.

"What was your impression of Dain?" he asked Edwards.

"Loser. Pain in the neck. Weak. Not someone I wanted to waste my time on."

"Did you think he had done something to Elysse? Kidnapped or murdered her?"

"That was the most likely scenario, sure. The whole ploy of getting Elysse's fans involved... some people love the spotlight. That's what it looked like. She was getting all the attention. They had a fight. She wanted to break it off. No more attention, no more spotlight. He got mad, hurt or killed her, then turned the media circus on himself."

"Looking at his social networks... he was never an active poster like Elysse. He was just adjacent to her. Shows up in her feed sometimes, reposts some of her stuff, or refers people to it. Didn't post much of his own content; it was usually something to do with her."

Edwards shrugged. "Which means... what? What are you getting at?"

"I'm just not sure he wanted that much media attention. He was only 'famous' as Elysse Allan's boyfriend. If it hadn't been for her following, no one would have known anything about him. Or only five people."

"I don't see how that means he didn't want the attention. Plenty of people would like to be a rock star but don't have what it takes to become one. Being a terrible singer doesn't mean you wouldn't do anything to become one."

"Well, I guess," Zachary admitted, nodding. "So you got the feeling that he was a media hog. And that he just did this—whatever this was—to get his time in the spotlight."

Edwards nodded his agreement. "Yep. So we gave him all the attention he could handle." He laughed. "Made him think twice about whether he really wanted to provoke us that way."

"Did you find anything out about Elysse during that time?"

"We learned a good deal about her... nothing particularly helpful. Nothing that was going to help us find her."

"Do you think he was involved in her disappearance? Do you think he knew where she had gone, or that she just wanted some space, and he reported it just to get the attention?"

"We looked into her, investigated their relationship... and I think I got a pretty good bead on the kind of person she was. After hearing about their relationship and watching her press release when she reappeared... I suspect she just went off on her own and he had nothing to do with it. That's my first instinct. I could be completely wrong, but I think she wanted him out of her life."

"He didn't say anything in his interrogation that made you think he had hurt her?"

"He said plenty during his interrogation that made me think he was guilty as hell. But he wasn't. She was still alive and unhurt. Reviewing everything after the fact, knowing that she was okay, I would say he was not involved. It was a whole different scenario than the one we had imagined. All our premises and assumptions were wrong."

Zachary nodded slowly. He had a long drink of his coffee, considering. When Dain had reported Elysse missing, the police had assumed that she had just gone off on her own and there was no reason to suspect foul play. Then Dain had done his magic, putting the department at the center of a maelstrom of social media activity, forcing them to act. At the point at which they opened the investigation, he became a suspect in her disappearance. The intimate partner was always the primary suspect, unless she had actually been seen being abducted by someone else.

Dain was that person. Statistically, he was the most likely person to have killed her. He had no alibi. He was making a nuisance of himself. A certain kind of killer loved putting himself in the middle of a media circus. He wanted to be recognized, wanted people to see how smart he was, how he had managed to pull off the perfect crime. He was egotistical, self-aggrandizing, and believed that everyone admired him. It tickled his ego for people to see how brilliant he had been in pulling off the crime and being recognized, yet not being charged with it.

But eventually, the police department and everyone else who cared would find out that he hadn't actually committed any crime.

"What did you find out about the argument before Elysse disappeared?"

Edwards rubbed his chin, thinking about it. He didn't refer to any notes, but relied completely on his memory. Had he reviewed his notes before the meeting?

"The kid went through several versions of the argument. Always trying to put himself in the best possible light, of course. There were a couple of witnesses and some video taken at the time. People who recognized them or were concerned about the violence of the argument."

"Did they get physically violent? I've seen some trimmed video that shows Elysse taking a swipe at Dain, and he admits she slapped him. But do we know whether he hit her? That day or some other time?"

"Most of the fight that day was only verbal. She did slap him partway through the fight, and he didn't leave or hit her back. They knew there were witnesses nearby. She figured she could still get away with slapping him, and she was right. People aren't outraged by a woman slapping a man like they are with a man threatening or hitting a woman. You can bet we would have heard about it if he had hit back, even in self-defense."

"According to the witnesses, what was the fight about?"

"They couldn't make most of it out. They could see what was going on and hear the yelling but couldn't agree on the actual content of the argument."

"Dain told me it was about them not having time together on the vacation trip."

Edward sucked in his lip and shook his head. "I doubt that's the truth. Not the full truth, anyway. But he came up with so many versions of the fight that it's anyone's guess."

"You couldn't tell from the recordings?"

"Just a word here and there. And neither one is facing the camera, so no chance of reading their lips."

"Did you have conversations with Elysse's family and friends?

About what kind of a relationship the two of them had or what they thought had happened to Elysse? Where she would go if they had broken up?"

Edwards swirled his cup, but only a dribble of coffee was left in the bottom, and he didn't drink it.

"Her family... an interesting group of people. I wish I could say that they had been helpful. But I'm not sure... how much they cared about finding her."

11

Zachary sat back in his chair, looking at Edwards. Edwards leaned back and glanced around as if checking to make sure no one could overhear them.

"If I hear that repeated anywhere, I'm denying it," he warned Zachary. "I would never say such a thing."

Zachary nodded his understanding and waited for more details. Edwards looked around again, then continued.

"Her mother and sister spoke to us. I think there was also an aunt who gave part of an interview on TV. They said they were concerned about her and were worried that Porter might have done something to harm her. They seemed more concerned about impressing on us what a piece of trash he was than about finding Elysse."

Zachary had gotten a strange vibe from her family during the TV spots as well. They seemed to enjoy the attention, excited to be on the news. They had not appeared to be devastated by the news that their daughter was missing. Possibly murdered.

But a fact Zachary had repeated many times was that a person's apparent reaction to stress or grief was not always what it seemed. Someone who barely seemed to register bad news or react to it could be deep in mourning. Another person who appeared to be frantic, crying buckets of tears over a missing loved one, might turn out to be involved. Mothers wept over carjackers stealing vehicles with babies in them and turned out to be cold-blooded murderers. There was no telling what was going on in someone else's brain.

"Did you have any leads?" he asked Edwards. "Had you managed to track her at all?"

"You would think that in today's world, it isn't possible to go very far without going by a license plate scanner or without law enforcement being able to track your GPS. But the stuff they show on TV… that's the future. Where the technologies exist, they don't work as well as portrayed on TV or are not connected to the databases that would give the results you see in fiction. I can't just ping your phone or activate the GPS in your car on a whim and get real-time results on my police department computer. And when you get into travel between states and you are trying to coordinate the information in a man search across the country, with no idea as to the direction the person actually took, things get even more complicated."

Edwards rose from his chair, stretched, walked over to his window, sighed, and turned to face Zachary again, leaning his arms on the back of the chair as he stood behind it.

"We had thousands of people looking for Elysse Allan, trying to spot her all over the country. But it was a fiasco. We were getting tips from every single state, including Alaska and Hawaii. We focused on anything that showed up between Vermont and JFK, where Elysse was supposed to catch her flight home. That is also where the fans focused, so we had hundreds of sightings to sift through. Meanwhile, we had search parties tramping through the woods near the gas station where they had the argument and the sites where Elysse was supposed to go next."

"But no luck. She didn't even stay in Vermont, much less go on to New York. Instead, she backtracked and went back to the Grand Canyon. Why did she do that? Any idea?"

"She would not talk to the police when she returned. Not here, and not in Arizona or Oregon. And as an adult who had not been involved in any crime, she wasn't required to. There wasn't any way to make her. You can go by her interview with the reporter where she said she wanted to go back to see the stuff she had missed when she had been there with Porter because there was so much to do, and she had done what he wanted rather than what she did. And if you believe that…"

"I think I believe Dain—that she was the one who set the itinerary, and they saw the things that she wanted to see."

Edwards nodded his agreement, peering at Zachary over the brim of his cup.

"Then why did she go back?" he prompted.

Zachary shook his head. "I have no idea."

"And neither do I."

"Maybe it was to throw people off her trail. She just didn't want to be followed. So she did the opposite anyone would have expected her to. Foiled the search teams, the scent dogs, the fans who thought they would be able to catch up with her at the airport…"

Edwards agreed. "I thought of that."

"And discarded it?"

"No. I still think that's probably why she did it. She didn't want to be followed. She wanted to be alone. Whether she was into something shady or just wanted to have some breathing space for once, I don't know. Was it some kind of mental breakdown? I don't know. Maybe one day she'll tell her fans. Maybe write a tell-all memoir."

"Did you know she's not posting anymore?"

"Yeah?"

Zachary had a feeling Edwards already knew that.

"Yeah. I wondered if it was some kind of breakdown. Dain said that she hadn't been the same since it happened. That's one of the reasons he is so intent on finding out what really happened. He wants to help her."

"Or so he says."

"Yes. So he says."

"You can't always trust what people say," Edwards pointed out.

"Especially one like him; we already know he lies, and his story changes."

"Under police duress."

Edwards gave a nod, not arguing.

Zachary figured that his own story would probably vary wildly if he were questioned by the police for hours on end. He recognized that he was the type of person who would spin his story differently depending on who was asking and who he was trying to protect. He would want to adjust it to suit his interrogator. He knew that about himself. He had watched himself do it in front of so many foster parents, teachers, and social workers. It was like an out-of-body experience, watching himself and being surprised what came out of his mouth when he was confronted about something.

Edwards turned his wrist to look at his big black watch. "Well, I hope that has been helpful to you, Mr. Goldman. That's about all the time I can spare right now."

"I appreciate you taking the time to talk to me. Can I call you if something comes up in the course of my investigation?"

"You can try." He didn't promise results.

"I'll tell Kenzie you say hi," Zachary offered, reminding Edwards that he and Kenzie were connected and he wanted to stay on good terms with her.

"Yeah, you do that. I'm sure we'll have the opportunity to work on other files together in the future."

"She does tend to get involved with homicides."

Edwards chuckled. Zachary stood up, and Edwards walked him toward the door.

"It must be an interesting relationship," Edwards commented. "Private investigator and medical examiner."

Zachary grinned. "It is," he agreed. "It isn't often I meet someone I can talk about murder and forensics with. She doesn't get grossed out over autopsy photos at the dinner table."

Edwards grimaced. "I wouldn't recommend it."

"No, we try to stay focused on each other over dinner, to enjoy each other's company and build our relationship. But it was a body that brought us together and, like I say… there are not many people I can talk to about bodies."

12

Zachary returned home to do some computer work and figure out his next steps. As he drove, Zachary reviewed his interview with Edwards, formulating plans and pondering unasked questions. He could call Edwards if other questions became more important. He didn't want to play the favor-for-Kenzie card too soon or make a pest of himself. It needed to be subtle so that Edwards would be open to working with him again in the future. Especially on an open case. It was one thing for him to be talking to a civilian about a closed file, and one where almost all their activities had already been publicized far and wide. Giving Zachary information on an open investigation would be a different matter. Police did *not* give tips to private investigators.

At home, he turned the TV on with the volume low and sat on the couch at his laptop desk. He saw he had an email from Heather and knew he had missed a couple of calls from her over the weekend. He knew what she was calling him about, and it wasn't urgent, but he needed to stay on top of administrative matters, so he sat down and tapped her name on his contact list.

Heather was his other older sister, and she had been doing work for him for the last couple of years, since he had helped to resolve a cold case for her and started her on the path of reunification with her with the son who she had given up for adoption. Heather had been looking for something to do with her life and had eagerly taken to the work he had given her on skip traces and other investigative work she could do from her computer at home. Heather had also taken it upon herself to organize Zachary's business and life in areas where his ADHD and other issues made things challenging. She was now his executive assistant and bookkeeper as well as doing some of the routine investigative work for him.

And the reason she had called was to set up the new file for the Elysse Allan investigation.

"Zachy!" Heather saw it was him and launched into the conversation without preamble. "It's about time! I take it you took the weekend off?"

"More or less," Zachary agreed. Though she would see from his time records that he had still put time in on the Elysse Allan file, and should have talked to her about it on Saturday, at least. "Kenzie and I went down to see Mr. Peterson and Pat."

"That's nice. Good for you. Did you see Joss?"

"Not this time. Maybe in a couple of weeks. I try not to impose on her too often. Have you talked to her?"

"It's been a few days." The two oldest girls generally kept in touch, though Zachary didn't know how often they ended up talking to each other. "No news. Everything is fine with her, as far as I can tell. So tell me about this new file."

But she didn't give him a chance to introduce it. And he didn't really need to. He had opened the file under Elysse Allan's name. He had filled in a couple of the fields necessary to open the file, which would give Heather enough information to ensure that all the accounting information was set up and the file-opening tasks checked off.

"Elysse Allan! How did you get that file? I remember what a big thing it was when she went missing. It didn't matter whether you knew who she was before that or not, you did once she disappeared. And it wasn't just Vermont local news, either. It was all over the world."

Zachary nodded. "Well, you remember the boyfriend, Dain Porter—"

"Everyone thought he had done it."

"Yes. But Dain hadn't done anything, and now he is looking for more information about what actually happened when Elysse disappeared."

"She already explained it to everyone. It was... well, according to her, just a misunderstanding. I'm not sure *misunderstanding* is accurate, but it was just a matter of her going off in a huff after an argument, wasn't it?"

"Maybe," Zachary said cautiously, "or maybe not. She said that was what happened, but that doesn't make it true."

"But it fits with the video taken of her before she disappeared. They had a fight. She left. She wanted some time to herself. Or maybe to punish him, embarrass him in front of their public and make him worry about her."

"Maybe. I don't have any evidence that it was anything other than that. But... it could have been. That's why we are investigating."

"What else would it be?"

"Do you follow her at all on social media?"

"No. I looked at Elysse's accounts when she disappeared to see what the fuss was about. Honestly, she's not really my kind of thing. I'm just an old lady as far as these young social influencers are concerned. They're my kids' generation, not mine. I don't have any desire to follow her every move. I don't care what she had for dinner or where she went on her vacation, or what her opinion is on this product or that." Heather paused, and Zachary thought she was finished, but when he opened his mouth to comment, she added. "I like cat videos."

Zachary laughed. "Who doesn't like cat videos?"

"If you've got a cute or loud cat, I'm your guy. But fashion and aesthetic... that's just not my thing."

"I don't even know what an aesthetic is."

"You and me, Zachy, we're getting old. We're not young and hip anymore."

"I was never hip."

"Me neither, to be honest. I was a hermit. And now I'm too old to be hip."

13

"If you did follow Elysse on the social networks, you would know she hasn't been posting since it happened. She's been silent ever since she came back," Zachary explained.

Heather was silent for a moment, considering. "She hasn't been posting anything?"

"Nothing. Complete radio silence. Or whatever you call it on the internet."

"Well then... it doesn't sound like she just needed some space. Time to get her head back on straight. It sounds like... something a lot bigger than that. Is she done? Burned out or retired? What is she doing if she isn't posting?"

"All these questions and more will be central to our investigation," Zachary told her in a dramatic radio announcer voice.

Heather laughed. "I guess so. I love investigations. What other profession lets you dig into people's lives and snoop around to find out everything you can about them and people actually pay you for it?"

"There are not very many of them. And I wouldn't want to be a cop."

"No, me neither," Heather agreed. "I'll stick to the private side."

"Me too."

"So what do you need me to do? We already have basic background on Elysse and Dain. They have biographies all over the internet. They can't take a step without the world knowing what they are doing."

"That might be how it seemed, but she fell off the map completely when she wanted to. And there were obviously things going on off-camera that the fans didn't know about. But I don't think you'll find any of that with a Google search. We're going to need to go deeper than that."

"Yeah, I guess so. You want me to do financial, family background, that kind of thing?"

"Yeah, whatever you can find. You'll find some information already saved to the file, I did some of the basics. They are originally from Oregon. I'm not sure if she has gone back there. We'll need to know at some point, so if you can find out where she is physically, that would be helpful."

"Okay."

Zachary could hear Heather typing and, on a slight delay, tasks appeared on the task list on his computer screen.

"If you come across any internet friends who seem to be very close to Elysse or Dain, let me know. I need to talk to people who know either of them personally."

"That's going to be difficult. The people who know them personally aren't going to want to talk to anyone, especially about private, undisclosed stuff."

"We'll figure out the approach after identifying them and how they know Elysse or Dain. Find them first."

"Will do," Heather agreed.

"Good. I think that's everything for now."

Heather was good at identifying other things that might be helpful on a file. She would follow her instincts, chasing down rabbit trails to uncover any hidden details. He trusted her to do that. All he needed to do was start her off in the right direction, and she would perform beyond his expectations.

"Before you go, Zachy?" Heather stopped him from disconnecting the call.

"Yeah?"

"I just wanted to know… how you're doing. Is everything good?"

Zachary considered the question. "The letter bomb?"

"Well… yes. That was a pretty big deal. You do seem to find your way into… trouble."

Zachary cleared his throat. He was well aware of his talent for finding trouble. The letter bomb had not been his fault. He had not said or done anything that anyone could have foreseen as being dangerous. He had just been interviewing the old school friend of a victim. He hadn't identified her as a suspect. He hadn't known that because of what he had unwittingly seen and heard, she had identified him as a threat that needed to be eliminated.

"I'm fine," he assured Heather, "almost totally healed. The next time you see me, you won't be able to tell anything happened. I can walk around in public and no one looks at me funny."

The scabs on his face made people think he was a meth addict, and they looked away from him even faster than they did when they just perceived him as an unshaven bum. Certainly, no one looked him in the eye.

"And emotionally? Being… targeted like that, opening the bomb without realizing the danger, that can't be easy to handle. The trauma."

Zachary blew out his breath. "Well, that will probably take longer to get over. But I have practice in dealing with… trauma stuff."

"You're talking to someone about it? I worry about your depression."

"I'm seeing my therapist every week. We talk about it when it is relevant."

Less than Dr. Boyle would have liked. Zachary was more inclined to ignore new trauma than to deal with it. But Dr. B was working on him, bringing it up regularly and probing around the edges.

"Okay, good," Heather approved. "Glad to hear it."

14

F inding people who might be able to give him insight into Elysse and her relationship with Dain was not proving to be an easy task. Zachary had left messages with various family members or friends who had spoken to the media, figuring they were the most likely to agree to talk to him. But it was obvious that not everyone who talked about her knew her. Those who were truly close friends would be less inclined to speak with him.

When he tired of leaving phone messages likely never to be returned, Zachary again went to the internet. This time, he wasn't looking for Elysse's social media or what her fans had posted on her profile; he was looking for deeper discussions about Elysse's disappearance and what had happened while she had been gone.

He dug down deep and started posting in chat rooms and discussion threads with new aliases. Nothing that would lead back to him. He looked for the people who seemed to know something rather than just the wild speculations about alien abductions or rants about entitled social influencers being babies and having meltdowns. Somewhere out there, someone knew more about what had happened to Elysse. Zachary didn't believe she hadn't seen anyone for five days. Someone must have known where she was. Her phone had been out of service, but she must have run into someone, talked to a friend, or maybe called someone from a borrowed landline, old payphone, or burner phone.

He recalled from Elysse's interview on TV that she'd been in possession of a burner phone when she had been discovered in the Grand Canyon. The interviewer had made a point of bringing it up.

He mused over its significance—why get a phone and then not contact anyone?

The police would not have been able to get her phone logs; there was no crime in Elysse disappearing or buying a new phone. No crime in leaving her old phone and old life behind and starting up somewhere new.

With a burner phone, Elysse could have been in constant contact with friends or family members, despite going dark for the rest of the world.

Zachary had seen an unknown number ring through on his phone, but he had been deep in his research and had decided he didn't want to be interrupted by a potential telemarketer. When he next looked at his phone, he saw that he had a voicemail message. His heart speeding, he tapped it to find out who had called. It could still be a telemarketer or spammer. He got plenty of voicemail messages from purported agents of the IRS or Homeland Security claiming that he needed to call them back right away to avoid prison time.

But it wasn't a spam call this time.

"Mr. Goldman, I am returning your call. This is Kristy Echols from… you know who I am. You have my number; give me a call-back. I'll be available for a couple of hours."

Kristy Echols was on Elysse Allan's staff. Or at least she had been when Elysse had been in Vermont. It was quite a break in the case for her to be willing to contact Zachary. Zachary tapped her number to call her back.

Recognizing his number, Kristy answered after just a couple of rings.

"Mr. Goldman."

"Thank you for calling me back, Ms. Echols. You can call me Zachary; I'm not big on formality."

"Then you can call me Kristy. How can I help you, Zachary? Are you a photographer?"

"Well, I am, actually, but that isn't why I was calling you. What exactly is it you do?"

Sensing a possible opportunity, Kristy was eager to give him the details.

"Think of me as a caddy for photography. A golfer has a caddy to hand him the club he needs for his next shot, to give him advice on the direction the ground breaks, hazards, and techniques to use. I do the same thing with photographers, especially those taking pictures for social media. I can set up your tripods and equipment for you, advise you on trending posts, topics, or challenges, help you establish an aesthetic, and even suggest what hashtags to use or time of day to post."

"Wow. I didn't know there was so much involved in posting pictures to social media."

"It depends on your goals. If you want to extend your reach and get your pictures trending, you need more expertise than just sharing pictures of your kids with your extended family. Some people are happy just to share with a small group of close friends and family as a way to stay up to date on what people are doing."

"But if you want to become an influencer like Elysse Allan, you need more expertise."

"Well," she gave a bit of a laugh. "I'm not going to promise you I can get you up to Elysse Allan's level of fame. But I can certainly get you onto more phones than you are now. I have plenty of experience and deep knowledge of the industry. You might think that it's simple to post a picture to social media, and it is, but if you want it to *trend*, you have to either be very lucky or you need someone like me, who is actively studying the platforms and knows the best practices to widen your reach and spread your brand."

"That would be a lot for me to learn by myself in a short period of time."

"Exactly," Kristy agreed. "Just like there is a difference between someone making a peanut butter sandwich at home and a restaurateur designing a sandwich menu for his venue. You don't get to be a chef at a three-star restaurant by making sandwiches."

"That makes sense," Zachary told her. "It must be a fascinating job. You would be exposed to a lot of interesting people and products."

"Yes." She sounded more stressed than excited. It probably wasn't easy to work with people who thought they were good enough to become world famous and expected Kristy to promote their brands. A lot of egos to be stroked and redirected. People who probably didn't take direction well.

"How long were you working with Elysse Allan?"

"About... a year, I think. I would have to check my records to see when I started working with her."

"So you had been with her for the entire vacation tour?"

"Yes. I would often go to a location ahead of her, set up the gear, analyze the lighting and view lines, then she and Dain would arrive and I would run them through what they should do and give them the posting instructions. If the photos were complicated or we needed 'couple' shots, I would stay and help take the pictures. If not, I would go on to the next location and get started there."

"What were the posting instructions? They knew how to post on all the social platforms by this point, didn't they?" It didn't seem to Zachary like it was that complicated. Once he posted a few times on a social network, he knew what he needed to do.

"Like I said, if you want it to trend, you need to know what hashtags to use, too. There are filters, stickers, certain trending tags or challenges, and it all had to be consistent with Elysse's brand so that she would reach her target audience and they will recognize her posts from one day to the next. Someone scrolling should be able to recognize her aesthetic immediately, without seeing what account it was posted from."

"And that's good."

She didn't answer immediately, seeming thrown by his question.

"Uh—yes. You want people to recognize your content and to stop to read it, comment on it, or engage with it. That helps to boost it so that more people see it. And the more people who see or engage with your content, the better. That's how you make money as an influencer. By getting lots of views and engagement. No one will hire you to promote their product if you don't have a proven viewer base."

"Is that the only way to make money by posting to social media? Sponsored product placement?"

"No, of course not." She sounded irritated, but quickly smoothed out her voice so that it was simply informative. She had experience in explaining social media monetization to the uneducated. "You can enable ads if you are getting enough viewership, so you get money every time someone is exposed to an ad while they're on your feed. If you're getting millions of views, that is a significant income stream. You can sell directly and use social media as your advertising platform. You can establish yourself as an expert in your industry to establish social cred and trust. You can engage directly with customers to build relationships. There are a lot of ways that social media allows you to build your business, whatever it is. What exactly is it you do, Zachary?"

"Well, I haven't done much with my photography. Some family and friends have suggested that I should do more. Post it on social media, maybe publish a coffee table book or sell digital wallpapers. There are a lot of opportunities out there, I guess, but I've never pursued them."

"I assume you have a day job. What is it you do again?"

15

"I'm a private investigator. That's why I called you about Elysse Allan."

Zachary had been quite clear about that on his voicemail. Kristy had apparently gotten distracted by her own upsell.

"Oh, right." Kristy gave a little chuckle. "Well... you found me. I haven't had a lot of people reach out to me about Elysse. It wasn't like she mentioned me in her posts or had anything branded with my business. Most people wouldn't realize that she had a social media consultant or the amount of work that I put into her posts."

"They thought she just did it all on her own."

"Yeah. And that's how it should be. My contribution should be invisible. It should boost her bottom line but not be obvious to her followers. They want to see her, not me."

"I wonder if we could get together to talk? Where are you located?"

"I'm in Nevada right now. Have a client who is kicking off a new brand. I don't think a face-to-face is going to be possible."

"Oh, okay. We could maybe video chat later if I need to follow up on something."

"Mmm." She didn't sound too excited about that fact. "I don't know what you are looking for, but I think we can cover it in a quick voice call. I'm not going to share confidential client information with anyone. If you want to get in touch with Elysse, you'll have to reach out through other channels. I won't be sharing any private email addresses or phone numbers with you."

"No, no, of course not," Zachary tried to put as much shock as he could into the words. "I wouldn't ask you to do that. I'm just making some inquiries for Dain. You worked with him, so I'm sure you understand how concerned he is for Elysse and what she has gone through."

"I'm sure he is," she said with reserve.

"They were very close. They'd been together since their school days," Zachary pointed out.

"I saw them together, Mr. Goldman. I think I understand their relationship better than you. You can't believe everything Dain tells you."

"I know they were a passionate couple. They had their share of disagreements and short breaks. But they had stayed together this long. I think Dain knew her better than anyone else. He's concerned about what happened to her and how she is dealing with it."

"What do you mean, what happened to her?"

"About what happened to her during the time she was missing. I'm sure you know she didn't just go off on her own like she told the press."

"I don't know what you think happened," Kristy said coldly. "I only know what Elysse told the media."

"She didn't say anything to you before or after she disappeared? You must have felt pretty irritated. You were there for her, ready for the next shots, all set up, and she didn't show. And didn't show at any of the next locations. That messed things up for you, didn't it?"

"My contract covered the full tour, whether she showed up or not. I knew it would be paid for."

"But still… you must have been concerned when Elysse just didn't show up. Unless she had already told you something about it."

"I wasn't very concerned. People with big followings can be very self-centered. Always looking inward, not thinking about how their actions affect others. It isn't unusual for a client to change their mind about something or not show up at a previously planned shoot. They get distracted by something else, decide to go somewhere else with their campaign, whatever."

Zachary nodded. He couldn't imagine what it would be like to constantly work with people like that, who just bailed on their commitments and jumped to the next fad or shiny object. Kristy said she had been paid either way, but it would still be irritating to put up with such childish behavior.

"At some point, did you start to be concerned? Dain said she missed three locations where she was supposed to shoot."

"Yes. I was starting to wonder if something had happened, but I wasn't... that concerned. Dain was her partner, and it was up to him to decide whether there was anything to be worried about. He could call or text her or her family or friends. I just did the shoots. And if they wanted to pay me for sitting around..." She grunted. "Whatever. I could take some pictures myself, make some phone calls, work on other stuff on my phone while I waited around. Vermont in the summer is nice. Warm and green and not too crowded. I'd picked out the sites for her photos myself. I live in Vermont, so I know all the good spots. Told her she should take some pictures here before going on to New York."

"You'd been with them for the rest of the tour?"

"Yeah."

"How had things gone at the other locations?"

"Fine."

"Were there any problems? Things that didn't go well? Arguments?"

"Some teams like this are constantly arguing. It's nothing. People get really anxious when their success or failure could depend on just the right frame of just the right shot, with the perfect filters, hashtags, and caption. A lot rides on those little pictures, meant to look casual and carefree."

"So people were grumpy. Easily irritated."

"Sure. And if things went well, they got a good shot or had a post that was already trending, they were delighted. Bouncing around, excited like little kids, refreshing their screens every two minutes. Enjoying the ride."

"Did Elysse and Dain argue a lot? More than most couples? Less?"

"I don't know. I didn't think it was anything special."

"Did you ever see anything that concerned you? Maybe… physical abuse? A bad display of temper? Concerns that someone could get hurt or things could go too far?"

"I don't know what you mean by physical abuse. Did they fight? Sure. Did I see them beating each other in front of me? No."

"A verbal argument, maybe some nasty names or threats thrown in. Trying to humiliate each other in front of an audience. Or even coming to blows."

"A slap?" Kristy asked tentatively.

"Yes. Elysse is reported to have slapped Dain at the gas station when they were arguing."

"I can see that. But I wasn't there when it happened."

"But she had slapped him before?"

"Yeah. On occasion."

"And had he slapped her? Or done anything else that could be construed as physically abusive?"

"He might slap her or shove her, sure. But it wasn't like there were injuries. No one was getting hurt."

"But they did put their hands on each other. Both of them."

"Yeah, they both did. So they deserved what they got."

"Did it ever go further? Not just a slap or a shove? A closed fist? A weapon?"

"I don't know. Not that I ever saw."

"Did you ever see anything else? Hear about it from someone else?"

"There were rumors, but I don't give those any credit."

"What kind of rumors?"

"If I didn't believe them, I'm not going to share them with you. That would be slander."

"You can tell me a rumor without saying it was true."

"No. I'm not telling you anything I didn't see with my own eyes."

"Okay." Zachary thought, considering what else he could ask her about. There weren't very many people with the insider view like Kristy. She was a valuable resource.

"Did you ever see anyone hanging around? Someone you didn't know? Someone who shouldn't have been there?"

"We were out in public. I couldn't stop anyone from being there. We weren't going to pack it in because there was someone else around. We would just go ahead with the planned shoot."

"So there had been people around."

"Sure. People hung around. Got in the way. Asked questions. Decided that they wanted autographs or selfies or something else that slowed our progress."

"Any stalkers? Groupies? Fans who followed you or preceded you from one place to another? Always there, underfoot?"

"Uh… sometimes. People were always showing up, popping up and getting into shots, asking endless questions. But a stalker…? I don't know. I can't think of any one person."

"It could be important."

"The cops asked whether anyone had been hanging around, and I told them no."

It wasn't exactly an assertion that she hadn't seen anyone.

"Maybe you've had a chance to think about it since then and realized there was someone," Zachary suggested.

"Well, there was this one guy. I don't know his name, and I don't know what sites I saw him at. He might have been a friend or just someone interested in what they were doing and wanted to be at the next scene."

"What did he look like?" Zachary sat with his fingers poised over the computer's keyboard, waiting.

"Big guy. Bushy beard. But there are so many people like that these days. I'm not big on the beard craze."

"Let's stay focused on him for a minute. How big is big?"

"I don't know. Over six feet tall. Broad. Overweight."

"Okay, good. And did he say anything to anyone in your

74

group? Did he approach Elysse? Talk to Dain? I don't know what other… uh… workers they had helping them out. Dain said there was sort of a convoy, with all their equipment and the people who were involved with the shoots."

"He might have talked to Elysse. I don't think he was interested in Dain."

"Was she uncomfortable having him around? Ask anyone to get rid of him or to stay around so she wasn't alone with him?"

"Nothing like that. Elysse would just move on and do the next shot. He kept watching. Might show up at another shoot after we left. I don't know if he knew the itinerary or was just guessing where we would go next. Or maybe it was being leaked by someone who worked with them."

"Was anybody worried about this guy?"

"No. I don't think so. There were always fans. Some of them are more persistent than others. But it wasn't like he was breaking into her hotel room or threatening her. Just showing up on the tour."

Zachary would look into it further. "Do you have any pictures of him? Did he show up in any of Elysse's shots?"

"I'd have to check. Sometimes, fans do get into the shots. Or they take selfies of their own. You might want to check fan feeds and see if he shows up somewhere with her over his shoulder."

"It would be helpful if you could look and see if you recognize him. I won't know him."

"He wears a baseball cap. Knicks, I think."

Zachary shook his head. Why hadn't she started with that? He typed this addition to her description. "That will help. If I find someone I think is him, can I send it to you? Get you to confirm that it's him?"

"Sure, I guess. I don't want to get the guy in trouble. I don't think he did anything to hurt Elysse."

"No, not likely. But if he hangs around her, he may be aware of someone else who was stalking her that you didn't know about. He might have seen things go on that you didn't, whether it was with a fan, or Dain, or a family member."

"Okay. Well, I hope you find something."

"Before you go—" Zachary could tell she was winding up the conversation, "I just had a couple more questions about how she was. Did she seem extra stressed? Depressed? Jittery? What was her emotional state like before she disappeared?"

Kristy let her breath out slowly. "I don't know. I try not to get wrapped up in my clients emotionally. I just focus on the pictures and postings and let them worry about taking care of the crap in their lives. Elysse was better than a lot of them. She wasn't on drugs, as far as I could tell. Didn't spend a lot of time drinking. She and Dain had a needy relationship, but whatever. It takes time to sort relationships out. At least neither of them had helicopter parents buzzing around trying to control everything."

Zachary had never had that problem himself, but he knew that many of the younger generation had parents who were unwilling to let their little fledglings take flight. Neither Elysse nor Dain seemed to have that problem. Their working-class parents were probably too busy taking care of themselves and any younger siblings to try to hold on to the older ones. Probably single moms or divorcees who never made their child support payments.

"So did you think Elysse and Dain's relationship was pretty solid? Or could you tell it was coming apart? Dain said that they'd had breakups before. Did you expect them to get back together after that last argument?"

"I didn't see the argument, so I don't have any opinion on it. Yeah, they fought often enough, and sometimes, one or the other would take off for a few days or say that they were done for good. But they were always back together again afterward. I don't think they ever made it to a week away from each other. They were always back for more."

16

When Heather called, Zachary was on his way to the medical examiner's office to pick Kenzie up from work. He answered the call over his Bluetooth earbuds.

"Hi, Feathers."

"Hey, Zachy. How's the investigation going?"

"I'm not sure I'm much farther ahead," he admitted while rubbing his forehead in frustration. "But I'm gathering bits here and there. It will add up and, eventually… something will break."

"How much do you know about Dain's past?" Heather asked, skipping over any further pleasantries.

"Not much yet. I was more focused on Elysse's. They're both from rural Oregon. Grew up together, went to school together, and were childhood sweethearts. I don't know if he has any family, but no one who is trailing him on his road trip across America or that he has mentioned in our conversations."

"Yeah, that all fits together. But this relationship that has been going on since childhood…?"

Zachary glanced at the phone with interest, even though Heather had not connected with a video call. "I take it you are skeptical about that part?"

"I can see about getting a librarian to pull his yearbook pictures and any mentions of them being a couple during school, but there seems to have been a period of time when they were not together."

"From what I understand, their relationship has been rocky. They have had breakups. A few days here and there. Was there a longer break that I haven't been told about?"

"He was charged with sexual assault a few years ago. Sounds like date rape, from what I was able to find. I've ordered court records."

"Was he convicted? Pled down?"

"Convicted, served a year, and was released. That's all I know so far. But if it was date rape, then he was seeing someone other than Elysse at the time. Or if it was not date rape, then…" Heather trailed off, unable to find anywhere to go with that.

"Either way, Elysse knows that he was convicted of sexual assault. He didn't just go away on an exchange program for a year."

"Yeah. I don't know how I would feel about being with some-body with that on his record. Actually…" she amended her statement, saying what Zachary had already been thinking. "There's no way I would be with someone who had been convicted of sexual assault. Period. No way."

"I know," Zachary agreed. "It's hard to believe that anyone would. But people do make that choice. Elysse was young and had known him since they were little; she might have just believed he was innocent, even though he was convicted. He might have given her some kind of story about it being a false accusation. Maybe that the woman had regrets after getting together with him. You hear that quite a bit from accused rapists."

"Even so—that would mean that he had been together with another woman, even if it was consensual. If he and Elysse were together since childhood, then he was cheating on her."

"Or got together with this woman when they were on a break."

"If they were only ever on a break for two or three days at a time… that's pretty quick to be jumping into bed with someone else."

"Yeah. But Dain might have said he didn't even know the woman. Or maybe Elysse just didn't care."

"I suppose."

"Well, thanks for letting me know. Would you believe Dain never bothered to tell me about this?"

Heather snorted. "I'm shocked."

"Anything else?"

"Not yet. Waiting for searches to come in from a few different sources. Anything else you need?"

"If you feel like scrolling through social media channels, you can look for an Elysse fan who wears a Knicks cap. Big guy, bushy beard, Knicks cap."

"Yeah? I can do that while I'm watching TV with Grant. He won't mind."

"Okay, let me know if you find him. And if anything seems off about him."

"Who is he?"

"Possible stalker. Possibly just a fan who saw something. Maybe nothing."

"Got it."

"Not high priority. But you never know. He might be an important piece of the puzzle."

After disconnecting from Heather, Zachary pulled in to the curb in front of the police station. Kenzie wasn't there yet, but would be in a couple of minutes. He didn't always pick her up, but it was nice when he did, because she then had to get off at a predictable time, instead of letting herself be pulled into doing just one more thing as it gradually got later and later. If he were picking her up, they usually had dinner in good time and had some time to spend together during the evening.

He scrolled through his emails on his phone and then switched over to his social networks. He didn't spend much time on social networking, and it seemed strange to him that it would be the center of anyone's life. But for both Elysse and Dain, it had been what they focused all their time and energy on. It had been their livelihood, and any ups and downs and the vagaries of the algorithms of each one would have been a huge cause for concern.

Likewise, the people who watched Elysse's feed had considered themselves part of her life. Every little thing she did, every post she posted, was of vital importance to them. She was more important than the characters in any book or movie fandom. Zachary had known foster kids in some of the homes he had been in who inhabited fictional worlds, who were so enamored by the literary or movie universe that they refused to live in the real world. For them, everything was hobbits, aliens, superheroes, or some other fictional race. They spent every waking moment immersed in their chosen fandom's legends, reading or watching it on TV.

These people were just as involved in Elysse and watching every step she made.

At least, some of them were. Zachary was sure that plenty of regular, everyday people went about their business, going to work, doing chores, and raising children, and only checking their feeds occasionally throughout the day to see what their favorite internet celebrities were up to.

He was so lost in scrolling through his phone and looking at each person who had mentioned Elysse's name in their posts that he just about jumped out of his skin when Kenzie abruptly opened the door.

He managed to hang on to his phone rather than flinging it across the car, but he did let out a little yelp, and his heart jumped in his chest and started racing like a piston. His body was sure he was in some kind of danger he needed to run away from.

Kenzie bent down and looked at him in amusement. "Are you okay?" she asked through the door.

Zachary cleared his throat and jammed the phone into his pocket. Kenzie got in, settling into the seat next to him.

"You just uh… startled me a bit," Zachary told her.

"I thought you were going to jump right out through the window. What were you doing?"

"Just looking at my phone. I didn't see you coming."

"Are you going to be okay?"

"I'm fine. I'm fine. How was your day?"

"Pretty good." Kenzie's expression sobered. "I'm sorry. I shouldn't be laughing about scaring you. I don't like to be startled. Especially now."

She didn't say "since the abduction," but he knew what she had meant.

17

While Zachary didn't like to rely too much on social media or rumors, he was waiting for information on other fronts. He had left messages with or sent emails to Elysse's friends and family members, was waiting for the results of the public information request he had put in with the police department and BCI, and hadn't yet been able to nail down Elysse's current location or a way to connect with her. But there was plenty of other information to sift through online.

Many fans shared information and speculation on the mainstream social media platforms Elysse had posted on. It would have taken a cadre of investigators a year to go through everything that had been posted while she was missing, so he had to search, filter, and narrow it down to what was relevant, a nearly impossible task.

Besides social media, mainstream media had also been busy speculating about what might have happened to Elysse or the rumors of where she might have gone or been spotted. It was all anyone had wanted to hear at the time. Everyone had been searching for the one clue that would help the police to track Elysse down and ensure her safety.

Most of the videos posted were just talking heads, reciting the story over and over again, and talking to family or friends or "experts" who were supposed to know something about disappearances like this. The police, of course, had no comment other than requesting anyone who had information on Elysse's whereabouts to come forward.

Zachary imagined they regretted asking people to come forward. They must have been swamped with calls, emails, texts, and tips of all kinds. At least no monetary award had been offered. He could only imagine what kind of chaos that would have caused.

But beyond what showed up on a quick Google search, there were sites where other information was shared. Posted by the Elysse fandom, the conspiracy theorists, the skeptics, the internet sleuths that had hoped to find something even before the police.

Some of the information might be true and some was clearly wild speculation. Zachary started to collect information, trying to organize it in some way that made sense. He mostly focused on photo and video evidence because he could at least trust that it was closer to the truth than the written opinions, rumors, and speculations. And it was easier for him to consume than walls of text.

He set up several subfolders in the case folder and started saving videos and photos, changing the filenames to descriptive names and tags that he could skim or filter later to keep track of what he would find in each and what he still lacked. He displayed them as large thumbnails so that he could also connect them visually.

Gradually, the various pictures and video snippets started to fit together like the pieces of a puzzle. Far from answering the question of what had happened to Elysse during the five days she had been missing, they instead raised additional questions. And so far, Elysse hadn't made herself available to answer any of them.

He didn't want to go to Dain without more ammunition. The other person he knew had been with the two of them regularly throughout the social media tour who might be able to answer some questions for him was Kristy Echols, the "caddy" who had been helping with setup, branding, and advice. She had been with them for weeks and had seen Elysse and Dain together and apart. She might not want to speculate on any abuse, but she could report what else she had seen.

"Kristy," she answered briskly. "Oh, Mr. Goldman, what can I do for you? Decide you need someone to advise you on your social media presence?"

"Well, considering I don't really have one…" he laughed. "I had some more questions about Elysse's disappearance, if you don't mind, Ms. Echols."

"Kristy."

"And it's Zachary."

"Okay, Zachary, sorry. Don't you think you had better establish yourself as an internet presence and get good social cred for the future? It is the first place people look for information now. Not in books or directories. You may get some business by word of mouth, but you need an internet platform if you are going to succeed. Even if you don't want to set up a website, you still need something on the main social networks where people can find you."

"Well, I guess sooner or later, I'm going to have to catch up with the modern world," Zachary admitted. "I'm a little resistant."

"Don't wait until your business is in the toilet. You need to get established now. It takes time. If you are successful, that is exactly when you need to jump on board and establish your reputation now. If you wait until you're not getting business from anywhere else, you won't be able to get any traction."

Zachary cleared his throat. "Well… do you have a price list? A beginner package or introductory offer?"

"Of course. Give me your email address and I'll get something to you right away."

Zachary figured if he was going to ask her the questions he was about to, he needed to offer something in return. She was probably right about needing to establish an internet presence before it was too late. He gave her the requested information and answered a few questions about where he advertised and how he got most of his business. He then pressed to get back to the topic he had called about.

"I needed to ask you a little bit more about Elysse and Dain and how things went down before Elysse's disappearance."

"I don't think I can give you anything more than I did. We covered all of that."

"I wanted to ask you a few specific questions about Dain's and Elysse's relationship."

"We already talked about that."

"Not really. I asked you about the argument, and I asked you about what you knew about the possible abuse in the relationship, but I have some new questions."

"Romantic relationships are not my area of expertise. Customer relationships. Fan relationships. But their personal lives are not my business."

"There aren't many people in this part of the country who saw them together and can answer questions for me. I'm not looking for professional expertise here, just some thoughts on how they got along."

"We already talked about that," Kristy repeated stubbornly.

"What kind of a relationship did they have?"

"Like we talked about. Elysse and Dain were a couple. They had arguments. Sometimes, they broke up for a few days, but then they got together again. That's really all I can tell you."

"And they saw other people."

There was a few seconds of silence on the other end of the line. Kristy cleared her throat. "I don't have anything to tell you about that."

"You never saw them with other people?"

"Sure. Elysse was a celebrity. She was often with other people. You have to be willing to get out there in the public. Meet people, talk to fans, press the flesh like the politicians say."

"That's not what I'm talking about. I mean romantically. Intimately. Did they see other people?"

"How would I know what goes on behind closed doors?"

Zachary said nothing, hoping that the discomfort of the silence would be enough to make her reconsider and tell him something about what she really knew.

"Look," Kristy said. "What they do outside of the publicity shoots is up to them. I'm not their mom or their pastor."

85

"I'm not asking you to make a judgment. Just what you saw or knew about. When Elysse would get upset and disappear for a day or two, where did she go?"

"I have no way of knowing."

"Did she have another boyfriend she went to?"

"There were always other people hanging around. Groupies. Fans. Roadies. I don't know who she talked to. She could have other relationships that I don't know about."

"So she didn't go off on her own. She went off with another man."

"Maybe. Sometimes. I wasn't with her all the time."

"You had your suspicions," Zachary suggested. "You saw or heard things and suspected she was seeing someone else."

"Yeah, sure," she finally agreed, casually, as if it meant nothing, and she hadn't just been fighting him on it.

"Who?"

"The only people I knew were Elysse and Dain and some of the guys who helped with the equipment and packing stuff from one place to another. I didn't know anyone she was romantically involved with, other than Dain."

"I have pictures of her with other men."

"Okay. So why do you need me?"

"Did Dain know about these other men?"

"As far as I could tell, yes."

Zachary was floored by her answer. Not that Dain might have suspected or had confronted her about it or scared off another boyfriend, but just that he knew.

"He knew that she was seeing other men?"

"Not everyone is constrained to the one boy-one girl monogamous dating structure anymore," she informed Zachary. "Things are a lot more open now. For some people, anyway."

"They were dating since school; I thought they were... committed."

"Yeah, they were. But maybe sometimes they saw other people too."

"It was an 'open' relationship?"

"That's right," she agreed.

"Dain saw other people too?"

"Sure."

"Did the two of you ever get together?"

"Me and Dain?" She scoffed. "Never. He's not my type. It might… complicate things."

Zachary laughed. "It would be for me. I have enough trouble with one partner. Throwing other people into the mix…" He shook his head to himself. "Relationships take work."

It had been hard for him to commit to Kenzie in the beginning, with his ex-wife Bridget still in the back of his mind. They were over. He knew that. He knew logically that there was no way they were ever getting back together, but he had been unable to let her go, even after she was with Gordon. For a long time, Bridget had been a specter in his relationship with Kenzie.

Juggling more than one active romantic relationship at a time? It would have been impossible for him.

"I'm sure there are plenty of open relationships that work out great," Kristy said. "I've just never seen one that lasted. Sooner or later… there are jealousies, inequalities, someone in the relationship wants something more. More time with one person or more… diversions. Some people say that men aren't programmed for monogamy, but I don't know if that is true."

"Is that why they argued, then? It was about the time the two of them shared, or didn't share? Too much attention given to someone else?"

"I don't know. I didn't get involved in their arguments."

"But you would have had a pretty good idea if it was over someone else. Dain says they were just passionate people. That it was just the stresses of the tour. Being on top of each other during the vacation. That Elysse just needed more space."

"Maybe she did."

"Or maybe he didn't like her seeing someone else. Or didn't like the person she was seeing. Or didn't like the amount of time she was spending with him or talking about him."

"Sure, could have been any of that."

"I think you would know. You would overhear bits and pieces."

"Maybe there were some arguments over other people."

"Maybe?"

Kristy was reluctant to give him any more than that. "Like I said, their relationship is their business. All I want is for them to be there for the shoots and to pay their bills."

"And you got paid for the tour? All the stops, including the ones that Elysse missed?"

"Yes. The full bill was paid. So if they don't show up? *Pfft.* Then I have time to do something else."

"When you're not being harassed by the police or nosy private investigators."

Her voice was a little warmer. "Luckily, that doesn't usually happen."

"Do you know who else Elysse was seeing?"

"I've seen her with other guys, but I don't know whether they were… involved or just friends or fans. I couldn't tell you."

"Did you tell the police that she was seeing someone else?"

"They didn't ask."

"You didn't think it was relevant to her being missing? She could have been with another boyfriend."

"That's the cops' job, not mine. I wasn't going to 'out' her. If she was just shacked up somewhere, they would figure that out."

"Did Dain ask you if you knew where she was?"

"I don't know. Things were pretty confused. I don't know if I told him she didn't show up for the shoot or if he asked me where she was. We were both looking for her, checking in with each other to see if they knew where she was."

"Did he ever try to involve you in their relationship issues? Asking if you had seen her with someone else?"

"No, they just kept it to themselves. Didn't flaunt it for everyone to see. I knew what was going on, but I don't know that anyone ever said anything explicitly. Just a raised eyebrow or a nod. You know."

"Yeah. How about the others who helped with the setup and

transportation? Did they know? Was she involved with any of them?"

"No, they kept it business with the roadies. As far as I know."

"And her fans?" Zachary had read enough of the posts on Elysse's accounts to know that only Elysse and Dain were pictured on her feeds. Not her and another man. No mentions that he had seen about having other guys on the side or Dain being off with other girls. "Did they know she had an open relationship rather than a committed—rather than a *monogamous* one?"

"I never saw or heard of her posting anything like that. We would have had to work to make it fit her branding. The whole 'childhood sweethearts' thing." Kristy was silent for a moment, thinking this through. "Yeah, that would have been pretty hard to swing." She chuckled. "To *swing*," she repeated, "get it?"

Zachary groaned. "Yeah, I get it. So you don't think it was something that her fans knew about or that she wanted them to know about?"

"No. It wasn't."

"So she may have had reason to go quiet and disappear for a while. If she wanted to get together with another guy, she wouldn't want any of the fans to know about it. Even if Dain knew. Shutting off her phone and not posting so no one could track her... she might have done that on purpose just because she didn't want anyone being able to find her and another boyfriend."

"Yeah. I was never really concerned if I couldn't reach Elysse. She'd get back to me sooner or later. I wasn't worried when she didn't show up for the shoots; just irritated. Dain was the one who got worked up. He was upset and calling the police when I figured she might still show up. And if she didn't..." she shrugged. "It would be a few days before I started to worry, honestly. She'd dropped out of sight before."

"So what was different this time? Why was Dain worried?"

"I don't know. Like I said, I wasn't worried yet."

Zachary made a few more notes. He thought about the burner phone. She had still been in contact with someone. If not Dain, then who? Another boyfriend? Her family? It was too bad the police didn't have any reason to check the phone logs on that burner.

18

Zachary had told Dain that he wouldn't take the case if Dain lied to him. But it was clear that Dain was still keeping things from him. Only parceling out the information that he thought Zachary needed to know. It was frustrating but not new. Clients often had things they wanted to keep private. They didn't think they would really affect Zachary's investigation, so they held back. But Dain had to know that the fact that Elysse had other intimate partners would be relevant to the investigation.

He tapped his contacts list to find Dain's number and pressed it. Dain picked up within a few rings, so Zachary didn't have to think about what to say in a voicemail message. Not that it mattered; people in Dain's generation didn't actually listen to voicemail messages.

"Hello?"

"Dain, it's Zachary," he introduced himself in case Dain hadn't seen his name on the caller ID and had just auto answered the call.

"Yeah, Zachary. How is it going? Have you already found something?"

Zachary leaned back on the couch, closing his eyes.

"Well, I have found some interesting facts. Not necessarily what was going on with Elysse when she disappeared, but… some interesting points."

"Yeah? You think it might be relevant?"

"I'm wondering why you didn't think it was."

"What? What are you talking about?"

"I thought you were going to tell me everything you knew."

"Of course, yeah."

"Who else did you call when Elysse was missing?"

"What do you mean? I called her. Some of the crew that might be with her. Called her mom to see if she'd said anything to her. But they didn't really get along, so I didn't expect her to know anything."

"Is that all?"

"I don't know what you're looking for. I called the cops. They said to check with hospitals in the area. Said she would probably show up. It took a while to get them moving, you know. I already told you about that."

"You didn't call anyone you thought she might be with?"

"I told you… some of the people in the crew… But she was supposed to be at the maple farm and she wasn't. There wasn't really anyone else to call."

"What about her boyfriend? Or boyfriends, however many there were."

"What are you talking about?"

Zachary waited. It wasn't like Dain didn't know what he was talking about. What was the point in pretending that he didn't know what Zachary now knew? Maybe he was afraid of revealing something more than Zachary had guessed or found out.

Uncomfortable with the silence, Dain cleared his throat. "So… what did you hear? From who?"

"I am an experienced investigator. That's why you hired me, right? So I could dig up the truth."

"Yeah, of course."

"But you didn't think I would find out about your relationships? That you weren't just childhood sweethearts in a monogamous relationship."

"Well, I didn't think it was relevant."

"Really."

"What would that have to do with her disappearing on our tour?"

"Because maybe she took off with one of the other men in her life."

"No," Dain said firmly.

"I asked you: Who did you call when she disappeared?"

"Well… yeah, I checked in with other people who might know where she was."

"I will need the names and contact details of any other boyfriends. And your girlfriends, too, while you're at it."

"What would they have to do with Elysse disappearing?" Dain demanded, his voice rising in outrage.

Zachary waited a few seconds before answering. "Your relationships and where you were and who you were each with matters. Let's not pretend that it doesn't."

Dain waffled, looking for some further objection that might work. "This is a waste of time," he said eventually. "This isn't about our partners. If Elysse had been going to someone else, she would have just told me."

"You were both completely open about the time you spent with others."

"Sure. That was what we had decided. There wasn't any reason for Elysse to keep it from me."

"She would just tell you she needed time with this other guy."

"Well, we didn't like it to interfere with the influencer stuff. She had a certain persona to project. She needed to make her appearances and keep posting to bring in the income that we needed. But if we weren't working, and one of us wanted to go out with someone else, we would just work that out."

"She would tell you she was going on a date with someone else."

"Yeah. If we didn't have plans. If we had plans of our own, then she would wait until a better time."

"Would she? Or would there be an argument, and she would go away anyway?"

Dain made a noise that sounded like a growl.

"Come on, Dain," Zachary pressed. He opened his eyes and thumped his finger on the computer desk for emphasis, even though Dain couldn't see it. "What was your argument about the day she disappeared? I don't believe it was just because the two of you were stressed. Was it about the relationship? About her wanting to meet up with someone else?"

"No."

"No? About you?"

"This is ridiculous. It doesn't matter what we were arguing about. The argument didn't have anything to do with Elysse's disappearance."

"How do you know that? If you don't know what happened to her, as you claim, then you don't know what it had to do with. You don't know if she went to another man and ended up getting in a fight with him. Or deciding to run away with him. Maybe she was upset with you for something and decided he was a better provider. Or that she liked him better. Maybe she decided there had been too many other women in your life, and she wanted to be monogamous with someone. How am I supposed to figure out what she did and where she went if you don't tell me what was going on?"

"You're just supposed to... track her. I don't know. I heard you were a good private investigator, and I thought you would be able to track her and figure out where she was during that time."

"Where do you think she was? You don't think she just decided to double back on your trail and go back to the Grand Canyon, even though that is where she was found. So where do you think she went? Who do you think she went to?"

"I talked to Mike. She wasn't with him. I would have been able to tell if he was lying and she was hanging out there. But there would be no reason for her to lie and not to tell me where she was going."

"No reason you can see; that doesn't mean she wouldn't have a reason. Were you the only two partners she had? You and Mike?"

There was a slight hesitation before Dain's answer. "Yes."

"Are you sure you would know if there was someone else?"

"I… don't know. We never said that there had to be any limits. I don't think there was anyone else."

"Did you tell the police that you both had other relationships?"

"No."

"You just expected them to be able to find Elysse without that information."

"What difference would it make? They would still use the same methods to track her, wouldn't they? Looking for her car, her phone, tracking dogs in the places she was supposed to be, the public appeal. It's all the same stuff as they would have done whether they knew about the others—about Mike—or not."

"Except they would have had other people to ask. Other possible witnesses. Other people who might have had something to do with her disappearing." Zachary realized he was nearly shouting, and tried to lower his voice and talk calmly. "You know now that she doubled back on her trail, but you didn't know that then. For all you knew, someone might have killed her and stuffed her in the trunk. Mike. Someone else you haven't told me about. Your girlfriend, or however many of them there are. You didn't know if she was okay. Why wouldn't you tell the police all the details?"

"I knew how they would act. They already thought I was a suspect. I didn't want them focusing on me or any of the others. None of us did anything to her. I wanted them to find her. In case something *did* happen to her."

"You didn't know that none of you did anything."

"I did know," Dain said stubbornly. "And what do you think would have happened if I told the cops that we were in an open relationship and were both seeing other people? They would have spread the word around that we were some perverted sex club and that she was just off with someone else. They wouldn't look for her. They would out us to all the fans. I had a hard enough time getting them to open the investigation without them knowing that part."

He was probably right that the police would just have assumed Elysse was off with another partner. Especially after having had a public argument with Dain, even having slapped him in front of witnesses. She wouldn't want to be with him. She would go to her other boyfriend. Or someone else she was attracted to. They wouldn't see her as a vulnerable girl who might have been waylaid by a predator in the Vermont wilderness. Just as a girl who was off somewhere with a friend.

"Did Elysse know about your past?"

"My past?" Dain repeated, "What are you talking about? I told you that we've been friends since school. Of course she knew all about me."

"So she knew that you had been convicted of sexual assault."

Dain swore. "How did you find out about that? You can't go spreading that around. Do you know what that would do to my reputation? To Elysse's?"

"It's public record. Anyone willing to do some general background on you can find it. You're lucky none of the reporters working on Elysse's disappearance found it. They certainly should have, as soon as you were suspected in Elysse's disappearance. *I* would have."

"I pled that charge out. Because I didn't want to face twenty years in prison if something went wrong during the trial. They said that she had a solid case. She was believable. People would believe her before they would believe me. Accused means guilty these days. Where there's smoke, there's fire. If you didn't assault this girl, you probably assaulted someone else. That kind of karma just follows you around. You treat women like that and, sooner or later, you're going to get caught, and you're going to have to pay."

"You pled guilty and served a year."

"Yeah. To get it over with so I could live my life. If I went to prison, I wouldn't be out until my forties. My life would be over."

Zachary rolled his eyes at the limited view of youth. But his lawyer had probably been right. If they thought there was any chance Dain would be convicted and sentenced to twenty years or more, it was best to plead down and see what kind of deal he could get.

"And Elysse knew all of this? What you had done or been accused of? Why you pled out?"

"Yes, of course. Elysse knew the girl who accused me. Trust me, it was all just regrets. Telling her parents she hadn't been with me voluntarily. She was still their good little girl."

"She was friends with both of you? Did she know that you were with Elysse? That you guys had this... open arrangement?"

"Sure. She was Elysse's friend. Elysse introduced us."

Zachary decided he didn't want to go any further into the details. He had the answers he had been looking for.

"Okay. So, if I talk to Elysse and happen to bring it up, she won't be surprised or shocked. She knows all about what happened?"

"Why would you bring it up with her? Have you talked to her? She won't answer when I call."

"No, I haven't talked to her yet, but I hope to. And I don't want to hear from her that you were lying to me about this, too."

There was silence from Dain at first. "Yeah, fine," he said finally. "I told you, she knows it all. We were open with each other. Talked about everything."

"And this never got out on Elysse's social networks?"

"People post ugly stuff all the time. Any time there was any hint of anything, we would report it and get taken down. People knew that Elysse and I were committed to each other."

"Just not that you were seeing others as well."

"Yeah. That wasn't any of their business. We wanted to keep the brand clean. Something like that can totally throw everything into chaos. We consulted with more than one expert who said to make sure it stayed out of the media if we wanted to keep our sponsorships."

"Elysse's sponsorships."

"What?"

"Elysse's sponsorships. Not yours."

Dain grunted. "We were a unit. You don't understand that. People liked the ship. It was all a part of the brand."

"The 'ship'?" Zachary repeated.

"The friendship. The relationship," Dain said impatiently. "Elysse and Dain."

The *ship*. Zachary scratched it down in his notepad. The next time he heard it, he wouldn't have to ask.

"Look," Dain said, his voice firm, trying to get control of the conversation. "This isn't why I hired you. I don't need you looking into our relationships. I already know all that stuff. And my conviction. Sheesh. Stay out of it. If I hear you've repeated that to anyone, I'll sue you for slander."

"You can't sue someone for slander when they say something true. You can't sue me for saying you have a conviction for sexual assault, because you do."

"I don't care. I'll sue you anyway. You can't go around repeating that kind of thing. You'll wreck my reputation."

"I don't plan on repeating it to anyone. But you must understand that all this ties in to Elysse and what happened to her after your argument that day. You can't separate it out like that. You can try, but the relationship between the two of you and between you and others may all relate to what happened. I have to look into it if you want me to find out what happened to Elysse."

"Just stay out of it. Stick to tracking Elysse. Find out where she went and when. I want to know what happened. That little story she told the TV reporter was a big fat lie. I want to know what really happened."

"I'll do my best to figure it out," Zachary agreed.

He didn't say he would leave the relationships out of it. He'd already explained why it was relevant. As he moved forward with the investigation, he would continue to look at Dain, Mike, and anyone else involved with Elysse or Dain.

19

Wednesdays were therapy day. Either Zachary's individual therapy or couple's therapy, generally on alternating weeks.

Zachary saw Kenzie looking at her calendar and grimacing as she mentally planned her day over breakfast. She scratched her head.

"It is couple's day," Zachary reminded her, even though he was one hundred percent sure she remembered this and was already considering it. It was a compulsion he couldn't restrain. She knew that Zachary worried about her missing therapy on couple's day. And he knew that she tried to get there and would if it were possible and no emergencies came up. But he couldn't help being anxious about it. It was one of those things that just threw his whole day off. His whole week.

As much as he tried to stay quiet about it and just be flexible, he couldn't.

Kenzie sighed and nodded. "So... we're supposed to have dinner with Mom and Dad in Burlington tonight, and I don't think I can take off the afternoon for couple's and then go to Burlington for dinner. I could skip therapy so that I have more time for my workload and then go out to Burlington after you're done therapy, or I could take the afternoon off for couple's therapy and then go back to work when we're done to finish my work for the day."

Zachary didn't want her to have to go back to the office after therapy. Therapy was exhausting and left them emotionally raw. They liked to relax afterward with ice cream and something mindless. It wasn't fair for Kenzie to have to go back to work afterward. And it wasn't fair for her to have to cancel the planned dinner with her parents.

But the solution was easy. "I'll just do individual therapy today, then. We can do couple's next week."

"Are you sure? I know you don't like me missing."

"You're not missing it if we reschedule. That's different."

He couldn't explain why one made him crazy and the other was a relief.

"Are you sure?" Kenzie checked. "I don't like to bail on you."

"You have work that needs to be done. Neither of us is in the middle of a crisis. It's fine to put couple's off for a week."

"And how will you be after your session? You won't want to go all the way out to Burlington, will you? I mean… you'll be tired and want to spend the evening recovering. Dinners with my parents aren't exactly… relaxing."

Zachary shrugged. "It should be okay. I'll chill during the drive."

Highway driving was as good as meditation for Zachary. Better, because it was easy for him to stay focused on the road and nothing else. Meditation with nothing to focus on was impossible. Not without plenty of medication and possibly hypnosis.

"We shouldn't have scheduled it for a Wednesday, but Mom said that was the only day she had, and I really want to see Dad and make sure he's okay."

"It will be okay. You finish the work you need to do and call me when you're done. I'll be back from therapy by that time, and I'll just pick you up and we'll head out. Unless you want to come home for a shower first. Maybe we should plan for that."

"I shouldn't have any autopsies this afternoon. I think I can get by without a shower, as long as I take some evening clothes with me."

Her comment reminded Zachary that he would have to remember to shave and change into suitable clothes before picking Kenzie up. She would *not* be happy if he showed up looking like a homeless person.

"How fancy is this dinner? Do I need to wear a suit?"

"No, no suit or tie. Just..." Kenzie looked at Zachary and gestured toward his shabby work-from-home clothes. "Pants with a crease. Shirt with a collar. No sneakers."

Zachary nodded his understanding. Her clear guidelines made it easier for him: No sweats, no jeans, no t-shirts or hoodies. Formal dress was not required, but he needed to be clean-shaven and neat.

"I'll clean up and change before I go to therapy so I'm not rushed," he promised. "But... if you could talk to me sometime in the afternoon just to remind me... I'll set an alarm, but sometimes I just shut them off."

Kenzie nodded her agreement. "Okay. I'll try."

As it turned out, Zachary managed not to ignore his alarms. He was shaved and neatly dressed when Kenzie called to remind him. He felt good going to his therapy session with Dr. Boyle.

"You look good today," his therapist commented, looking him over. He didn't usually dress up for therapy appointments and she had seen him at his worst, shepherding him through some very challenging times or encouraging him to get additional help when he needed it.

Her eyes lingered on his face, and Zachary's cheeks heated slightly. She was, he knew, looking at the healing cuts on his face, revealed and, in some cases, irritated by the close shave. She knew about the package bomb. He had not tried to keep it from her.

"It's healing," Zachary said with a shrug, looking away from her to break the eye contact. "I'm fine."

"You were lucky. How are you feeling about it?"

"Fine. I think it was probably worse for Kenzie than it was for me. She was the one who had to see me like that after the explosion. All bloody and panicked. It must have been really hard for her."

"Have you talked to Kenzie about it?"

"Not much. She doesn't like to discuss it."

"You need to make sure that you keep those lines of communication open so that if she is looking for a way to talk about it, you recognize it."

Zachary nodded. "Yeah, of course."

She gave him a look that meant his "of course" was too glib. He hadn't put any thought into what effort he needed to exert to ensure that Kenzie felt like she could talk to him about the bomb and how she had felt about it.

He ran his fingers through his short-cropped hair and thought back to it. How calm and reassuring Kenzie had been after the explosion. She had recognized immediately that he was stuck in a flashback to the fire that had taken his family home when he was ten. She had reassured him that everyone had gotten out and had made the firefighter treating him repeat her words, just as the firefighters who had rescued him from the fire that day had assured him that his family had all gotten out safely. Zachary hadn't been able to get unstuck until he knew everyone had been saved from the inferno.

"I'll let her know I'm open to talking about it whenever she wants to," he assured Dr. B.

"Good. She might be afraid to bring it up, worrying it will trigger you."

"Yeah. I'll make sure."

"It's fine if she doesn't want to talk about it, too. Sometimes, we need time and distance before we're ready to deal with a traumatic event."

Zachary nodded his agreement. "Yeah, I know."

20

D r. Boyle nodded. "And how are you dealing with it?"
"Fine. No trouble."
"Really? None? You haven't noticed any increase in symptoms? Anxiety? Compulsions? Rituals?"

He shifted in his seat. "Well... I mean, I get anxious; that's natural after something like that."

"After something like what?"

Zachary took a breath. He was using avoidant language. Not saying the words that might trigger an emotional reaction and prove him wrong. "After the explosion. The detonation of the package bomb." He waited for his racing heart to slow back down before giving Dr. B a longer answer about the aftereffects that he was experiencing.

"I get nervous whenever I know a package is being delivered to the house. I got one of those electronic explosives sniffers online so that I can check out any package that I get before opening it. Even if it is something I am expecting. I just really need to know it's not going to happen again. Which is silly because the culprit is behind bars. She can't do it again, and it's not very likely that someone else would do the same thing."

"Most people don't have to deal with a bomb once in their lives, let alone twice."

She was referring, of course, to the fact that he *had* dealt with two bombs during the past year. Although the first one hadn't even been wired properly. The chances of another criminal planting another bomb for Zachary to detonate during his lifetime were extremely low.

However, the chances of Zachary being attacked were considerably higher than the average person's as long as he kept investigating violent criminals.

It was probably good that the Elysse Allan case was just a missing person case, and he already knew she had survived the ordeal, whatever it had been.

"It's perfectly reasonable to be using an explosives sniffer after that," he told Dr. B, who nodded.

"Certainly. I think it is a very reasonable response to being targeted and the injuries you sustained, which could have been much worse."

"I don't want Kenzie to get hurt either."

"No. You're very protective of your family."

"We're going to see Kenzie's parents tonight." Zachary knew it was tangential. They had been talking about his family, not Kenzie's. But he worried about Kenzie and how she was managing the stresses in her life and the memories of her abduction just a year before. "She's really worried about her dad."

"Why do you think that is?"

"I know why. Even though Walter has never admitted to being kidnapped before Kenzie was, she believes he was. He wouldn't cooperate with the kidnappers when his life was in danger, but he changed his tune as soon as they kidnapped Kenzie."

"So she worries about him and what else the kidnappers might do. They were never caught?"

"It's not just one or two guys. It's… an organization. There wasn't enough evidence for any arrests. She knows the organization, but not who exactly ordered it or the individual players. And the police can't bring the entire cartel down."

"That must make it difficult for Kenzie to let it go and feel safe."

"Yeah. She says that she's okay. She's moved on. But… I know she still really worries about her dad. And she's still really triggered by things that remind her of the abduction, especially now, the same time of year."

"That's not surprising."

"No." Zachary hesitated, wondering if he had sounded like he was judging her or was implying that she was overreacting. "It makes sense to me. I wish she would talk about it more. But I know it can be really hard to talk about something so traumatic."

"You have your own traumas that you're not ready to talk about yet."

He wanted to protest and say that he had dealt with all those things, as evidenced by his going to therapy appointments every week. Clearly, he was doing everything in his power to deal with his past traumas.

But there were things he still could not talk about. He had never talked about his own abduction and the torture he had endured at the hands of Archuro. And he didn't know if he would ever be able to. He didn't want to think about it, let alone talk about it and share it with another person. He didn't want to hear the words spoken aloud, even by himself. He was still trying to bury what had happened to him.

He'd been able to work through some of the aftereffects of the abuse he had suffered, to regain the ground he had lost in his intimate relationship with Kenzie due to the experience. But some things were still too difficult to talk about.

Zachary was glad for the highway drive to Lisa's mansion in Burlington. He had told Kenzie that he would be fine going to her family dinner after his therapy session, but he didn't know if he would have been able to manage it without the hypnotic effect of a couple of hours on the road.

He and Kenzie asked each other about their days, and then Kenzie fell silent, occupying herself with her phone and watching out the window. He didn't think she was upset with him. Tense about the upcoming dinner, maybe. Worried about Walter. But mostly, he sensed she was just giving him the space he needed to decompress, and he appreciated it.

Eventually, he turned into the winding driveway that led up to the house. Kenzie put away her phone and checked her reflection in the visor mirror. "That didn't seem like it took very much time at all. How are you doing? Okay? We can tell them you're not feeling very well tonight and keep it short if you don't think you can manage... the usual."

Dinner at home was a brief affair, having a chat while they ate their meal and then spending the evening cuddling, watching a movie, or spending time together doing something else. But dinner with Lisa and Walter was a long, drawn-out affair. A before-dinner drink and conversation that might last as long as an hour. Individual courses served in the dining room, drawn out, with conversation, sometimes drinks or palate cleansers served between courses. And after all of that, retiring to the study for after-dinner coffee or drinks. It took the entire evening, and then they had another two-hour drive home afterward. Kenzie had to be up early to attend at the medical examiner's office in the morning. For that reason, they didn't usually have dinner with Walter and Lisa on a weeknight.

"I'm fine," Zachary assured Kenzie. "But if you want to shorten things up a bit so you can get home and to bed, feel free to use me as an excuse."

Kenzie nodded. "I might. We'll see."

"I don't mind."

He should probably feel guilty for using his mental health as an excuse to get out of dinner early. But he didn't. It was for Kenzie.

After parking, he opened his door and quickly walked around the car to open Kenzie's door and escort her to the house. Lisa opened the door as they approached. She and Kenzie air-kissed, and Lisa offered her cheek to Zachary.

"It's so nice to see both of you," she said. "I know this wasn't the best night to meet. We'll try to keep things short so you can get back home in good time."

"Oh, don't worry about that," Kenzie murmured, despite the fact she'd just been talking about engineering it so they could get out early. "Where's Dad?"

She hadn't seen him since Lisa had informed them that Walter was retiring, telling people it was due to his poor health. It was all a cover, a ruse to get him out from under the thumb of the cartel that had abducted Kenzie. If he were too ill to work, he could no longer lobby for or against the bills that they wanted him to in the Senate.

Even though Lisa had said that it was just an act and Kenzie had been able to talk to her father on the phone, she still needed to see him to convince herself he was not suffering from a stroke or other infirmity that they were trying to keep from her.

21

L isa smiled and led them to the study, where they usually partook of pre-dinner drinks. The smell of old leather-bound books and a trace of bourbon tickled Zachary's nose.

Lola, the dog Lisa had rescued, followed. She nudged Zachary to give her attention. Zachary bent down to scratch her ears as they reached the study, stroking the delicate, silky fur. Kenzie had tunnel vision, not even glancing at the dog. She hurried into the study ahead of everyone else. Zachary and Lisa hung back, giving her plenty of space.

"Dad!" Kenzie approached Walter, who was standing by the wet bar. She hugged him tightly and then stepped back to look him over.

Walter looked well. He still seemed to be losing weight, which Kenzie was convinced was because of the trauma of the kidnapping or some as yet undiagnosed or unannounced disease. Walter swore he was just taking care of himself better, but Kenzie didn't believe it. Zachary wasn't sure what to think.

But there was no sign of slackness in his face or unsteadiness in his stance. Nothing that suggested a stroke or convalescence.

"I told you I'm fine, MacKenzie," he said in an amused tone.

"As far the rest of the world is concerned, my health is failing, but you and I know that I'm still in the pink of health. Now, you stop worrying about it."

"I know what you said. I just… had to see it for myself. I've been really worried about you." She blew out her breath in a long sigh of relief. "You must be getting cabin fever not being able to go to the Senate, cooped up here all day."

Walter poured himself a drink, barely covering the bottom of the tumbler. He took a sip and put it down. "I must admit, it has been a shock to my system. I am used to being out all the time. Busy in the senate, talking to people, devising strategies, dinners out. It is very different being home all the time. Like I am under quarantine, except I'm not actually sick, so lying in bed all day is out of the question."

"We've been doing what we can to keep him occupied," Lisa contributed, stepping into the study to join the conversation. Zachary and Lola followed her in. "He jogs around the property. Uses my gym equipment. We've installed a putting green in one of the upstairs rooms."

"I'm catching up on all of the movies that I've said I'll watch someday," Walter said with half a smile. "All of the cult classics from the past twenty… or forty years."

"All the important stuff," Kenzie laughed.

"I'm doing crosswords and sudoku religiously. Keep the brain active. But I need something else to occupy it. Maybe I should learn computers. I'm not a Luddite, but there is more that I don't know about computers than I would like to admit. I'm sure I could find a lot more to do if I knew my way around the computer better."

"You'd probably enjoy research," Zachary suggested. "Not just following current events or scrolling on Facebook, but digging into the meat of issues that you never had a chance to before. You're very well-read and knowledgeable in many areas. You know, there are online research projects you could join. Or crowd sleuthing."

Walter poured a glass of wine for his wife and for Kenzie when she nodded. He looked at Zachary. "A Coke, Zachary? Fruit juice?"

"Coke," he agreed.

"What kind of research projects?" Walter asked while pouring him a glass. "And what exactly is crowd sleuthing?"

"There are sites you can sign up on or projects you can join. Helping to solve cold cases or to process information that the police post. Say the police have an unknown man in a five-year-old photo. They run facial recognition on him, but it doesn't get a hit in his jurisdiction's police database. He doesn't have the resources to do anything else with it."

Zachary took a sip of the Coke.

"So, he posts it on a crowd sleuthing site, asking for assistance. A thousand people around the globe, some law enforcement but mostly civilians, start searching through archives and running facial recognition against social media and public online videos of sports games, train stations, celebrations, all that kind of thing. If each of those thousand people spends ten hours on it—and many times, it is more like ten thousand sleuths spending fifty hours on it—that is ten thousand man-hours that the police department could not afford, and they might turn something up."

"Do they really do that?" Walter asked with interest, "And they solve crimes that way?"

"There are people who spend all day doing nothing but look for children that have been posted on missing person sites. People who comb through public records of John Doe murders trying to identify the victims. There are innocence projects where they are trying to get innocent people off of death row. There's an incredible amount of work being done by volunteers and retirees. And the more tools that become available for civilians, the more they can do."

"That's fascinating! I had no idea."

"I used crowd sleuthing on a recent case, and they matched my missing person with an unidentified homicide victim dumped in Canada ten years ago. Within twenty-four hours."

"Amazing!"

Zachary had been tempted to use crowd sleuthing on the Elysse Allan case to figure out where Elysse had been on what days, and who she might have been with. But with Elysse having such a large fan following, he would not be able to keep his investigation a secret from her fans, and he could just see Elysse threatening to sue him for implying that her story was a lie or taking out a restraining order against him. Her case, unfortunately, had to be kept as far as possible from the crowd sleuths. No one could know that he was trying to track her movements and figure out what had happened to her during the missing time.

"That's a really good idea," Kenzie said, sounding surprised.

Surprised that Zachary had thought of something that would help to keep her father busy? Surprised that her father was interested or that such projects existed? He raised his brows at her.

"I mean it," Kenzie said. "That sounds like something Walter would be really good at."

"I'll need some training," Walter said. "Would you be interested in helping me with that? Then, who knows? Maybe I could help you with some of your cases."

Kenzie flashed Zachary a warning look. She had warned him against getting involved in anything Walter approached him about before. Walter was the kind of person who always had an ulterior motive. If he was offering Zachary something with one hand, Zachary had better be on the alert for the other hand picking his pocket. After a couple of such encounters, Zachary came to understand that Kenzie knew what she was talking about and that it wasn't just resentment over how he had disappointed her as a child. Walter had a brilliant mind and was always several moves ahead of everyone else, but he worked for himself and his own interests.

But in this case, Zachary already knew why Walter was doing it. He was interested in it because he was bored. It was a way for him to keep working and doing good in his own little corner of the world, even if he was trapped in front of a computer and unable to pursue the political agendas that had occupied him for the past forty years. This time, there was no danger that Walter was just trying to push through—or block—a bill that Zachary had no interest in or operated against his interests.

"I'd be happy to help," Zachary agreed. He thought about the best way to approach the new project, which had just come to him while they'd been talking. "I'll pull together some of the sites and projects that I'm aware of and let you know what they're working on, and you can see what kind of project you would be interested in working on. Then we'll know what specifically to teach you to do."

Walter nodded earnestly. "That would be great. I would love to be able to still do something... that makes a difference in the world."

"What about the family foundation?" Lisa asked, frowning. The Kirsch family foundation was technically Walter's family legacy, but Lisa had been the one running it since it had passed into his hands. She had been eager to have him put more time into it now that he was "retired."

"I'll still work with the foundation," Walter promised. "I told you I would. But it won't take up all my time, and I don't want it to."

Zachary sipped his Coke and watched the two of them anxiously. He had not intended to cause tension between them.

"Fine," Lisa said flatly. "As long as you are going to do what you promised."

"I will," Walter reiterated. "But it was never my life's dream to run the family foundation. We have the board to direct it, the staff to run it, MacKenzie to take it over one day. It is not my passion. But I'm not going to let it founder, either."

Kenzie didn't look too thrilled at Walter declaring it would be her responsibility one day, even though of course she knew that was the plan. It wasn't her passion, either. Lisa had taken well to running the foundation. She had always been involved with charitable ventures. But Zachary thought it was getting to be a strain. She didn't want to be the only one involved in running it. She wanted her husband and daughter to step up and do their bit, too.

"I will help with the foundation," Walter reiterated. "But this will give me something else to do, too. You wouldn't want me tinkering and making a bunch of changes to how the foundation is run, would you?"

Lisa raised her brows in mock horror. "Dear me, no! Do you think I would let you dismantle everything I've worked so hard to set up?" She put her hand to her heart and shook her head. "The very thought!"

Walter's laughter was a low rumble.

After eyeing everyone to reassure himself that they were all reasonably onside with his proposal to help Walter dip his toes into the world of cyber sleuthing and justice, Zachary asked one further question.

"What kind of work would you be most interested in doing? Is there a particular area I should focus on?"

The older man scratched his chin thoughtfully. "Your mention of the innocence projects is intriguing. I imagine there would be a lot of work to be done on legal research—statutes, case studies, legal arguments, that sort of thing. That is the area that is closest to the skills that I already have. I can read bills and statutes all day long."

Zachary nodded. "Great. I'll focus on that."

22

Zachary was pleased to be able to pick up the copies of the documents he had been granted access to as a result of his public information request after he dropped Kenzie at the medical examiner's office the next day. After paying the fee for copying costs and administration time, he was given a nice thick file to take home.

It took most of the day to sort it into piles and to start plotting the places that Elysse had been seen on the map. There had, of course, been Elysse sightings all over the country, but the police had tried to narrow it down to the actual sightings. Places more than one person had seen her. The direction she was likely to go. They had been so certain that she would be headed toward New York that they had discounted any reports that had her doubling back on her trail and heading west toward the Grand Canyon.

He dropped pins on a virtual map, one for each report, ignoring the police department's bias. Elysse had many fans. They were far more likely to spot her than the average missing person.

Clusters started to form. While there were a lot of outliers, he could definitely see several steps leading back to the Grand Canyon. Those were the reports he would follow up on.

He couldn't listen to the hours of interviews with Dain Porter.

Instead, he scanned the transcripts of the interviews into his computer so that he could search for specific keywords and phrases. He tapped a few searches in as he tested it out.

"Mike" had a few false positives before Zachary came across a hit that was actually good.

Dain had once referred to Mike Milton as a roadie. Although both Dain and Kristy denied that Elysse was involved with any of the roadies or other crew, Zachary suspected this was Elysse's other lover.

It took a few searches to track down the right Mike Milton. Not a resident of Vermont, but of Oregon. He occasionally commented on Elysse's social media posts. Zachary brewed more coffee and spent a few minutes building a profile of the man before calling him.

He was not the bushy-bearded possible stalker. But then, Zachary hadn't expected him to be. If he was one of the roadies, Kristy likely knew him and would not misidentify him as a possible stalker.

Mike was a redhead with a thin beard. Taller than Elysse, but skinny, likely not outweighing her. Unlikely to have kidnapped her, at least not by himself with physical force. There were other methods. Threats or manipulation, drugs, the use of a weapon. Recruiting help. A hood over her head so that she couldn't see her attacker and realize that he was smaller and lighter than she was. Though, if they were lovers she would presumably recognize his voice.

Zachary found what appeared to be Mike's current phone number, and called to see if he could get anywhere with him as a witness.

"Hello?" the voice was lower than he would have expected for such a skinny man.

"Hi. Mike Milton? My name is Zachary Goldman, and I wondered if I could talk to you for a few minutes about Elysse Allan."

"Sorry, I think you have a wrong number."

"This is Mike Milton, right?"

"Yes," he admitted after a second or two of hesitation.

"Right. And I wanted to talk to you about Elysse Allan."

"I don't have anything to say about her... sorry."

"Do you know where she is right now?"

"Who are you? A reporter? I don't know why you people won't leave Elysse alone. You know she isn't missing anymore, so why won't you just let her live her life?"

"No, I'm not a reporter. I am looking into the circumstances of her disappearance. Trying to sort out the true story."

"What are you talking about, the true story? She already told her story to the press."

"Sure... but she didn't tell them anything they didn't already know, did she? I don't know about you, but I don't believe the story about her just wanting some space and going back to the Grand Canyon because she didn't get a chance to see everything she wanted to when she had been through there with Dain."

"Well..." Mike was still hesitant, but he sounded intrigued by what Zachary had said. Not ready to hang up on Zachary. Not yet.

"And the fact that she hasn't posted anything at all to social media since she came back... well, that says something, don't you think? Nothing in six months?"

"What do you think it means?"

"Well, I'm still trying to figure that out. But I think it means there was a bit more to her disappearance than just wanting some space for a few days."

"Uh-huh."

"Have you been in contact with her at all? She hasn't had any contact with Dain. Is that because she is with you, or because she's avoiding all contact?"

"I don't see how that's your business."

Zachary didn't argue that it was. Because, of course, it wouldn't be, except that Dain had made it Zachary's business. If he were reading the man's signals right, Mike was just as curious about what had happened to her in the missing time as Dain. Given a little time, he thought he could get Mike on his side without telling him anything about why he was looking into Elysse's disappearance six months after the fact.

"She hasn't answered my calls," Mike said eventually. "I don't know what's going on, why she just cut me off. Both of us. I think... maybe she is depressed."

"Could be," Zachary agreed. "I wondered about that. I wonder if she's cut herself off from everyone. She could be so traumatized by what happened to her while she was missing that she can't leave the house or talk to anyone about it."

"Uh-huh."

"Have you been to her house?"

Dain had not been there physically. He'd honored Elysse's desire to be left alone and had not gone to her house when she wouldn't answer his calls. Maybe she had told him at some point that if he did so, she would charge him with trespassing or harassment. But could she keep him away from her house if they had been living together? What about his possessions which had collected at her house? Even if they didn't live together, he had probably left a few things at her house for when he was there. Had she boxed them up and shipped them to him with the warning not to bother her at the house?

"I tried once or twice," Mike said. Which probably meant three or four times, or more. "She just says to leave her alone. I don't think she has left the house. Not while—I mean, not that I could tell. It looked like she's just been at home."

Not while he'd been watching, Zachary finished Mike's inter-rupted thought in his head. So Mike had felt the compulsion to sit outside her house, waiting for her to go for a walk or to drive some-where in her car. Zachary had been on enough stakeouts—and had spent enough time in front of his ex-wife Bridget's house when he shouldn't be—to understand the growing anxiety over a woman who never left the house. Was she sick or injured? What else could be wrong? How long would it be before she left the house? What if she never left the house?

23

"Have you talked to anyone from her family?" Zachary asked. "Is she talking to anyone? Or has she totally cut herself off?"

"They don't know me. I wouldn't call them."

"They don't know that you're involved with her?"

"Who exactly are you?" Mike asked, irritation clear in his voice. "I don't even know who you are. How do you know me or anything about me?"

"I'm a private investigator. Hired by someone who is concerned about Elysse and what happened to her. The same way as you are concerned."

"Who hired you? Dain?"

"I'm not at liberty to say."

"Well, it certainly wasn't her family. Had to be Dain."

"Are you the only two she was involved with? As far as you know, I mean."

Zachary decided to plant a seed of doubt. Imply that there was someone else. Or more than one other. Mike had been willing to share Elysse with Dain. He had probably come onto the scene after Dain, so he'd accepted that he was second fiddle and would have to take whatever time Elysse was willing to give him. But how would he feel if there were someone else? Someone who hadn't been around before him. Or who Elysse hadn't bothered to mention.

"Yes," Mike asserted. "It was just us. And she said..." He trailed off.

"What, that she was breaking up with Dain and then it would just be the two of you?"

"Well... the two of them weren't that compatible. Elysse had been with Dain for a long time. They argued. Drove each other crazy sometimes. She said she was going to break up with him permanently. Not go back to him."

"Is that what you thought happened when she disappeared in Vermont?"

"Well... I didn't know. I thought maybe she decided she'd had enough. And then when she didn't answer any calls or respond in any other way..." There was a long, painful pause. Zachary could imagine all the scenarios that must have gone through his head. "I was worried... that Dain had done something. They had a big blowup and... I don't know—he hit her or strangled her. Killed her by accident and then reported her as missing to take the focus from himself. But of course... everyone thought he'd done it, especially the cops. Then, when she showed up in the Grand Canyon, and she was okay..."

His voice broke slightly. Zachary heard the relief Mike had felt on learning she was still alive and then the realization that she'd blocked him, just like everyone else. She had let them all think that she had been murdered.

Zachary wondered again what had prevented her from calling anyone. Had it been her choice? Had something happened to her? She'd emerged from the Grand Canyon with a new phone.

"Did you talk to the police while she was missing?" Zachary asked, knowing the answer to the question already. He had the police reports in front of him. He'd spent all day going through them. They had not talked to Mike, despite the fact that they were intimate partners. No one had told the police.

"No. I never talked to them."

"You didn't think it was important for them to know everything you did?"

"About what? I didn't know anything."

"When you had last seen her. What kind of a mood she was in? Whether you thought she had run away or would harm herself. If you thought that someone else might have harmed her."

"Well… no one came to me. They could have asked me and I would have told them."

"But you didn't want word to get out that you and Elysse were seeing each other."

"She didn't want that to be public," Mike's voice took on a brittle quality. "It might damage her brand."

"So I heard."

"Her *brand*," Mike sneered. "I thought the whole point of these social networks is that they give you a chance to express yourself, to be who you really are and connect with like-minded people. What's the point in establishing a persona that isn't your own? For everyone to fall in love with and applaud someone who doesn't exist? To have to pretend to be this… model… this shell that you created? Her *brand* was supposed to be her true self. Not someone made up."

"And you wanted her to admit that… she was with you? Or that she was with multiple partners?"

"What's the difference? Either way, it wasn't going to happen. She wouldn't break it to her fans that she and Dain weren't the real deal. Her one true love." Mike made a gagging sound. "Seriously. Did anyone really believe that? Did they think she was a real person or a made-up character? Who stays with one person for their whole life? From elementary school? Come on; that doesn't happen. Did she really think she could sell that? And keep selling it forever? She needed to admit that it was over with Dain and get on with her life."

"What about other guys?"

There was a definite chill on the other end of the phone call.

"What are you talking about?"

"Other guys she was seeing. You and Dain weren't the only ones, right? Who else do I need to talk to?"

Silence from Mike.

"Do you really think she didn't call anyone during the five days she was missing?" Zachary probed. "She had a phone with her. She let the one you had the number for run out of juice, but she had another one."

24

"She wasn't seeing anyone else," Mike told Zachary flatly. "Just Dain and me. That's it. I don't know why she had that other phone. Maybe she found it. Maybe she lost the charger for her regular phone, so she had to get a burner until she could get back to civilization. Maybe she just needed space."

"Then who did she call? She didn't call you? Dain? Why did she get a phone if she wasn't going to call anyone?"

"For safety. People do that, you know. Especially women. They don't feel safe if there isn't a way for them to call 9-1-1. She wanted to be on her own, but she still needed a way to call for help if something went wrong."

The explanation would have passed muster if not for the fact that Elysse had let her regular phone die. If she didn't want to be bothered or tracked and just wanted something in case of an emergency, all she had to do was power off her phone. It would keep it charged for when she needed it. Eliminate the annoying ringing. All she had to do to call for help was turn it back on.

Something else could have happened to the phone. Elysse could have dropped it over a cliff or into the river. But she hadn't said that in her TV interview. It would have been dramatic and exciting, just the kind of thing to include in a TV report. Instead, she had said that it had run out of juice.

There were chargers everywhere. The store where she had picked up the burner had doubtless sold replacement charge cables. There were portable battery packs to charge phones while away from civilization. Solar chargers, even. There was no reason for her to be left in the wilderness with no power on her regular phone, but an extra phone on hand.

"Do you really think that's what happened?" he asked Mike. "Does it make any sense?"

"She wasn't seeing anyone else," Mike insisted. "She just ran out of battery. I'm telling you. She just wanted to disconnect. There's nothing criminal about that. There's nothing wrong with it."

"Kristy and Dain both said Elysse was not involved with any of the roadies."

"Yeah," Mike agreed, clearly missing the point.

"But weren't you one of the roadies?"

"Well…" Mike sounded guilty. "I wasn't actually a roadie, no. I helped with some of the set-up, so it looked like I had a reason to be there. But I wasn't one of the staff."

"So everybody knew that you weren't a roadie?"

"Everybody? No. Dain knew, of course. I don't know if Kristy did. But she was…" Mike hummed as he tried to think of the word he wanted. "Kristy was sort of… separate. She wasn't part of the road crew. She was independent. She didn't want to know about anything other than the locations and the campaign plan. Just the stuff that she was directly involved with. She didn't have anything to do with the roadies and… looked the other way when any personal stuff came up with Elysse."

"She didn't want to know about any of the personal drama. Just the business."

"Yeah. And even then, just enough about the business to do her job. PR stuff. Getting the branding right. Getting the right shots and the perfect posts. Anything else… she was invisible. She didn't want to see it."

Kristy was invisible? Or she was blind?

"Was Kristy involved with anyone on the crew? Or with Dain?"

"With Dain?" Mike scoffed. "No. She wouldn't have anything to do with someone like him."

"What does that mean? Someone like him?"

"She was very... picky about who she would have anything to do with off camera."

Zachary wondered whether that meant Mike had pursued Kristy, and she had turned him down. Or whether Dain had tried to get Kristy's attention and he'd been rejected.

"So you don't know whether Elysse was seeing anyone else. Any of the other roadies? A fan who met up with the group every few days? Someone at home?"

"No one else," Mike insisted.

"Who else was Dain seeing?"

"Dain?"

"It was an open relationship, right? So that must mean that he was seeing other people as well. Isn't it usually the guy who wants an open relationship because he wants to see other girls? He doesn't want to break up, but he wants to be able to see others."

"That's... a generalization. It doesn't always work that way. It could just as easily have been that Elysse wanted to see other men."

"You."

"Maybe. The relationship with Dain was old, established. She didn't want to give it up, even though they were not good for each other."

"Were you trying to get her to break up with Dain?"

"I knew better than to encourage a breakup. Elysse was like a toddler who would do the opposite of whatever you told her. If I'd told her to break up, it would have had the opposite effect."

"So you had to pretend to encourage it. Or at least to be neutral."

"Yeah. And to hope that she would see for herself how toxic that relationship was becoming."

"What made you think it was *toxic*?"

The hesitation on the other end of the line made Zachary sure that Mike knew about the physical abuse between Dain and Elysse.

But Mike didn't know whether to say anything about it. He didn't want to be slapped with a lawsuit for slander.

"The physical abuse?" Zachary asked.

"I'd... heard that."

"You never saw any physical abuse yourself?"

"No. Nothing much. I mean, maybe some minor contact. But nothing... serious."

"What would you consider serious?"

"Well... broken bones, internal injuries. She had bruises, but I never saw Dain..." Mike cleared his throat uncomfortably.

"What kind of bruises?"

"I don't know. Sometimes Elysse had bruises, but I thought they might just be... from a game."

"The two of them were into S&M?"

"I don't know. We didn't do that," Mike emphasized. "She never asked me to do anything. But... I don't know; she and Dain had been together off and on for years. Maybe they were bored."

"Or maybe it was abuse."

"I don't know. She never said there was."

25

Kenzie had gone out to buy groceries. Zachary looked out the window a few times, waiting for her return. They often did grocery shopping together, so when Kenzie sent Zachary out with a list, he knew what brands to get and where to find everything she liked. But he also got on her nerves when she shopped, saying the wrong thing, distracting her, and drawing attention to things she might want to buy when she just wanted to pick up the things on her list and get out of there.

And there had been a couple of incidents at the grocery store. A couple of scares where one of them had been stalked or surprised by a suspect.

He would think that would make her want him to be there with her, that she would want the protection he could provide. At least a second person who could dial 9-1-1, since Zachary didn't carry a gun and was not exactly a trained ninja.

But instead of Kenzie wanting him there at her side to be a second set of eyes and to protect her from stalkers and sneak attacks, his presence seemed to trigger her anxiety even more. She jumped or tensed every time he checked behind him or swiveled around to look at something.

And it had been worse lately, with the anniversary of her abduction. She had been more jumpy and irritable for weeks, but Zachary hadn't realized why until Sergeant Campbell had asked him how she was doing with the anniversary of the kidnapping.

So as much as he wanted to help Kenzie with the errands on her list and to be there to comfort and support her, he knew he had to just stay out of her way and let her do things for herself and work things out on her own.

He saw Kenzie pull to the curb in front of the house to park. He went to the door to put on his boots and help her carry the groceries in. At least he could do that without upsetting her.

Kenzie and the car were out of sight while he was at the front door putting on his boots, but that was only for a few seconds. He was moving quickly so that he could get to the car to help her before she grabbed everything from the trunk herself.

He heard a screech of tires and yanked the door open to see what was happening. A white van had pulled in hard behind his car. Kenzie was standing in the space between the two vehicles to get the groceries out of the trunk. She was half turned around, looking at the van, her eyes wide in alarm. Her face was as white as the undisturbed snow in the front yard. Zachary took a couple of steps out of the house, frowning, trying to process what was happening. He didn't recognize the van. A delivery truck? Someone visiting a neighbor? Why was it driving so recklessly and pulling in so close to Kenzie like that?

The side door of the van slid open, and two men jumped out. No coats. Black balaclavas. Big, muscular men. Zachary was running toward them even before his conscious brain had come to a conclusion.

"Hey! Get out of here! I called the police!"

He had worried in the past about having to run. He had not regained a natural running stride after a spinal cord injury sustained several years earlier when he and Kenzie had been in a car accident. Anything faster than a walking pace was awkward and he always felt like he was going to trip over his big, ungainly feet.

And it happened. He didn't know whether his foot caught on the edge of a sidewalk block or the heel of his other foot but, suddenly, Zachary was flying through the air, hands outstretched to catch himself. He hit the pavement with a bone-jarring crash and slid forward with the momentum of his brief sprint.

Ignoring the pain of his landing and the embarrassment over his clumsiness, Zachary scrambled awkwardly to his feet and kept going.

He shouted incoherently at the men, more concerned with distracting them from Kenzie than saying anything sensible. He wasn't going to talk them out of what they were there for. It wasn't the time for reason or argument.

The men turned toward him, white skin and wide eyes behind the holes of the black balaclavas. Their hands were up, ready, prepared to fight him, but they were thankfully unarmed. At least Zachary wasn't going to die from a gunshot in the next few seconds.

"Get away from her!" he screamed at them, "Get out of here! The police are on their way!"

He flew into the attackers, like crashing into a brick wall. Both of them were solid and twice his size. He was thrown back from them, to trip again and land on his back this time, the wind knocked out of him. But he managed to avoid hitting the back of his head on the pavement and knocking himself out.

He started to get to his feet a second time, bellowing like an enraged bull. One of the men swung his foot and made contact with Zachary's rib cage, landing with the dull thud of a watermelon smashing. Red and black splotches crowded out Zachary's vision and, for a few seconds, he was fighting blindly, swinging wildly and hoping to at least touch one of them.

He took a couple of blows to the face and then they seemed to be retreating. Zachary forced himself to his feet again, worried they had counted him out and were turning back to Kenzie. He screamed at them, followed them back to the door of the van like a yappy dog nipping at the heels of a bear, totally outclassed but determined to protect his mate.

They jumped into the open van, and he grabbed at them, trying to pull them back, to pull off their masks, something. One of them managed to kick him square in the chest, throwing him back as the van first reversed, then pulled out and screeched away as they rolled the door shut.

Lying on the sidewalk, Zachary hoped Kenzie had the presence of mind to get at least part of the license plate number, as he was at the wrong angle to see it and was too slow to get to his feet before it was out of sight.

26

Zachary could hear shouts in the distance. Neighbors or passersby who hadn't been close enough to help during the attack were now rushing to his aid. In the distance, the high keen of sirens and, closer to the spot where Zachary had landed, the roar of powerful engines. The klaxon of their security alarm.

He struggled to get to his feet, adrenaline still burning in his veins, heart beating wildly, his primitive brain sure that the fight was not yet over. There might be more attackers. A second wave. He needed to banish all foes, to be sure that they were safe from enemies who would hurt, steal, or kill.

"It's okay," someone said firmly beside him, pushing him down gently but insistently. "Just stay down; they're gone, and you're hurt."

"Kenzie!" Zachary tried to get to her, flailing ineffectually against the hands that tried to hold him down. "Kenzie!"

"I'm okay." Her voice was faint and far away. "I'm okay, Zachary. I'm fine. It's over."

"No. Let me go!"

He managed to push away those trying to help him and crawl

to his feet and then stagger over to Kenzie, who was still standing frozen behind the car, trunk open, her eyes as big as saucers.

"Kenzie." He wrapped his arms around her and held her tightly, trying to convince himself that she was okay. The danger had passed and he had done everything necessary to protect his partner.

Kenzie clung to him.

There were slamming car doors as the racing engines stopped in a wide arc around Zachary, Kenzie, and Zachary's car. Looking around, he took in the sight of the armed and vested men from their security company. They strode up, looking around, trying to identify what had just happened.

"Sir? Ma'am? How can we help?"

Zachary held to Kenzie tightly. She didn't squirm like she wanted away, so he didn't let go.

"A van," he told them sharply. "White van. Just left. License plate…" He looked wildly around at the neighbors who were trying to help, those creeping out of the houses to see what was going on, and anyone who might have been on the street and gotten a good look at the van. "Who saw the plates? Anyone get any of it?" He pushed back slightly from Kenzie to look in her face. "Did you see the plate?"

Kenzie shook her head. "No. I didn't see anything. I was just… paralyzed."

"It's okay." He hugged her to him again. She was starting to shake. "She's cold. A blanket?"

One of the security men returned to his car. He popped the trunk and pulled out a red and white first aid box and folded blankets. The neighbors helped to unfold the blankets and drape them around Kenzie's and Zachary's shoulders.

The sirens got closer and, finally, a police car pulled up to the scene. It seemed like a feeble effort after the three cars from the security company. A uniformed cop got out and looked around.

"What's going on here? An alert was sent to the police from the security company. Was there a break-in?"

Zachary shook his head. "Attempted abduction."

"Abduction? Is everyone okay?" The cop looked at Zachary,

shaking his head. "You should sit down. Come sit in my car where it's warm."

"No," Zachary clung to Kenzie, unwilling to release her or move anywhere else. He kissed the top of her head. "We can go into the house. Sit together."

"Is it clear?" the cop asked, looking toward the house and the security company officers. "Was there a break-in?"

"No, no break-in," Zachary insisted.

"I'll check it out," one of the security employees offered. He approached the house, hand on his holster.

A minute later, the klaxon alarm from inside the house was silenced and everyone let out a breath. It was suddenly unnaturally quiet. The guard came back out of the house. "It's secure," he told them. "Let's get these folks off the street and somewhere they can be treated."

Zachary allowed himself to be shepherded back into the house. He released Kenzie from the tight embrace and walked with her, one arm around her body, back into the house. They sat down on the couch together. But Zachary found himself unable to stay there. He bounced to his feet, looking out the window for further danger.

"Someone needs to bring the groceries in," he muttered, pacing across the living room and checking out the hallway and the kitchen himself, even though he knew that it had already been checked out by the security guard and that the chances someone had snuck inside while he'd been trying to fight off the intruders were very slim.

"Please sit down," the cop told him, motioning back to where Kenzie was sitting.

"Come on," Kenzie encouraged, patting the seat next to her.

Zachary couldn't have settled down enough to sit under any other circumstances, but Kenzie needed him to sit with her. So he could do it.

"Are you okay?" He pulled Kenzie close to him once more to kiss her and look her over to make sure.

"You're bleeding," Kenzie told him. "You need to let them take a look at you and fix you up, or go to the emergency room."

"I'm not going to the emergency room," he said immediately.

She had obviously anticipated this response. "Then you need to let them look at you."

Zachary rolled his eyes at the security guard with the first aid kit. He nodded his agreement. The man approached him and started an examination of his head and face.

Zachary looked down at his hands as the guard looked at his face, vaguely aware they were part of him and should be hurting. They were badly skinned, ripped up from catching himself after tripping, sliding them across the ice and concrete. They were bleeding and one large flap of skin was peeled back, almost completely torn away. Zachary's eyes moved from his hands to his knees, also torn and scraped, but somewhat protected by his pants.

Kenzie was shaking and shuddering. Her breath came in gasps and sobs. "I can't believe it. I can't believe they came after me again."

She drew a long, shuddering breath, trying to pull herself together.

"Again?" the cop demanded.

"A year ago," Zachary told him. "She was taken a year ago and then released."

"Taken?"

"Abducted."

Kenzie just sobbed and shook, unable to answer. She hadn't been able to even say the words 'kidnapped' or 'abducted' since it had happened. She still had nightmares. She still worried every time she left the house that it was going to happen again.

The cop's eyes were riveted on Zachary as the guard used gauze to clean up Zachary's face, one after another coming away wet with blood. It didn't hurt. He might have been working on someone else's face.

"What happened a year ago?"

Zachary swallowed. He had been told the story, but he hadn't been there that day. Would he have been able to stop them if he had been? Did they let him today? The two men had been much bigger, stronger, and more skilled than Zachary. Had they left because it hadn't gone smoothly and they knew the police would be there soon? They could have just tased Zachary and Kenzie and thrown them into the van, worrying about properly securing them afterward, using duct tape or handcuffs to ensure there would be no more resistance.

"The same as today," he told the cop. "She was getting something out of the trunk of the car. They drove up behind her. Grabbed her and threw her in a van. Drove away."

"Do you know who was behind that abduction?"

"Russian mob." Zachary looked at Kenzie, worrying. Was this the Russians' response to Walter's retirement? Did they think they could scare him back out of retirement by kidnapping or threatening his daughter again? "They didn't make any arrests. There wasn't enough evidence as to who exactly did it. But we know it was the Russians."

"And have you had further problems with this gang?"

Zachary looked at Kenzie again, trying to discern how much information she wanted to give and answer appropriately. "Nothing specific. Nothing targeting Kenzie."

"Have you had threats?" the cop looked at Kenzie. When Zachary opened his mouth to answer, he held up his hand, stopping him. "I asked the lady."

"No," Kenzie shook her head. "No... no threats."

But had the killing of Senator Neufeld's wife been a warning to Walter? Did that warning also apply to Kenzie, since she was the one wedge they had that worked on Walter in the past?

"Can you describe the people involved in this attempted abduction?" He was speaking to Zachary again.

The security guard had stopped mopping blood, using sharp-smelling alcohol wipes to sanitize the cuts and suture strips to hold them closed. Zachary was lucky he hadn't broken any teeth tripping and landing face down on the sidewalk like he had.

"Two males, maybe six feet tall, heavyset, muscular builds. Black shirts and balaclavas."

"Did you know them?"

"Not with balaclavas on."

"Did they speak to you? Did you recognize any voices?"

"They didn't say anything." Zachary looked at Kenzie. "I don't think so. They didn't say anything, did they?"

"No."

"They didn't make any threats? They didn't call you by name or give you any warnings? Shout at you to put your hands up?"

Zachary looked at Kenzie. She shook her head. "No. Nothing. They just drove up and were getting out of the van when Zachary raced out of the house and went after them."

"You decided to attack two six-foot-tall men?" the cop asked Zachary in disbelief, as if shocked that he had no sense of self-preservation. "You didn't think to maybe do something safer, like calling the police?"

"There wasn't time," Zachary objected. He nodded to the security guard. "I pressed the panic button on the alarm before leaving the house. They got here faster than you did."

"Hitting the panic button was the right choice," the guard assured him. "We were able to get here and get the police here very quickly. But I would not recommend attacking intruders."

"They would have taken her if I hadn't," Zachary said stubbornly.

But he wondered if it were true. They had left without their quarry. That didn't make sense to him. One of them could have kept him busy while the other grabbed Kenzie. Neither Zachary nor Kenzie were trained fighters. So why had the abductors just turned and left?

27

T he guard performing the first aid moved on to Zachary's hands, grimacing as he looked at them. "What we need is a basin of warm water and clean towels."

He glanced in Kenzie's direction, but she didn't move. Zachary tensed to stand and the guard shook his head. "Check the kitchen," he told one of the others.

It took some time to treat Zachary's hands and knees. Kenzie sat numbly watching. The adrenaline in Zachary's bloodstream dissipated, and he started to crash. Like Kenzie, he started shaking and suddenly found that he was exhausted. He didn't want to do anything but go to the bedroom, crawl into bed, and sleep. And he could manage without the first two. The dip in adrenaline also meant he started to feel his injuries.

While his hands, knees, and face burned, that wasn't the worst of it. He had dealt with burns being debrided when he was ten. The cuts and scrapes from the sidewalk and ice couldn't compete with that. But as he shifted, looking for a more comfortable position, the pain in his ribs and sternum made him gasp and curl his body, trying to guard against any further aggravation. Kenzie put her hand on his shoulder.

"We need to get you to the hospital. I couldn't see everything, but you took a few really good hits and kicks. Have you got broken ribs?"

Breathing shallowly, Zachary nodded. But there was little point in going to the hospital. They wouldn't do anything but prescribe him some painkillers and tell him to take it easy for a few weeks until he started to feel better. They wouldn't bind them up. They didn't do that anymore.

"You could have other internal injuries." Her voice was shaky. "We need to check. Get a few scans to make sure there's no bleeding."

"I'm not going to the hospital to sit around for hours," Zachary told her, keeping his voice as calm and soft as possible. "You'll be able to tell if there is anything wrong. It's just a few bumps and bruises; I don't want to have to hang out at the hospital just to have them tell me to come home to sleep when what I want to do is just stay home and sleep."

"We need to make sure you are okay!"

"I am," Zachary assured her. She didn't usually get emotional over his injuries, and he didn't like hearing her voice break. "Everything will be okay. I just need to rest, right? That's what they would tell me. I've had broken ribs before."

"I can't believe you went running out there! Don't you know how dangerous that was? Attacking two guys like that? And there was someone else in the van, too, at least the driver. What were you thinking?"

Zachary blinked at her. "I was thinking I wasn't going to let them kidnap my girlfriend."

"Well, you're lucky they didn't kill you and k-kid—and take me! What if they'd had guns?"

"She's got a point," the cop said.

"No. I wasn't going to let them do anything to you. I wouldn't just stand by. If there was anything I could do, I was going to do it. I love you. I couldn't do that."

Kenzie covered her eyes with both hands, sobbing.

He wanted to assure her that they were both okay. There wasn't anything to cry about. But it was probably just the relief. Everything hitting her now that she knew they were safe. She just needed to let out a little bit of the tension.

Zachary patted her leg, trying to convey his concern and reassurance.

Things were happening outside. More police arrived, talking with those already on the scene, taping off a small area behind the car where the van had been and where Zachary and the men had fought. Or, more accurately, where they'd beaten Zachary. He wasn't even sure he'd landed a blow on either one of them. He certainly hadn't done any damage. To himself, yes, but not to the potential kidnappers.

Another cop entered the house. Zachary could hear him giving instructions to the others, his slow, purposeful voice clear and calm. He walked into the living room and looked them over.

"Dr. Kirsch."

Kenzie didn't uncover her face. She just shook her head.

"How is everything going here?" The cop got close enough for Zachary to read his name badge. Detective Cameron. He knew that Cameron had worked with Kenzie on a couple of cases.

"She was doing all right," the cop said, sounding slightly defensive. "I think it's just… it's just the shock. It's just hit her."

"You're Zachary?" Cameron held out his hand for Zachary to shake. "Detective Cameron." Zachary squeezed it and then withdrew his hand, pulling the blanket he wore closer. "Is there something we can do?"

"I think… she just needs some space," Zachary said. "A little time to get herself together."

Cameron nodded. "I'm sure it was pretty traumatic. Do you want to go to the bedroom? Take a few minutes?"

Zachary squeezed Kenzie's shoulders. "Do you want to?" he asked.

"No."

"No?" Zachary was confused. "What do you want, then?"

"I want all these people out of my house," Kenzie said sharply. "Everyone. Get out of my house and leave me alone."

She continued to sob.

Zachary's face heated as he looked at the security guards and cops who had been taking care of them. Not pushing hard for information, but being kind and relaxed and helping them out. Taking care of Zachary's scrapes and bruises. Finding out what had happened.

"Uh, sorry," he apologized. "We just need... it's been rough..."

He didn't want to imply that they had done anything wrong or that Kenzie was doing anything wrong by asking them to leave. He understood that sometimes Kenzie might just need to do things her way to process her emotions. They were different people, and her needs were different from his.

"We'll need to get an official statement," the cop who had been talking to them pointed out.

"It can wait," Cameron told him. "They are clearly in no state to be giving one right now. Let's just give them the house. We'll process the scene outside, and if Zachary feels up to coming out and walking us through what he remembers...?"

"I don't know. Just let me take care of Kenzie first. You already know what happened. Signed statements can wait a day or two."

"Your video extends out to the curb, doesn't it?" one of the security company guards asked. "In case someone messes with your vehicles?"

"Yes."

"So you have video of what happened."

"Uh... yeah, I guess we do. Can you run a copy for the police?"

"I sure can. If I have your verbal password?"

Zachary gave it to him, and the guard nodded. "I'll do that now."

28

The various cops and guards filed out of the house. Zachary escorted the cops and security guys out. He returned to Kenzie, who was still crying, though she had lowered her hands from her face.

"I don't know what's wrong with me. I'm never this emotional. I just… nothing happened. There's nothing to cry about. But I can't stop myself. I just feel like…" She broke off, shaking her head, and sobbed.

Zachary could identify with her better than she probably realized. How many times had he lost control in the throes of a panic attack, of a compulsion he couldn't resist, or some other reaction that was beyond his control?

"It's okay," he assured her. "Just give yourself some time. Trying to control it… will just make things worse."

"What could be worse than this?" Kenzie demanded, again giving way to loud sobs.

"Do you want to lie down? We can cuddle. I can get you a cold drink. It really helps."

"I don't want anything, just to feel better. How can I not be safe in my own home? How can they just walk up to me, my house, my car, and take over? Isn't there any way to protect ourselves? We've got the security system, but that doesn't stop anyone from just walking up to me anywhere and…"

Zachary swallowed. He, too, had been snatched, although he had been drugged and didn't remember the details clearly. Maybe that had been a blessing, so that his brain didn't know what to be afraid of, wasn't triggered by similar circumstances. He already had enough other triggers.

"It's going to take some time," Zachary tried to assure her.

"They can just walk up to my house and take me!" Kenzie shouted at the top of her lungs. The cops outside the house heard her through the closed windows and heads turned toward them. Zachary ignored them.

"I'm going to call Dr. B," he told her.

It wasn't a question. Zachary wasn't asking Kenzie for permission or for her opinion. Kenzie needed someone to get her through this, and Zachary wasn't a therapist. He was more damaged than she was, and the last thing she needed was for him to have a meltdown or to scream back in her face. It was all he could do to hold himself together when faced with screamed, unreasonable demands and accusations. His body wanted to react. Fight or flight. He couldn't stand there and take it without reacting.

Kenzie didn't stalk out of the room and slam the bedroom door. She just cried, as heartbreakingly as if he had screamed at her. Zachary removed himself from the room. As much as he wanted to hold her and soothe the sobs away, he couldn't help her now.

Dr. Boyle answered after several rings. "Zachary. How can I help you?"

"There's been… you know when Kenzie was kidnapped? How she told us it had happened? It's happened again, they pulled up in a white van. Guys in balaclavas got out to grab her—"

"Zachary! She was kidnapped again?"

"No. They didn't get her. I went out there. The security alarm. The police. They took off again. She's safe, but…"

"Oh, dear. Where are you? The hospital?"

"No, at home. Do you think… I didn't know whether to take her to the hospital. I don't know if she *would* go. She wanted me to go for X-rays, but I think she would object if I said that she needed to be admitted. And I don't know if she does. She's just... upset. And it's perfectly normal to be upset after something like that, right?"

"Of course. Give me your address so I don't have to dig it out of the files. I'll come right over."

Zachary told Detective Cameron to let the doctor through when she arrived. Then he sat with Kenzie on the couch, rubbed her back, and tried to keep her calm until Dr. Boyle could get there. How many times had she comforted him during a panic attack or flashback? She always provided a comforting hand, a soothing voice, and the anchoring that he needed to get back on a stable footing. Now, it was his turn to try to give Kenzie some of that back.

Roxboro was a small town, so it did not take Dr. B long to get there. Cameron escorted her to the door so she didn't have to fight her way through the cops. Zachary was waiting in the doorway and let her in before re-arming the security alarm. She watched him, and then, when he had checked the alarm a couple of times to make sure it was properly armed, he motioned for her to go ahead of him to the living room.

The therapist looked around the room. She had never been to the house before. She sat down on the couch, not touching Kenzie.

"Kenzie? It's Dr. Boyle. How are you doing?"

Predictably, Kenzie was too upset to answer her, but continued to sob. She did raise her head long enough to reach out and touch Dr. B's leg to acknowledge she was there, but nothing escaped her mouth except sobs.

Zachary hovered in the doorway to the living room, unsure where he should be.

"We're probably going to be a while," Dr. B told him. "I can come find you if I need you. Is there something you could do to occupy yourself?"

Zachary nodded. He stepped closer to grab his laptop. "I'll be in the bedroom. No, the office. Better if I work at the desk. And then, if she wants to lie down, I'm out of the way."

Dr. Boyle nodded. "That sounds good. I imagine she'll be very tired and she might want to."

With how tired Zachary was feeling, he agreed. He wouldn't mind lying down himself, even though he rarely napped during the day. There was a spare bedroom; if Kenzie wanted her space, Zachary might just stretch out in there in the next hour or two. He had taken painkillers for his ribs, but every breath he took caused a deep, burning pain.

"Are *you* okay?" Dr. Boyle asked. "I can understand why Kenzie wanted you to go to the hospital. You look like you took quite a beating."

"I'm okay. It's Kenzie I'm worried about. She's the one who needs support."

"We *all* need support, and you've gone through an ordeal too. You and I will talk later."

Zachary nodded. He retreated to the home office at the end of the hall and set up there.

He didn't try to listen in on Kenzie and the therapist. He wanted to know that she was okay and that Dr. B could help her calm down and move forward from the attempted kidnapping, but he knew that Kenzie needed space. Away from him.

If he were in the room, he would feel compelled to answer Dr. B's questions in Kenzie's place, explain all of what had happened, and put his own spin on what Kenzie was feeling instead of just waiting for her to speak up for herself. But stepping in to explain things for her would not be helpful. And if she wanted to vent about Zachary, about what he had or hadn't done during the attack or afterward, he should be out of the way so that she could talk openly and not worry that he would overhear and get upset about her feelings.

He needed something to occupy his time. Dr. B had said it might take a while, and he didn't know whether that time would be measured in minutes or in hours. Or whether they would need to go to the hospital eventually. As hard as it was for Zachary to know when he needed to admit himself to the hospital, it was even more challenging to know what someone else's emotional needs were.

Kenzie had never been hospitalized for mental health issues. He had always been the one who had needed the extra support.

If Kenzie were admitted to the hospital, Zachary would have to call Lisa to explain what had happened, and that was going to be a difficult conversation.

29

Zachary opened his computer. He didn't go to his email inbox or social networks. If he started on one of those apps, he would just scroll mindlessly, thinking about the attack and Kenzie and feeding his own anxiety.

He needed a project that he could really dig into and lose himself in, something that would require all his concentration.

He pulled up the map that he'd been working on for Elysse. What he needed to focus on was each location she had definitely been seen at. He would define that as five sightings in a small town or isolated setting or ten sightings in a big city, no matter where they were, whether they were on the route he expected Elysse to take or not. The police had been blinded by their investigative bias, focusing solely on sightings that were on the route from Vermont to New York. They had been taken entirely off guard when Elysse had shown up in the Grand Canyon, caught flat-footed looking for her on the other side of the country.

If he could find definitive proof that she had been in a place, it didn't matter whether it matched his expectations or not. Currently, no one knew where she had been. They assumed she had taken a direct route from Vermont to the Grand Canyon, but that wasn't what the preliminary clusters seemed to indicate. Elysse had the money to go wherever she wanted to, by whatever means she wanted to. She could have flown to Paris before returning to the Grand Canyon. Zachary didn't know whether she'd been driving her own car when she was discovered. Even if she had, someone else could have driven it there. Elysse and her car might have taken completely different routes to get there. He couldn't make any assumptions. He was looking for *proof* of where she had been.

He started working through the locations witnesses said they had seen her at. He would rate police tips as the most likely genuine sightings, and then search for social media posts that confirmed she had been in a particular location. With everyone carrying a camera in their pocket, there was a good chance that wherever she had been, someone had taken a picture of her.

In smaller towns, he searched for hotels and noted them down with their phone numbers. He would call to find out whether Elysse had been checked in there. See whether they had any video surveillance footage that he could review. He wouldn't say he was looking for Elysse, of course. He would come up with a good cover story. But what he would be looking for was video confirming that Elysse had been there.

Where had she been? Had she been by herself or with someone? If she was traveling alone, had she been stalked? At some point, had it changed from a voluntary disappearance to an abduction? She might have flounced off after the argument with Dain, still planning to be at her next shoot, but then something had happened to prevent her.

She might even have gone missing on purpose, wanting to draw attention to herself and to get her fans worked up. It wouldn't be the first time something like that had happened. As long as her fans didn't figure out that it had been on purpose, they would welcome her back with open arms and be even more enthusiastic followers in the future.

If Elysse had been abducted or coerced in some way, why had she not reported that to her fans? Why hadn't she said anything about it when she was interviewed on TV? To the police? To Dain or Mike? Instead, she had just withdrawn, not even posting anything online after that. Unless she had created new social accounts under different names and email addresses, Elysse had not posted a single thing since her disappearance. Not an "I'm back" post, "Sorry I was out of touch," or even a post saying that she would not be participating in social media anymore and was taking her life in another direction.

He started to group the pictures he found online according to location. Some of them were extremely grainy, low-light, or taken from the wrong angle so that her face could not be seen. But a few were clear and appeared to show somewhere she had been. Sometimes, she was wearing the same clothing in pictures taken by different fans, which increased the likelihood that it was her. He had a fairly good facial recognition app that he used to search internet pictures and profiles, but the fan photos were rarely good enough quality to use the app on. It returned percentages like "10% match," indicating that the results were not reliable.

He worked away at it, going down the list of locations in order of the number of police tips. He switched pin colors on his virtual map, starting to drop blue pins where he had pictures or video that he considered good enough to prove Elysse had been at the location.

30

"Zachary?"

Zachary pulled himself away from the project and looked around. He had been so completely immersed in the job that he had forgotten where he was. In the office. Waiting for Dr. B to let him know how Kenzie was doing and what their next step was. And now she was in the doorway, waiting for him to orient himself and switch his focus to the here and now.

"Sorry, Dr. B. I lost track of time... how is Kenzie?"

She glanced around the office, but there wasn't a good place for her to sit down to chat. "Do you want to meet in the living room or kitchen?"

"Yeah. Sorry." He stood up quickly, and the resulting knife of pain from his ribs and sternum had him gasping for breath and holding on to the desk to keep from keeling over. He'd forgotten his injuries while sitting nearly motionless in the chair, hyperfocused on his project.

"Are you all right?" The doctor was at his side, touching his arm, ready to provide support or to help him sit back down again.

Zachary took a slow, shallow breath, waiting for the pain to subside enough for him to move again. "Yeah. I'm fine."

"Fine?" she repeated with clear disapproval.

One of the rules he and Kenzie had agreed to follow, both in therapy and in their personal communications, was never to say that they were fine or any other polite social reply to brush off the question. His answer needed to be thoughtful and honest. If he didn't want to be honest about his feelings, then an "I don't want to talk about it" was acceptable. But not saying he was good when he was not.

"I'm… pretty sore," he revised. "Physically. I forgot for a minute and moved too fast. If I take it easy, I will be—if I take it easy, it won't hurt so much. I want to sit down and talk about how Kenzie is doing."

Dr. Boyle kept her hand on his arm, escorting him toward the door and then letting go when they arrived at the hallway. She let him walk ahead of her, watching carefully. He could choose the couch, which would be more comfortable but more difficult to get back up from. Or he could choose a kitchen chair, which would be supportive and easier to get up from when they were done.

The kitchen was a good choice. Zachary got them each a glass of water before beginning and started brewing a new pot of coffee. He looked sideways at the clock, totally disoriented about the time of day, and saw that it was late in the evening. Maybe too late to offer guests coffee.

"Thank you." Dr. B took a sip of the water. "Talking, especially when there is lots of emotion involved, is thirsty work."

"Kenzie is lying down?" Zachary asked. It was a simple conclusion based on the fact that she wasn't in the living room or kitchen. And he hadn't heard her leave the house. Granted, he had been deep into his research project but thought he would have heard the door open. It would have been concerning enough for his unconscious brain to send a warning to his consciousness that someone was coming or going.

"Yes. Hopefully, a few hours of sleep will help Kenzie to recover more quickly."

"Is she okay? You don't think she needs to go to the hospital?"

"I think she will fare better here, where everything is familiar, and she doesn't have people hovering over her. She needs some time to process what happened." Dr. Boyle tapped the side of her glass lightly as she thought. "The negative of staying here is, of course, that this is where both the abduction and today's attempted abduction occurred. Will she have negative associations with it? Will being here make her more anxious rather than less? It may be a while before we have the answers to those questions."

"It's Kenzie's house… I hope she doesn't… I wouldn't want her to have to move somewhere else because of what happened here. Because she doesn't feel safe."

"How about you? Do you feel safe here?"

It was a good question, because Zachary had been attacked there more than once. Not just outside on the street, but inside the house. A break-in where he was assaulted. A letter bomb. And those were not the only incidents. But he still felt like it was home. He didn't like to think of moving.

He had moved so many times as a child that he tended to get overly attached to places. Kenzie would have to initiate a move because he didn't want to even consider it.

"I feel safe here," he told Dr. B. "Mostly. We've got a security alarm."

"That didn't help you today. That doesn't help when something happens outside the house."

Was she trying to make him more anxious?

"It did help today. I hit the panic button and the security company arrived in minutes. They have a very fast response time."

"But you were the one who had to intervene physically. What would have happened if they'd been a little longer?"

"I don't know." Zachary shook his head slowly, thinking back on it again. "I don't know if… I don't know how committed they were to snatching her… Maybe it was just intended to scare her."

"Really." Dr. Boyle studied him, small frown lines appearing between her brows. "Is that what you really think, or is it something you made up to make yourself feel better?"

Zachary sipped his water and thought about it. *Was* he just trying to make himself feel better about it? Telling himself that they weren't really in danger and the Russians didn't really want to snatch Kenzie, but had just been sending a warning to her father? Seeing how Walter would respond?

"There were two guys," he said slowly. "Both of them twice as big as me. I don't lift weights or fight. I don't know any martial arts. I've done a little self-defense training, but I'm not skilled. These guys probably live for the next fight. They had no trouble throwing me around like a rag doll."

He indicated the damage to his face and breathed slowly, trying to keep his body from reacting to recounting the story. He didn't need to relive it. He was just talking.

"Kenzie isn't any more a fighter than I am. They could still have grabbed her. Just swatted me out of the way or sucker-punched me so I couldn't breathe. Or tased or shot me. But they didn't even try. They didn't have a hood to put over her head or zip ties that I saw. If they were really going to snatch her, they could have had her in the van before I got to the end of the sidewalk. They could have had weapons. Point a gun at her and one at me, and we couldn't have done a thing to stop them."

Dr. Boyle nodded. "Okay, I'm convinced. Either they were not professionals and didn't know what they were doing, or they never actually planned to take her."

"I think it was just intended to scare her."

"Well, they did that," the therapist said with a sigh. "They did a very good job of that."

Zachary nodded. "Is she going to be okay? I know you can't say for sure, but... Kenzie was already having trouble before this happened. We haven't discussed it much in therapy because she wasn't ready. But... I think it has been bothering her a lot lately, with the anniversary and her dad deciding to retire."

"She's having a hard time," Dr. Boyle admitted. "A very hard time. As you would expect. Is it something she will be able to get over easily? I'm afraid I don't think so. I've asked her to try an anti-anxiety prescription for a few weeks. If we can get her through the next little while without any major setbacks, I'll be much more confident about her recovery."

"What does that mean? That she won't have to go to the hospital? That the prescription will only be temporary? What about work?"

"One day at a time," she warned him. "And for now... one hour at a time. Don't worry about the future; worry about now. Supporting her recovery right now, this minute."

Zachary nodded. He wanted to know how the whole picture would turn out when they had hardly even put pencil to paper.

"So... today." He glanced toward the bedroom. "She's going to have a sleep and see how she feels when she gets up. You gave her a prescription. Has she taken anything yet?"

"Yes." Dr. Boyle outlined the protocol she had prescribed for Kenzie. Zachary had more than passing familiarity with the medications, how they worked, and what side effects Kenzie might experience.

"You'll be a good resource for her because you're familiar with these prescriptions. And with how difficult it is to admit that you need help. You've had your own challenges with not wanting to take anxiety meds, so you can empathize with her. But... don't encourage her to just see how things go without them. She needs the med support for a little while or she *is* going to end up in the hospital."

"Okay."

Dr. Boyle nodded. "I guess that's it, unless you have any other questions or concerns."

"What about work? Should I encourage her to take some time off? Or to go if she feels like going? Is she required to tell them if she's on medications?"

"No, it's up to her. She can decide how she feels and what she wants to tell them. She might want to get out of the house and to do something to keep her mind off things, or she may feel like she can't handle anything right now. Or she may go into the office and decide twenty minutes later that she can't handle it and needs to go home."

"Yeah. Okay. So just be there and let her figure out what works for her."

Dr. B nodded. "I would also like her to consider individual

therapy to help work through the aftermath of the abduction. And now this incident as well. I've given her three names to choose from. I know we've talked about it before and she has held back. But I think we are getting to the point where it is no longer optional. She needs to take care of her mental health."

"Yeah. I hope Kenzie listens to you."

The therapist smiled. She had dealt with Zachary enough both in individual therapy and couple's therapy to understand that he was saying he wasn't going to push Kenzie into it. Dr. Boyle could do the pushing; hopefully, that would be more effective.

31

After Dr. Boyle left, Zachary fixed himself a snack and got back to work, though he moved his laptop back out of the office and into the living room, where he preferred to work and could watch out the window so he knew when the police were gone. There weren't many left out there, and the security guards appeared to have left. He didn't need them there anymore, so that was just fine.

He reviewed the work he had already done, each place he could establish that Elysse had been, and what day or days she had been there. The shape of the trip was starting to gel, but he wasn't sure how much more he knew now about the reason for her disappearance. Learning where she was and why she was there were two very different things.

He tried to keep one ear cocked for movement from the bedroom, not to get so immersed in the work that he ignored Kenzie. Today, she needed him. Right now, she needed him to stay out of the way and let her sleep but, in an hour or two, she might need him to listen, fix her a snack or nightcap, or make phone calls on her behalf. He didn't want to be oblivious to her needs.

It was a couple more hours before he heard her moving around, first in the bed and then getting up to use the en suite bathroom.

He went to the bedroom door to talk to her when she returned from the bathroom.

Kenzie was slightly startled when she came out of the bathroom and saw him from the corner of her eye. She blew out her breath and nodded.

"Hey. Sorry, I guess I screwed up our evening together."

Zachary shook his head. "You didn't screw anything up. How are you doing?"

"I feel all… muzzy. I guess it's better than bawling my eyes out. But I just feel thick-headed and gross."

Zachary just nodded and didn't comment. She might be feeling that way because of the medication, her long nap, the letdown from a burst of adrenaline, or the emotional fallout of the experience.

"Are you hungry? You should probably have something to eat." It had been a long time since her last meal, and she would have burned through extra energy with the attempted kidnapping.

"No, not really."

"Ice cream?"

Kenzie gave him a tired smile. "I know ice cream has magical properties, but I'm not up to it tonight."

"Okay. Just let me know if you change your mind, and I'll make it for you."

"I can probably manage to get ice cream for myself."

"Not today. Today, it's my job," Zachary told her firmly.

Kenzie didn't argue. She rubbed her eyes with her palms. "Are they finished out there?" She looked toward the bedroom window, which faced the street. But the blinds were shut so she couldn't see.

"Yeah, it looks like the last of them are gone. Just you and me now."

"Good. I know they were here to investigate and try to catch these guys, but having them out there made me antsy."

"Did you want to do something for a couple of hours? Or are you going to go back to sleep?" He wasn't sure whether she would have her second wind now and be unable to sleep even though it was late, or she would want to just climb back into bed.

"You're probably ready for bed."

"Me? No." Clearly, she was hoping he didn't want to go to sleep now. "You want to put on a movie? Cuddle? Work out some tension...?" He waggled his brows suggestively.

Kenzie shook her head. "Not up to any extra-curricular activities tonight. A movie sounds like a good idea if you really don't mind staying up for a couple more hours."

32

K enzie fell asleep as they watched movies, her head resting on Zachary's shoulder. He stayed there, not daring to move, while she breathed heavily. A few times, she startled awake, snuggled close, watched the TV, and fell asleep again in a few seconds. Zachary stroked her hair and back in a way he hoped was comforting.

Long after his arm fell asleep, he decided she was finally deep enough asleep for him to move. He put throw pillows around her, trying to build them up as he slid away from her, gently transitioning her to sleeping against a pile of pillows in a roughly Zachary-shaped configuration. He moved his computer to the other end of the couch and kept working. His ribs were burning, and his brain had been telling him for a long time that it was time to go to sleep, so he finally rested his head on the arm of the couch and one remaining throw pillow and fell asleep.

In the morning, Kenzie did not wake up until the coffee was brewing. She was used to being woken up by her phone alarm, and she had left her phone in the bedroom. Zachary had decided she needed to sleep as long as possible, so he did not retrieve her phone for her or tell her that it was getting late. He knew the ringtone that would indicate she had been called out to a scene, but that one didn't sound, so he let her sleep. Kenzie had talked to Dr. Cook before about being able to work on her own schedule, starting later if she had to, so it wasn't like she would get fired if she didn't get in at the usual hour.

Eventually, she started to stir. She sat up amid the pile of pillows he had put her to sleep on and rubbed her eyes, sniffing the air.

"What time is it?"

"Eight-thirty."

"Eight-thirty? I should be out of here!"

"You needed to sleep."

"Well, not that long! Why didn't you wake me up?"

"I thought you needed sleep more than you needed to get there at a particular time. You didn't say you had any meetings this morning."

"You can't decide that for me," she snapped. "You should have woken me up and asked if I wanted to sleep late."

"Then you wouldn't have been sleeping. You would be awake, and you might not be able to get back to sleep. You certainly wouldn't have been able to get the sound sleep that you had."

"You still should have asked."

"Next time."

"Is that coffee?" Of course she knew it was. It couldn't be anything else. "Bring me some. I have to wake myself up."

"Are you sure you don't need to sleep longer?"

"After eight-thirty? No way. I never sleep that late."

"You were up late. You had a rough day yesterday. You needed it. If you're worried about what Dr. Cook will say, have Dr. B write you a note."

"I don't need a doctor's note! I *am* a doctor. And I have the flexibility to start at whatever time I want. I don't need a note."

Zachary held back from pointing out that her concern about being late seemed unnecessary given her flexible schedule. He took her a cup of coffee, not in a travel mug, and sat down beside her. Hovering over her might make her feel like she had to get up and get moving on her morning routine. If he sat with her, then she would want to stay with him, have a short visit, and not feel like she had to rush the morning.

At least, that was his plan.

Kenzie took a sip of the coffee and then blew on it. "Hot."

"Scalding," he agreed. "Don't burn yourself."

"I should let it cool while I shower and get dressed."

"Or you could just sit here for a while and relax."

She grunted, and she didn't get up. That was something, anyway.

"Do you want to take a vacation?" he asked.

Kenzie scowled. "Because you think I'm too traumatized to work? No."

"Because I need to check out Elysse Allan's travel route. I thought maybe… we could do it together."

"How can you check out her travel route? You know what route she took?"

"Roughly," he agreed. "Places Elysse slept or ate, where people spotted her. The police discounted the tips that were outside of the area they thought she should be in. If she'd had a falling out with Dain, she would want to go home, not back to the Grand Canyon. It would take a few days driving long hours to get there, but it was only a short drive to get to New York and catch her flight home."

"But she never did that."

"No. But by the time they started to expand their search, she was long gone. And then she was found."

"It was a crazy case. Why did Elysse go back to the Grand Canyon? Why didn't she tell anyone where she was or what she was doing? It was so bizarre when you called me to tell me they had found her alive, acting like a tourist in the Grand Canyon. Totally opposite to what I thought they would find. I was still expecting her to be brought into the morgue one day."

She sipped her coffee after blowing on it, and it was cool enough to take a couple of tiny sips.

"So can you?" Zachary persisted. "Today is Friday. Tell Dr. Cook you're dealing with some family business. Take the next three days off. Tell him it might extend to Monday. If we catch a plane rather than driving, we can visit the top priority locations in three days. You can get away—" Zachary glanced out the window at the street and the car by the curb. "Get away from the snow and cold weather. Pamper yourself at a nice hotel for a couple of days. Take some time away from the death and the stress."

"That sounds really good, but…"

He waited for her to explain why she couldn't. Kenzie sipped her coffee.

"It hasn't been *that* busy this week," she mused. "Dr. Cook can handle it if anything urgent comes up."

"You haven't had a vacation, even a long weekend, in how long?"

She rolled her eyes. Probably not since she had been suspended. And that hadn't been voluntary. She loved her work and didn't like to leave her responsibilities for too long. Especially with Dr. Wiltshire being away. She wanted to be responsible and reliable. But she had already proven herself many times over.

"If you had the flu, you'd have to take at least three days," Zachary suggested. "They have to be able to cover you for that long."

"They can," Kenzie admitted. "But it's so last-minute. I don't like to do that to Dr. Cook."

"If you were sick, he wouldn't have any warning."

"No, that's true."

Zachary just sat sipping his coffee. He knew if he said too much or pushed it too hard, she would think of all the reasons she couldn't go on a trip with him. He wanted her to think of the reasons she could and should go.

Everyone needed a break now and then for mental health. Kenzie had been stressed, so it would be nice to take a little break. A few days wouldn't set her back that much. If there were a mass casualty event, she could fly back.

"I don't know." Kenzie gave a little laugh. "You really think I could? Just take off for a few days? And that will be long enough for your investigation?"

"If it's not, I'll extend it. You can decide whether to continue with me or to go back. But it shouldn't take longer for me to follow her trail than it did for her to travel it in the first place."

"She was gone for five days."

"Yes."

"So it shouldn't be more than five days. That's not long, when two days are a weekend. That's only three business days."

Zachary nodded his agreement. He was getting excited. He could see she was seriously considering it and was on the edge of saying yes. It would get her away from the site of her abduction. She could sleep in hotels without worrying about someone coming after her. It would be a fresh start and help get her back on track. That, combined with the anti-anxiety pills, would ensure that she was rested and calm and ready to go back to work on Monday. Or Tuesday or Wednesday, if it went a bit longer.

"I'm just going to talk to Dr. Cook," Kenzie said, rising from the couch. "See what he thinks."

Zachary watched her walk out of the living room to make the call from the privacy of the bedroom. He started a mental list of what he would need to pack for the trip and the route they would take.

They worked in tandem, each packing their bags and discussing what they did or didn't need for the trip. Zachary was used to packing light, and Kenzie tended to take more than she needed, just in case.

"You should let your mom know you're going to be away," Zachary suggested.

Kenzie stopped packing and looked at him, her face a frozen mask.

He swallowed. "What?"

"I should tell her about what happened?"

Zachary's mind raced and he replayed his own words in his head, checking to see whether that had somehow slipped out in place of what he had intended to say. He shook his head, frowning.

161

"That's not what I said."

Kenzie swore. She clearly wasn't hearing him, thinking about the voice in her own head that was telling her she had to explain to her parents what had happened. Telling her mother that she had nearly been kidnapped again. Telling her father that the Russians were still trying to keep their hold on him. Telling either of them how anxious and emotional she was about it, her therapist insisting that it was bad enough that she needed to be medicated for a few weeks at least.

"Zach…"

"I'm not going to make you do anything," he promised. "You decide what you want to tell them or not, and I won't say anything to them."

"How am I going to tell them all this?"

"Maybe you don't. Maybe you wait until we get back and see what you feel like telling them when you've had some time to think about it."

"No," she sighed heavily. "I can't do that. I have to let them know what happened and where I'm going. They deserve to know. I would be really upset if they didn't tell me what was going on. I *was* really upset when they didn't tell me what was going on with Dad and Maksim. I was really upset that they didn't think they needed to tell me something that important."

Zachary said nothing, folding his clothes into small packets and fitting them into his carry-on.

"They are going to freak out," Kenzie groaned.

"Then maybe it's a good thing you're leaving town."

33

Kenzie was right about her parents not being happy to hear the news of the recent attack. Normally, Kenzie would have gone to another room to make a personal call to her parents and avoid disturbing Zachary's work. This time, however, she called with Zachary sitting beside her, using speaker-phone so they could both participate. Kenzie wasn't sure she would be able to explain what had happened without getting emotional.

Zachary thought she had every right to be emotional and should not be so worried about crying in front of her parents. Or on the phone with them. She was a human being with emotions, and they were family.

But the Kirsches had some very clear ideas about how to behave in various social situations, and Zachary assumed she had been told in the past not to cry over some upsetting situation. Or maybe Lisa and Walter had just modeled the stiff upper lip. Maybe Kenzie had learned not to show her grief when her sister Amanda had been sick or when she had died, and in the dozens of fundraisers where her life and death had been discussed since then. Grief was a private thing; she had been taught one way or another that one should only shed tears in private.

Of course, Zachary wasn't much better. He couldn't count the number of foster homes or other situations where he had been told that boys didn't cry, that he had nothing to cry about, or to wipe those tears away and act like a man. His ex-wife Bridget had been mortified by any show of emotion or weakness by Zachary in public and castigated him in private.

It had taken a lot of therapy sessions, both with Kenzie and alone, to get to the point where he wasn't so embarrassed and afraid to cry in front of Kenzie or Dr. Boyle. He still felt like a failure when he couldn't contain his emotions.

But he thought Kenzie should feel more free to cry. Her parents were supposed to be educating themselves on mental illness, trauma, and other issues that should have taught them that expressing emotion, especially during a traumatic situation, was a good thing, not bad.

"MacKenzie," Lisa greeted warmly, "what a wonderful surprise. I wasn't expecting to hear from you. Are you at work?"

"No, Mom. I need to talk to you and Dad. Is he there?"

Since they were pretending that Walter was convalescing at his ex-wife's home following a stroke, he couldn't very well be anywhere else.

"Yes. Is everything all right?"

"I wanted to talk to you both together if I could. That would be easier than having to repeat myself. Is he available? Or is he napping?"

"He may be retired, but he is not yet taking naps. Unless you're talking about him 'resting his eyes' while watching C-SPAN."

"Could you get him?" Kenzie prompted.

Zachary could already hear Lisa's heels on the floor as she walked across the house to wherever Walter was entertaining himself.

"Walter? It's MacKenzie."

"What's wrong?" Walter asked in the background.

"I don't know. Hold on while I figure this out... Okay, have I got you, MacKenzie? You're on speaker."

"Hi, sweetie," Walter greeted.

"I've got Zachary with me," Kenzie told them.

Everyone exchanged polite greetings, but the tension was palpable.

"Mom, Dad... Everything is okay. But I needed to let you know what's going on."

"What is it?" Lisa asked worriedly.

"Yesterday..." Kenzie breathed out heavily. She looked at Zachary for help, but he wasn't sure whether she wanted him to take over. He squeezed her hand. "When I got home from buying groceries, a van pulled up behind me, and..." She choked up, unable to go on.

Zachary rubbed her back, proud of her for getting as far as she had. His own throat was tight and hot and he didn't know if Kenzie's parents would be able to hear the strain in his voice.

"Two men jumped out of the van," Zachary told them. "They... it was... another abduction attempt."

There was a stunned silence from Walter and Lisa and then they were both talking together, talking over one another, trying to get all the details.

"Are you okay?" Lisa demanded. She swore, something very rare for her. "I can't believe something like this happened! Did you call the police? What happened?"

"Kenzie is fine," Zachary told them. "They didn't lay a finger on her. We scared them off before anything could happen. The police came and are looking into it. But it was very difficult for Kenzie, very traumatic after the... the other kidnapping."

Kenzie shook her head, trying to stop Zachary. "I'm okay; it's not that bad."

"She talked to our therapist and she's okay," Zachary assured them. He didn't reveal that Kenzie was now on anti-anxiety meds or that she was supposed to get further counseling. That was something Kenzie could choose to share or not. "Everything is fine. But you needed to know."

"Yes," Walter agreed. His voice was clipped and angry. "They will pay for this! I can't believe they would go after you again. I'm supposed to be recovering from a major stroke, and they are still trying to coerce me?"

"No, Walter," Lisa insisted. "You cannot respond to this. Not... not the way you are thinking."

Walter stopped short in his protestations. "What do you mean?"

Kenzie was wiping at her eyes. Trying to stay under control even when they couldn't see her crying.

"They are testing. Seeing whether you can be moved the same way you were before. But you can't respond to them. Not this time. If you cave and go back to lobbying, you will never be able to escape their grasp."

"What did you mean, then, not the way I am thinking?"

Walter's reaction was typically male. To go after the people who were threatening his little girl, to use some kind of threat or violence to convince them that he could not be coerced this time, that they could not continue to use his daughter to manipulate him.

Zachary thought he could see where Lisa was going. This was a test; if they did not respond correctly, they would never be free of the Russians. If they did, though...

"You need to have another stroke," he told Walter. "A major setback. The stress of this attack on Kenzie makes you worse, takes you to death's door."

Walter made a noise of protest, but Lisa immediately agreed. "Exactly. They think they can use Kenzie to manipulate you into doing what they want you to. They think this might all be a lie, a strategy, so they are testing you. But no matter how angry you are at them, you can't go up against the Russian mob. Even against that one oligarch. Their reach is too far. There is nothing you can do, even armed to the teeth, even threatening them with exposure. We can't prove that they did this."

"I'm not going to be intimidated into hiding—"

"You need to follow through on the act. You need to make them believe you can't do anything for them anymore. You need to finish what you started."

"They won't believe it."

"You need to make them believe," Zachary told him. "Get a

private ambulance service over there right away. You have lots of contacts in the medical community with all the donations you have made. Make them believe that you are being taken to the hospital in dire condition. Plant a false trail there. A wealthy patient whose name cannot be entered into the hospital's computer records, a private room, secret doctor visits, someone important and influential close to death after an emotional shock."

"Do I have to stay there?"

"You have to make sure they will play along with you. They can't actually get into your hospital room to see if you are there, but any inquiries should confirm that you are there, but no one can know about it."

"What about MacKenzie?" Lisa asked. "It's dangerous for her to stay at home. They could come after her again, try to get the truth out of her."

"They have a security system," Walter pointed out.

"Kenzie and I are going to go away for a few days," Zachary told them, glad they had already made plans. "I have an investigation that is taking me to Arizona. We will be out of the way."

"But she wouldn't go to Arizona if I was at death's door," Walter protested.

"If you and Lisa thought her life was in danger? You're doing everything you can to keep her safe. Including sending her away."

"Well..."

"We'll stop at the hospital first," Zachary said. "Tell us what wing to visit after arrangements are made. We'll go in for a few minutes, and then hustle out. Put on a big show. Then we'll head straight for the airport while apparently trying to hide our identities."

"Do you really think that would work?" Lisa asked doubtfully. "They won't think that you're trying to deceive them? That we're all just playing a game?"

"The more misinformation you can plant, the better. It's going to mean lying to your friends as well as acquaintances. Unless someone is one hundred percent trustworthy, you cannot tell them the truth. Make sure it gets onto social media. The other lobbyists

Walter worked with. Everyone." He thought about Elysse. "Just like with Elysse Allan, you have to make sure everyone hears the same story."

"Elysse?" Lisa repeated doubtfully.

"She's the woman who disappeared a while ago. A social influencer. No one knew where she had gone. Everyone thought she had been killed by her boyfriend. Until she showed up in the Grand Canyon."

"I know who Elysse Allan is," Lisa told Zachary. "I just... don't know what that has to do with this story about Walter, or Kenzie leaving town, or spreading lies to our friends."

"I've been interviewing friends and coworkers about her. And no one really knows what went on during the time she was missing. She didn't tell the people who were closest to her. Even now, six months later, she hasn't told them what the deal was. She just sticks to her story, saying that she decided she needed some time and space for herself, and that's why she disappeared."

"You're interviewing people about her? For what?"

"That's why we're going to Arizona too. We want to know what happened to her while she was gone. There are some witnesses, there were pictures taken at certain locations. So I'm following up."

"You were hired to find out what happened to Elysse Allan? Or you're just doing this as a diversion, because you had to find a reason to get out of town?"

"I was hired by the boyfriend, Dain."

"Hmm. I was always curious about what happened to her. But it seems like now... no one would really care about it anymore. It's old news. She was found. She didn't want to say what happened to her, made up the story about it just being over the argument, and went on with her life."

"Except she didn't. She hasn't gone on with her life. She never went back to posting on social media. She's not communicating with Dain or others who used to help with social media. Or... other friends. No one really knows what she is doing now."

Things came together very quickly. As far as the rest of the word was concerned, Walter Kirsch had a massive heart attack and was taken to a private suite of rooms at the hospital. A hospital with an entire wing named after its major donor, the Kirsch family foundation. It was all hush-hush, of course. The Kirsches had always kept to themselves, and they didn't want the details of his ailment broadcast to the world. His diagnosis, doctors, and treatment were all kept strictly quiet, and only those who were involved with his care knew anything.

Zachary and Kenzie visited at the hospital. It was a fleeting visit. They already had their bags packed and their flight booked. Those who were not "in the know" thought it very strange that the two of them would leave when Walter was in such desperate straits. But families like the Kirsches did not share their reasons.

34

Kenzie placed her in-flight magazine back in the pocket on the back of the seat. She shook her head.

"You're sure that Elysse went to Canada? Why would she do that? It isn't on the way to the Grand Canyon. It isn't on the way to New York. Why just strike off in a random direction?"

"Maybe that *was* why." Zachary had been thinking about it, too. "Because it *was* a random direction. Somewhere no one would think of looking for her."

"She didn't want anyone following her? You think she was planning from the start to disappear? It wasn't just that she decided to do her own thing or go back to see the Grand Canyon after the argument with Dain, she actually planned right from the start to cause a big fuss? To make people think that something had happened to her?"

"I don't know. I have a lot of questions to ask before I can come to any conclusion."

"Canada. Why come to Canada?" she mused again.

It was only a one-hour flight from Burlington to the Greater Sudbury airport. But factoring in the time they had to be there ahead of time to allow check-in on an international flight and to wait for baggage because Kenzie had insisted on checking luggage rather than using only carry-on, it was going to end up taking about the same amount of time for them to fly as it would have taken Elysse to drive.

Assuming that Elysse hadn't had any trouble getting past the border. She'd probably had enough camera equipment in her car to convince the border guards that she was a tourist. Or maybe she hadn't taken her car, but had rented something in Burlington and left her own vehicle behind. Somewhere it hadn't been discovered? Or had it been impounded long ago? By the time it was found in long-term parking at the airport or somewhere else, Elysse had been found and the police investigation had been closed.

Why Sudbury? Had she had someone to see there? It wasn't exactly a huge tourist destination. The pictures he had looked at online were gorgeous, but she hadn't used it as a backdrop for her social media pictures. She hadn't posted any social media pictures at all. She might still have taken pictures, but her purpose had apparently not been business-related.

Elysse had not booked one of the big hotels. There were plenty of hotels in Sudbury that were fancier and better known than the little independent place Elysse had been spotted at. It had not even shown up on Zachary's initial searches. He'd had to search for the Hideaway Inn by name before he'd come across a couple of internet listings for it. A "budget-friendly" motel, which meant no Wi-Fi, no pool or hot tub, and only basic cable on the TV. There were no queen beds. They were primarily double beds that were intended for single occupancy, as attested by the one wooden chair tucked into the kneehole of what was supposed to be a writing desk. No writing paper was on the desk, and there were no pens in the drawer.

"Are you sure she stayed here?" Kenzie asked, looking around. "This doesn't seem like the kind of place an internet celebrity would stay at."

"I'll find out," Zachary told her.

After plugging in his laptop, Zachary pulled up the photos that had been geotagged with the motel's location. Kenzie looked over his shoulder as he reviewed the pictures of Elysse from a couple of different angles. In the parking lot. In the lobby of the motel checking in or out. The faces were slightly blurred in the pictures, but it looked like Elysse, and his facial recognition program said that it matched her measurements with 90% accuracy.

Kenzie walked to the window and looked out at the parking lot, and over toward the lobby. "Well, it looks like the pictures were taken here. But are you sure that is Elysse? I couldn't swear it from the photos."

"Every indication is that it is her. These were not tips that were called in to the police, but pictures posted on the internet after the news that she was missing. But the police wouldn't have followed them up anyway."

"Different country, and no reason for her to be here. They expected her to go to New York."

"Right." Zachary agreed.

"Do you want to take a look at the lobby? I could do that, if you want?"

He grinned at her eagerness to be a part of the investigation. He had worried that he would be dragging her against her will, that she wouldn't be interested in the case or in seeing any sights while he investigated. That she would be wondering why he bothered to bring her on the trip. Or that she would be anxious, watching out the window for stalkers or kidnappers, unable to relax and enjoy herself.

But so far, she had been game, not only to fly out to a place she had never dreamed of going, but to investigate alongside him. She seemed to have left her anxiety back in Vermont. Part of it was, of course, that she was now taking antianxiety meds, but he thought that it was more than that. She had left the Russians behind in Vermont and did not have to worry about them. They were safe, her father was safe, and they could just immerse themselves in solving an interesting puzzle.

"We'll both go," he told her. "I'm hoping to be able to find someone who remembers seeing her here, or to confirm that they have a record of her registration."

They walked across the parking lot to the lobby. Sudbury in winter was not the green, lush place pictured in the images Zachary had looked at online. And the hotel was not in a natural setting, but on a street lined with similar motels, light industrial businesses, and a convenience store or two.

The snow on the ground was dirty and trampled. Brown, gravel-strewn slush on the street. It was bound to look nicer in the summer, but it was not where Elysse would have been taking pictures to post online. She had been there for other reasons, whatever they were.

The old man in the lobby didn't look up when they entered. He was tapping on an iPad, looking very intent. Maybe playing a game with a friend, since it didn't look like he had much business. The carpet was thin and threadbare in places. His name tag was a friendly "Hi, I am JACK."

Kenzie went over to the vending machines in the corner to look at the brands of the snacks, some of them familiar and some of them not. Zachary stood waiting politely at the desk. He didn't want to aggravate Jack, or he wouldn't be open to answering questions.

After a few long minutes, Jack looked up and raised his brows at Zachary.

"Yes? How can I help you?"

"Hi," Zachary gave him a warm smile. "Listen, I have a friend who stayed here a few months ago. Maybe you remember her. Elysse was her name." Zachary showed the man his phone, one of the pictures of Elysse at the motel.

He studied the picture. "Nah, I don't remember her. You sure this is the hotel she came to?"

"That's it in the background, isn't it?" Zachary questioned, indicating it.

"Well, could be, could be." the man said, though he didn't sound too sure. It was his own motel, and he didn't seem to recognize it. Maybe he was not the right person to ask whether he recognized a face.

"Oh, well," Zachary shrugged. "I was just wondering which

room she was in. She was telling me about the artwork on the wall, and I wanted to get a look at it. I'm interested in vintage paintings, and would like to get a look at the one she described."

Zachary had surveyed the room they had booked to try to find something of interest, and the painting was all he could find to talk about. The only unique feature of the room. An actual painting rather than a reproduction, so each room had to have a unique piece rather than being identical.

"What was the picture?" Jack asked.

"Flowers," Zachary hazarded. The ones in his room were flowers, so several others probably featured flowers. "If you could just look up which room she was in, then I could have a look..."

"We don't do that. Private records."

"For a room number? I just want to get a look at the artwork. I'm not asking if she was there alone or meeting someone."

"That's not our policy..."

"Are you the owner? If not, maybe I could talk to the manager. Maybe he would be able to give me the room number. Then you wouldn't have to feel like you had contravened any rules."

"He's not going to give you the room number either."

Zachary nodded. He looked down at his phone and scrolled through pictures. People hated silence. They hated someone who made a request and didn't back down or accept no for an answer. They felt the need to actively do something. To remove the irritant.

"I told you the answer is no," the man repeated.

"It's too bad. That painting could be valuable. But I can't make a judgment if I don't see it. If it is valuable, then obviously you and the owner don't know it, or it wouldn't still be hanging on the wall. Someday, maybe someone will come along who recognizes its worth and they'll just take it with them when they go. You'll have to find another painting to fill that spot and will never know what it was actually worth."

The man sputtered and tried to come up with something to contradict what Zachary said. But he couldn't say that he recognized the value of the painting in question, because that wouldn't get him anywhere. The owner or manager could hire an appraiser to go to each room and look at the paintings, but that would cost money, and here was a guy who would tell them for nothing. Telling the owner and leaving the decision up to him would take the responsibility from the man, but he wouldn't get anything out of it. On the other hand, if Zachary told him of a valuable painting, he could then tell the owner about it and hope to get something out of the deal, or the painting could disappear and be replaced with a ten-dollar flea market painting. All the profit would go into Jack's pocket.

"What's your friend's name?" he finally demanded.

"Elysse Allan. If she registered under her married name. You don't recognize her from the picture?"

"I haven't got a clue." The man typed Elysse's name into his computer. Zachary didn't hold out much hope that Elysse had registered under her own name. Why would she if she were trying to disappear?

"Elysse Dane?" the man asked.

"About six months ago?" Zachary asked, giving him the date in the photo's metadata.

"Yeah."

"That's her." Zachary shot Kenzie a triumphant look, but she seemed to be mesmerized by the vending machines and didn't share in his victory.

"Room 103," the man told him.

"Great!" Zachary didn't actually need to look at the room. It wasn't very likely that there would be any remnant of Elysse's stay there months earlier. Though the housekeeping did not appear to be stellar and the room turnover probably wasn't very high, judging by the number of cars in the lot. Just enough to keep the hotel running. But he needed to complete his performance. "Can we go see it?"

"Follow me." The man grabbed the door key for the room in question and led the way. Zachary walked up to Kenzie as he headed toward the door, giving her a nudge.

"Are you coming? Did you hear all of that?"

"Did you see these?" Kenzie asked, pointing to the coins

pictured on the vending machine. "They have dollar and two-dollar coins. Look at the two-dollar coins; aren't they cool?"

The coins were two metals in concentric circles. Zachary had to admit that they were pretty cool.

"Yeah. You want to get some while we're here? Start a coin collection?"

Kenzie chuckled. "I don't know. Maybe I will. Memento of our first road trip together."

They walked out of the lobby back into the parking lot and followed the man to room 103.

"She *was* here," Zachary pointed out, in case Kenzie hadn't been paying attention to their conversation. "That's confirmation that she did come here after leaving Vermont."

"Canada." Kenzie shook her head. "I still can't fathom why she thought that was a good idea. Having to cross borders when she was trying to vanish? What if the border guards recognized her? What if they had bulletins with her picture on them?"

"I think she probably crossed the border before being reported missing. But that does make it harder for her to leave the country without anyone catching on. Going back into the US after the bulletins had been issued and it was all over social media and TV. It would have been very easy for her to be recognized. Canadians watch TV. Read social media posts. Being a smaller population helps, but Elysse could still have dozens of followers in Sudbury. We know that at least a couple of people recognized her and took her picture."

"Maybe she didn't think she had any Canadian followers," Kenzie said. "A lot of people think of Canada as this tiny, isolated, permanently frozen country. Not part of the modern world with technology on par with the US."

The man opened the motel room, and Zachary walked in and took his time studying the paintings on the wall. The small room was set up identically to the room he and Kenzie had booked. The paintings were slightly different but of the same vintage.

He had been right in his guess that there would be a flower

painting. There was also a mediocre landscape, thoroughly unin-
teresting.

Zachary looked for a long time at the flower painting, leaning
close and studying it from two inches away, then turning his face
and shining his phone's flashlight LED across it obliquely, studying
the brushstrokes and wondering what else a real expert would
look at.

"I was hoping," he said slowly, "but it looks like this is a copy.
The brushwork is not right. A good copy, and very pleasant, but…
not authentic." He *tsked.* "Well, it is disappointing, but thank you
so much for letting me look at it."

"It's not worth anything?" the man demanded. "As a copy? It
must be worth something…"

"Maybe in another fifty years," Zachary encouraged. "You never
know."

"Fifty years?" the man repeated with disgust. "I'm not waiting
fifty years!"

Zachary took a glance around the motel room for anything that
would answer the question of what Elysse had been doing there.
But as he had expected, there was nothing personal left behind.
Nothing that Elysse had dropped six months earlier, no note
pleading for help tucked away somewhere with just the corner
showing. No message written on the dusty window with her finger.

"Was she here with someone, do you know? Was it single or
double occupancy?"

"I thought she was your friend, telling you all about her stay
here?" Jack sneered.

Zachary shrugged. He hadn't expected an answer, but it had
been worth at least asking.

"I couldn't remember whether this was the trip she took with
Jose or not," he told the man.

"Why would anyone bring someone else *here?*" Jack looked at
Zachary and Kenzie, and shook his head. He obviously did not
have a very good opinion of his place of employment.

35

Zachary lay in bed, his arm resting over Kenzie's body, listening to her breath, feeling the rise and fall of her diaphragm. Her breathing was soothing—a peaceful, rhythmic sound. Kenzie had fallen asleep almost immediately. She was still recovering from the attack. Something so emotional and traumatic could be very hard on the body, demanding a lot of energy.

Zachary's body was suffering and could also use the sleep. Every breath he took was painful, and whenever he moved, he had to be very careful to avoid aggravating his bruised and broken ribs any more than he had to.

That in itself would have been difficult enough to sleep through. It was his brain that was causing the worst problems.

If it was just pain, he could take painkillers and maybe a sleep aid and be able to get a few hours of sleep, all that he needed to keep going.

But he was worried. Everything he had said to Kenzie and her parents about being out of the way of danger and leading the Russians to believe that Walter was, in fact, at death's door had been true. The chances that any of them would follow Kenzie and Zachary out of Vermont and out of the country were very low. The two of them leaving the state did not cause the Russians any problems. It removed Kenzie from their reach at least temporarily, but they had already seen that Walter could no longer be manipulated by an attack on his daughter. There was no reason for the Russians to follow them.

But Zachary sensed he was being followed. Not just followed, but pursued. Somewhere behind them, somewhere nearby, maybe even in the same motel where they were sleeping, dangerous men who were targeting them were also sleeping. Or not sleeping, because they could be creeping down the sidewalk, preparing themselves to attack any second.

He listened closely for the scrape of a shoe, a whispered voice. A reflection in the window or light racing across the wall.

There were plenty of noises to try to identify and lights and reflections that would have driven a cat crazy. That meant that Zachary couldn't sleep. He was not relaxed and calm like Kenzie. He was on high alert.

Kenzie jerked in her sleep and murmured something, making Zachary jump. He commanded himself to slow his breathing and pounding heart, to go back to normal, to relax, and to go to sleep, but none of his orders had any effect on his body or hyper-alert brain. He wiggled his toes and flexed and relaxed the muscles in his legs, trying to find ways to stay still despite not being able to fall asleep.

He tried progressive relaxation exercises. He tried anxiety-reducing breathing patterns. He visualized the best outcomes for the things he was worried about. Having a great trip with Kenzie, finding out everything they had been wondering about Elysse, getting home to find that the Russians had backed off and were not interested in Walter, who could clearly no longer be of any service to them. Getting a big paycheck from Dain for the resolution of the case. Kenzie going back to the medical examiner's office feeling calm and relaxed.

But none of it worked. Zachary's mind just kept returning to the noises. To the certainty they were after him. The Russians, the bomber, Elysse's friends or enemies, Teddy Archuro. Everyone who had attacked or hurt him in the past, no matter how impossible it was for them to be there.

Between his anxiety and his broken ribs, he could barely breathe. He knew that the drowning feeling meant that he needed to exhale fully. To expel the carbon dioxide and to keep fluids from accumulating in his lungs. To help reduce the overinflated feeling of doom. Impending disaster.

Eventually, he couldn't stay in bed any longer. At home, he could get up and pace, watch TV, do some routine work on his computer. There was little he could do in the tiny motel room without the risk of waking Kenzie. And if she woke up, she might not be able to get back to sleep. She needed her sleep.

He paced a few steps back and forth across the room, remaining as silent as possible. It helped a bit. He tried to recite a mantra to keep his breathing slow and regular. When his body was too exhausted to walk, he sat down in the uncomfortable wooden chair and looked at his phone, checking email and social networks and watching a few entertaining videos.

But they all reminded him of Elysse and the questions that still hung over his head about why she would suddenly quit, walking away from the life she had built for herself. What had caught up with her? An outside party? Her own demons? Something to do with her relationships with Dain or Mike? With someone else? He had heard stories of other people just walking away from their lives. Sometimes, with the explanation that they'd had a head injury or some other trauma. Sometimes, with no good explanation at all. They just walked away and left it all behind.

"Zachary?"

Zachary turned his head at Kenzie's soft query. He put his phone down, rose from the chair, and returned to bed.

"Hey." He moved slowly and carefully, his ribs protesting every movement, to get closer to her and put his arms around her again. "It's okay. It's not time to get up yet."

"Where were you?" Her voice was faint. "Did you go to the bathroom?"

"Yeah. Did I wake you up?"

"No, no. My body just thinks it's time to get up."

"Not yet."

She breathed softly and slowly, and he thought she was asleep again.

"Zachary?"

"Yeah?" He moved so that his mouth was right over her ear, breathing warm air onto her, inhaling the scent of her sweat and shampoo.

"Don't go away."

"Okay. I won't."

"Did you go to sleep?"

"I will. I just wasn't tired yet."

He was so tired. So bone-achingly, mind-numbingly tired. He needed sleep. Every fiber of his body told him that. Yet he couldn't bring himself to take a sleep aid. He could not leave Kenzie unguarded. The flimsy locks and chain on the motel door would do nothing to protect them from an attacker. There was no security team hardwired in and ready to respond if something went wrong. If something happened, he was on his own. No one would be coming to his aid this time.

36

Kenzie stirred. She moved around restlessly for a little while, then she was rubbing her eyes and sitting up to look around, maybe disoriented not remembering where she was. She gazed at Zachary across the room.

"Is that coffee I smell?"

He got up from the uncomfortable wooden chair and stretched his legs. He poured Kenzie a cup of coffee and returned the small carafe to brew another. It only brewed a couple of cups at a time, and he would need a few more.

"Thanks." Kenzie closed her eyes and savored the coffee after a couple of sips. "That's actually not too bad."

It was probably the only thing in the motel that was up to par. Maybe the previous occupant of the room had bought his own grounds and replaced what had originally been left in the room.

"What time do we have to go?"

"We've got about an hour if you want to shower. We can eat at the airport."

"Good idea. Then we won't be too rushed. You want to get us checked out? I have a feeling it may take a while."

"Are you saying the service here has not been stellar?" Zachary teased. "I don't see a 'rate your stay' survey card…"

"Why would they? They have to know this is about the worst fleabag motel in the city."

Zachary chuckled. "If you want grab the clothes and toiletries you need, I'll put everything else in the car so we'll be ready to go."

She agreed, taking her time to pick out an outfit and anything else she would need. "Okay, you can take everything else, except my carry-on."

Zachary agreed. He waited until she was in the shower and he was sure she wasn't going to ask for anything else before taking everything out to the rental car. He scanned the parking lot and the street for any sign of surveillance. He had done his best to keep an eye on things during the night, but the view from the bedroom was limited and he hadn't wanted to leave the curtains wide open.

The checkout was surprisingly quick. Maybe they were used to people being in a hurry to get out of there. Zachary paced around the parking lot, waiting for Kenzie to finish getting ready, keeping a sharp eye out for any surveillance. He was less paranoid in the full light of day, but he still couldn't shake the feeling that they were being stalked. Would the Russians really give up that easily? Or did they not even care that Kenzie had left town?

Had that been Elysse's reason for the strange jaunt to Canada? Was she trying to shake off a pursuer? To have a chance to watch her back trail to see whether someone was following her? Hoping a stalker would not be able to cross the international border?

Kenzie came out of the motel and looked around for him, slightly confused to find him on the other side of the parking lot rather than in the hotel room, car, or lobby.

"All ready to go?" Zachary asked as he got over to the car.

"Yeah." Kenzie studied him. "Are you okay?"

"Okay? Sure. I'm…"

He had been about to say that he was fine, but that was not the truth. Part of their agreement was not to brush her off by saying he was fine or mask how he was really feeling with another glib phrase.

He cleared his throat. "I could be better. Bit of a rough night."

"A bit of a rough night," she repeated. "Your normal night is worse than my bad nights. So how bad was it?"

Zachary shrugged.

"Did you sleep at all?"

"Not really."

She motioned him away from the driver's side of the car. "You're not driving."

"It's just to the airport."

"Yeah, and I will take this leg of the trip. You're going to relax for a few minutes while I do. Grab a nap on the plane, and I'm sure you'll be fine to drive in Salt Lake."

"I'm okay to drive now."

"Nope." Kenzie opened the driver's door and got in.

There wasn't anything for Zachary to do but to get into the passenger's seat. He did up his seatbelt while Kenzie adjusted her seat position and mirrors. There wasn't any point in arguing about it, so he sat back and watched out the window, alert for anyone watching them go or falling in behind the car once they pulled out.

"How was your sleep?" he asked.

"Not bad. I don't usually sleep great at hotels, but I felt like I needed to catch up, and I think I did. I'm feeling a lot calmer today."

"Part of that will be the anti-anxiety pills."

She nodded. "Yes, I'm sure it is. But a good night's sleep makes a big difference, too. I think... being away from the house for a few days was a good idea. I feel like I can relax."

"Good."

Zachary was paranoid enough for both of them.

Once they had made it past the airport security and were waiting for their flight, Zachary felt a little better. Getting past airport security with a weapon wasn't impossible, but it was not easy. Even someone who was trained to kill with his bare hands would still have to find a way to get Zachary or Kenzie away from everyone else to do the deed.

So he had another cup of coffee and a chocolate chip muffin

and was able to relax enough to visit with Kenzie and look forward to the next leg of their journey. No one else knew their itinerary. Following Elysse's erratic trip had the added benefit of being unpredictable, no one could anticipate where they were going next.

Unless someone knew the route she had taken and that Zachary was following it.

"Now go to sleep," Kenzie told him once they were in the air. She pulled a paperback out of her carry-on.

"I don't know if I'll be able to sleep on a plane."

Zachary had not had much opportunity for air travel during his lifetime. He had flown only a handful of times and was usually hyped up and looking out the window or following their route on a map.

"Close your eyes and relax. We're in the air for four hours. What else are you going to do?"

He looked at his carry-on, which, of course, included his computer. There was plenty he could do while they were in the air. Kenzie shook her head. "Not until you've had some sleep."

After the events of the last couple of days and the anxious, sleepless night, Zachary's body was crying out for sleep. He knew by the frayed-at-the-edges feeling that the lack of sleep was affecting him. He sighed, settled back in his seat, and closed his eyes.

He was completely dead to the world until Kenzie woke him up, shaking his arm gently so as not to startle him. Zachary still awoke with a start, jolting his broken ribs. He gasped and held still for a moment, waiting for the pain to subside enough that he could breathe shallowly.

"What is it?" He looked around to see if she had woken him up for drink or lunch service.

"We're landing."

Zachary blinked. He rubbed his eyes. "I slept the whole time?"

"Like a baby. I guess you needed it."

That was longer than Zachary slept at home in his bed many

nights. He took a deep breath and let it out again, wincing at the expansion and contraction of his rib cage. He was feeling a lot more clear-headed and energetic. Amazing what a few hours of sleep could do.

"Sorry, I guess I wasn't very good company."

"I had a book. I didn't need any conversation." She tucked it back away in her bag.

Zachary couldn't imagine being able to read a thick novel for entertainment. He could, if pressed, read through large amounts of material with the aid of his ADHD meds, But the idea of reading for fun was foreign to him. The challenges of dyslexia, ADHD, and PTSD in those early years had prevented him from developing a love of reading.

Even at school when they had been instructed to put their heads down on their desks to listen to a beloved children's novel read by the teacher, he had not enjoyed it. Sitting still and being quiet were not his wheelhouse, and there were many times when he had been banished to sit in the hallway alone so that other students could listen to the teacher undistracted by his restless movements.

It had been pretty obvious he wasn't going to grow up to be a reader.

"Please fasten your seatbelts," the flight attendant instructed.

Zachary reached down to buckle his up and saw that he had never unbuckled it in the first place. He relaxed and watched out the window as the plane glided out of the clouds and toward the runway.

37

O f course they had to wait for Kenzie's luggage but, eventually, they were on their way again. With several hours of sleep under his belt, Zachary was allowed to take over the driving again, heading towards a mall where several people had reportedly sighted Elysse.

The reports had been discounted by the police because, of course, they weren't anywhere near Vermont, New York, or Elysse's home in Oregon. The authorities were focused on the areas where they expected to find her, especially the wilderness areas in Vermont that could have swallowed her up so easily.

Places where her body could have been disposed of and not found for years except by chance.

They had been so sure she was dead, and that Dain had killed her.

Was that what they were supposed to think? Had Elysse planned to disappear, be presumed dead, and never resurface again? To start another life under another name and identity? Was she so disenchanted with her life that she had been willing to kill her identity and start again?

The fans who had found her in Arizona had wrecked any

chance of that happening. Elysse had probably not realized just how recognizable she was and how quickly she would be forced to return to her old life.

Zachary and Kenzie examined the pictures of Elysse at the mall downloaded from social media and discussion boards. They looked for recognizable objects in the backgrounds of the photographs to establish where Elysse had been and walked around the mall to find the stores or other locations pictured.

Zachary went into the first store that Elysse had been seen leaving, a women's clothing store. One of the saleswomen approached him, smiling but reserved.

"Hi, can I help you with something?"

"Hi." Zachary had not entirely decided on the approach to take to confirm the sightings. "I'm wondering… were you working here six months ago?"

She looked curious but said that she had been. The turnover of staff at retail stores could be pretty quick, so Zachary was happy to have found someone on the first try who was there when Elysse disappeared.

"Great. This might be a stupid question, but do you know Elysse Allan? The social influencer… Elysse?"

She was wary. "I know *of* her," she said stiffly.

"She was seen here six months ago, during the time she was a missing person. Do you know who was on shift when she was here?"

"Why?"

"I'm investigating her activities during that time," Zachary told her vaguely. "There are a number of pictures showing that she was in this mall and in this store."

"So what?"

"I'm just wondering if anyone remembers her being here. If they can confirm her presence."

The young woman bit her lip, thinking about this. She looked around the store as if she didn't know who was there with her.

"I don't know what it matters. So what if this woman did come to the store? Why not? Who really cares?"

"I am investigating her disappearance."

"But she was found."

"Yes, but the story she told the public wasn't true."

"I don't know who was here or if anyone talked to her. I remember them talking about her, but…"

"Who talked about her?"

She looked around the store again. Kenzie was walking around the store, looking through the racks of clothing. Another saleswoman approached her to see if she needed any help. Kenzie started talking to her about the clothing lines and what she liked or didn't like.

"I'll ask around," the saleswoman Zachary was talking to said. But she didn't make any move to talk to anyone else.

"Now?" Zachary asked.

"People are busy. We're working, you know. If we start chatting about other stuff, we'll get fired. If you want to buy something…" She gestured around her at the racks of dresses and other women's clothing and gave him a little smile. "See anything you like?"

"I don't think you have anything in my size," Zachary laughed.

She looked at him critically. "It's not like you're some big, buff guy. We've got plenty that would fit you."

Zachary laughed. "Okay, well, you'll talk to the other staff later, then? Can I give you my card, and then you can call me? Or whoever saw her in person can call me to confirm?"

She reluctantly agreed to take his card. Zachary could tell she was not eager to call him back. She was just hoping to get rid of him and his questions. He would be lucky if he got a call back from anyone in the store.

Kenzie was still having an animated chat with the other salesclerk. Rather than motioning for her to follow him or joining the conversation, Zachary drifted out of the store and checked out some of the other stores nearby. It was possible that workers or employees of other stores had seen Elysse while she had been there.

He tried starting a few conversations, casually mentioning that he had once seen Elysse Allan there, hoping someone else would chime in and say they had also seen her. Mostly people just looked at him as if wondering what some old dude's interest in the young social influencer was. He felt dirty just mentioning her, as if he were doing something wrong.

Kenzie caught up with him eventually. It seemed like she'd had a very long conversation with the clerk at the clothing store.

"How did you do?" Zachary asked. "Did you buy anything?"

She grinned at him. She held up a shopping bag. "I bought a blouse. Can I expense it?"

"Expense it?"

"As a business expense for interviewing the salesclerk."

"Did you find something out?"

"We had a long conversation about brands and clothing lines."

"Uh-huh."

"About how it was odd that Elysse Allan would come in there when she didn't normally wear any of those brands."

"Oh. So she remembered Elysse?"

"Yes, she did." Kenzie grinned broadly.

"Great! So we have a confirmation that she was here. Did they talk? Did she know who Elysse was when she was in the store?"

"Yes, she knew who Elysse was and talked to her."

"Perfect. Great job."

"Aren't you glad you brought me along?"

"Definitely. You've earned your place on this trip. Talking to her about clothing brands—that never would have occurred to me."

"You probably don't spend much time talking about women's clothing brands."

"That's true," Zachary admitted. "Hardly any. I'm obviously going to have to bone up on women's fashion."

They went to the food court to get some lunch, and started conversations at strategic locations about Elysse Allan to see whether they got any responses from anyone else who had seen her there.

Sitting with a milkshake and looking around the food court, considering any other approaches that might be successful, Zachary's eyes caught on a familiar logo. A Knicks cap. Someone standing behind a group of people. Funny that he should see a

Knicks cap at the same time as he was thinking about the Elysse Allan case. He waited for the person wearing the cap to come into view.

Eventually, the crowd thinned, and he could see the wearer.

A big, heavyset man with a bushy beard.

38

Zachary jolted before he could control his visceral reaction. Not a great PI trait, showing everything he was thinking in his face. Kenzie saw the reaction and turned her head to see who he was looking at.

"Don't look," Zachary warned her. "Don't do anything to attract his attention."

She pointed her nose back directly at him. "Whose attention?"

"A man just came in... he matches the description of someone seen multiple times on Elysse Allan's tour."

"Matches his description? You haven't seen a picture?"

"No."

"Is he distinctive?"

"Well... not unique," Zachary admitted, watching the bushy-bearded guy peripherally while talking to Kenzie, trying not to give away that he was paying any attention to the man. "Big guy, big bushy beard. Wears a Knicks cap."

Kenzie arched an eyebrow. "That description must match dozens of men. Hundreds, maybe. How many people would you see in the stands at a Knicks game? How many of them would be big guys with bushy beards?"

Zachary tried to envision a stadium full of fans. How many

people would it hold? How many of them would match the description? Kenzie was right. He had no reason to get worked up over seeing one guy who fit the profile. It had just startled him. It was a coincidence.

But seeing a lot of big guys with bushy beards at a stadium during a Knicks game was not the same as seeing a man somewhere other than a Knicks game in Vermont or Utah. There were far fewer people wearing Knicks caps while they were out and about.

"We should go over there and talk," he suggested.

"To him?"

"No. Just close by. So he might overhear."

"Okay," she agreed, unperturbed by the suggestion.

Zachary's gut was getting a workout as they walked across the food court, getting closer to the bushy beard guy. Was it wise to approach him? He did not have anything to do with the case. It was just a coincidence that Zachary saw someone who matched the potential stalker's description while following Elysse's back trail.

Why would the man with the Knicks cap care about Zachary's investigation, even if he were the man who had been following Elysse? He didn't even have any way of knowing about it.

Certainly, there was nothing dangerous about talking to him. And they weren't even going to start talking directly to him but would only slide into a conversation if he responded to their fictional discussion.

Kenzie looked at Zachary, confirming whether they were going ahead. Maybe she sensed his anxiety.

Zachary swallowed and nodded.

They stopped near the bearded man. "And the last time I was here, you wouldn't guess who I saw."

"Justin Bieber," Kenzie suggested promptly.

Zachary stared at her. She grinned. He wondered whether her suggestion was prompted by their recent visit to Canada.

"Not Justin Bieber," he told her firmly. "Elysse Allan."

The bearded guy, who hadn't turned a hair at the mention of Justin Bieber, turned quickly toward them. Zachary ignored the reaction, pretending not to see the man.

"Really?" Kenzie asked. "What would Elysse Allan be doing here?"

"I don't have a clue. Shopping, I guess."

"In Salt Lake City?" Kenzie scoffed. "It couldn't have been her. It was someone who resembled her. Maybe."

"No, it was her, for sure," Zachary insisted. "Don't ask me what she was doing in Salt Lake City. Maybe it was part of a media tour."

The man was turned fully toward them, clearly wanting to be involved in the conversation.

"Excuse me?" he had a rich baritone voice. "I couldn't help overhearing, did you say you saw Elysse Allan here?"

"Crazy, right?" Zachary asked. "I mean, she lives in Oregon, so what would she be doing in Salt Lake?"

"I heard she was here too," the man contributed, encouraging him.

"Zachary Goldman," Zachary said, holding his hand out to introduce himself.

The man hesitated, then shook. "Marvin Haroldson."

"Good to meet you, Marvin. Are you a big Elysse Allan fan?"

Marvin wasn't sure whether to admit it or not. Zachary appeared to be unembarrassed about being a fan. But maybe Marvin had been mocked in the past about being a fan. The millions of fans around the world couldn't all be teen and twenty-something girls. Maybe Marvin could find in Zachary a friend and confidante—an Elysse Allan groupie closer to Marvin in age and gender.

"Well, I've been following her for a while," he offered tentatively.

"Me too," Zachary told him enthusiastically. "I know it might seem like a strange choice for a guy my age, but she's so… genuine. I really miss her postings. I wish she would come back from this… hiatus."

Marvin nodded his agreement. "She was posting every day, several times a day, and was just soaring in popularity. And then suddenly, she stops. Just flat-out stops. I can't understand her leaving everyone in the lurch like that."

"I guess it was when she disappeared," Zachary contributed. "But I thought she would start up again once she was found."

He studied Marvin's face, trying to read everything he could there. Hero worship? Love? Lust? Obsession? What had made him follow Elysse Allan and how had he responded when she had stopped posting? Or had he been part of the reason she had disappeared?

"She should have," Marvin agreed fiercely. "Why would she just stop? All of us out here, waiting for her to start talking to us again. Waiting for some word or picture, some piece of her life... but she just stopped sharing."

"She must have been traumatized by her disappearance. Something must have happened, don't you think?" he suggested.

"What could have happened? Traumatized? She just had a fight with Dain. Took off to have some alone time. Why would that stop her from posting? Maybe she got hit in the head. You hear about things like that. People losing their memories, losing their identities and having to start over."

"Do you think that's what happened?" Zachary pictured Marvin hitting Elysse over the head. Was that why he'd made the suggestion? Had he tried to approach Elysse? Been spurned by her and ended up in a fight? If she'd suffered a head injury, that could explain her not reaching out to anyone.

But did it explain the erratic travel pattern? Going to Canada? Elysse must have told the border guards something about why she was going to Sudbury. If she'd said she didn't know who she was or what she was doing, they wouldn't have let her cross the border without some kind of intervention.

But then she had come to Salt Lake City, to this mall, and that was where they had found him. Had she met Marvin there? If so, had she done so on purpose, or had Marvin engineered it?

"We should sit down," Zachary suggested, motioning to the tables and chairs of the food court.

Kenzie raised her brows. Probably wondering how either one of them was going to be able to eat anything more.

"Just a coffee," Zachary told her. "But when we meet another fan… we should take a few minutes to talk. Not everyone shares our interest."

Marvin looked unsure, then nodded and sat down at the table.

"You guys stay here. I'll go get the coffee," Kenzie told them.

Zachary sat down with Marvin. He didn't say anything, waiting to see if Marvin had anything to confide now that it was just the guys.

"So, how long have you been following Elysse?" he asked when Marvin didn't offer anything.

"I don't know. A couple of years, I guess. I can't believe she would abandon her fans like that. After how loyal we have been to her, how much time we've spent following and supporting her."

Zachary nodded. "It's hard being left without someone you have been with for so long."

For him, that person was Bridget. But he figured Marvin felt the same way about Elysse. Obsessing over her, worrying about her, wondering what had happened to her and whether she was okay now.

Marvin leaned toward him. "You *get* it," he agreed. "After all that time together, suddenly she's gone, and it's like… she left an empty hole in my life. I don't know how to fill it. Other people roll their eyes at me, and they say if I'm missing her posts, I just need to find someone else like her. Anyone else. And they think that will be enough. Then I will be… fulfilled. But it doesn't work that way. You can't just substitute one person for another. They aren't swappable."

"Of course not. Would they say that if you lost a spouse? 'Well, just go out and find another woman'?"

"That's right. Exactly. You can't replace someone like Elysse."

"Did you ever try to get in contact with her? Find out what was going on?"

"She hasn't even been in contact with her family. No one knows why she's just gone quiet. But I think it's like I said… she must have been hit over the head or something. Lost her memory. And she's trying to build her life again, but how can she when that big part of her is gone?"

"I was in Vermont when it happened. You should have seen the response... how many people were looking for her, searching everywhere. The number of fans who flooded the area, hoping to be able to find her."

Marvin opened his mouth, on the edge of confessing that he had been in Vermont too. He had been following her, had been showing up on her shoots. Talking to her and getting his picture taken with her, or working up his courage to do so. His eyes were alight and his mouth opened.

"Here we go," Kenzie announced, plopping the coffee cups on the table and distributing them.

Marvin sat back, startled, and closed his mouth.

"I bought some cookies," Kenzie told them, setting a small box of big, round cookies in the middle of the table. "Figured you guys might want something a little sweet with your coffee."

"Thank you," Marvin said politely, reaching for one of them, "that was very kind."

Zachary helped himself to one as well, though he was full and didn't know if he would be able to do much more than nibble it. But he wanted to mirror Marvin's actions as much as he could. Establish a relationship between them. Mutual love of cookies, coffee, and Elysse Allan.

39

In the end, Zachary and Kenzie didn't manage to get much of anything from Marvin. Zachary was sure that he *was* the bushy-bearded man Kristy had referred to. But she hadn't known whether there was anything going on with him, whether he was dangerous to Elysse or just another non-threatening fan.

Zachary took a few selfies with Marvin to send to Kristy. They exchanged phone numbers, Zachary noting Marvin's down carefully and giving his own with the digits reversed so Marvin couldn't track him down or start harassing him. He would have Heather do some deep research on the man and see whether there was anything suspicious in his past.

After discussing whether to stay in Salt Lake or go on to their next stop, they decided to go on, so Zachary booked a flight to Phoenix. This was a shorter flight, and Zachary was rested and eager to learn more about what had happened to Elysse in Arizona. It was only a short flight, and he didn't sleep through it this time.

The weather in Arizona was balmy. No more snow or winter coats. They both carried their winter clothing and breathed in the warm air deeply. Too deeply for Zachary. He held his hand over his protesting ribs, trying to calm the flare of pain.

"It's nice here," he told Kenzie in a strained voice.

She looked at him, frowning. "Yes, it is. It's lovely. I think I understand why the snowbirds like to stay here."

Zachary tried to imagine what it would be like to stay that warm all winter. There was fruit on the trees, and people were walking around in shorts. It felt like stepping into another world.

"I've lived in Vermont my whole life. I've never known anything but snow during the winter."

Kenzie nodded her agreement. "This is much nicer. I always thought I would miss snow at Christmas. But looking around here... I'm not so sure I would. I could always watch snowy Christmas movies on TV."

Zachary chuckled. It really was different. Christmas was barely behind them, but it couldn't feel farther away.

Using his phone to do a little research, he found there wouldn't be time to get to the Grand Canyon to do anything constructive that afternoon. Instead, he would have to use the time to contact the law enforcement officers involved with Elysse's reappearance and arrange to see them the next day.

"Dinner and a movie tonight?" he suggested to Kenzie.

She looked surprised. "I thought this was a business trip. You'd be breaking out the laptop and doing some more research."

"It's also a getaway weekend. The laptop can stay put away one night."

"Well, that sounds very nice. I'm still full from our business lunch, but maybe an early movie and late dinner."

"I could do that."

"Better see what's playing," she motioned to his phone. "We'll need time to get the luggage, rent a car, and maybe a hotel room before the show."

Zachary ducked his head and buried himself in making arrangements for their date.

The movie was pleasant, as was the restaurant. They didn't know which hotel Elysse had stayed at while she was in Arizona, so they were free to book something nice, an upgrade from the Hideaway Inn. It wasn't hard—anything was an upgrade from the Hideaway Inn. Zachary found a nice suite with a king-size bed and a hot tub and, after dinner, they relaxed in the hot tub, liberated a few sweet snacks from the minibar, and cuddled before bed. Kenzie was horrified by the bruises she could see when he undressed for the hot tub, but he did his best to convince her that his injuries looked worse than they were and to distract her attention from them.

They didn't have any wine, since alcohol was contraindicated with Kenzie's meds. Zachary considered whether to take a sleep aid to make sure he got a better sleep but, once again, he couldn't bring himself to. Not when someone could easily break down the flimsy hotel room door. It was a card key door rather than a traditional key lock, and Zachary knew only too well how easy they were to hack with the right equipment. And the security lock on the inside of the door was no barrier at all to an experienced burglar.

Even with no electronic equipment, a well-placed battering ram or kick beside the lock could easily break through the door frame.

Kenzie fell asleep curled up against him, the smell of her curly hair in his nostrils, her body warm and soft and comfortable. But he couldn't fall asleep himself. He again needed to keep watch over his mate, to make sure that nothing could happen to her.

Even though there was nothing at all he could do if two masked men burst through that hotel room door intent on harm.

40

Zachary put a couple of ice packs over his eyes briefly before Kenzie woke up in the morning, hoping to eliminate any redness or bags under his eyes so Kenzie would not suspect that he had not slept again.

By the time she woke up, Zachary had already ordered room service, and her traditional toast and marmalade breakfast was on its way.

"What's on the agenda today?" Kenzie asked, yawning widely and stretching. "How much time do we have?"

"There's time for breakfast and a shower, and then we'll drive to the Grand Canyon and meet with one of the Rangers who talked to Elysse when she was found."

"Are they going to tell you anything?"

Zachary shrugged. "Well, I told them what I am here for, and they said to come in, so I hope they aren't just going to slam the door in my face when I get there."

"It would be pretty bad to make the trip all the way here just to be shut down."

"Well… if I can't talk to one of the investigating officers, I'm sure I can find someone else who was around when she was found.

It was big news. A lot of people were involved in 'rescuing' her. Maybe I could talk to the reporter who interviewed her."

"She wouldn't tell you anything other than what was on TV."

"Maybe not," Zachary agreed. "But maybe she would at least give us a hint."

"If she knew that Elysse's story was a lie and that she had really been somewhere else, she would have broken that story. That would have been big news."

"Not if she didn't have any proof about what happened. That doesn't mean she doesn't know anything. Or wouldn't be interested in meeting someone who might know something."

"What would you tell her?"

Zachary pursed his lips. "I'm not sure what, but it would have to be something worth her while."

"Yeah, and so far, you don't have that."

"I have the trip to Canada. And the stalker in Salt Lake City."

"Well... yes."

"Neither of those things have been reported on yet. They would be eager to get some of the information I have."

A hotel employee arrived with the room service breakfast and they sat down to eat.

"Did you have a good night?" Kenzie asked.

"Better than the night before."

Even if he hadn't gotten any sleep, the larger suite meant that he could walk around without fear of waking Kenzie up, lie down on the couch if he thought he might be able to catch a few Zs, and work on his computer with a Wi-Fi connection. There were a hundred or so channels on the TV, but he just turned it on quietly to the first familiar channel to keep the restless, worried part of his brain occupied while he worked.

"Well, it couldn't have been much worse," Kenzie laughed. "I'm glad you had a better night."

Ranger Eric Poulsen was in his thirties, ruggedly handsome, just as Zachary had expected a ranger working in the Grand Canyon to be. He assumed there was a whole crew of law enforcement officers working in the area, varying widely in age and gender, but this cop was right out of central casting. The epitome of a National Park Service Ranger. Short dark hair under his Ranger hat, a muscular, well-proportioned body under the crisp uniform, and an air of competence.

He met them in his office, a small, rustic building on the North Rim that looked out onto the scrubland. The fresh air wafting through the windows of the station was scented with dust and pine.

"So…" Poulsen motioned to the visitor chairs for Zachary and Kenzie to sit down. "I'm not sure I can be of any help to you. I understand that you are following up on the disappearance and reappearance of Elysse Allan last year, but… I'm not sure what help I can be to you."

"Well, you're the one who found her," Zachary pointed out. He took a sip of his coffee. Not bad for the ancient-looking coffee machine that hissed and burbled on the counter on the far side of the room.

"Well, not exactly. I talked with Elysse after she was discovered, but I wasn't the one who found her, and she was not in need of any services."

"What kind of condition was she in?"

"She seemed fine. Like most of the tourists around here. Hot and sweaty. A lot of them are not used to hiking or haven't antici-pated how much physical activity is involved in exploring the canyon, even if they are with a tour company. Elysse looked like she'd been around for a few days. Other than that… I mean… there wasn't anything that stood out to me. Other than the fact that she was the person pictured in the 'missing person' bulletins that went out from Vermont."

"You had no doubt?"

"No, of course not. The pictures were clear. And there were plenty of other pictures available online if there was any question. A person that well-known can't exactly be misidentified."

41

Zachary nodded. "So... tell me about it. How was she found and how did you get involved? Did she have a medical emergency or call for help?"

"No. The girl didn't want to be found." Poulsen considered what to say. He tapped his pencil on the desk. "Well, that might be overstating it. She wasn't trying to be found. She wasn't lost. She didn't reach out to us. But she wasn't exactly hiding."

Zachary looked out the window at the vast expanse of wilderness. He had done a little research on disappearances in the Grand Canyon and discovered that while many people were reported missing temporarily, most were found within forty-eight hours. But there were still a number of people who had disappeared there and never been found. They were, he assumed, people who had wandered off the trail and ended up in situations they had not bargained for. It was just too vast an area to search and, like the wilderness areas in Vermont, could hide human remains for years.

And that was people who had not intended to disappear. If someone were actually hiding there, actively avoiding detection, how long would they be able to go without being found? It was impossible to tell. Properly provisioned, someone could be out there for weeks.

But Elysse had not been; she had been there for two or three at the most. Had she been trying to avoid detection? He didn't believe she had just gone there to look at the sights she had missed while there with Dain.

"So she was just... wandering around? Was she on her own? Part of a group? Did she pay for a tour?"

"There are a lot of self-guided tours. Tourists can take walking pathways from one place to another. Obviously, you can't go as far on foot as on one of the donkey tours, but you can get around."

Zachary nodded. "Was she here by herself?"

"Yes."

"You're sure?"

"Yeah, she was on her own. She was just... touring the canyon like hundreds of other visitors. I assume she wanted to stay anonymous and enjoy her time exploring, but she couldn't because she was so well known. Someone recognized her. Insisted that the police get involved."

"How did they do that?"

"Called the police, said that she was a missing person, that she was in trouble, might be in danger. Whatever it took to get us out there."

"And this was just a random tourist? Someone who happened to be a fan? You didn't get the feeling that it was staged?"

"What do you mean? That the woman who called us was supposed to do that? That she was in on it?"

Zachary raised his brows, waiting for the Ranger to consider it.

"I don't think so, no. Miss Allan was not particularly happy about law enforcement being called. Insisted that since she hadn't done anything wrong, there was no reason for the police to be involved. She understood that she had been reported missing, but she said that wasn't a crime. And she was right, of course."

"But you still had to investigate."

"Sure. Establish her identity. Confirm whether she was there under duress, whether she or anyone else was in danger. Whether any crime had been committed. Just generally to get it straightened out."

"The fan was just a random fan? Hadn't been there looking for her?"

"Yeah. She was there on a pre-booked tour. With a group. Nothing suspicious. There wasn't any reason to investigate her."

"Did you get her name?"

"It's in my notes, but I don't see how that is relevant. I would say that is private information that you don't need. We took down her information for a witness statement, but there wasn't anything else for us to investigate."

"What did Elysse say about why she was here?"

"Well..." Ranger Poulsen picked up his big coffee mug and took several swallows. "The first thing she did was to deny that she was Elysse Allan. Claimed that it was a matter of mistaken identity. She gave another name—I can't even remember what it was. It wasn't relevant to anything—and said she was just there on vacation to see the Grand Canyon. Canada... I think she said that she was visiting from Canada."

Zachary looked at Kenzie. Canada again. Had something happened in Canada? He hadn't found any Canadian connections in her background. It was probably just on her mind because she had initially fled to Canada. And she had gone there because she wanted to avoid detection, didn't want the Vermont police or FBI to be able to find her.

"Did she have any identification showing that she was from Canada? How did you establish that she was Elysse Allan?"

"Well, I mean..." Poulsen shrugged. "It wasn't hard. She didn't want to give her name or any identification. But everybody in the country saw the coverage of her disappearance. Law enforcement across America had her picture and the details of her disappearance. And if that wasn't enough, all I had to do was to check social media for more pictures. They were plastered everywhere. I recognized her as soon as I saw her."

"But she denied it."

"For a while, yes. But it wasn't a charade she could keep up. I recognized her. So did the woman who had reported her. Others in the group believed that it was her as well. She had on a cap, had her hair pulled back, a few things like that which made her look a little different, but it wasn't enough to completely disguise her. With the number of pictures of her that were available, she would have needed plastic surgery to avoid detection."

Failing that, if Elysse Allan had wanted to avoid being recognized, she would have had to keep out of sight. Hat, surgical face mask or balaclava, stay in a hotel room and order whatever she needed to be delivered. She would have had to stay completely out of sight.

Going to a tourist destination, arguably one of the top two or three tourist destinations in the country, was not the way to stay anonymous. It was the way to be found.

Elysse Allan had clearly not been hiding any longer.

42

"And you think Elysse was by herself?"

"She was," the Ranger agreed.

"There wasn't anyone else in the group who knew her? Who could have been giving her instructions or directions? Someone she looked at sideways? Who corrected her? Made eye contact with her?"

"Well…" Poulsen thought about that. "I mean, this was six months ago now. That's a long time to remember something like eye contact."

"It is," Zachary agreed. "But not impossible. Replay it in your mind. Think about the other people in the group. The woman who called it in. Anyone who stepped in to speak up for Elysse or to make a scene. The woman who called it in would do whatever was necessary to get the police there, you said."

"Yes, she made no secret of the fact that she wanted the police there to identify Miss Allan and force her to… reveal herself."

"And you don't think that they were ever together? They didn't arrive together? They didn't know each other?"

"No. I can't see it. The woman was overwrought. She insisted that Miss Allan must have amnesia. A brain injury that had caused her to wander off and disappear. That if law enforcement didn't get there, she was in danger of... falling off a cliff or getting eaten by a mountain lion because she was impaired. She really did think that if there wasn't any intervention, Miss Allan might just disappear off the planet for good."

"Was there anyone else in the group that might have been with her? Someone who appeared to be a bystander, but was more engaged for some reason? Interfered or talked with her directly?"

"There was... one man in the group who seemed more interested in her personally. But I wouldn't have guessed that they were together."

"Big guy? Bushy beard?"

"No. Clean shaven. Someone I might have thought was a highbrow type businessman on a forced vacation. You know, his work or his wife says he has to take some time off. More of a... father figure."

"Significantly older than Elysse?"

Poulsen nodded.

Zachary thought about that. He didn't know much about Elysse's family situation, but he hadn't heard a father mentioned at all. Nor an uncle or any other man who might have fit into that role. He'd heard of a mother and sister, maybe an aunt and more extended family, but Elysse's family members seemed to be primarily female.

"That's interesting. What did he think of everything? Did he talk to her? Stay with her?"

"He hung around. I don't know whether he was with her or not. Maybe gave her some advice. I didn't pay that much attention. I was trying to figure out how to handle her reappearance and to get the story from her. But she didn't want to say anything about where she had been or why. Said it was none of my business." He shrugged. "And really, it wasn't."

"No." Law enforcement's involvement ended once a missing adult was determined to be voluntarily missing. Poulsen would be expected to write his report, file it, and stay out of her business. "Who called the TV network? Who got the reporters involved? Was that Elysse?"

"No… I'm not sure who called the TV networks. They just started showing up. More than one network. There were half a dozen of them here with their TV cameras and reporters trying to get interviews with her. It was a mess. I can't kick reporters out of the park just because they are a nuisance. Had to allow them to stay and get their footage."

"And Elysse cooperated with them, even though she hadn't been the one to call them."

"Miss Allan didn't want to deal with all of them, so she picked out one network and told them that was who she would deal with. Very sensible. But I guess she knew how to deal with media."

Even though mainstream media was different from social media, Elysse had still had enough experience with both to know how to address the press and make sure she got her own way. Once they knew how famous she was, they would bend over backward to do what she wanted.

But who was the man? Had he been pressuring her or coercing her somehow? Had she managed to get away from him once the cameras were rolling and he didn't want his own mug to be recorded?

"Do you have surveillance video of her and the rest of the group? Anything that would show the man?"

"Well, I don't wear a body cam. We have some cameras out there, but…" Poulsen squinted, deep in thought. "I don't think they were close to any of them. And anyway, it was six months ago; we don't keep video for that long."

"Would you have any pictures that were taken that day? People must have been excited about seeing Elysse and being part of the recovery effort."

"I don't have anything. But I'm sure plenty of people probably posted about it online. If you went through the photos that were posted around the event…"

"Yeah, I will," Zachary agreed. "Anything about this guy that will help me to identify him?"

Poulsen shrugged. "He wasn't exactly the touristy type. He probably looks out of place, if he was caught in any of the pictures.

I don't mean that he was dressed wrong for the weather or anything like that… just that he was not a hiker, not a photographer, not someone who looked like he was here on purpose or of his own choice."

"But he wasn't with his wife? Daughter? Coworker?"

"No, by himself, as far as I could tell. Like I said, it looked like an enforced vacation: 'Take two weeks off to relax, and I want to see pictures.'"

Zachary grinned and looked at Kenzie. She was just the type who would have to be forced to take a vacation. She hated to leave the medical examiner's office in someone else's hands. Even in the shape she had been in after the abduction attempt, it had taken some talking to get her to agree to go on the trip to the Grand Canyon with him. And she had probably only agreed because of the attack and not wanting to have to look over her shoulder for the Russians all the time,

Kenzie rolled her eyes. "You didn't have to force me to take time off," she told him. "You only asked."

"But what if I'd said two weeks?"

She cleared her throat. "Well… two weeks is a long time to be away from the office. I would have had to get someone to cover for me…"

Poulsen chuckled. "Some people just aren't built for vacationing."

43

B ack at the hotel, Zachary sat on the couch with his laptop and worked his way through social media pictures posted of Elysse before and after the press release where she confirmed her identity and tried to explain that she hadn't been trying to make anyone worry about her; she had just wanted some time alone after the argument with her boyfriend. The ensuing panic was just an innocent mistake.

There weren't many people who fit the ranger's description of the businessman on vacation. He had stayed well back from the cameras when the media had been broadcasting, but there were social media photographs taken around the same time that showed him among the group of tourists who had "discovered" Elysse.

Poulsen's description had been good. The man wasn't over-dressed or wearing the wrong clothes. He wasn't obviously out of place, and yet he *was* obviously out of place. A fish out of water. And his eyes were trained on Elysse in all the photos they could find of him.

"Who are you?" Zachary mused, staring at him. He tried running the man's face through several facial recognition apps, even though it wasn't the perfect angle and resolution. There were no good matches, but that didn't really mean anything. The databases

Zachary had access to were public access, not mugshots or prison records. Not that the man looked like he'd ever been at odds with the law.

There was a knock on the hotel room door, and Zachary looked up, rubbing his eyes and wondering how late it was. Had Kenzie already ordered room service? He should have taken her out to a restaurant, but maybe she was hungry and had given up on his tearing himself away from his computer.

Kenzie answered the door, but she didn't return with a food tray. She waved a thick envelope at Zachary.

"Delivery for you."

She tossed it onto the table. Zachary leaped to his feet, hands out protectively, heart jumping to his throat.

Kenzie startled at his reaction. "Sheesh, you scared me! What's —" She cut herself off, looking at the package that had landed on the table and back at Zachary. "Oh, man. I'm sorry. I didn't mean to startle you."

They both stared at the package for a moment, not moving.

"Do you want me to open it?" Kenzie suggested.

Zachary shook his head. His heard was pounding a rapid rhythm and he was breathing quickly, which was burning his ribs. "I don't even want you to touch it."

"Well, what do you want me to do? What are you going to do? Did you order something?"

Zachary might forget ordering items online when he was at home and it was routine, but he hadn't ordered anything while they had been at the hotel.

Who knew that he was there, other than Heather? They hadn't told anyone other than Kenzie's parents that they were leaving town and had not shared their itinerary with Walter and Lisa.

Could the Russians have followed them from Vermont, to Canada, to Utah, and then to Arizona? It seemed unlikely that anyone could have followed them all the way to Arizona unless they had a tracking device on them.

When it had become apparent that Kenzie was going to pack more than just a carry-on no matter what he said, Zachary had taken advantage of her suitcase space to add a few more devices that he didn't have room for in his carry-on. That included both his bug sweeper and his explosive sniffer.

Without explaining his thought process to Kenzie, he retrieved the two items from her suitcase. He first ran the explosive sniffer around the small packet Kenzie had thrown on the table. Thanks to her rough handling, he already knew it didn't have any kind of motion switch. But it could still have a pull-string like the last package bomb he had received, a timer, or remote detonator.

The sniffer was silent. No lights and no audio alerts. The display showed all zeros. Nothing of concern. But that still didn't explain where it had come from or how anyone had known how to find him. It was Zachary's name on the envelope. No return address. He didn't recognize the handwriting. If it had been the Russians, it would have been Kenzie's name, wouldn't it? Unless they had been smart enough to realize that might set off alarm bells.

He turned off the sniffer, trying to smile reassuringly at Kenzie. "No explosives. Should be perfectly safe."

He ran the bug sweeper over their luggage, clothing, and all around the hotel room. No hits. If they hadn't been tracked there, how had anyone known to send a package to him?

Zachary sat back down and tapped Heather's name on his phone shortcuts.

"Hi, Zachy," she greeted. "How is the vacation?"

"Interesting," he said briefly. "Uh... you didn't tell anyone we were here, did you?"

"Oh. Well... there was an email from a photographer that you had contacted. You gave her your card; I just handled the email because it was routine. She had a USB drive she wanted to send to you, so I just told her that's where you are... you figured you'd be there at least another day, and I thought you might want her pictures and videos right away..."

"*Who* was this?"

"Uh... let me just check the email." She faded out for a moment and then returned: "Kristy Echols."

The photographer who had been working with Elysse and Dain on the tour. The "caddy," to use her own description.

Zachary's shoulders relaxed. He took a deep breath. "Oh, Kristy. Okay, that's great. Not a problem."

"Good. I'm sorry, I just assumed that you would want to see what she had as soon as possible."

"I do. I just didn't know what was in the package or who knew we were here. Freaked me out for a minute."

"Oh, I didn't think about that! I should have given you a heads-up. I'm sorry."

"No, it's okay. We didn't quite get around to immersing it in a bucket of water."

"I hope not. I don't think USB's work too well when immersed."

"No," Zachary agreed. "Well, thanks for letting me know. I'll talk to you later."

He ended the call and nodded to Kenzie. "It's okay. It's safe."

Kenzie took a deep breath in and released it. "Well. Now that you've got my heart going. I hope you know I'm not going to be able to sleep tonight."

"Then we can stay up together," Zachary teased. He reached for the package. His heart was still pounding and the pain in his ribs pulsed with his heartbeat. He knew he needed to take a painkiller, but he didn't want to do it in front of Kenzie and let her see how much pain he was in. She would have something to say about his traveling all over the continent with his broken ribs bothering him as much as they were. He'd learned in his early years not to let pain slow him down and not to let anyone see his vulnerability. It was a hard habit to unlearn.

Zachary was having trouble controlling the anxiety he felt about opening the delivered package, even knowing that it had come from Kristy and not one of the Russians or another enemy. He knew that pushing through the anxiety was the only way to overcome it, so he tried to pretend to himself that he was not panicking about opening it and blowing himself to bits.

He tore the pull strip across to open the end of the brown paper envelope.

There was no boom, no loss of consciousness, no time jump. He was still standing in the hotel room, looking at Kenzie as if nothing had happened. He looked down at the package and slipped his hand inside to grasp the USB drive and pull it out.

"Kristy is a photographer. She was going to go back over her footage from Elysse's tour and see what she could get for me," he told her, his voice barely cracking. He cleared his throat. "Let's see what she's found."

He plugged it into his computer. Again, nothing blew up. Nothing bad happened. His computer didn't crash; nothing threatening came up on the screen; his computer just brought up the directory for him to look at. He glanced over the files and tapped to preview the first one in the directory.

His heart rate started to slow.

As Zachary sat down again to look through the photos, Kenzie sat beside him on the couch. They both leaned in to see if there was anything new and enlightening in Kristy Echols' pictures.

44

After reviewing the photos and video Kristy had sent him, Zachary called her to discuss what they showed. He put her on speakerphone when they connected.

"It's Zachary Goldman," he told Kristy. "I've just been looking through the photography you sent me."

"Oh, good. Your assistant said that if I sent it right away, it would catch up with you before you left your hotel, so I thought I would send it through. It was too much to try to share by email, and I don't know about you, but I always prefer physical storage to a cloud-sharing link."

"Yeah, that works for me. Then I don't have to fight with the system and hope it lets me download files. Especially with hotel Wi-Fi, which is always a little flaky and might cost extra."

"So you had a look? I found a few pictures of the bearded guy that I remembered."

"Yes. And we saw him in Utah. I wondered whether it was the same guy or not. Now I have confirmation."

"In Utah?"

"Yeah."

"Huh. I guess he had to live somewhere. So you really didn't need me to spend all that time going through my pictures."

"It was helpful," Zachary protested, not wanting her to resent the effort she had put into it. "I really appreciate it. It could have been two different men. I also wonder whether you saw someone else that we are looking for while you were reviewing your pictures…"

"Someone else? Really?"

"Sorry. I'll text you a photo when we get off the call. He was a dad type. Maybe a businessman. Someone who seemed a little… out of his element. Probably not like the other fanboys that followed Elysse around. Maybe someone she knew from back home; we're not sure yet."

"So, like, forties or fifties, corporate type?"

"Yeah. Dark hair and eyes, clean shaven, dressed like he was on vacation but wasn't comfortable with it."

"Doesn't ring a bell with me. Sorry. That doesn't mean it wasn't someone Elysse had a relationship with. Just that it's not someone I remember seeing on the shoots. She could have been seeing him, but I wouldn't really know that. I just knew her public persona."

"Her brand."

"Exactly," Kristy agreed. "She always tried to stay on brand when we were working on a shoot. You have to, or you end up screwing up and posting something that doesn't fit the brand. And that can be suicide."

"What do you mean?"

"Well, because she has to keep… 'in character' for all her appearances. She endorses certain products, and if she did anything to harm a product she endorses because of something someone saw her do… it could result in the loss of that contract and a significant amount of money. She had to *be* the person that the sponsor was paying for."

"So if her sponsor was… say, a baby product, and her brand or persona was a nurturing mother. Then she posted something online where she was swearing and ranting at someone, or making threats, or even just doing something bad for the environment…"

"Yeah," Kristie agreed. "Suddenly, she's no longer the earth mother type, and she loses those endorsements. She wouldn't be able to do work for them anymore because she's burned that brand. It's really important not to do that. To always be aware of your messaging every time you post something."

"It must be exhausting."

"Some people do find it difficult. Elysse was pretty natural, but even she could make a mistake and, more than once, I told her not to post something, or that she needed to tweak her hashtags, or whatever."

"That was part of your service."

"It was."

"Were you seeing her?" Zachary asked on instinct, trying to identify the nagging feeling he got while talking to her.

"Seeing her?"

"Well, we both know she and Dain were not exclusive. And even though you told me she didn't have anything to do with the roadies, I assume you knew she was in a relationship with Mike."

"Mike wasn't *really* a roadie," Kristy protested. "He was... he played at being one of them so that he had a reason to be around. But he wasn't really."

"You didn't answer my question." Zachary knew she was avoiding it. She could have just told him no, but she was trying to find her way around it so she didn't have to actually lie. He'd already caught her in a half-truth.

"Well... I don't know what you want me to say. I worked for Elysse. We had a business relationship."

"And also a personal one?"

"Maybe... a little. We were friends," Kristy hedged.

"You didn't tell me that when we talked the first time. You pretended that it was all just your professional services."

"Well, that was *mostly* true."

"And you had an intimate relationship with her."

"Mr. Goldman..." she said stiffly.

"It's still just Zachary. You and Elysse had a relationship outside of your work relationship. I assume you had the opportunity to see whether Dain was physically abusive or not."

"Not exactly. Elysse... had bruises sometimes. But that might have been Dain, or it might have been Mike… or it might have been someone else. And I don't know what kind of a relationship she had with anyone else. Maybe some of them were more… physically demanding than others."

Zachary rolled his eyes at Kenzie, who was pretending not to listen in on the conversation but was not succeeding in looking oblivious. She shook her head. Zachary tried not to laugh, as it was too painful.

"I'm going to let you off the hook for now," he told Kristy, "but I might circle back with some other questions later. And I want you to think about what you might have seen. And whether you think that someone was abusing her or if she was just… having a good time."

"Okay," Kristy agreed, sounding relieved. "There was one thing I wanted to tell you about, though. When I went over the media coverage after looking at my photographs, I noticed something."

"Uh-huh?" Zachary reached for his computer keyboard and prepared to write down notes.

Kristy didn't say anything immediately. Zachary waited a few seconds.

"Kristy?"

There was no answer. Zachary looked at his phone, which no longer showed an active call on the screen. He muttered a curse under his breath and touched the screen to bring up his contact list again. He tapped Kristy's number and waited for it to reconnect.

The phone kept ringing and eventually went to voicemail. Zachary hung up. He tried one more time, reasoning that she might be trying to call him back at the same time he was trying to get her, or her phone might have crashed or reset for some reason and was booting back up again. He'd had that happen randomly before, which was annoying, especially if he was right in the middle of an important conversation.

The second time it went to voicemail, he sighed and left a message for Kristy to call him back, even though he was sure she would call back once she got things straightened out on her end.

45

Zachary waited for Kristy to call back, working on a few notes of his conversation with her, but she didn't.

"Maybe something came up," Kenzie suggested. "She might have had a client in a big crisis or something. Something that had to be dealt with right away. I'm sure she'll get back to you."

Zachary nodded. Sooner or later, he would reconnect with Kristy.

"Dinner?" Kenzie suggested. "I'm starving."

"Uh, sure. Did you want to order from room service or go out?"

"Go out. I saw a few interesting restaurants nearby. We might as well act like it is a vacation, even if it is a working vacation."

"Sure. Lead the way."

Kenzie had scoped out the nearby offerings, so she ran through the options when they got to the car. Zachary gave his input, but really didn't care which one they went to. Something to eat, a little time relaxing with Kenzie, then back to the hotel room to watch TV and get ready for bed. Once Kenzie dropped off to sleep, he could get back to work.

They sat down at what Zachary thought was an authentic Mexican restaurant. At least it was more likely to be authentic than what passed for a Mexican restaurant in Vermont. The air was redolent with hearty, spicy aromas. They ordered an appetizer platter. Zachary fingered his phone.

"Tomorrow is Monday," he pointed out. "You said you didn't mind staying one more day. Do you want to be back at the office Tuesday morning? What time should we aim to be back in Vermont?"

Kenzie hesitated, which Zachary assumed meant she needed to get back. He wondered whether they could catch a red-eye. They might have to return to the hotel room, pack, and get right onto a plane. Kenzie could sleep during the flight and get back for an afternoon at the medical examiner's. If he could get the arrangements made right away.

"I actually wouldn't mind taking another day," Kenzie said, surprising him. "I'm enjoying this, and… I've been emailing with Dr. Cook, and he's okay with me taking another day or two. The thing about dead bodies is they aren't going anywhere. They can wait, as long as there is no political pressure. And if something needs to be done urgently, Dr. Cook can do it without me."

"Is that allowed?" Zachary asked in a shocked tone.

Kenzie laughed.

He relaxed, glad he wouldn't have to make a last-minute, all-night flight back to Vermont.

"We could go on to Oregon tomorrow," Kenzie said, "I know you were hoping you might be able to talk to some of Elysse's family. It's less than three hours."

"You checked?"

She smiled, eyes dancing. "I checked."

"Great. I'd love to be able to talk to them. I'll see who I can get ahold of tonight. Arrange for a time for us to meet."

Zachary knew that after the previous sleepless night, he should take a sleep aid to help him get caught up, but there was still the problem of knowing that the hotel room was not secure and, if he were asleep, especially under the influence of a heavy sleep aid, he would not be able to protect himself and Kenzie from intruders.

He probably wasn't much more capable short on sleep, unarmed, and without any special martial arts training, but he felt safer awake than asleep, and promised himself he could sleep on the airplane in the morning. Once he was in the air, he would know he was safe from intruders. Airplanes might not be totally secure, and they might be a lot more vulnerable than the general public thought them to be, but he would be much safer in the air than on the other side of a flimsy hotel room door.

He reviewed the photographs Kristy had sent him again and wondered what had happened to her. Why hadn't she returned his call? Or at least sent him an email or text? He checked his email, his spam folder, and the task list that Heather helped him maintain to see whether Heather had processed an email from Kristy and set up a follow-up action from Zachary.

But there was nothing. Zachary sent an email reminding Kristy that she had been about to tell him something she had noticed while she was going through the photographs and videos she had of Elysse's tour.

46

They caught an early flight to Portland, breakfasting in the airport lounge after checking in. So when Zachary finally rested his head against the headrest and closed his eyes on the plane, he had a full, satisfied stomach and felt safe for the first time in a couple of days.

"Zachary."

Zachary opened his eyes. He glanced out the window. They were still on the runway. He closed them again.

"Yeah?"

"Time to wake up, sunshine."

He opened his eyes again, looking out the window. It was brighter outside than it had been when he had closed them. "How long have we been sitting on the runway?" He rubbed his eyes. "I must have dozed off."

"Yeah, you dozed off for four hours and slept through the entire flight. It's time to get off."

Zachary turned his eyes to the cabin, and he saw that people were getting up to disembark, rather than getting settled into their seats as they had been when he'd first closed his eyes.

"Oh." He yawned and scrubbed his eyes again. "Okay. Getting up."

He grabbed his carry-on and stood up. Kenzie's carry-on was in the overhead rack. She got it out, and he caught her giving him a frown.

"What?"

"I'm just wondering how much you're sleeping at night."

"Oh." Zachary cleared his throat. "I'm sure it will be better once we get home. It's just hard in an unfamiliar place. I don't sleep soundly."

He didn't tell her he was sleeping, so he wasn't lying. But he also didn't want her to know that he wasn't sleeping in the hotels at all. It would just cause unnecessary worry.

Kenzie didn't say anything further about it. Since she was seated on the aisle, she led the way off the plane. Zachary left Kenzie to wait for her luggage and headed to the car rental counter. When Kenzie caught up with him, the rental counter guy led them out to their vehicle. Zachary and Kenzie stared dubiously at the big red truck.

"I reserved a compact," Zachary pointed out.

"We don't have any. This is what we've got."

"But... I didn't want a truck."

"It's the same price."

"Well, the gas mileage isn't the same. Or the maneuverability in traffic."

"Trucks are safer in traffic. You'll be glad you've got it. Much better 360 visibility, and people get out of your way."

Zachary had always hated how aggressive truck drivers tended to be, thinking that they could just bully the smaller cars out of the way.

He looked at Kenzie for her thoughts. They could try one of the other rental counters, but they were already cutting it close to get to the appointment he'd set up with Elysse's family. If he took any longer, he would have to call them to tell them he would be late.

"Can you drive a truck?" Kenzie asked.

"Yeah, I've rented them for moves before."

"So let's just go with it. I know it's a pain and they burn

through gas like crazy, but you can just charge your expenses back to the client. It's not your fault you got a truck."

He sighed. "I guess so."

They went ahead and walked around the truck to check for any dings in the paint and signed the contract on the rental guy's iPad. He handed them the keys, and they were on their way.

The Allan family lived in a small town in a more rural part of Oregon. Before long, they had left the streets of the city and were on a long stretch of highway. The tires hummed over the asphalt.

As Zachary had observed when he had researched Elysse's background, the area that her family lived in was poor. One of the poorest in the state. Lots of unemployment, people living hand to mouth, barely scraping by. The houses were low, patched, and looked like they would be blown away in a strong wind.

The GPS led them to the address of Elysse's aunt Esther, where he had been told everyone would meet him. On one hand, Zachary would have preferred to meet them individually and not have their stories contaminated by each other. But he also didn't have the benefit of time that he would have had if they were interviewing in Vermont. Seeing them all at the same time would shorten the amount of time required for interviews. And he still hoped to be able to see Elysse, though he hadn't succeeded in arranging an interview time with her. Maybe he would have a better idea of how to get somewhere with her after talking to the family.

"Here they are!" a woman stood at the door and shouted back over her shoulder. She turned back to face Zachary. "You found us! Did you have any trouble?"

"No, the GPS—" Zachary started to tell her.

She started talking over him and grabbed his arm to pull him behind her into the house. "A private investigator, can you believe it? It's like we're in the middle of a movie! One of those noir detective flicks?"

She pulled him through a kitchen area with sticky linoleum worn through to the wood into a living room area with seventies-era brown carpet that reeked of stale smoke.

"Can I be the leggy blonde?" asked the youngest of the three women.

"You're not blonde," Zachary pointed out, a little breathless with the sudden assault on all his senses.

"That's easy enough to fix," she told him in a whispery voice, leaning closer. Then she laughed in a long, loud bray that completely overwhelmed the flirty, breathy voice she had been affecting. She punched Zachary on the arm, a little too hard for a friendly nudge.

Zachary raised his eyebrows at Kenzie, who had followed him, hoping for rescue. It was one thing to deal with dark, menacing figures who lurked out of sight or made ambiguous threats toward him and his investigation. He would take them over a houseful of rowdy, teasing women any day.

Kenzie smiled at Zachary in amusement. She introduced herself to the women, and they responded in kind.

47

The two older women were Priscilla and Esther, Elysse's mother and aunt, but he had trouble keeping straight which was which. They were both obnoxiously loud and cheerful, excited to be interviewed by a private investigator and ready, it appeared, to spill all the family secrets. The third woman, the youngest one, was Celine, Elysse's sister.

All three were tall, brash, bony brunettes. Elysse was blonde rather than brunette but, as Celine had suggested, that was a change easy enough to effect with a bottle of bleach. Zachary didn't know whether Elysse's hair was naturally blonde or helped along by chemicals.

"Have a seat, please," Esther told Zachary, pointing him toward a couch with a stained zebra-stripe slipcover. Zachary wasn't sure when he sat down on it whether there were cushions under the cover or suitcases. Whatever it was padded with, it was not comfortable. He perched on the edge, and Kenzie sat down with him. She shifted uncomfortably a few times, then was still.

"Mr. Goldman," Priscilla simpered, "what a great name for a private eye. Like Goldfinger from James Bond! Do you get that a lot? Goldfinger?"

"Uh, no, Not usually. And I just go by Zachary, so please, feel free... Priscilla..."

"Zachary," she repeated, smiling at him coyly. "You're not putting the moves on me, are you Zachary?"

"No ma'am," Zachary protested. "I just... don't go my last name much. Everyone just calls me Zachary."

"Or Zach?" she suggested, "I'll bet people call you Zach."

"Uh, sometimes. A few people."

"How about you?" Kenzie asked. "Do you have a nickname? Do people call you Prissy?"

"Never liked that nickname," she declared. "Because I'll tell you, prissy I am not!"

All the women laughed. Zachary rubbed the bridge of his nose. He was getting a headache. It was too early in the morning for all the noise and drama.

"I sure appreciate you meeting with me," Zachary told them. "It's very helpful, as I'm trying to figure out what happened to Elysse, to be able to talk to her friends and family. No one is closer than family, am I right?"

Of course they all agreed. One of them seemed to be in motion at all times. One woman would sit down and another would pop up. Celine got up to fill a couple of chipped mugs with coffee for Zachary and Kenzie. Zachary sipped the fragrant beverage gratefully. He didn't care whether the cup was clean or not; he needed the caffeine if he were going to get through the morning with the covey of women. The coffee was piping hot and strong. He took a few gulps.

"So, are the rest of you into social media?" he asked them. "Are you all influencers?"

He knew very well they were not. He would be surprised if they all had social media accounts. But he knew they were not active on social media. None of them had followed the trail Elysse had blazed into the forest of social media.

They cackled with laughter.

"I don't even have Facebook," Priscilla bragged. "I haven't got a clue how to do any of that stuff. And wouldn't want to spend all my time scrolling mindlessly through that crap. Have you seen the kids? How they don't even turn them off when they go to bed? I'm surprised they aren't all waterproof. Do they put them down when they're in the shower? I know they don't on the crapper. Gotta be scrolling, always gotta be scrolling."

Celine nodded. "You just don't understand. You don't know how to do anything on your phone or computer. It isn't that you're so much more virtuous than anyone else. It's just that you're a Luddite. That means you don't understand how to do anything online."

"I wouldn't want to even if I did," Priscilla declared loudly, not denying her ignorance.

"So, you know what I'm here about," Zachary started in a slow, calm voice, hoping that if he were slow and deliberate, the women would be too. He needed them to think carefully about their answers, not to fly from one thing to another and make jokes. He needed the answers only they could give him. "I'm trying to trace Elysse's movements during the time she was missing over the summer."

Priscilla wrung her hands. "You can't imagine what that was like for me, her mother, to sit and watch the coverage, day after day, and wonder where Elysse was. Whether she was okay. I don't understand why she disappeared like she did. I think there must be something wrong with her. Is that what you think? Do you think she was hit over the head? Or drugged? I can't understand why she wouldn't call one of us to tell us what was happening or ask for help if she was in trouble. If she just wanted some time on her own, that's okay; who would have cared about that?"

Zachary nodded. "It does seem strange that she wouldn't at least let you know she was okay."

"She should have. What kind of child doesn't think it is important to tell her parents where she is and what she is doing? We wouldn't care if she wanted to spend a month in the Grand Canyon as long as she was happy and safe there."

"It's common courtesy," Kenzie agreed. "You would expect it

from anyone. That they would let you know what was going on in their lives and that they were safe."

"That's the way she was raised! Do you think any of us go anywhere without telling the others where we're going or what we're doing? We're always calling or messaging back and forth to tell the others what is going on."

"Even if Mom can't do anything else on her phone, she knows how to call and text," Celine said in a teasing voice.

"That's right. If I can do that, anyone can! It isn't like Elysse didn't know how. I don't know why she didn't."

"Before she disappeared, was she usually good about letting you know about things? Where she would be and what she was doing?"

The women looked at each other, all heads nodding vigorously. "Yes, of course. She was part of this family. She always let us know what she was doing. I mean... okay, sometimes it was a few days between when she was on a tour or just caught up with things. But she would always let someone know sooner or later. And if we called or texted, she would get back to us."

"And she was posting online all the time," Celine pointed out. "So if you wanted to know what she was doing, you just looked at her timeline, and you could see it."

Silence fell momentarily. Zachary looked at Esther, who was scowling.

"But she stopped posting online at all. You didn't hear from her at all during that time?"

"I told her not to go out east," Esther said. "I told her there would be trouble. Everybody knows the kind of people you meet out there. No offense, but..." Zachary had noticed the tendency some people had of saying "no offense" when they were about to say something very offensive. "Easterners just aren't as friendly as westerners. You can't trust them. All kinds of gangs and psychopaths... she wouldn't even agree to avoid New York City. New York City! She thought she could just walk the streets there like anywhere else. She thought people were the same all over, that she could just strike up a conversation with anyone. But believe me, I remember how New York City was in the eighties! You can't just take a girl from backwoods Oregon and plop her down in the streets of New York!"

"It's not the same anymore, Auntie Esther," Celine protested. "Things have changed. It's much safer there now than when you were a kid."

"It still isn't safe," Esther insisted, shaking her head. "People get killed in New York every day."

48

"**D**id you know of anyone who was harassing her?" Zachary asked, sliding his gaze over to Priscilla, who he assumed was more likely to know about an issue with her daughter. "Was anyone causing trouble for her? Someone she might have been afraid of?"

"You think that someone did something to her?" Priscilla asked, her lip protruding in a pout, "She said she was just camping out in the Grand Canyon."

Camping? Zachary highly doubted Elysse had been doing any camping while she had been there.

"I'm pretty sure that she was not entirely honest about what she was doing or what happened to her while she was gone," Zachary said slowly. "I wouldn't want to call her a liar, but I do think... there was a lot happening that she was unwilling to reveal when she spoke to the press."

"But we are her *family*," Esther emphasized. "We weren't just the people on the other side of a TV screen. We gave her a start in life. She wouldn't exist if it wasn't for us. You can't lie to your family."

Zachary knew plenty of families who lied to each other. Some of them constantly. He would guess, based on the way the women's

233

eyes went back and forth, examining and monitoring each other, that there were plenty of lies in this one, too.

"You must have been very close to Elysse," Zachary told Celine. "How close are you in age?"

"Just a year apart," Celine agreed with a nod. "We were always together, joined at the hip. Until…"

She stopped, hesitating. Zachary waited to see if she would finish the sentence.

"Until she got to be a famous influencer?" Zachary suggested finally.

"No. I couldn't care less about that. Having a famous sister isn't all it's cracked up to be. But she's still Elysse. She's still my sister. No, it's just that…" she trailed off and left it hanging. Zachary waited for her to finish, then looked at the others to see whether this was an old gripe they all knew about. Chances were, because they were so close and Elysse and Celine had been "joined at the hip," everyone else would know exactly what she was talking about.

"You're sisters," Priscilla said sternly, "Sisters should never let a boy get between them."

A boy. Zachary thought about Elysse out east on her publicity tour, juggling various partners, her sister back home nursing a grudge against her for the boy that got between them.

"Dain?" he guessed.

There were nods. Celine shook her head, tears escaping her eyes. She had remained dry-eyed when talking about her sister missing and presumed dead.

"Dain was interested in me, not in Elysse. She was the stupid kid sister. He didn't want her. He wasn't interested in her."

"I thought they went to school together."

"Sure, we all went to the same schools together."

"But she was younger? She and Dain were not in the same grade?"

"No. He was a year older, in my class. But she had to go after him. Had to… seduce him and take him away from me."

It wasn't impossible that the younger sister had seduced the older one's boyfriend, but it was far more common for the roles to be reversed, the boyfriend forgetting his interest in the one sister to explore a relationship with the other. Was the grass always greener on the other side? Did Dain prefer blondes? Did they just get along better? Have more in common? Or had Elysse done it intentionally to spite her sister for some perceived slight?

"That's not what happened," Priscilla disagreed.

"You weren't there, Mom. You don't know what happened."

"I know what I saw. Two girls making fools of themselves over a boy instead of being loyal to each other and kicking him to the curb."

"You blame Dain?" Zachary asked her.

"I didn't raise Dain. I did raise the other two." She gave Celine a sharp look. "They knew better than to both get involved with the same boy."

"He was mine first," Celine insisted. "It isn't my fault Elysse decided to go after him. I wasn't the one in the wrong."

"It's silly to stop talking to each other over a boy."

Celine shrugged and folded her arms stubbornly.

"So is that why Elysse hasn't been in contact with you?" Zachary suggested. "Because you had a falling-out over Dain?"

"We were still talking," Celine said. "Sometimes, anyway. We weren't best friends like we used to be, but we still talked to each other and messaged each other. Elysse stopped when she disappeared, and I thought... I thought he had done something to her."

"A lot of people thought he must have harmed her. I'm sure it was all over the news here, just like in Vermont."

Celine nodded. "She wouldn't answer any calls or texts. I thought... they got in a fight. They were always fighting or arguing or something. I thought that if he killed her in a fight, then it was my fault. It should have been me. Because I was the one who was supposed to be with him. If he had done something to her, it was my fault."

Priscilla left her seat to go over to her daughter and hugged her fiercely.

"It isn't your fault. Whatever happened or happens to Elysse, it isn't your doing. She's made her own choices. She's been the victim of circumstances. None of it has anything to do with you."

Celine swiped at a few more tears. Zachary wasn't sure now whether they were tears for her loss of Dain or the near loss of her sister. Feelings could be very complex.

"It's this influencer stuff," Priscilla said. "She should never have gotten involved in all of it. It isn't good, honest work. Posting pictures of yourself online and expecting people to look at you or to pay you for it. That's just... exhibitionism."

"She didn't do that kind of picture," Esther said dryly. "That wasn't her 'brand.'"

"No," Zachary agreed. "I've seen lots of her pictures, both selfies and pictures of other products, landscapes, and so on. It wasn't anything racy. Nothing questionable."

"It wasn't honest work," Priscilla repeated. "I warned her from the start that wasn't the way to make her way in the world. A woman has to learn a trade. How to make things with her own hands, clean, cook, those are the things she should be getting paid for, not online pictures."

Zachary nodded his understanding. He wasn't going to argue with Priscilla about Elysse's choice of vocation. Especially since that career had apparently come to an end. Elysse was no longer posting.

"How often do you see her now? Not very often because of your falling-out?" He looked at all of them to see what they would say, what their faces would give away.

"She's been a total hermit since the disappearance," Esther told the room in general. "She won't come over here, and if we go to her house... she won't have anyone in. We are her family, and getting past the front door..." She shook her head. "You should be able to go see your own kin. We brought that girl up. This is the thanks we get."

"Has this all been since the tour and her disappearance? She would see you before?"

Priscilla nodded. "Before... I can't say she was always welcoming. She was so 'busy,' you know? She couldn't spare a few minutes to visit with her family because she had all of that 'work.'" She rolled her eyes. "Posting pictures. That was 'work,' and she couldn't afford to take a day or an afternoon off to go shopping, or to a family birthday, or just to hang out and visit."

"But it was bringing in pretty good money."

"Yes," Priscilla seemed to disapprove of this as much as everyone else. "She made her money off her pictures, displaying herself online, and then she had to move away, and she had to have nice things for her home, and she had to go out to eat and go to big black-tie events. Having money changed her." She shook her head. "It always changes you."

"It was good she got her own place," Celine protested. "I want to get my own place. I want to get enough money to afford my own place too, and decorate it to make it look nice and have nice things. It's not bad to have nice things."

"It is if it changes you," Esther backed Priscilla up. "Not caring about your family anymore, not talking to them or having anything to do with them. That's not the kind of person you want to be. You don't want to be like her in that way."

"She cares," Celine said, her voice lowered slightly as if they might not be able to hear her. "She's just... I don't know. Something is wrong."

"You think she's scared?" Zachary suggested. "Maybe she has anxiety about leaving her house or having anyone in since her disappearance. Maybe something traumatic happened and it is affecting the way she can interact with you and the rest of the world."

"Scared? Why would she be scared to leave her house or for us to come in?" Esther argued, shaking her head vehemently. She got up from her seat and went over to the bookcase, where a few bottles of alcohol shared space with some books that looked like they hadn't been opened in the last century. She poured several glugs of high-test fluid into her coffee cup. "If she's scared, then she needs to come home. We will take care of her. We'll make sure that nothing can happen to her."

"I'm sure that would mean a lot to her. That you want to protect her. But she might not feel like you are able to."

Thinking about his own anxiety and being unable to sleep in the hotel rooms with the flimsy doors, Zachary could empathize with Elysse. However much she might want to come back home to her family or allow them into her house, she might feel too anxious to do so. Anxiety could keep a person locked up as a prisoner in her own home for years. Decades.

"If she's scared, why doesn't she have Dain look after her?" Celine sneered. Then she laughed. Dain wasn't a big guy, or highly trained, or the type to carry a gun. There wasn't a lot he could do to protect his girlfriend if she were too scared to leave the house.

"Do you really think something happened in the Grand Canyon?" Priscilla asked Zachary. "I mean... what could happen? She goes camping, sleeps rough for a few days, then comes clean and makes a statement on TV, and goes home to her nice, warm home. How traumatic is that?"

"I'm not sure she was alone. I'm not sure why she felt the need to abandon her old life to disappear, or to stay hidden now. The fact that she's not even posting on social media anymore, that doesn't strike you as a disturbing change in behavior? You don't think that means something?"

The women looked at each other, exchanging shrugs and head-shakes. "We didn't want her doing it in the first place. If something happened to knock some sense into her..." Esther held out her palms. "That's good. We're glad that she's coming around."

"But not if she's scared," Celine said, defending her sister and former best friend, not quite liking Esther's "tough love" approach.

"I'd like to get in to see her," Zachary said. "I read online that she had sold her house. Do you have her current address?"

"She didn't sell it," Celine said. "Not really. She transferred it to a holding company that didn't have her name on it anywhere. So her address wouldn't show up on any public records and she could have some privacy."

"Do you think she would answer the phone if you called or texted her? To see if I could talk to her for a few minutes? You don't need to say who I am or who I'm working for… just that you have a friend who thinks he might be able to help and he wants to come see her."

"Haven't you been listening?" Priscilla demanded. "Haven't you heard a thing we've said? She doesn't want to talk to us anymore. She doesn't want anything to do with her family."

"Maybe I could get her to." Predictably, it was Celine who offered. "Sometimes she answers me. Or at least reads what I have to say. You can tell when someone has read your messages on some of the apps."

Zachary nodded. "Would you give it a try? Maybe I can say or do something that will help. I can't promise anything, but I'd like to give it a try."

49

After extricating themselves from the Allan household despite numerous attempts to convince them to stay for lunch, watch the soaps, or have a longer gab session, Zachary climbed up into the cab of the truck, rested his forehead on the top of the steering wheel, and sighed.

It was quiet in the truck.

He felt like the Allan broads, as Esther had referred to them, had sucked the life right out of him. Their constant chatter and bickering with each other wormed into his brain and he felt like it was still echoing around in there.

Kenzie stayed talking at the door for a few minutes longer, which gave him a little time to himself before she also climbed into the truck and settled herself into the passenger seat.

"How are you?" she asked, a mixture of sympathy and amusement in her tone.

"I'm… still in one piece. I think."

"You sound worse than you did after fighting the… Russians."

Zachary chuckled, which hurt his ribs and reminded him of just how difficult that encounter had been. "Physically better. Mentally… I'm not sure yet."

She laughed. "I don't know how you do it. I'm amazed you

could stay in there as long as you did. I wasn't even sure about going inside in the first place."

"Well… I've seen worse. But the noise, the way they're always talking, and with such… force and conviction. I don't know. I find that really difficult."

Kenzie nodded. "I can understand why. I'm pretty good at listening to several people talking over each other, but those ladies take it to a whole new level."

Zachary nodded. Kenzie sat for a minute watching him.

"Are we actually going to move?" she asked eventually. "Like, put the key in the ignition and go somewhere?"

"I need to think."

"Can we do that somewhere other than in front of the house? I think if we stay here too long, they're going to come out and offer us lunch again."

Zachary glanced toward the house. The door was still closed, but Kenzie was right. He didn't want to stay right there where they were watching him, waiting for him to leave, or speculating on why he was still just sitting there.

He started up the truck and let it warm up for a minute.

"Do you want to get something to eat?" Kenzie suggested. "A little fuel for the brain engine?"

"I'm not hungry."

"We still need to fuel. We were up early this morning, and have only had coffee since the airport lounge."

"I'm okay." Then Zachary realized he wasn't the only one to take into consideration. "Oh, you're probably hungry, though. Sorry, I wasn't thinking. Just trying to… settle down my brain, and I didn't think about it. What do you want?"

"Just a sandwich place would be fine. We can be in and out and have something reasonably healthy. Nothing too greasy or calorie laden."

Zachary nodded his agreement. He put the truck into gear and drove away from the house, thinking over what he had learned from the Allan ladies.

"Why aren't there any Allan men?" he mused.

Kenzie laughed. "The Allan men had other ideas," she told him. "How long would you survive with them all?"

Zachary shook his head. "I've lived in some pretty chaotic homes. But it would be... challenging."

"I think that's why there are no Allan men around. And the one who was around had to choose between the two sisters, which I gather didn't go over too well."

"Dain and Elysse are both okay with an open relationship. I guess Celine wasn't."

"Dain could have gone with both sisters, you mean? I'm not sure how that would have worked."

"Seemed to work for the polygamists. A lot of them marry sisters in the same family."

"As long as he could find somewhere quiet to sleep," Kenzie teased.

"And to think," Zachary agreed with feeling.

He sat in the sandwich shop for a long time, staring into space and working through his notes and what he'd heard from the Allan family. He picked at his sandwich. There wasn't anything wrong with it, but his thoughts were far away.

"We have Elysse's address," Kenzie said after a while. "Do you have a plan for approaching her? I know you asked Celine to try to break the ice for you and get you in the door, but do you really think you'll be able to when she won't talk to her own family? I don't see what her motivation will be to talk to a private investigator. The other ladies were happy enough to talk to the mysterious Goldfinger, but I don't know if Elysse will be equally enthralled. Especially not if she is suffering from agoraphobia."

"That's being afraid of going outside?"

"More or less."

"I don't think she has a phobia."

"Anxiety, then. Not an illogical fear, but the response to something that happened to Elysse during the time she was missing. Do you have an idea of what happened to her? You don't think she just ran away from her life."

"Not without a reason."

"But everyone has a reason. But was it a reason you and I would understand and find compelling? Or just something that made sense to her? Or she's at the end of her rope and just overwhelmed by anything to do with her own life."

"I'm starting to put together a plan. You know, it's lucky we have the truck today. That's actually going to come in handy."

"You have a plan that requires a truck?"

He nodded.

"You're not planning on turning her house into a drive-thru, are you?"

Zachary smiled at the thought. "No. Nothing like that. In fact, something very quiet and unobtrusive."

"With a big truck. Well, I'm very interested in finding out what it is. Do you want to tell me what you're planning?"

Zachary smiled and tried to decide how much to involve Kenzie in his crazy plan.

50

When Elysse answered the door, her confusion was clear. She peered around the large refrigerator box at Zachary, her brows furrowed in confusion.

"What is this? You've got the wrong house."

"Zachary Goldman. Celine told you to expect me, right? Nod your head like you were expecting this delivery and let me in."

She stared at him, trying to process this.

"Smile and nod," Zachary encouraged. "I'm here to help."

She still wasn't sure how to respond to his sudden appearance and the strange set-up. Finally, she forced a smile and nodded her head. It didn't look convincing, but hopefully if she were under surveillance it would pass. Zachary hadn't been able to see a surveillance car or anyone out of place on the street, but it had been six months since Elysse's reappearance. If she were under surveillance, it was probably via a tiny camera mounted under the eaves of the house across the street or a co-opted doorbell cam rather than someone sitting on the street. There could be a camera inside the house, but he would have to take that risk.

Elysse opened the door wide so that Zachary could maneuver the dolly with the unwieldy box into the front hall of Elysse's house.

It was definitely an upgrade from Esther's house. It was a big, clean, spacious home—not a mansion, but definitely comfortable. It was in a nice neighborhood with good access to schools, shopping, a library, a swimming pool, and a gym. Zachary glanced around the front hall, looking for any obvious surveillance.

He pulled his phone out of the large pocket in his deliveryman coveralls and turned it to face Elysse.

I'm here to help. Is there a camera or bug?

She read it, then shrugged, spreading her hands apart.

"Lead the way to your kitchen and we'll get this installed for you," Zachary told her out loud.

Elysse apparently decided that since she had already let him in, she might as well follow his instructions and see what happened. She led the way through the open living room area to a large kitchen in the back of the house. It was, of course, equipped with new-looking brushed-metal appliances, including a double-wide fridge that was bigger than the box he had on the dolly.

"You're going to love this new unit," Zachary told her, ad-libbing features that might, in theory, make the new fridge a good addition to what Elysse already had since it obviously wouldn't be a replacement for the existing appliance. "The built-in water purification system will give you crystal-clear ice cubes available on demand with an anti-jam delivery mechanism. The separate refrigeration zones are programmable for the type of food you are storing. Soft fruits and berries, hardy fruits, salad greens, solid vegetables, root vegetables, and, of course, meats or dairy. The fridge will maintain the optimum humidity and temperature for each."

He opened the box, which was empty other than a chair and some cinder blocks to keep it weighed down and bolster the illusion that it contained a heavy appliance.

Zachary swiped to the next message on his phone and held it out for Elysse to read.

Make yourself comfortable in the box and I will take you out of here.

She looked from the phone to the box. If Zachary had

misjudged the situation and she was, in fact, just living as a recluse of her own free choice, there was no way she was getting in that box and going off with a stranger, even if Celine had tried to prime her for Zachary's arrival.

"We'll just get it plugged in over here," he said out loud for the benefit of any bugs. Hopefully, there was no camera to capture what was going on in the kitchen. And if there were, then the person monitoring the house would not have time to get there to do anything about it.

Elysse moved slowly, walking into the box and turning around to examine the interior surfaces. She looked at the chair and back at Zachary.

He swiped to another message.

Leave your phone and any other electronic devices here.

She took out her phone and handed it to him. She patted her pockets, indicating that there was nothing else.

Then she sat down on the chair.

Zachary left her phone on the kitchen counter and closed the box, hiding Elysse inside.

"There, that looks good. I'll get rid of this old stuff for you. Let the fridge run for ten hours before using the ice maker. Scan this QR code for the online manual on setting up the refrigeration zones. If you could sign here… and here…"

He tipped the dolly backward slowly. Definitely more weight in it this time. He felt the chair with Elysse sitting in it settle against the back of the box.

"You have a nice day now, ma'am. My card is there if you have any questions on the installation."

He wheeled the box to the front door. Down the two shallow stairs, careful of his cargo, and to the truck. The ramp was still down. It took some effort to push the dolly up the ramp, with Elysse's weight now added to the box, but it wasn't too bad. The exertion did make him breathe harder, which caused a flare of pain in his ribs. He rested a moment and secured the box with a couple of straps. They certainly didn't want it tipping over or flying off as they drove.

51

"What the heck is this all about?" Elysse demanded when Zachary opened the box at their destination.

Zachary put his finger to his lips and motioned her out. Elysse stood in the middle of the storage locker, her eyes wide. Zachary scanned her with his bug sweeper, moving slowly and being very thorough to ensure that she wasn't being bugged or tracked. Then he turned it off and smiled at her.

"Hi. Zachary Goldman, private investigator."

"Uh… yeah. That's what Celine said. But what is this whole…" she waved her hands around, "this whole kidnapping thing and the charade at the house. What the heck is this all about?" Her eyes went to Kenzie. "And who are you?"

"I'm Dr. Kenzie Kirsch from the medical examiner's office in Roxboro, Vermont. At one point, I retrieved and analyzed human remains presumed to be yours."

Elysse licked her lips. "Yeah, I heard about that."

"I'm glad to see that you're in better shape than she was." Kenzie looked at Zachary. "Now, maybe you could tell both of us why we had to go through this big production instead of just visiting Elysse in her house."

"Because I believe that Elysse might still be under surveillance. Under the control of the man who kidnapped her in Vermont."

"I wasn't kidnapped," Elysse scoffed. "Didn't you watch the press coverage? I just needed a break from... the tour and being a social media influencer, on display all day, every day."

"A six-month break? And you won't even visit with your family? The sister you grew up so close to? That sounds more like a break-down than a break."

"So what if it was?" Elysse shrugged. She looked around the interior of the storage unit, musty and dusty, the fluorescent tubes overhead flickering and humming. "Can we get out of here? This is creeping me out."

"Of course," Zachary assured her. He motioned for her to leave the unit ahead of him, hoping she would feel free to do what she wanted rather than being herded by him. She'd put up with enough coercion over the past six months. Her heels clicked as she walked out ahead of him. She squinted in the sun and looked around.

"We can go wherever you want," Zachary said, pointing to the red truck. "Wherever you would feel most comfortable. Although," he grimaced, "I would prefer it wasn't your Aunt Esther's house. I'd like to be able to talk, and I can't get a word in edgewise over there."

Elysse laughed sharply. She looked at the truck. "I'm driving."

Zachary opened his mouth to object. It was his rental, and he was responsible for it. He always drove, as long as he could convince Kenzie to let him. Never her "baby," of course, and some-times she wanted to trade off when they both used his car during the winter. He had been planning to drive the truck.

But Elysse hadn't had any freedom of movement for six months. She needed to know that she was safe and in control. She knew the town and would know where to go to feel safe. He looked at Kenzie, then offered the keys to the truck to Elysse.

She snatched them from his fingers quickly enough to make him jump. But he didn't protest. She was still anxious, unsure whether she had the choice to do what she wanted. Watching the two of them, Elysse climbed up into the truck. She could just drive away before they got in. Once behind the wheel, she seemed to relax and motioned for them to climb in. Zachary nodded for Kenzie to enter ahead of him, assuming that Elysse would feel safer with a woman beside her than a strange man. Zachary climbed up last and pulled the door closed.

"Anywhere?" Elysse asked.

"Wherever you want," Zachary agreed. "Wherever you feel safe and don't think he will be able to monitor you."

"What makes you think anyone is monitoring me?"

Zachary didn't answer. Elysse turned the key in the ignition and drove the truck out of the self-storage lot. In a few minutes, they drove up to a pancake house and Elysse led the way in. They were seated at a booth by the hostess, who left them with menus while she went to get their drink orders.

"I think," Zachary said slowly, "that you were kidnapped when you were still in Vermont. You were coerced to go with the man or men. Maybe by threats and maybe by physical force."

Elysse's eyes were big. She didn't deny it, but she didn't confirm it either. Not in so many words.

"He forced you to do and say whatever he wanted. Maybe he threatened your family. Being discovered at the Grand Canyon wasn't the end of it. Maybe that was all part of the plan. Maybe it wasn't. But you did and said exactly what he wanted you to, so that you could come back here. Only when you got home, you found you were still a prisoner."

She looked around the restaurant, scoping out all the staff and customers. Did she know everyone who was involved in the operation by sight? Would she recognize anyone who had been involved? Or was it possible that other people who had not revealed themselves had been part of the kidnapping but would feed information back to the man in charge about where she was, what she was doing, and who she was talking to? They had, hopefully, gotten her out of the house and to safety without anyone being the wiser, but sooner or later, they would find out. After putting so much time and effort into controlling her, they would not be happy to find out that she had slipped out of their grasp.

"You have a great imagination," Elysse told him.

52

K enzie was watching Zachary, with occasional glances at Elysse. Her expression was thoughtful as she considered the bare bones of his story.

The waitress returned with glasses of orange juice and a pot of coffee, and asked whether they were ready to order.

"This is awesome," Elysse said, looking down at the menu. "You do not know how much I have been craving waffles. Really good waffles, not the ones you stick in the toaster." She placed her order for a big breakfast platter. Zachary and Kenzie, having already eaten before starting the operation, were not quite ready for another full meal, so they ordered a plate of fries to share. The waitress noted everything down carefully and left them alone again.

"Did you know the man before he approached you in Vermont?" Zachary asked, trying to ease Elysse into the story. She must want to share it with someone after having to keep quiet about it for so many months.

"You really think I got kidnapped," Elysse said, raising an eyebrow. "Why?"

"It bothered me that you haven't been posting since you got back. That you just completely cut your fans off. You cared so much about them and about keeping them satisfied before you disappeared. That was your whole life. And I don't believe that you left just because you had an argument or were burned out."

"You're the kind of guy who knows everything and doesn't listen to what anyone else tells him, aren't you?" Elysse demanded.

It was almost eerily similar to what Joss, Zachary's oldest sister, complained about. How he would go to her for advice, talk everything through, and then make a decision that was counter to everything she advised. And even though he recognized that he did so, he couldn't force himself to approach it differently, or to follow Joss's advice even if it ran counter to his own opinion. He had to make the choice that was right for him, even if she told him he was being stupid and making the wrong choice.

"I guess I am," he admitted. "But I'm right."

"You're the one who practically kidnapped me. Coming to my house, pushing your way in, making me get into a fridge box, spiriting me away. The cops could arrest you for that, you know."

"Only if it was against your will. If you wanted to get out of his clutches and we helped you to do that, it isn't kidnapping."

Elysse looked away from Zachary. Her eyes again roamed over each person in the restaurant. Checking. Double-checking. She had been held against her will for so long. She would probably be hyper-vigilant for a long time.

Look at how anxious Kenzie was after being abducted, and she had only been held for a few hours. Not six months. The only injury she had sustained had been a bump on her head. Who knew what kind of injuries Elysse might have sustained, physical or psychological.

Zachary didn't ask questions or direct Elysse to go to the police to report what had happened to her. She needed time to learn to be with people again and to decide what she was willing to tell Zachary or anyone else.

"I'm so sorry anything happened to you," Kenzie offered. "I had... I had something happen to me a year ago. Not as bad as all of that... I was only held for a few hours, but..." Kenzie shook her head. "I can't even imagine what it must have been like for you."

Elysse studied Kenzie with a scowl, lines deepening between her brows. "You had something happen to you?" she repeated. "What does that mean? You had what happen to you? Because I'm pretty sure it was nothing like what I've been through."

"No, I'm sure it wasn't," Kenzie agreed. She looked at Zachary and he saw that she was sweating. She didn't say she wanted him to take over the explanation, so he kept quiet and let her work through it. It was best if she learned to tell the story herself, learned how to get through it without triggering anxiety or flashbacks. But Zachary knew how hard it would be. There was stuff that he still couldn't put into words. Stuff that he tried to keep pushed down out of his conscious memory so he didn't have to deal with it.

Kenzie cleared her throat. She took a sip of her juice. "I was grabbed off the street," she said in a rush, getting all the words out at once before they could get stuck in her throat. "It was quick, and I wasn't... I didn't have to stay there for long. My dad, he... I don't know; he talked to them and arranged for them to let me go right away, and he took me home." She swallowed strenuously a few times, then had another sip of orange juice. "It was over fast, but it still bothers me a year later. I don't know... how long it will take me to get over it. Or if I will get over it completely."

There was another period of silence. The smiling waitress came over with their dishes and made sure they had everything they needed.

"Ketchup?" Elysse asked curtly, and then when the woman raised her hand to adjust her glasses, Elysse shied away. Zachary's stomach knotted at this evidence of her level of anxiety and how she had been treated since her disappearance. The man had not left her alone for the past six months; Zachary was sure of that.

Elysse dug into her big breakfast platter, taking a bite of each food, eating quickly like she was starving. Zachary couldn't see any evidence that she had been starved. She was still about the same weight as before her disappearance. But she hadn't had the social interaction or ability to eat outside her own home and was perhaps hungrier for those things than for the actual sustenance.

"They grabbed you off the street?" Elysse asked Kenzie, her eyes flicking back to the other woman before returning to her meal.

"Yes," Kenzie agreed. "It was... so scary." Her voice broke. Zachary put his hand over hers, trying to give her the strength and support she needed, even though there was nothing he could do to erase those memories or to go back in time and stop it from happening to her. When she had been abducted, he had been in the hospital, utterly oblivious to her plight. In the hospital, fighting his own life-and-death battle against depression and suicidal thoughts.

"They had masks. And a van." It was too hard for Kenzie to explain step-by-step what had happened, as she had tried to do when telling Zachary and Dr. B about it. But those little details were enough to fill out the story. Masks. A van. Zachary's fingers curled tightly around his coffee mug as he remembered fighting off the Russians the previous week. They had not tried to grab him and throw him into the van. They had been satisfied with just knocking him to the ground, and hitting and kicking him.

"They came back last week," Kenzie told Elysse in a hoarse whisper. "I can't... I couldn't even move. Couldn't do anything but look at them."

"You can't," Elysse agreed. "They do that... they hit you so hard... terrorize you... so that you can't even think about fighting back. You can't even imagine doing anything but what they tell you to do."

It was the first bit of confirmation that she let them have. Yes, she had been kidnapped and terrorized. She shared that experience with Kenzie. Even if Kenzie had not been kept for a period of months.

Months. It always horrified him to think of people like Elizabeth Smart, held hostage day after day, week after week, month after month. He didn't know how Elysse could have kept her sanity after that long. How she could still have any humanity left. How she could sit there and talk to them about waffles and the ordinary things of life. To be angry with him for taking her out of her home in a box, rescuing her from her captor.

He knew that she had still been a prisoner in her own house, no matter what she said to him about it. No matter how the man had ensured her compliance. How he had forced her to stay there and do what he said, a prisoner in her own house despite the fact that she wore no shackles and that there had been no one else in the house with her.

Those things were physical. Elysse had been tortured psychologically. She had been terrorized and threatened. The chains were invisible, but they were still there. Elizabeth Smart had denied who she was even when stopped on the street and questioned by a cop. She knew she had to keep acting the part her captor had pushed her into, that there was no escape. Until she had finally been taken somewhere safe.

53

Elysse started to slow down in her consumption of the waffles. She studied Zachary, looked at Kenzie, then returned her gaze to Zachary. He supposed being a man made him the dangerous one. The one who could have concocted this whole thing just to draw her out and hurt her again. Zachary continued to pick at the French fries, not making eye contact.

"I didn't know him," Elysse told Zachary finally.

He nodded, waiting for more.

"When I first saw him in Vermont. I didn't know him. Didn't know anything about who he was or what he wanted. He said he was a fan. That he wanted an autograph. I'm so used to signing autographs for people; it is automatic. Everywhere I go, there is someone who is a fan and wants my signature on something."

"You hadn't seen him before?"

"I don't know. Sometimes, I see people a few times at different shoots. They'll show up at a bunch of fan stuff when I am in town. Maybe he'd been to an event before. But I didn't *know* know him."

"Was there just one? Or several people?"

"I only ever saw one. But there were others. I know there were. He had people working for him. Watching me, arranging things, making sure that I did what he said to do… or not to do."

"Did you hear him talking to the others? Or see evidence of them? Or you just knew they were there, watching?"

"What's the difference?" She waved the questions away irritably. "That first day. The shock of it…" She swallowed hard and stopped shoveling food into her mouth. "I've been hit before." She swore and rolled her eyes. "I'm no shrinking violet. I've had my share of hard knocks."

Zachary had guessed as much.

"But this was just… over the top. Like some drama on TV. *Taken.* He reached out to hand me a photograph to sign. And I went to take it, and then…" She shook her head, still looking shaken by it, "I was on the ground."

"He hit you?" Zachary asked. "Knocked you down?"

"No. It was an electrical shock. A Taser. I couldn't do anything about it. I just went down."

Zachary nodded his agreement. "It's physiological. You can't stop your muscles from going rigid when it hits. There's no 'relaxing into it.'"

She stared at him, her eyes piercing. "Who *are* you people?"

She wasn't asking their names. She couldn't understand how they'd had the experiences they had. How they could understand what she had gone through. Kidnapped. Tasered. Other ways that she had been brutalized. Not just over a day or two, but over a period of months.

That was where he got stuck. He had been in terrible situations. The places that he had been in for months had been foster homes, group homes, institutions. Places where he was supposed to be treated like a human being, like a member of the family, and they had instead treated him like a dog or worse. But it hadn't been like it had been for Elysse, taken away from everyone else, isolated, kept from contacting the outside world. No fans, no family, no friends. Just her, by herself, in that house, unless the man was there.

"We've… been through some stuff," Zachary told her. "and we've gotten through it. Just like you will. You'll be able to look back at this. It will be in the past."

She shook her head. "You don't have any idea. You say you know what I'm going through, but you don't. You *don't*."

"You can talk to the police," Kenzie said. "We'll help you. They can arrest this guy, protect you from him, make sure that he can't do anything to you again."

"Police?" Elysse's eyes got big. She shook her head in alarm. "You can't bring the police into this. He'll go after my family."

"He doesn't know you're gone. He thinks you're still at the house. So you can talk to the police, tell them who he is and what he's done, and they can arrest him before he even knows you are gone."

"No. He'll know." Elysse looked down at her plate, dropping her cutlery with a clatter. "What am I doing here? I can't be here. Doing this. I have to go back." She looked at Zachary. "How are you going to get me back in there?"

Zachary hadn't thought about returning her. He had thought that once they got her away from the house, away from the man who was monitoring and threatening her, she would be free. She could tell them all about who had been threatening her, get him arrested, and she would be free to go back to her own life. Or do something else, if she didn't want to be a social influencer. She had her whole life ahead of her.

But Elysse's face looked pinched and pale. She had enjoyed a few minutes of freedom—that little taste of waffles, being able to walk free without being under constant surveillance and threat of violence. But now they had to figure out how to help her get free of the man or return to her cage.

54

"Tell me what happened," Zachary told Elysse calmly, as if he had everything under control and wasn't suddenly panicking about what to do. "We'll figure this out. We'll find a way for the police to find him and arrest him, so that you don't have to worry anymore."

"That won't work. He'll get out on bail. It takes years to prosecute a big case, and who knows how it will turn out. They could find him innocent. Or they could find him guilty and he'd have to serve a year for stalking or harassment. What good does it do me if he only serves a year?"

Zachary frowned, shaking his head. "He's not going to get off with just stalking. He was doing a lot more than just following you around, wasn't he? You said that he used a Taser on you in Vermont, kidnapped you with it. That's a lot more than just harassment. That's aggravated kidnapping. He can get over 20 years for that. You don't need to worry about what he could do to your family."

"He could get out on bail. Then he can do whatever he likes. And don't try telling me that the police can protect my family because you and I both know that's just TV stuff. In real life, the police don't have the time and resources to guard someone."

She rubbed the bridge of her nose, and her next words were muffled by her hands being held over her face. "Besides, you said you met them. Can you imagine anyone trying to guard my family? All of them? The Allan Broads would eat those poor cops for dinner."

Zachary laughed. "Yeah. Is that what happened to their husbands?"

Elysse made a noise somewhere between a laugh and a sob. "They never do seem to stick around for long."

"But Dain did," Zachary told her. "Dain is still loyal to you. Still wanting to get back together with you. He's the one who hired me. He knew that what you told the press was a story and that there was something else going on."

"Dain." Elysse sighed. "I wish he would meet someone else and leave me alone. We're not good for each other and... I don't want him mixed up in any of this." She dropped her hands from her face and looked at Zachary. "You can't tell him any of this. He'll try to do something, and Dain's no fighter. He would get hurt. I don't want anyone getting hurt because of me."

"It isn't your fault. This is not on you. You didn't do anything wrong."

"I should never have gotten into the social media stuff. I was greedy. I thought it was a great way to make money, easy, and people loved me. What could be better? They loved me just for posting stuff about my life. And I could make good money at it. The products that I posted about went viral. Companies loved me. One or two mentions, and I could make their year. So I kept raking in the money, kept showing up, posting more, trying to make it better, penetrate the market further. Until all my time was spent pimping out other people's products. I should have just stopped. Just cut back and said I wouldn't do it all. That I needed time for myself, my relationships, and my family."

"This did not happen because of you selling products on social media," Kenzie told her, echoing what Zachary had said. "This is because some creep got obsessed with you and didn't know where the line was. Or he knew, but he didn't care. You're not to blame for someone else's obsession."

"But it wouldn't have happened if I wasn't out there. If I was like my mom and didn't do social media, or like Celine and just did a bit of personal stuff on there for my friends, he never would have come after me."

"Well, for whatever reason, he did," Zachary said flatly. "And now we have to trap him. Get him arrested and off the streets so he can't hurt you or your family anymore. Make the police and the judge see that he is too dangerous to let him out to terrorize someone else. And then you can be free. You can do what you want to with your life without being afraid of him. You don't have to worry about him hurting your family or Dain."

Elysse sniffled. She picked up one of the napkins and wiped her nose. "I suppose Celine told you that I stole him from her."

"She might have mentioned something like that."

"I never stole him. I never did anything to take him away from her. That was Dain, all him. She wasn't what he wanted. She's just… a little country mouse. Vanilla. No excitement. He wanted someone more interesting. Challenging. Spicier."

Zachary's cheeks warmed. He was sorry that he had shaved before going to see the Allan women that morning. At least whiskers would have hidden his blush as Elysse continued to add adjectives.

She sniffled and blew her nose. "I don't see how we can do anything to stop him. There's no way to ensure he stays in jail until he's tried and convicted. If there is enough to convict him. He was careful, you know. Always cleaning up after himself. Wiping down fingerprints and vacuuming and eliminating all the evidence. How can I prove anything?"

"First, by telling us what happened," Zachary told her. "We've worked with the police before. I'm sure we can get some corroborating evidence." He snorted. "It's not like they've cleaned that hotel room in Canada since you were there."

"That was the most horrible place," Elysse said, shuddering. "I thought he was going to kill me. I really did. I thought that's why he took me to Canada. To dump me in the wilderness out there, and no one would ever be able to find my body or to identify it because I wasn't supposed to be there."

Zachary nodded. He wanted to put his hand over Elysse's on the table, to let her know that they were there for her and that, somehow, they would sort everything out. But Elysse didn't need anyone touching her. She'd had enough of that, Zachary was sure. Turning the tables and thinking of someone trying to comfort him with a touch, his skin crawled. Only Kenzie. She was the only one that he could let comfort him that way, and he had worked hard with her on developing that trust and the ability to stand physical contact without freaking out or dissociating.

55

"Why did he take you to Canada? Did he have a friend or relative there? Did something come up that made him change his plans and bring you back to the States?"

Elysse wiped her nose with the rough napkin again. The skin around her nose was already getting inflamed. What she needed was three-ply tissues with moisturizing cream in them. Zachary loved those.

"I was going to go to the next shoot," she told him, not answering his question but instead going back to the beginning of the story. "Had that stupid fight with Dain. I was tired of fighting with him. Told him it was over. I didn't want to have to deal with him anymore. Thought I was hard done by, having people who cared about me, who smothered me with too much attention." She rolled her eyes.

"So he was irritating," Kenzie said. "Guys are irritating. There's nothing wrong with realizing that."

"Huh." Elysse took a sip of her orange juice and grimaced. It was probably too sour after maple syrup on the waffles. "I was supposed to go to a maple bush," Elysse said, looking down at what remained on her plate. "I always loved maple syrup. I wanted to see where they made it. Tapping the trees, boiling the syrup, all that stuff. There was this guy, as I was driving up to the next shoot. He waved me down, getting me to stop. Acted like he was in charge. He was a suit, a corporate type, so I thought he must be the president or the owner or something."

Zachary nodded. He imagined Elysse driving to the property and being waved off to the side. The forty- or fifty-year-old businessman was thoroughly nonthreatening. Who would have thought he was violent?

"He told me where to park my car, where I was supposed to go, and who I was supposed to talk to. It was a bit different than what they had told me on the phone, but that happens sometimes. Things don't work out how they initially told you, or someone got the message wrong. Then he stopped me, reached into his pocket, and said that he had something for me. I thought it was a picture to sign. I told you, people were always handing me junk to sign."

Zachary pictured Elysse turning back toward the man, reaching toward him to take the proffered photograph from his hand, an automatic reaction. And instead of pulling out a picture, he had pulled out a Taser.

"He didn't warn me or tell me to get in the car or to do anything. He just pulled the trigger, and there was this... pain, and I was on the ground wondering what was going on. I didn't know what had happened. Couldn't figure it out at first; my mind was so muddled. And he just kept doing it. If I tried to get up, or crawl away, or open my mouth to scream, it didn't matter what I did. He just hit me with another shock."

Zachary had faced his own psychopath wielding an electrical behavioral modification device. The pain had been excruciating. It had been much stronger than the Tasers sold as personal defense devices or what the police used to subdue suspects. They had been worried that it had done permanent damage, but he had eventually come through it relatively unscathed, the physical damage healing over time.

"It's a power thing," he said. "Some people like causing pain."

"I think I know that," Elysse told him sharply.

Zachary grimaced. "Yeah, sorry. I'll just listen."

"Actually… it helps me to have someone who reacts. I've told myself so many times that none of it mattered. Looked at myself in the mirror and told myself that no one would care. I kind of like… someone caring what happened."

Zachary smiled. He had experience dealing with abrasive people, especially his oldest sister, Jocelyn. She tended to be sharp with him, but she was still his sister, and he loved her. And he knew that, despite her often-angry attitude toward him, she really did love him, so he put up with it.

He didn't mind putting up with a few sharp comments from Elysse as long as he knew he wasn't actually aggravating her.

"Did he say anything to you?" Zachary asked. "Anything to indicate what he wanted from you or why he was doing this? Was it just because he was obsessed, or was there something else going on?"

Elysse shook her head. "That first day… I hardly knew what was going on. He kept zapping me any time I tried to ask questions. He just shoved me into the car while I was still wonky and he got in to drive. But he had needles, and he injected me with something. I was so doped up. I didn't know where he was taking me or why. It was all just… like going down a tunnel. Everything dark, and moving forward, and nothing to hang on to or look at. Like a nightmare."

"Do you know what he gave you?" Kenzie asked, leaning forward with interest.

"I don't know. Roofies, maybe. Between the Taser and whatever he injected me with, I didn't know whether I was coming or going. That's when he took me across the border."

"How did he get you across the border in that shape? Didn't the border guards notice there was something wrong?" Kenzie queried.

"He just… told me what to do and I did it. Maybe it was the drugs. He said to smile and tell them we were going on vacation. And if the guard acted worried about me, just say I wasn't feeling well and wanted to get to the hotel to lie down."

"And that worked?" Zachary asked. "There wasn't any trouble?"

"No. They were all nice and said they hoped I would feel better soon. It's not easy being sick while you're away from home. He said it was probably just a twenty-four-hour bug, and I'd be fine the next day and could enjoy my holiday."

"Did you know your kidnapper's name then? Or do you know it now?"

She shook her head. "You can't do anything about him. You can't touch him. No matter what we do, he will get away with it. I just know it."

She had been conditioned right from the start not to ask questions, but to believe what he told her absolutely. He'd had power over her every movement and she believed there was nothing she could do but obey his instructions. If she didn't, bad things would happen to her.

Elysse looked around the restaurant again. "I have to get back. You have to help me get back so he doesn't know I was gone."

"We will," Zachary assured her. "But we need to hear the rest of the story."

"What else is there to tell?" Elysse protested, agitated. "He took me from one place to another. He threatened me. He made sure I would do exactly what he said, or he'd go after my family, too. You think I wanted Celine going through the same thing? My mom or auntie?"

"No. You wanted to protect them. Do you know why he took you to Canada in the beginning? It doesn't make any sense, other than to take you in an unexpected direction. But why cross an international border and risk people seeing you and realizing something was wrong? Did he have a friend there? Someone who met him? Someone who was supposed to help him out?"

"No. It was just him." She thought about it. "He left a few times, but I didn't think he was far away. I was worried that if I tried to escape, he would be right there, outside the door, with the Taser." Her voice broke. "I couldn't deal with the Taser anymore."

"Of course not," Kenzie said encouragingly. "You were conditioned. You were afraid."

Elysse ran her hand over her face. "He said if I left, if I talked to the cops, I would be arrested. I'd crossed the border, lied to the border guards, and he'd had other stamps added to my passport, saying that I'd been in the Middle East. He was going to make it look like I was a terrorist. That's what they do, you know, they go to Canada, come into the US from there so that there's no flight from Iraq or Afghanistan or whatever."

"But you are an American citizen."

"It doesn't matter. Americans can still be terrorists. They go overseas to train, then they come back, and… they're moles until they're ready to attack a target. That's the way it works." Her voice rose, challenging Zachary to argue with her about it. "Do you know how my fans would react if they thought I was a terrorist?"

Zachary kept his mouth shut. What did he know about International travel and how terrorist cells worked? From what Elysse was saying, it was lucky that the man *hadn't* radicalized Elysse and turned her into a Patty Hearst, ready to commit a bank heist or some other crime for him. She was terrified of him and, for six months, she had sat at home, unable to break free, to do anything against his will. Whether he had been there or not, whether he had actually had her under surveillance or not, she was entirely under his control.

To the point that she wanted to go back home and take her place there again before he could discover that she had escaped.

56

"How did you get from Sudbury to Salt Lake?"

Elysse looked surprised at Zachary's question. She rubbed her temple, shaking her head slightly. If she'd been in a fog from roofies and repeated tasings, maybe she didn't even remember.

"We drove again. But not the same way, not back to Vermont. It was a different border crossing. Into Michigan, I think?"

Zachary had studied the maps of the area and different travel routes. "Sault Ste. Marie?" he asked, pronouncing it how it was spelled. *Salt Stee Marie.*

Elysse gave a little nod, but she was laughing. "That's not the way they say it. They pronounce it *Soo Saint Marie.*"

Zachary shook his head. "Soo Saint Marie? Why would they say it that way?"

"French, I think."

"Okay. So that's the border crossing you used?"

"Yeah. And then we caught a plane in Traverse City and flew to Salt Lake City."

"Why did he want to go to Salt Lake?"

"I don't know... I thought it was probably just because it is a hub. Maybe there weren't any flights from Traverse City to Portland… or Phoenix… I didn't really know where we were going or why. When we went west, I just thought we were going back to Oregon. He kept telling me that he was going to take me home. But then he took me to these other places, and I had no idea why." Elysse pushed food around on her plate. She took a sip of her coffee and looked around. "We should go soon," she worried.

"We will. I'm thinking about how to get you back without anyone realizing. The more you can tell me about what happened and what you know about him, the better. Do you know his name?"

"You can't find him, he's a ghost."

"Is that what he told you?"

She nodded. "Yeah. He said no one could identify him; they would never be able to track me back to him."

"Your passports were used together twice."

She shook her head. "He said no one would be able to connect us. That he was a ghost. If they tried to grasp him, he would just slip between their fingers like smoke."

"So Salt Lake was just a stopover?" Kenzie asked. "You were just there to kill time?" She was frowning.

"I guess so. I don't really know. We had to get some supplies. Changes of clothing, toiletries, stuff like that."

"You were seen at the mall."

"Yeah. A few people recognized me there. I was trying to stay low profile, but I couldn't stop them from seeing me. I wasn't exactly in disguise."

"But you didn't ask anyone for help?" Kenzie asked.

"No! I just did what he said to do. I couldn't tell anyone that I needed help or that there was anyone with me. He told me what to say, what to do, so I did."

"You did what you had to do to survive," Zachary soothed. "That's all you could do."

Elysse nodded vigorously.

"And then, Salt Lake City to Phoenix and the Grand Canyon."

"Yes." She knew what he was going to ask and shook her head. "I didn't know why we were going there. I think… it was just a test.

Seeing if I would do everything I was told to, whether I understood why or not."

"What did he tell you to do? You went on a tour together?"

"Just self-guided tours. We were there for more than a day. It's hard for me to remember… the timeline is all screwed up. I can't remember when I was there. I wasn't sleeping very well. It's all… distorted like a nightmare."

"Was he still drugging you?"

"No. He said he wouldn't if I did everything I was told. And I tried to do everything he said, exactly the way he said to do it. When the fans recognized me in the Grand Canyon, I told them no, they were mistaken. But they knew, and they called the police, and they questioned me, and someone called the media, and I had to do a press appearance to quiet everything down. He told me what to do and say. He said it would all settle down if I just did the one interview and told people it had just been my own idea, that I was just… taking a break from everything."

She swirled the ice that remained in her glass of orange juice. "That reporter who did the interview… she did not like me. After the interview, she said how irresponsible she thought I was. That I had caused this huge manhunt, costing thousands of dollars, all the people putting their time and energy into it. And all the time, I was just on a little vacation. I couldn't tell her any differently. That was the story he said to stick with."

"And after the Grand Canyon, you came back here."

"Yeah. Finally home." She sighed. "I thought I could relax, go back to my old life."

"But he had other ideas."

"I guess it could be worse," Elysse said. "I mean… I was trapped there, his prisoner. He could have done anything. But he didn't. Just told me what to do and reminded me that he could do to my family what he had done to me. That we could all be his prisoners. His robots. Under his control."

"And what did he want you to do?"

Elysse chewed on her lip. "Are we leaving? We need to get out of here. What if someone sees me? I need to get back to the house before he knows I'm gone."

"We will. What did he want you to do? You transferred the title to your house. Was he the beneficiary of that?"

"No. It's my own company. One I had set up before to handle certain financial transactions. He said that if I transferred the house out of my name, people wouldn't show up on the doorstep looking for me. It would keep the reporters and stalkers away."

"And what else did he want you to do?"

"It was more... what he didn't want me to do."

Zachary met her eyes. "Not posting to social media."

She looked surprised at this, but nodded. "Yeah. Nothing at all."

"And you weren't allowed to talk to your family?"

"I couldn't... explain to anyone what was going on. I couldn't tell anyone what was up. I couldn't have anyone in. He didn't want me talking to anyone but him."

"That's why you have the new phone. So he can stay in communication with you."

"Yes. But not anyone else. He killed the phone I had."

Zachary mused on her use of the word "killed." Not that he had broken her phone, or ditched it or thrown it out, but had killed it. She mourned its loss. That phone had been her lifeline, her livelihood, her means of staying in contact with her friends and livelihood. By destroying that phone, he had effectively killed her old life. She had lost everything it represented.

The new burner flip phone probably didn't even have email on it. No access to her old social media or contact list.

But she had somehow still kept a connection open with Celine. Celine had somehow been able to warn Elysse that Zachary would be coming. Maybe she had a second burner. One that her sister had given to her on one of their brief doorstep conversations. Hidden from the man and the rest of the world, only used covertly when no one was around and she knew she could not be overheard. Maybe in the bathroom with the water running to defeat any bugging devices in the house.

"We need to get out of here," Elysse insisted again. She stood up, looked around for the waitress, and approached the closest one, not the one who had served them. "Please, we need to pay our bill. I have to get out of here."

"Be right with you, honey."

They waited. Elysse picked up her knife, studying the edge, and eventually put it down in the middle of her plate.

"You know what to do?" she demanded. "Have you figured out how to get me back inside without anyone seeing? You can't do it in another refrigerator box!"

"I know," Zachary assured her. "I'm working something out. But we're going to get you out of there. I'm going to figure out how to help you. So... hang in there. Don't give up hope."

"You don't know what he's like. You can't outmaneuver him. He'll just... hurt someone else you love. I can't let him do that to my family."

"You can't continue to live like this."

"I can," Elysse insisted. "It's better than the alternative."

The older waitress came over and fiddled with the point-of-sale machine for a few minutes before finally offering it to Zachary. He paid the bill and motioned for Elysse and Kenzie to accompany him.

57

*Z*achary had gotten a good look around when he had picked Elysse up from her house. He had been walking in blind and had tried to construct a scenario that would succeed even if Elysse was in a busy neighborhood or under direct surveillance. But there had been no sign that anyone was sitting in a car watching her, in the house, or in a neighboring house.

There had been no obvious reaction when he had taken Elysse. If the man did not know that she had been removed from the house, he would not be watching for her to come back. He would assume that everything was as he had left it. If he were monitoring a street cam nearby, he would only know that Elysse had gotten a delivery. If there were bugs in the house then, hopefully, her abductor did not monitor them constantly or have a program set up to alert him if things got too quiet because Elysse had left the house.

Zachary felt a lot more conspicuous in the big red truck than when he went out in his anonymous compact car, but it would have to do. Elysse was too anxious to get back and would not want to wait while they tried another car rental place to see if they could get a less noticeable vehicle.

Zachary drilled Elysse on the locations of and approaches to the other entrances to the house, of which there were two.

Once they were within a few blocks of the house, Zachary pulled over, and he and Elysse got out of the car. He checked his watch. "Ten minutes?" he checked with Kenzie.

She looked at the time on hers and nodded. "I'll be there in ten minutes," she agreed.

Elysse led Zachary through the streets toward her house until they reached the back alley right behind it. Zachary looked up and down the alley, using one hand to motion Elysse to be quiet and still while he made sure that they would not be observed.

She was fidgeting like a junkie hurting for a fix. They were so close to getting back into the house that she could barely stand waiting.

"We do this right," Zachary whispered to her. "What would be the point of going through all of this just to be seen coming back?"

She bounced on her heels. "I could have come out to the alley to take out the garbage. It doesn't matter if he sees me go back in from here."

"Do you want this to be clean or not?"

She did, of course. So she clenched her teeth and waited for him to give her the "all clear." Zachary eventually decided that the alley was safe. There was no surveillance, no neighbors watching from their back porches, and no obvious cameras pointed at Elysse's house.

"Come then," he murmured to her. "Just into the yard. We wait before going into the house. You let me make sure that it is safe, and we wait for Kenzie to do her part. Understood?"

Elysse nodded. She was pale, but at least entering the yard was helping to settle her down. She was on her own property. If the man were looking for her, she was where she was supposed to be.

Zachary traversed the yard, looked around, and approached the house. There was no back door surveillance camera. Elysse had said there were no outdoor cameras that she was aware of, but a camera might have been mounted without her knowledge. That was part of what Zachary did. He knew how easy it was to mount a button-sized camera where no one would see it unless they were looking directly at it. And maybe not even then. But he couldn't see any spy cameras where he would have put them.

Elysse had given him the key code for the back door lock, so he punched it in. The door unlocked and he turned the handle and pushed it open, then listened. He looked into the cute little back entryway with clean white paneled walls, cubbies, and coat hooks. There was no sign of anyone there. There was no burglar alarm, no hint of any covert movement in the house.

He looked at his watch, noting that he had arrived sooner than expected. But the time for Kenzie to make her appearance was past, and he didn't hear anything. He looked back at the corner of the yard where he had left Elysse and did not motion for her to come forward. He looked back down at his watch again, staring at it as the seconds ticked away.

Something had held Kenzie up.

That was fine. She might have taken a wrong turn or twisted an ankle stepping off a curb, or been held up by a nosy neighbor wanting to talk. Kenzie was smart, and she understood the plan. She would be able to adapt if something had gone wrong. She would either show up or she would send him a message explaining what had happened. Elysse was the one who had been putting pressure on them to get her back there quickly, and she was okay now that she was inside the yard. They would have her back into the house soon, but there was no reason to rush it and end up showing their hand.

It was better if the man didn't know she had ever been away. Didn't suspect that anyone knew his secrets, what he had done. That was the most important part. They didn't want him going after Elysse's family for revenge.

The doorbell rang, making Zachary jump, even though he had been waiting for it. The doorbell was quickly followed up by hard pounding on the door. And a few more rings for good measure.

Zachary nodded at Elysse, and she flitted around the yard staying against the fence, as agreed, rather than crossing the middle where she might be observed. Zachary pushed open the door and she entered. She would pick up her phone from the counter as she walked through the kitchen, and go straight to the door.

Kenzie hammered on the door some more. Elysse took her time getting there, as if she might have been across the house or having a nap. Then she opened the door.

"What is this? What's going on?" Elysse's voice carried across the house.

"This is so exciting!" Kenzie fangirled from the front step. "It really is you. They all said that you'd moved out and didn't live here anymore, but there you are! I can't believe it's you! Elysse Allan. Can I get your autograph?"

"This is my private residence," Elysse snapped. "You don't come to my private home. That's intrusive! You want me to call the police?"

"I'm not doing anything wrong. I'm just asking you for your autograph! Say cheese!"

"Put that thing away!" Elysse protested the use of Kenzie's phone camera shoved in her face. "You're trespassing on private property. If you don't get out of here and leave me alone, I'm going to call the police."

"How can you treat us this way? Your fans have always been loyal to you, and you've just completely cut yourself off. I *had* to come here just to find out what had happened to you. You can't just abandon us and cut us out of your life when we have been there for you. How is that right?"

Kenzie sounded just like an upset fan, lots of emotion in her voice, excited at seeing Elysse and frantic that she was going to lose her opportunity for more contact just as fast. She was good.

"You don't have any right to come to my house like this," Elysse said. "I don't owe you anything. I can't post anymore, okay? Just go away. Don't come back here. I can't do this anymore. I… can't give you what you're asking for." Her voice was emotional, too. Zachary couldn't help but wonder how much she missed that life. Was she saying the things she really wanted to say to her followers but wasn't able to? It had to be a lonely life, especially after all the attention that she'd been used to before the abduction.

"Please, can't I come inside to look around? To talk to you?" Kenzie coaxed.

"No. Please leave. Please go and don't come back again."

"Please…"

"No."

Eventually, the door clicked shut. Kenzie would retreat, heading back to the truck. Zachary quietly pulled the back door closed as well. He slipped around the yard along the fence, out the gate and across the back lane, and retraced his steps back to the red truck.

58

Taking different routes, Zachary and Kenzie arrived back at the truck at about the same time. Zachary smiled at Kenzie to congratulate her on her performance and to confirm that he believed they had re-inserted Elysse without her kidnapper being any the wiser. Kenzie's commotion at the front door would have drawn the attention of anyone in the area, distracting them from Elysse entering quietly in the back.

There was always the possibility that Elysse's return had been recorded by a hidden camera, but chances were, no one would be scrubbing all the video to find out. They would be interested in Kenzie's appearance on the scene and Elysse handling her, and would look no further, having no reason to suspect there was anything else to see.

"We need to get home," Kenzie said in a strained voice.

At first, he thought it was a joke, teasing him with how Elysse had been so insistent on getting back home, maybe joking that they now needed a big, complicated plan to get themselves back home.

But Kenzie didn't smile and, taking in her expression and body language, Zachary could see that it was not a joke, and quickly dropped the smile that had come to his lips.

"What is it? Did something happen?"

"I got a call from Dr. Cook."

"He had said that he didn't mind you being away. He could just proceed with any autopsies he needed to and put off the rest for a day or two. This is the first time you've taken off in months."

"It isn't that. He wasn't calling to tell me I had to come back. He called to say that we had a homicide coming in. He knows that I want to be a part of any of the homicides, if I can. Wanted to know whether I expected to be back or whether he should just go ahead on his own."

"Oh. So you want to go back for it?" Zachary wouldn't have minded one more day in Oregon, just to tie up a few more loose ends. He knew what he had set out to discover—that Elysse had not simply walked away from her life, but had been kidnapped and coerced and was still being controlled by her abductor. But he didn't know why, or whether the man lived in Oregon and had simply gone to Vermont to grab Elysse, or whether he lived somewhere else. How much danger was Elysse in? Was she living in fear when, most of the time, her kidnapper was not even in the state? Did he monitor her remotely?

Of course, if Kenzie wanted to go back for the new autopsy, Zachary would do what she wanted. She had tagged along with him and been an asset on his road trip. And if she had something to do when she got home, she wouldn't just be sitting around worrying about the possibility of the Russians coming after her again. Hopefully, the road trip had distanced her from that anxiety.

But there was something in Kenzie's face as they both climbed up into the cab of the truck and looked at each other that made him wonder what the rest of the story was. She had something else to tell him. His stomach clenched and he wondered what could possibly have happened to put that expression on her face.

"The homicide victim is Kristy Echols."

Kenzie's words were far away and, for a minute, he couldn't even think of who that was, even though he knew. He almost could have predicted that was what she would say, just by the look on Kenzie's face. It had been written that clearly.

"Kristy," Zachary repeated, his own voice sounding very strange in his ears, like he was a completely different person. "Elysse's photographer."

Kenzie nodded gravely. "I'm sorry, Zachary."

Kristy had ended their last call abruptly. She hadn't called him back or answered his return calls or responded to the voicemail messages he had left her. He had assumed that she was just busy. Too caught up in her own work. Focused on herself and her own needs, too busy for Zachary's inquiries about her former client.

"This is… this is crazy. Kristy Echols. What happened? It was homicide? Did he tell you how? Or is he not allowed to say anything until you do the autopsy and see for yourself?"

"Apparent strangulation. But of course, that is just preliminary observations. We'll have to make sure that there were no other factors."

"And definitely homicide, not suicide?"

"She didn't kill herself."

Was it Zachary's fault? Kristy had been fine. She had gone on with her life after Elysse's disappearance. She had been just fine for six months. Until Zachary had gone around asking questions.

"She said she noticed something while going through the pictures," he reminded Kenzie.

"Yeah, she did."

"What was it? What did she see? Is it something we should have seen? Was it in the pictures she sent us?" He swore. "Why didn't she stay on the line long enough to tell me what she had found? Just a sentence. A few words. Something to point us in the right direction. Why didn't she answer the phone when I called her back?"

Kenzie just shook her head. "Maybe it wasn't that important. Maybe it was only a passing thought, not a real clue. And when she thought about it again, she decided it wasn't really anything."

"It *was* something." His brain seized on this. "I *know* it was something. But what? What could she have seen?"

Kenzie didn't answer the unanswerable. "We should see what flights are available. Catch the quickest one we can. If you can drive us to the hotel to pack up, I should know by the time we get there what kind of wait we'll have."

"Sure."

Zachary focused on the road and getting them back to the hotel quickly while Kenzie tapped on her phone, eventually booking a couple of tickets for them. They didn't have to rush, but they wouldn't have any excess time to sit around looking for something to do.

59

Once the seatbelt sign went off, Zachary grabbed his laptop and powered it up. He began sifting through the photos Kristy had sent him on a USB drive, along with those he'd downloaded from social media and various internet postings about Elysse's disappearance and reappearance. He watched video rants and tributes. He had watched Elysse's press coverage when she was discovered in the Grand Canyon about ten times in a row when Kenzie gave him a nudge.

"Hey."

He couldn't tear his eyes from the screen to answer Kenzie. "What?"

"I think you're stuck."

"Mmm." Zachary watched Elysse's eyes as she spoke to the reporter. Neurolinguistics would have him believe that if she looked up and to the right, she was lying or making up her answer. But Elysse had been filming her own videos and appearing in the media for a long time. She had a calm and practiced gaze, looking toward the camera without much variation, very focused and controlled. Not like how her eyes had been moving when she had been at the restaurant, back and forth and checking anxiously for the man or one of his minions.

Besides which, he'd never put much stock into that rule of thumb. People could have widely variant brains, and eye gaze could be consciously controlled and disguised. It was an interesting thing to watch for, but it wasn't of any evidentiary value.

"How many times have you watched that video?" Kenzie asked.

"One more," Zachary told her, trying to shut out any questions or comments she might have. He needed his complete focus and attention to be on the video. He needed to glean every detail he could from the interview. Elysse had been told what to tell the reporter. She knew that her life and the lives of her family were on the line if she failed to satisfy him. She had just been through five days of hell, being tortured and conditioned to fear him and obey him absolutely.

The reporter poked holes in Elysse's claim that she'd just had an argument with her boyfriend and had decided to double back on her trail and wander around the Grand Canyon for a while. He remembered watching it the first time, wondering what Elysse was hiding. She came across as cold and self-centered, caring only about herself, with no thought for Dain or her fans and followers. The interview had exploded across the media with just as much or more force than the reports that she had vanished and Dain had filed a missing person report. It had been replayed and analyzed by various experts, and none of them had been very complimentary about Elysse and what she had done.

But she had made her statement and moved on with life, leaving behind the reporters and everyone else who wanted to talk to her.

"Zachary. Blink, for goodness sake. Have a drink. You're not going to see anything new there the hundredth time you watch it."

But she was wrong. Zachary had made important discoveries in the past, watching videos over and over again. Just because he didn't see something the first ten times, that didn't mean there was nothing new to learn. Just because a hundred people had looked at it before he had, that didn't mean he wouldn't see something that every one of them had overlooked or thought unimportant.

He took the glass of juice Kenzie pressed into his hand and

sipped the cold, sweet liquid. He was very dry. Planes dehumidified the air, making it very arid inside the cabin, leading people to become dehydrated and thirsty.

"Thanks."

She put her hand over Zachary's, working the video control keys.

"Zachary. You aren't going to find anything else there."

"I might."

"Can we talk about it? What have you found so far?"

"I'm not... I'm not over the hump yet. It hasn't come together. But it *will*. Kristy figured it out, and I will, too. It's just a matter of time."

"Only if you are looking at the same pictures or video that she was."

"It's in here. I'm sure I'll be able to find it," Zachary told her stubbornly. She knew that when he was focused, when he refused to quit, he could find things that no one else did. Relentless. Like a bulldog. They sounded like negative qualities, but they were not. When he obsessed over Bridget or whether the doors were locked, that was irritating and unproductive. But when he was obsessed about a case and finding the one missing piece of the puzzle, obsession was good.

Zachary sighed, letting the video run to the end. He put his palms over his eyes to warm and soothe them. He *would* get it. Maybe not until Kenzie was at the medical examiner's office working on the autopsy, but he would find it. How could he not? How could he let Kristy down and let her death be in vain?

"You must be tired," Kenzie pointed out. "You slept on the last two flights. Why don't you let yourself go to sleep now? Then you'll be able to look at it with fresh eyes in the morning. I don't want you to stay up all night watching that video over again and again."

There were other videos. And there were other photos. There was a lot to be processed, and he would keep going through it until he made sense of it and found what he was looking for.

But Kenzie was right. He should sleep while he could, rest his dry eyes, and start fresh again in the morning.

60

I t was light out when they landed. Zachary rubbed the vestiges of sleep from his eyes and looked out the window at the dawning morning; dim, flat light playing over the gray buildings and black asphalt of the airport.

"How are you feeling?" Kenzie asked.

"Slept like the dead," Zachary offered. "But I want to get back to work. I have to figure this out. You'll let me know what you find out about Kristy? When she died, how, if the police have any suspects or leads?"

"I'll share what I can, but you know I have to be careful what I tell you. Don't want to be accused of leaking confidential information to the public."

"I'm not the public," he protested as they gathered their gear and prepared to disembark.

"No, not exactly," Kenzie agreed. "But I don't want to get in trouble. You can understand that."

"We need to find out what happened. Others may be in danger. Elysse herself. Dain. Someone else who saw what Kristy saw. Maybe she talked to someone or had an assistant. I don't know much about her life."

"I don't know how much of that information I'll be privy to. A lot of it depends on the detective assigned to the case. Some of them share a lot and make very detailed notes, and some of them don't want to tell me anything but the very basics."

"Well, let's hope it's one who is willing to share. If they know it is related to the Elysse Allan case, do you think they will share more or put more resources into it?"

"No, I don't know that they will. The missing person case was closed six months ago. People were sort of soured by her statements made after she was found. She turned a lot of people off, claiming that she had just gone on a road trip when they had put so much effort into trying to find her body."

While Kenzie waited for her luggage, Zachary grabbed coffee and donuts for both of them. Then, they retrieved Zachary's car from long-term parking. Kenzie stood, stomping her feet and sipping her coffee while Zachary examined the car, diligently checking for any bugs, trackers, or incendiary devices before opening the doors.

He knew that she thought he was going overboard, that it was just paranoia. But he had been targeted with explosives twice in recent memory, and once it had been in his car.

He did not trust airport security to keep his car safe and not allow any bad actors near it. He had put trackers on enough vehicles to know how quickly and easily it could be done, even in parking lots that were monitored twenty-four hours a day by security guards. They were bored, didn't expect anything to happen, and were easily distracted.

They might be able to keep cars from being vandalized or stolen, but they weren't going to stop some guy who looked like a business traveler from walking through the parking area looking for his car.

Eventually, he decided that the car was clean or that he had checked it as thoroughly as one man could with limited equipment in the middle of a public lot in the cold. Kenzie didn't complain but looked chilled despite her hot coffee. Zachary's coffee had probably gone cold while he had been inspecting the car.

He unlocked the doors. No extra clicks. No boom. Kenzie reached for the passenger door, but he motioned for her to stop. He opened the driver's door first, wincing a little as he did so. Again, nothing happened. Zachary looked around the inside of the car, including shining a flashlight under the seats. Eventually, he nodded to Kenzie, and she opened her door, climbed in, and settled into her seat.

"I should have just waited in the airport until you told me you were ready," she said. "You could have just driven up to the arrivals area and picked me up."

"Yeah. Probably should have done that. Sorry."

"I didn't realize there would be such a production."

"I had to be sure."

She didn't argue with him. Maybe after one kidnapping and then the attempted kidnapping, as well as seeing the aftermath of Zachary opening a package bomb had all convinced her that there was danger in the world that they needed to be aware of, and Zachary's carefulness wasn't all just paranoia.

"Do you need to stop at the house for anything, or do you want to go straight to work?" he asked her.

"That depends. Will you take the luggage into the house for me?"

"Of course."

"You won't have to put everything away; just make sure it gets into the house."

"Sure."

She looked at herself. She was dressed more casually than usual for work and was somewhat rumpled from sitting for hours in the airplane. But she was going to go straight into an autopsy, pulling on protective gear over top of her clothes. She wouldn't be sitting out in the reception area at her public-facing desk.

"I think I'm fine," Kenzie said. "Dr. Cook knows that I'm coming back from my vacation. I will just impress him more with my diligence in going to the office straight from the plane."

"Straight to the office it is, then," Zachary agreed. He put the car into gear. Nothing exploded. He hit the highway and pointed the nose of the car toward Roxboro and the medical examiner's office.

"Do you know which detective is on the case?"

"No, not yet. I'm sure Dr. Cook does, but I only got the bare essentials from him when he called yesterday."

"Is that why you were late getting to Elysse's house?"

"Yes. Sorry about that. I know I was a couple of minutes behind."

"Things happen."

"Yes, they do." She studied him, probably trying to decide whether he was *really* bugged by her being a couple of minutes late. Sometimes, what should have been a minor irritant wormed its way into Zachary's brain and made him more upset than he should be about it. Even if he knew logically it wasn't a big deal, it still ate away at him and he couldn't let it go.

But this was not one of those things. Zachary had been on enough stakeouts and other operations over the years to know that the unexpected often happened in the middle of even the best-planned operation, and a good investigator simply adapted and worked around it the best he could. He could never predict everything that might go wrong, things that might throw off the timing or sequence of events, people who might walk right into the middle of things without warning.

It hadn't been that big of a deal. He'd simply waited a few more minutes for Kenzie's arrival, and everything had gone as planned.

"It's fine," he assured her. "Really. Already forgotten."

"Okay."

Despite being upset about the news of Kristy's death, Kenzie had still been able to pull off the assignment he had given her, playing the rabid fan convincingly enough, distracting anyone's attention from Elysse's return through the back of the house.

They settled in for the drive back to Roxboro, listening to the morning news and some golden oldies as Zachary navigated the highway home.

61

When he arrived, Zachary was sure to take all the luggage into the house. Kenzie would not be pleased if she found out he had forgotten the one assignment she had given him. She was going out of her way to deal with an autopsy she didn't have to and would pass on what she could to him. The least he could do was take her clothes into the house for her.

He sat at his computer, prepared to start watching videos and looking through the photography again, looking for whatever Kristy had discovered. But as he booted up his laptop, it occurred to him that he needed to call his client. Zachary did not necessarily need to report everything he had found so far, but just touch base and make sure Dain was okay and that he knew Zachary was still working on the case. He didn't know whether Dain would have found out yet that Kristy had been killed. It might not have been public knowledge.

He found Dain's contact card on his phone and tapped his number. At the same time, he navigated to the email inbox on his laptop to see if there were anything that needed his immediate attention.

"Hello? Mr. Goldman?" Dain's voice was high, a bit strained.

He knew, Zachary guessed.

"Just *Zachary*. I wanted to check in with you. I just got back from Oregon."

"You were in Oregon?"

"Yes, I went there as part of my investigation. Talked to Elysse's family."

He wasn't sure whether to reveal yet that he had talked to Elysse herself or any of what Elysse had told him. He didn't want Dain hopping on a plane back to Oregon and banging on Elysse's door himself. He didn't want to make things any more difficult for Elysse. He needed a plan to get her out of danger. To find the man and see that he got arrested and couldn't threaten Elysse and her family anymore.

"You talked to them? Celine and everyone? How are they?" Dain sounded guilty. Because he hadn't talked to them himself? Because he felt guilty for what had happened to Elysse? Or for having dumped Celine for Elysse, a fact that both sisters had confirmed.

"They're getting along," Zachary told him, unsure what else to say about the Allan women. "But that isn't what I called you about. I didn't know if you would have heard... that Kristy Echols was killed."

"What?" Dain's voice was shocked. Zachary could suddenly hear his breathing. "Kristy Echols? What happened?"

"I don't know a lot of details yet. They are doing the autopsy today. Her body was found yesterday. I just talked to her on Monday. I know it's a shock."

"When you say she was killed... and there's an autopsy..."

"It was homicide. Preliminary signs are that she was strangled. I'm sorry, you were probably close to her..."

"I can't believe it. I just... my brain won't accept it. I'm sure it must be some kind of joke or mistake, even though I know you wouldn't do that to me. I just want... another explanation." Dain sighed heavily. "I want it to be a dream. I want to wake up from his whole thing. I want to find out that the whole thing with Elysse was just a nightmare and it's all over. That we are back together, touring... or just back in Oregon with each other. It's been so..."

"I know."

"Why would anyone kill Kristy? Oh, man. Elysse will just be crushed. Do you know if... she knows about it? I wish I could call her..."

"I think it's best if she doesn't know about it for now. She's going through a difficult enough time without adding that in."

"What's going on? You need to tell me. This is what I hired you for."

"I'll fill you in when I know more. But for now, I wanted to know... well, if you have talked to Kristy recently. On Sunday or Monday? She had some important information she had planned to give me, and then..."

"No, I haven't talked to her. I really haven't talked to her since Elysse disappeared. I talked to her then and tried to find out if she knew anything about where Elysse had gone or why, but since then... well, she was Elysse's consultant, not mine. And without Elysse, I can't do the social media thing by myself. The only reason people were interested in me was as part of the relationship. I haven't been able to get anything off the ground since then."

"But you still have money."

After all, he had hired Zachary and was paying his daily rate and expenses. His initial retainer had been deposited in the bank, and Zachary hoped that any further payments would be, too. If that had been the last of Dain's money...

"I'm writing a book," Dain said slowly, hesitant about sharing the news. "I'm writing about life with Elysse, and about what I went through when she disappeared, and how I have gotten by since then. It is going to be a bestseller, and there is a movie option. The network says that it will be the biggest release next year. So they're covering my living expenses right now, and I'm still getting residuals from the sponsors we worked for, though each check is smaller than the last. And then... I have money in savings and investments."

Zachary shouldn't have been worried about him. He had been

able to pay Zachary's initial retainer. He was still going strong, even if some of his income streams had run dry.

"So this book… it's coming out next year? You didn't mention before that you were working on anything."

Was Dain's book his reason for wanting Elysse's disappearance investigated more thoroughly? Maybe he wanted the book to tell the rest of the story. If so, it could be a big break for him. But Zachary didn't see how they could prevent the news of Elysse's kidnapping from getting out into the media before the book was published. They needed to free her from her kidnapper and get him put in jail where, hopefully, he could no longer have any influence on her.

But Dain didn't know all the details. At least not as far as Zachary knew. He had guessed that there was a bigger story; he might have had a clue as to what it was, but he had needed Zachary to investigate and work out the details.

"I didn't want to complicate things by bringing the book into it," Dain told him. "Your investigation isn't really anything to do with the book. I mean, it is adjacent, but…"

"But you didn't want me to think that the only reason you are investigating it is so that you can write a book about it."

"Well, yeah, that's part of it," Dain admitted. "I love Elysse, and I want to find out what happened and how I can help her… how we can get back together if that's possible. That would be amazing, and I couldn't ask for anything more."

"But the book succeeding as well as you hope and spawning a movie would also be pretty amazing. You wouldn't have to worry about money for a long time."

"Maybe never. But we have to get it out soon, while there is still interest in what happened. It's not going to be published in time for the anniversary. That would really have helped things along. But things are not going as quickly as I would have hoped. Publisher timelines are… long."

"And movie production, too."

"Yeah. I know. By the time it comes out, it's a retrospective. 'Do you remember where you were when…'"

Zachary thought that it could probably still make pretty good money. He saw true crime movies come out ten, twenty, thirty years after the actual crime had been committed, and people were still interested and talking about it. Speculating on "the real story," as well as whatever well-crafted conspiracy theories they had come up with during that time.

"Okay, well, thanks for taking my call. We will talk again later, but I wanted to make sure you knew about Kristy and to find out if you had been in contact with her at all. You'll let me know if you think of anything? Or if you find out she sent something to you by email or snail mail?" Zachary thought about the USB drive that Kristy had sent to him. Maybe he wasn't the only one. Maybe she had made a compilation for Dain to memorialize his relationship with Elysse or her social media journey.

But Zachary suspected she had not. She had sent Zachary the pictures he had wanted. She had been prepared to tell him about something she had noticed. But then her life had come to an end, and she would never be able to tell him what she had found.

62

Zachary disconnected the call with Dain and looked at his computer. There wasn't much in his inbox. Heather would have had a look over it already and would let him know if there were anything he needed to take care of immediately. He would call her once he'd had a chance to go through his task list. But he needed to look at the videos and photography again. He was sure if he spent enough time on them, he would be able to find something. It was right there in front of his eyes.

The phone vibrated when he put it down and Zachary looked at the screen. Kenzie.

He hadn't been expecting a call from her so soon. He scooped the phone back up and answered the call.

"Kenzie!"

"Hey, Zach. Hope I'm not interrupting anything."

"No, of course not. You can't be finished already. Not unless Dr. Cook went ahead and did the autopsy without you."

"No. We're just getting started here. But I thought I would let you know, preliminary indications are that Kristy died on Sunday. No activity Monday, no breakfast, bed not slept in, no calls logged on her phone or card swipes to her building."

"So after we talked to her. Within a few hours."

"You were the last call logged on her phone. Only incoming calls after that, a couple of voicemails. Mostly you."

"Yeah. I was trying to get her."

Kenzie sighed. "Yes. Okay, can't talk long. I'll let you go."

"Good luck... I hope you find everything you need to nail this guy. DNA under her fingernails. Fingerprints. Something."

"Me too, Zachary. Me too. Take care."

Zachary hung up and returned to his work. Kenzie would do her part to get justice for Kristin, and so would he. He went back to Elysse's social media accounts and the last messages she had posted before her disappearance. Before, as Zachary now knew, she had been abducted. Everything seemed so normal. There was no indication that Elysse had been worried about anything. No premonition. No mention of weird phone calls or people following her. As far as the outside world was concerned, she had been living a normal, fairly carefree life. And then all of that had changed.

He searched for the footage of her media interview after being "discovered" in the Grand Canyon, which he had already watched numerous times. He brought it up on his screen once more. He watched it without any sound, examining Elysse's face and body language without the distraction of her words.

He already knew her words off by heart. Her mannerisms and the dynamic between her and the reporter interviewing her.

He studied other parts of the screen as the footage continued to play. The set Elysse and the reporter sat in. Away from her fans, away from the Grand Canyon, physically separated from the man who had been terrorizing her, but repeating the story he had told her to give. She told his version of the story instead of her own, and no one knew the difference.

He wasn't on the screen with her. There were likely other people on the stage, but they were out of view of the cameras, all taking care of their tasks. Zachary zeroed in on Elysse again, looking at her eyes, her hands. She sat still and relaxed with her hands in her lap unless she was emphasizing or illustrating a point. Her gaze was direct. Her clothes were neat and presentable. She did not look as though she had just spent five days being tortured and terrorized as the man dragged her around the country.

Zachary scrolled down to look at the first few comments on the screen.

Even though it had been six months, the ticker for the views of the video was still rising. Zachary could only imagine how quickly the views had been leaping ahead when the report was live, or when it had just been freshly posted. People were still interested. They were still seeking out this video to watch her and hear her story. They were still commenting. Several comments had been made over the past few days. People who were still upset about her disappearance, about the way that she had come off in the interview, about the fact that she was no longer posting anywhere.

A commercial came up, and Zachary let it play as he thought about the comments and about Elysse's real story. The commercial ended and the interview resumed. The counter was still going up. Slowly, but steadily. After six months, it was still getting plenty of attention. If people found out about the murder of Elysse's photographic assistant and friend, views would likely increase even more.

Zachary clicked on the video to pause it, and sat there staring at Elysse.

63

There was a lot of work to be done, and it would go much faster if Zachary got some help. He wasn't used to having "people" to call upon.

The first was a volunteer. Walter was much wealthier than Zachary and might even have been insulted if Zachary had offered to pay him, but he had been interested in research work or crowd sleuthing when Zachary had brought it up. So he would see if Walter was ready to get his feet wet.

"Zachary?" Walter sounded surprised when he picked up the call. "Is everything all right?"

"Yes," Zachary assured him. "I just thought I would check in on your 'convalescence' and see how you are doing."

Walter grunted. "As you can imagine, sitting around all day doing nothing is incredibly boring. I can't work or even catch up with friends and business acquaintances over lunch. It's tedious."

"Well, I was hoping you might feel that way."

"You were?" Walter sounded confused.

"If I send you the links to a few crowd-sleuthing forums, do you think you could set up accounts and make some posting for me? And then… monitor whatever comes in on them."

"I'd be happy to," Walter declared. "What's the case?"

"I am trying to identify a criminal. I have a picture. But I need to find out who he is. I already know where to start, but it will take a lot more time than I have. If I can get this guy… a young woman who has been held against her will for months will be very happy."

"Oh, dear. Well, that is incentive, even if boredom were not."

Zachary explained about the man who had kidnapped Elysse. Until now, they had been unable to guess his motive for abducting Elysse, but now Zachary thought he knew.

"Okay." Walter sounded thoughtful. Zachary thought he was probably writing down notes of what Zachary had told him. "So you'll send me the sites you want this picture posted to. I'll ask for any other pictures of him and find out if anyone knows who he is or where he came from."

"Right. I have an idea of what we'll find, but I need as much corroboration as I can get."

"You got it," Walter agreed. "I'll do everything I can. And I assume this is… urgent. ASAP."

"Yesterday, if possible," Zachary agreed.

Walter chuckled. "That's the kind of deadline I'm used to. Well, Lisa will thank you for keeping me out of her hair for a little while. I think she's been a little… aggravated having me around so much lately. Oh, you know she tries to be nice about it. I have always been welcome here; that didn't change when we divorced. But having me underfoot constantly is a bit of a problem. It's a big house. I stay out of her way as much as I can. But we had never planned for me to be here full-time. Neither of us is equipped to handle it. We are both very… *independent* people."

Which was probably much of the reason they had gotten divorced in the first place. As Kenzie had described her childhood years, Walter had not been home a lot. He had mostly lived in Montpelier, working at the Capitol during the week and only returning home for weekends and holidays. They had divorced when Kenzie had graduated and been traveling away from home. Not much had changed in Lisa's and Walter's relationship.. Walter still returned to what was considered the family home when he needed to be in Burlington or wanted to spend time with his ex-wife or daughter.

But part of selling the story of Walter's serious illness was his not being able to take care of himself anymore, or at least not for a long period of recovery time.

"We could get you one of those big puzzles to put together," Zachary told Walter. "Give you something to do."

"Oh, please, no," Walter groaned, "I never could stand the things. I'll take your crowd sleuthing over jigsaw puzzles any day."

"Hey Zachy," Heather greeted, answering the phone. "Are you back home or still on your road trip?"

"I'm back. Anything worrisome while I was gone? Anything I need to take care of right away?"

"I think everything is in your task manager. No emergencies. How was the trip?"

"Pretty good. I'm glad I went. I did a lot and learned a lot that would have been impossible to figure out from here. And I think Kenzie needed to get away for a while, too."

"She didn't want to extend it for another day or two? I figured once she was away from the office, she would want to take a bit more time. She's been working so hard since Dr. Wiltshire broke his hand."

"Well, I think we would have stretched it out another day or two, but something came up here... the photographer that you gave the name of our hotel...?"

"Kristy Echols," Heather said promptly.

"Yeah. Kristy. She was killed."

Heather gasped. "No! Oh, no. That's terrible. Do you think it was related to the case? Is there any indication who it was?"

"I'm worried that it might have been. She had some other information to share with me, a theory, and she was killed before she had a chance. But I think I figured it out. And if she was killed by the guy who kidnapped Elysse... then I'm going to catch him.

We'll put him behind bars. Protect Elysse, help her to get her life back. We can't do anything for Kristy... but we won't let her death be in vain."

"Kidnapped her?" Heather repeated.

"She was kidnapped and terrorized. Her disappearance was not just Elysse taking a little vacation."

"And you think you know this guy's identity?"

"I will soon."

Heather's voice was thick with concern. "You need to be careful! I'm worried about this, Zachary. If this guy has already killed one person... you need to be careful. You can't just go jumping into this."

"Like I always do?"

"I didn't say that." Neither of them said anything for a minute, then Heather laughed. "But yes, that's what I meant."

"Once I have his identity, I'll go to the police. Let them take it from there."

"Why don't you give them what you have right now? Let them identify the guy and take him down."

"I need more. The police were involved from the start, but they think Elysse was just taking a trip. That she was gone voluntarily. To prove what happened to her, I need more."

"Can't she just tell them the truth? It seems like she's the one who is responsible for them thinking that she was missing voluntarily. That's what she told them."

"Because she's afraid. He has her under his control. He broke her and she'll do whatever he says to. She's afraid of what he could do to her and what he could do to her family. If they don't arrest him or don't keep him in custody until he can be convicted and sent to prison for the rest of his life, he could still harm her or her family."

"Yeah, I guess she has reason to be concerned about what he could do if he's still on the outside. But how are they supposed to do that if she won't tell them anything to put him behind bars?"

"I'm hoping... that once I identify him, we'll be able to prove that he killed Kristy, not just that he was responsible for kidnapping and terrorizing Elysse."

"Why would he do something like that? Was he just obsessed with her? I worry that this is what happens when kids put all their information online. A psychopath like this guy sees it and decides to…?"

Heather had kids who were young adults, and Zachary was sure she must worry about everything that could happen to them. She had lived most of her life in fear and, while she was doing better now, she was still a mom with all those fears. They had caught the man who had stolen her childhood, but there were more people like him. Too many more of them. People like Elysse's psychopath, who targeted strangers and took away their lives, even if they didn't kill them.

"In this case," Zachary said slowly, "it isn't random, but it isn't like any other case you've ever seen. I don't want to say too much about it yet. But yeah… he's a lowlife, and we need to make sure we've got enough evidence on him to put him behind bars permanently. There can't be any mistakes or technicalities that will set him free."

"So you didn't just call me to find out if anything happened while you were gone."

"No."

"What have you got for me?"

"I have a company that I need you to gather all the information you can about. It might be hard to get past all the PR, but I need to dig down and get more than just their annual financial statements and CEO's message."

"Okay. Maybe Grant can help me with some of that."

Heather's husband was an accountant. Zachary didn't know what kind of accounting he did or whether he would enjoy digging into all a company's records like Zachary was suggesting. But they would take whatever help they could get. Grant was very devoted to Heather. Zachary was glad she had someone looking out for her and helping her. Heather deserved every bit of pampering and attention.

He gave her the details on the company. It wouldn't be hard for her to find the basics. But he didn't know how much else they would be able to pull together to show what had happened over the past year or so.

"And I need all the pictures you can give me of employees of the company. Everything from upper management on down. Corporate headshots, pictures of company picnics, whatever we can get. I might need to surveil them to get pictures of the people who have never shown up in their literature, but we'll start with what's already available."

"You want me to save the pictures for you in a subfile for the project? Then you can just review them as I find them."

"Yeah. But message me whenever you save a new batch. I want to see them right away."

"Okay, will do. You don't have a sketch or description of the person you are looking for?"

"I need everyone you can get, I'll want to show them to witnesses to see if anyone else was involved in this. I'll send you a couple pictures of the guy I *know* we are looking for. And I guess I should tell you we have another operative doing some work for us," Zachary told Heather.

"What? Who?" She sounded a little offended that he would assign someone else work on the case. He probably should have told her before he did it. Made sure that she was okay with it. But it was too late for that now.

"Kenzie's dad. He's got cabin fever, not being able to leave the house… after his stroke." Zachary decided he'd better stick with the official story and not let on that Walter was actually in perfectly good health.

"Oh, I didn't know. Poor Kenzie. That couldn't have been easy, right in the middle of everything else. When…?"

"Just recently." Zachary didn't want to give a particular time-frame. "But he's starting with rehabilitation, physiotherapy, whatever. And he can do some computer work."

"That's great. And there's enough to go around. It isn't like I need to support a family on my paycheck. I'm mostly just doing it for fun."

"And you do a really good job. I'm not trying to replace you. Just giving him something to do too… spreading the work out."

"So what do you have him doing? I should add his tasks to the project as well so we can keep track of everything being done. And you should charge out his time too."

Zachary explained the task he had given Walter: find any more pictures taken of the man from the Grand Canyon and posted on social media.

"That's going to be quite a project."

"That's why we're crowd sourcing it," Zachary agreed. "And it will save me some eyestrain…"

"I suppose you don't have anything to do now that you have assigned us all your grunt work."

"There is still plenty for me to do. And Kenzie, too, for that matter. She's doing the postmortem today."

"Oooh… maybe you'd better buy her some flowers."

It wasn't such a bad idea.

64

As was usually the case when Kenzie had been doing autopsies in the afternoon, she was late getting home. When she arrived, she wanted a shower before she was ready to face dinner or the rest of the evening. She knew that Zachary would want to hear all about the postmortem findings on Kristy Echols and paused before heading toward the bathroom.

"We'll talk about it at supper, okay? I just need to wash away the sweat and smell before I get into it."

"Take your time," Zachary told her, "I know you need it."

She gave him a wry grin. "Do I smell that bad?"

Zachary sniffed the air. "Not from here," he said with a smile. "But maybe you shouldn't get too close."

She snorted and retreated to her bathroom sanctuary to rinse off the rest of the day. Zachary got up from his spot on the couch where he had been working and went to the kitchen. Kenzie hadn't said she had anything particular in mind for supper, and he wanted to make sure he had something ready for her. The easiest thing would have been to order in from one of their favorite restaurants. But they had been on the road for several days and had been eating fast food or restaurant food that entire time. Kenzie would really appreciate something homemade.

Of course, it would have been better if Zachary had thought this through earlier in the day, because when he opened the fridge, he found it pretty bare. He should have gone shopping to pick up some fresh produce and other ingredients.

He waffled about whether to order takeout. It would be better than nothing, and Kenzie wouldn't want to wait while Zachary went to the store.

He checked the freezer and cupboards and decided he had enough to work with. If Kenzie wasn't satisfied, she could fill up on ice cream, or they could go out for dessert or some other treat.

Zachary had told Kenzie to take her time in the shower, so he knew he would have at least half an hour to prepare, and that seemed like plenty.

Kenzie eventually returned to the kitchen, curly hair still damp, her cheeks flushed, and dressed in her comfy jammies. So they would not be going out anywhere for dessert. The smell of the warming soup and bread filled the kitchen. Kenzie looked at the table, already set, and wandered over to the stove to give Zachary a hug and peek into the pot.

"That smells delicious. I thought you might order in."

"Did you want me to?" Zachary suddenly doubted himself. Maybe he *should* have gone with that initial inclination.

"No, not particularly. We've been eating prepared food all week. It's kind of nice to have something homemade."

"Sorry, there isn't a salad. I didn't think about needing groceries earlier."

"We can do without salad one day. There are plenty of veggies in the soup."

He had warmed up one of the "handcrafted" soups she liked to get at the grocery store. They were full of chunks of locally sourced produce and came in fancy glass jars with raised curlicues framing the vintage-style label.

Zachary himself preferred a good old can of chicken and stars, but he was making the dinner special for Kenzie, not warming something up for his own solitary lunch. When he was at home, he could have a can of soup for lunch every day of the week if he wanted, though Kenzie warned him he should be watching his sodium intake.

"And you warmed up some bread?"

Zachary opened the oven door with a flourish to check on the loaf of French bread he had pulled from the freezer, thawed for the first few minutes, then split and spread with butter and garlic. If Kenzie got her special soup, he could have garlic bread. And it went with soup, so she couldn't accuse him of making it just because it was his favorite food. A puff of warm air washed over him. The garlic bread looked perfect, the butter melted and the loaf starting to get golden brown around the edges. Zachary carefully took it out and set it on the counter.

He had forgotten to put soup spoons on the table, but everything else was in order and, in a few minutes, they were both sipping the surprisingly good soup and dipping their crusty garlic bread into it. Soup wasn't such a bad way to get his vegetables. Kind of like spaghetti, without the noodles.

"So, the results of the Kristy Echols postmortem," Kenzie said after a few bites of soup followed by approving noises.

"Yeah. Dr. Cook figured it was strangulation?"

"Yes. That will be the cause of death."

"Murder."

"Yes."

"Was there anything else? Anything interesting or unusual? Unexpected?"

"We sent off tox screens and all of that to the lab. They will take a few weeks to be processed, but I don't expect them to find anything. Maybe some alcohol, her prescriptions, but there wasn't anything to indicate she'd been drugged."

"Any blows to the head? Signs of a struggle?"

"She fought back, but it was all over pretty quickly. I sent nail scrapings to the lab with a request for them to speed DNA processing in case she scratched him. We might get lucky there. But unless this guy is already in the system, we're going to have to find a way to identify him."

"I'm already on that." Zachary told her about the assignments he had given Walter and Heather.

Kenzie laid down her spoon and sat back, thinking about this. She grinned.

"I love that you're putting Dad to work for your own purposes. And if it helps him find something to do and helps Mom put up with him, that's great. And I think he'll be able to help you. He's always had his causes and has been willing to go to… almost any lengths to help them. Just be careful that he doesn't take an assignment like this further than you wanted him to, or use…" She looked up at the ceiling, fishing for the appropriate word, "more *controversial* methods to get answers. If you want to be able to take it to the police…"

Zachary nodded slowly. In his drive to find out who the man threatening Elysse was, he had forgotten about some of the finer points of Walter's personality. Walter had manipulated Zachary to get what he wanted on other occasions.

He had given Walter clear instructions on getting the information he needed, so he didn't think there was any danger in his going too far with that. But if Walter decided to use other means to try to "help" Zachary get the information he needed, it could be a problem.

Walter's decision to get involved with the Russians had proved to be a misjudgment on his part, and he didn't normally fall into that trap. Walter was an incredibly successful lobbyist, and he didn't get that way by making a lot of mistakes. His judgment was good and he was capable of thinking several steps ahead of his opponent and putting together very complex plans to get what he wanted.

Zachary would have to make sure that Walter understood he wasn't to go rogue on any assignment Zachary offered him. He would need to get permission before he decided to go off in his own direction.

"What are you smiling at?" Kenzie asked.

"Just… the thought of me telling Walter not to go off the rails. That he needs to be able to follow my instructions exactly."

Kenzie chuckled. "You mean because you would never do such

a thing yourself? I can just see the two of you both going off like hounds after a quarry—in opposite directions. One of you is going to have to be a stabilizing influence."

"I don't think I've ever been called upon to do that before."

"I've seen you do it... with Tyrrell or Rhys, or Mason. But it's going to be a challenge to keep someone like Walter under control. You might have to bring out the big guns."

"You?"

"I don't think I've ever been able to convince my dad to do or say anything he didn't want to in my life. He has... his own ideas about things. But maybe Mom. She *might* be able to redirect him."

"I'll remember that," Zachary promised. "Keep it in my back pocket in case I need it in the future."

65

Research could take weeks or months. Gathering evidence and getting enough information to take a case to the point where a suspect could be arrested and prosecuted could take years, even decades.

So it amazed Zachary how quickly information could be gathered by a group of untrained internet sleuths. Several hundred or thousand people working on a project together, and they could compile the information and find the answers that the police had been unable to, even when they had been putting all their resources into a case.

Of course, the police had *not* been working on the Elysse Allan case. Not since she had reappeared in the Grand Canyon and given her television interview. That had effectively put an end to any investigation into what had happened to her. Even if they had suspected she was covering up what had really happened, they couldn't continue to investigate it once she had reappeared and said she had just been on vacation.

The internet sleuths were much better than Zachary at digging up the pictures he was looking for on social media, photography sites, personal blogs, news articles, and other sources.

Zachary looked over the photos that had started to come in. The man was probably in his forties. Too old for Elysse, and yet the pictures of him almost always included her in the frame, her eyes on him, watching and waiting for every signal.

In the interview following Elysse's reappearance, she had smiled and been pleasant. She'd had a calm and relaxed manner. Focused, but not noticeably anxious.

But that had all been a mask. Elysse had been on camera enough times to know how to put any anxiety to the side and just focus on her public persona. Her brand, as Kristy had referred to it.

The shots she had been caught in prior to her TV appearance, however, told another story. The shots that had only accidentally caught her in the background with her captor showed her as anxious, hypervigilant, watching his every movement.

Zachary downloaded each photo of Elysse's captor and loaded them into the facial recognition app on his computer to build a solid model from which to work. Then he ran it against the pictures Heather had been loading into the folder for the case.

The facial recognition searches that appeared in the TV shows Zachary occasionally watched with Kenzie were always practically instantaneous. Of course, they had to be, given the constraints that TV show writers were given to work with. The case had to be solved in minutes. There was often a ticking clock to work against, a time bomb or anticipated terror event which, in the end, was foiled with only seconds left on the clock.

In reality, such matching took hours—if they even had the person's biometrics in their database, which was not a "given" as it was on TV.

But Zachary was working with a much smaller set of files. He had less than two hundred photos from the company's website and social media sources. He left the app working in the background, switching over to his inbox to see what other work he could do while he waited for a response. There was no guarantee that the man would appear in any of the pictures they had found. He might be a recent hire. He might be an independent consultant. He might just be camera-shy. Knowing what kind of work he had been assigned, he might actively avoid any and all cameras.

There was a two-tone alert, and Zachary flipped back to the facial recognition app, which had isolated three photos.

The first two photos were small and lower resolution, their suspect in the background of a larger picture. But the third had him as the main subject as he flipped pancakes at a company breakfast fundraiser. Zachary checked the filename, which referred him to an index sheet Heather had created. Navigating to the index sheet, he found the URL of the page it had been downloaded from. She was always very organized, thinking of ways to make things easy to understand or to find again. He clicked the URL and was taken to the page of promotional photos showing how the company had been involved in several charitable campaigns. Good PR for a big company, showing how they cared about the little guy and weren't just in it all for the money.

He scrolled down until he found the source photo which, luckily, was captioned.

Jordan Starr serves up flapjacks at the Kidney Cancer fundraising breakfast.

Bingo. They had a name.

Kenzie had informed him that Detective Cameron had been assigned to the Kristy Echols homicide.

He was the cop who had been called after the attempted abduction, and he had been polite and respectful. Zachary hadn't worked with him on any cases, so he wasn't sure how he would be to work with. Some cops Zachary had dealt with would never talk to a private investigator, even one who had information to give to them.

Kenzie had talked Cameron into meeting with Zachary, making time for him that afternoon. When Zachary sat down, Cameron leaned way back in his office chair, making the spring squeal in protest. Zachary gritted his teeth and tried to hide how much the nails-on-the-blackboard sound irritated him.

"So, Dr. Kirsch said that you have been working on a private investigation involving Ms. Echols and that you might have information pertinent to her homicide."

"Yes." Zachary leaned forward in his chair. He was eager to get the wheels moving on the arrest of Jordan Starr and to give Cameron the details that would clinch the arrest. "I believe that Kristy Echols was killed because she was helping us—helping me—with my investigation. She had just called me to follow up on some pictures she had sent me and to tell me what she had discovered as she reviewed the old photographs. But before she could… we were disconnected. And that's the last we heard from her. I kept trying to get her back, but…"

Cameron nodded. "Your calls were logged on her phone."

Zachary wondered why the detective hadn't bothered to call him as soon as he saw that. It seemed to Zachary that in a murder investigation, it was essential to interview possible witnesses as soon as possible, rather than waiting a couple of days before pursuing it, and then only because Zachary had asked Kenzie to set up the appointment.

"I believe that she'd figured out the motive for Elysse Allan's abduction. The only thing that explains why she was snatched and returned like she was."

"Abduction?" Cameron repeated. "Elysse Allan was not abducted. She was a voluntary missing. She had just taken off on her own and was out of touch when the search was started."

"That's what she told the reporter who interviewed her," Zachary agreed.

"That's what happened."

"No. She's been living under the terroristic threats made by the guy who snatched her for over six months. He has made threats to her and her family to keep her from saying anything about it. She is a prisoner in her own home."

Cameron clicked the top of his pen on the desk in front of him. "Is that so."

"Yes."

"And that's what she would tell me if I gave her a call?"

"No… she'll tell you she was just on a trip when she was reported missing and happened to be out of phone contact. And she'll keep repeating that as long as the kidnapper is still on the loose and holding the threat to her family's safety over her head."

"That's convenient."

"No, it's not. This would be a lot easier for all of us if she would tell her story. But she won't. Not until she believes she is safe. And right now, she still believes he could come after her at any minute. That he is monitoring every move she makes. And it's not convenient for *her*. She has to keep telling a story that isn't true and stay closeted up in her own home for months. It isn't convenient for anyone."

"So all you have for me is a story?"

"I'll start with the story and show you what evidence I've gathered as I tell it to you."

Cameron flicked a hand toward Zachary, palm up, inviting him to commence his presentation.

Zachary tapped the edges of the pages in his folder to square them. He took a deep breath and started the explanation.

"According to what we could get from Elysse herself, she was kidnapped when she was on her way from the argument with Dain to the next location she was supposed to be shooting at. She was supposed to meet Kristy and never showed up. She was stopped by a man who she thought was going to direct her to the location. He acted like he wanted an autograph, but then pulled out a Taser and zapped her."

Cameron raised his brows skeptically.

"He tased her and drugged her and took her to Sudbury, Ontario."

"Where is that?"

"Canada."

"I know Ontario is in Canada," Cameron said sourly. "I'm not completely ignorant. Where exactly?"

"North of Toronto."

"Nice place?"

"Generally, yes. But not the place where Elysse was held."

Zachary opened his folder and put the first picture sheet on the desk before Cameron. "These are pictures that were taken of Elysse when she was there."

His eyes flickered over the page. "Looks like she was alone. Where is this kidnapper?"

"She was being coerced. He's not in the picture. He didn't have to be right by her side to force her to do his will. She had been tased and drugged repeatedly, told that her family would be harmed if she didn't obey him. He told her he was setting her up as a terrorist and, if she said anything, that's what her fans and the police would think of her."

Cameron snorted.

"This is the information from Jack at the hotel, confirming that she had been registered there under the name Elysse Dane."

"Why would some kidnapper take her to Canada? Why risk crossing international borders with her?"

"There are a number of reasons, but I suspect the biggest one was to make a clean getaway. No one was looking for her in Canada. Far smaller population, she had no reason to go there on her own, any sightings or tips that were called in to the police about her being there were completely ignored."

"Uh-huh."

"She was transported from Sudbury over the Sault Ste Marie border crossing," Zachary told him, taking care to pronounce Sault Ste Marie the proper way. "Into Michigan. She then took a flight to Salt Lake City. I believe they drove across the border to avoid the more stringent security checks at the airport."

"Why would they take her to Salt Lake? Was it a stopover on the way to Arizona?"

"They didn't fly back out of Salt Lake immediately. Here are some of the pictures posted of her there."

The pictures of Elysse in the mall in Salt Lake were clearer than the ones taken in Canada. Clear enough that Cameron didn't express his doubt that it was her.

"And several people who saw her while she was there..." Zachary again presented Cameron with the confirmations she had been there.

"Now, this is key," Zachary said slowly. "I didn't see the significance right away because I didn't understand how these social influencers work. But I think this is what Kristy noticed as well."

66

"What's that?" Cameron demanded. Despite himself, he leaned forward to peer at the pictures, his curiosity about the case captured.

"Elysse herself didn't know why he took her there, what he was trying to do."

"What?"

"You can see her shopping in these pictures," Zachary pointed out. "And while we were there, Kenzie—Dr. Kirsch—talked to one of the witnesses about fashion lines and branding."

Cameron's nostrils flared, impatient with Zachary. And it was true that Zachary was drawing it out unnecessarily long, wanting to pull Cameron into the story as he withheld the necessary information.

"Then, she was seen in the Grand Canyon. There are several pictures where she is in the background. People hadn't recognized her yet; she just happened to be in the background."

Cameron looked over the pictures, nodding.

"You can see the clothes she is wearing," Zachary pointed. "These are the outfits that she bought in Salt Lake City. Or that her abductor bought for her."

"Yeah, so?"

"And for the first time, you can see the man with her."

Zachary tapped Jordan Starr's face in several of the pictures. Cameron frowned, looking at it. "Looks like an accountant. This is your kidnapper?"

"Do all criminals look like someone from central casting?" Zachary challenged.

Cameron grunted. He knew, of course, that there were plenty of people convicted of murder or other heinous crimes who looked like the boy—or girl—next door. Or a kindly old grandpa. Or like a mild-mannered accountant.

"This is just a representative sample of the pictures and video I have of her in the Grand Canyon. There is plenty more that you can view and have your forensic and behavioral experts look at. Look at the way she is watching him. Her body language. He is no stranger to her. He's not a friend."

Cameron looked over the pictures and nodded in agreement. A police detective was an observer of human nature. He saw plenty of conflict between people. Learned the language and behavior of people who were involved in domestic violence, human trafficking, drug use and trafficking, and all sorts of other situations where they might have been coerced.

"So, who is this guy?"

"I'll get to that," Zachary assured him. "Then we have the reappearance of Elysse in the public eye. The police are called. She won't talk to the ranger. The media is also called, and Elysse elects to talk to one of the reporters. Goes to their network and does an interview on their set, under the proper stage lighting,"

Cameron pursed his lips. "As if it had been planned that way? Not an off-the-cuff interview on location, but something properly staged and professionally filmed."

"Yes," Zachary agreed. He placed another set of pictures in front of Cameron. A few stills gleaned from the video of the interview. "Note again the clothes she is wearing."

Cameron looked at the pictures and shrugged. "It all seems appropriate."

"The clothes that she bought in Salt Lake City." Zachary

showed Cameron a printed page with product pictures and descriptions for the outfit she was wearing, backpack and day pack she was carrying, her shoes, and her cap. All with the triangular *Mystic Mountain* brand badge.

"Uh-huh."

"But these do not fit Elysse Allan's brand."

Cameron raised his brows. "What does that mean?"

"When Kenzie and the saleswoman talked in Salt Lake City, that's one thing the saleswoman said. The clothes Elysse bought did not fit her brand. One of the things that Kristy Echols helped Elysse with was keeping all her pictures and social media on-brand."

"So she couldn't buy whatever brands or lines or clothing she wanted to?" Cameron shook his head. "What would that matter? So she picked out a different brand than she normally would because she was going to be hiking in the Grand Canyon. So what?"

"Elysse was a very famous social influencer. Companies would pay her thousands of dollars to wear or use their brands in her postings. Hundreds of thousands of dollars for a few seconds in a couple of videos."

Cameron's chair thumped into a fully upright position. "Hundreds of thousands of dollars."

"Yes. It was well worth it to them for Elysse to be seen wearing their clothing brands. For a few seconds. But... Elysse didn't have a contract with Mystic Mountain."

Zachary teased the page with the pictures from Elysse's interview out from under the others and pointed to the time stamp in the corner of one of the videos. "Forty-three minutes. Forty-three minutes of Elysse Allan's time, in proper studio lighting, makeup, etc. after a five-day media event that captured the world's attention. Millions of people watched it live. And six months later, people are still watching it. Whenever anyone searches Elysse Allan's name and tries to find out what she is doing now, this is where they land. And they watch it again."

"Free advertising."

"Yes. For as long as anyone is interested in Elysse Allan. And right now, Dain is writing a book about their time together and her disappearance and, when that comes out, the interest in Elysse will skyrocket again. People will be searching her name and watching this video again."

"You think Dain had something to do with this?"

"No. He hired me to find out what really happened to Elysse, and if what really happened gets out, the Mystic Mountain brand will tank."

Cameron tented his fingers in front of him, considering the story. The pages were laid out on the desk before him, and he could review them again to see if the story held together. But Zachary's folder was not yet empty.

"Since it hasn't been a full year, the public doesn't have access to all the financial numbers yet. But here is a chart of the share prices of Mystic Mountain."

He laid the chart on the desk in front of Cameron, who looked at the huge spike in the value of the shares that occurred after Elysse had appeared on TV in her Mystic Mountain garb.

"The increase in production," Zachary laid the next chart down. "The increase in cost of their product lines. The overall value of the company."

Each chart he laid down showed huge spikes that dwarfed the business Mystic Mountain had been doing before Elysse's disappearance. Cameron picked up the last chart. He eyed the axis scale. "This is ten millions?"

Zachary nodded. The amounts boggled the mind. The increase in the value of the company was incredible. All due to the abduction of one young woman.

No, not just due to her abduction. Due to her abduction, her return to the public eye wearing the Mystic Mountain brand, and then posting nothing after that. All three events, taken together, continued to feed the machine, driving sales to a previously lackluster brand. Pushing a regional brand into an international monolith.

67

C ameron shuffled through the papers and pulled out the pictures of Elysse in the Grand Canyon. The man with her. Both dressed in Mystic Mountain togs.

"And this man. How does he profit from all of this? Who is he?"

"Jordan Starr. Manager of Marketing at Mystic Mountain."

"Manager of Marketing. So this was all his idea? This was his brainchild—kidnap a social influencer and coerce her into wearing the brand on network television. And then... force her to keep her head down and not post anything else."

Zachary nodded. "I can't tell you whether it was his own idea or someone else's, but he was the one that put it into effect. Elysse didn't know who else might be helping him. She didn't see anyone else who was involved in the kidnapping. She thinks other people are watching her, but that may be paranoia. I've gathered photos of other employees for her to review. She has been conditioned to fear Starr, so it's not unexpected that she will see danger wherever she goes, whether from him or someone else. Anyone who looks at her the wrong way..."

"Of course. Anyone could be working for the guy. She keeps herself cloistered because she thinks he is always watching her."

"And he could be monitoring her remotely. There could be bugs in the house, hidden cameras, key loggers on her computer, a tracker on her car, all kinds of things. All he has to do is say that he saw her do one thing, and she'll be convinced that he was there watching, or someone else was, all the time. He can just be in Salt Lake City doing his day-to-day corporate job, just checking on the cameras and security logs a couple of times a day to make sure she is still being compliant."

"He's in Salt Lake?"

"That's where the company is headquartered. Like I said, it wasn't a big brand when she was taken. Regional, available in a few states. Now it is much bigger, spread all over the world. But the headquarters is still in Salt Lake."

"That's why he took her to Salt Lake to get her outfitted."

"Both of them. He shopped for himself, too, so he wouldn't look out of place with the touring groups."

"And then they just walked around waiting for someone to notice her and make a fuss."

"I wonder if he expected it to take that long," Zachary pondered, "It must have been excruciating, waiting for his plan to play out and Elysse to get in front of the cameras."

"That's probably why she looks so scared," Cameron observed, looking at the picture. "He had probably been escalating while he waited for her to be recognized."

"Probably," Zachary agreed.

"Do you know where Jordan Starr is now?"

"Well, I can't track his phone GPS like the police. But we can assume that he was in Vermont on Sunday when Kristy was killed. If he knew that she found something in the pictures and was talking to me... then he might still be here, hoping to get a chance to... uh... talk to me."

Cameron chuckled. "And that doesn't make you nervous?"

"I'm talking to you, aren't I?"

He nodded. "That's probably a good idea. But you know we don't do 24-hour guards and safe houses like on TV. We can increase patrols past your house and look for anything out of place. You have a good security system."

"Yeah. We do. Security company hardwired in, they get there in two or three minutes. But it can be a really long two or three minutes."

"I imagine so. You own a gun?"

"No."

"Might want to consider it. A man has the right to protect his castle. And his damsel, for that matter."

Zachary nodded, but didn't give Cameron any explanation for his decision never to own a gun. He had survived so far without one, but he couldn't guarantee that he would survive if he had one when he went through his next bout of depression, even with Kenzie there.

"What traceable information do you have on this guy? You have his cell number? Vehicle make and license plate? Does this Mystic Mountain have an office here in Vermont?"

Zachary pulled the profile Heather had pulled together out of his folder and placed it in front of Cameron. A copy of the picture of him flipping pancakes. All the personal details Heather and Zachary had been able to find using the databases they had access to.

"Don't know if the guy has a record. Nothing in Utah, but our courthouse searches in Vermont and Oregon are still pending. Other states… who knows? You might have better luck than us. Be able to put it out on your networks and find out more. Closest relatives are there too. Don't know if any of them will be able to tell you where he is or where he is likely to go if he thinks his cover has been blown."

"You think he knows you're on to him?"

"Hopefully not. But my name and number were on her phone. And with Kenzie being the one to do the autopsy… that has to make him pretty nervous. Puts me too close to the action. I haven't made any of what I have found public. Elysse is still in her house in Oregon, afraid to leave or do anything that might set him off. I don't think she's in any danger. He won't want to kill the golden goose."

"Does he know Dain is writing a book?"

"I don't know. Someone must know that. I don't know how far the publisher and Dain have spread it. Since he is big into social networks, I assume he has announced it everywhere he is active."

Cameron was tapping his pen on the table again. "I'm not comfortable with the idea of Dr. Kirsch being targeted."

"I would hope not."

Cameron gave him a wry smile. "How much of what you've just shown me does she know?"

"Uh… nothing yet. Just what we found out firsthand when we followed Elysse's route and talked to her in Oregon."

"So she knows the route and that Elysse was being menaced, but not why or by whom."

Zachary nodded his agreement. "I'm going to see her next," he said, checking the face of his phone to see what time it was. "I was hoping I would have something more to tell her."

"Like what the police think of your wild theory and what they are going to do about it, if anything?"

"Yeah."

"Well, I can't answer that yet. I will need to run this up the flag-pole and see what my fellow detectives and the sergeant have to say about it. Talk about how we are going to proceed. But you can tell her that we are taking it seriously and we will get back to the two of you on our next steps once we've worked that out. I'll get started on getting access to his phone records and GPS coordinates, we'll try to pin down where he is right now. At least what state he is in."

"That will help inform you on next steps. Just remember… he could have left his phone in Utah and bought a burner while he was here. Or not even have a phone here."

"Seems almost impossible to survive without a phone in your pocket in today's society. But I guess people still do it. We'll do everything we can to get a location on this guy. Then I'll give you a call. Or Dr. Kirsch."

Zachary stood up. Cameron rose as well and offered to shake his hand. Zachary gripped it firmly and nodded. "Thanks. I look forward to hearing from you."

68

Kenzie was safe as long as she was in the morgue. At least
he could be confident of that fact. Security at the police
station was good and extended to her offices below the
building. Security checkpoints and guards patrolled the halls to
make sure that everything was in order. A criminal would have to
be crazy to think he could just walk into the police building and go
after her.

Kenzie was at her desk in the public reception area at the front
of the medical examiner's office. She had paperwork and filing to
catch up on. She had been away for a few days, and while there had
not been a lot of autopsies to worry about, there was always more
paperwork coming in. Lab results, police reports, reports to be written. A person could drown in all the paper.

But Kenzie, luckily, had a talent for taming the paper. She had
been initially hired for her administrative capabilities and, over the
past few years, she had been given more and more opportunities to
participate in the actual evidence gathering, forensic analysis, and
postmortems until she had enough experience to actually be called
an assistant medical examiner.

Kenzie looked up from her work to see who was approaching
the reception desk. She smiled.

"Zachary! What are you doing here? I didn't know you were coming by."

"I had a meeting with Detective Cameron."

"Oh." Kenzie nodded slowly. "On the Kristy Echols investigation?"

Zachary nodded soberly. "Yes. If we want him to solve it, we need to give him all the information we can."

"I've done my part," Kenzie acknowledged. "Were you able to give him anything useful? What does he think of the possible connection to the Elysse Allan case?"

"He's convinced."

"Really?" Kenzie raised her brows. She pushed aside the paperwork she had been working on. "I'm surprised. I didn't think he would see the connection."

"I had a good amount of evidence. He could see it."

Kenzie looked around. "Can we sit down for a few minutes? Do you need to go anywhere, or can we discuss it?"

"I was hoping you would have some time."

She nodded. "Let me forward the phone, and we'll just sit in the boardroom."

She put away any paperwork on her desk so that there wasn't anything sensitive if someone came down looking to claim someone's personal effects, fill out a public information request form, or talk to someone about the results of a postmortem. Sooner or later, they were going to have to get a full-time receptionist, because Kenzie's expertise was needed elsewhere much of the time now, leaving the public information desk unmanned. With forms available online to fill out, not many people came in person, but enough that they still needed someone out there.

After Kenzie finished putting things away, locking her computer screen, and forwarding the phone, she motioned for Zachary to enter the boardroom. They sat down with the door open so she could see or hear any arrivals.

"How did you convince Cameron of the connection between the Elysse Allan and Kristy Echols cases?"

"Well, the fact that I was the last person Kristy talked to probably helped," Zachary said slowly.

A stab of pain lightninged through his chest that wasn't anything to do with his broken ribs. It was guilt. Guilt that he had taken the case and questioned Kristy, had asked her for her help, all of which had eventually led to her death. He wasn't the one who had killed her, but had he signed her death warrant?

"He could see that she had talked to me close to the time that she died and that I had called her back a number of times. I told him that the reason was the Elysse Allan file."

"But it's pretty hard to say that her knowing Elysse and talking to you was directly related to her death, though. Especially since they believed that Elysse was just a voluntary missing person."

"I walked him through it, and he agrees that Elysse was under duress."

"How did you do that? I didn't think they would change their minds on that. With all the effort put into finding her, and then the press release where she said she just went on a vacation... I figured they would write her off. Not want to have anything to do with her or her case again."

"They did. But your dad did a good job of crowd sourcing pictures from the Grand Canyon and we were able to find enough with Elysse in them to show that she was not there alone. And her facial expression and body language strongly suggest they were not on good terms."

"But where does that get you when you don't know who he is?"

"We were able to identify him. His name is Jordan Starr."

"How did you do that?" Her voice rose in excitement. "Facial recognition? Was he already in the system?"

"I ran my own facial recognition against the pictures mined from the website and social media of the company I believed he worked for. And I found him."

"The company he worked for. Does that mean this was a contracted hit?"

"No. Kristy was killed to cover up what they were doing. Why they kidnapped Elysse in the first place."

Kenzie's fingers tightened around the arms of her chair at the mention of kidnapping. Even though they both knew that Elysse had been kidnapped, the word still triggered her anxiety and the memories of her own abduction. Zachary paused a few seconds, waiting for her body to relax and unclench before he went on.

"So why?" Kenzie demanded. "Why would anyone do that? It all seemed so random. A random target. Traveling randomly all over the continent. Keeping her holed up in her own house, afraid to go out. None of it makes sense."

"You hit on it accidentally when we were in Salt Lake. You remember talking to the salesclerk at the mall where she was seen."

Kenzie nodded slowly. "Yes. Of course."

"You got into a discussion with her about the clothes that Elysse had purchased."

"Yeah. That's right. We were talking about fashion, what was popular, and the fact that Elysse had bought clothes that were off-brand for her."

Zachary nodded.

"You think that was significant?" Kenzie asked. "Which part? If she was being coerced, then it makes sense that she would be behaving differently. She wouldn't care whether the clothes she brought fit her brand. She wasn't posting pictures anymore, so it didn't matter whether they fit her online persona."

"She bought clothes for the hikes in the Grand Canyon."

"Right. Of course."

"And so did the man that she was with. Jordan Starr."

"Okay. But I don't see what that has to do with anything."

"He was the marketing manager of the clothing brand. Mystic Mountain."

He watched Kenzie consider this and work through all the implications.

"He wanted her to dress in his clothing brand. To be seen in it."

"Yes."

"He *planned* for her to be seen in the Grand Canyon."

"Not just seen. He planned on it being a big media event."

"Just so that she could be seen in his clothing brand?"

"*Just* being seen in that clothing brand sent company sales skyrocketing. And they are still climbing, because every time someone searches for Elysse Allan to find out what she is doing now and when her last post was, they watch the video of her press release."

"Where she was wearing the Mystic Mountain brand."

Zachary nodded.

"You have proof of all of this?" Kenzie asked. "Actual evidence?"

"I gave it all to Detective Cameron." Zachary's cheeks warmed. "I didn't think of making you a copy. But I can show you tonight when we're home and I have my computer. I just have my phone right now and it's hard to juggle everything."

"No, that's okay. It's Cameron you needed to convince, not me. I already knew that there was something weird going on. That Elysse had been... coerced and that Kristy's death had to be related."

"He wanted me to assure you that he was taking it seriously and the police department will follow up."

Kenzie frowned. "He wanted to assure me? Why?"

"Because it is possible that... er..."

Her eyes widened. "They think I'm in danger? Why?"

"Jordan can connect Kristy to me, since I was the one she was talking to before... she died. So he knows I am making some kind of inquiry. And if he can connect that you are the one doing the postmortem report and that you and I are together..."

"That puts you in danger more than me."

"I guess," Zachary admitted. "But the police are more concerned about you. You're an asset. I'm just... a civilian."

Kenzie chuckled. "Or worse. An irritant. They don't really think that there is any danger, do they? He wouldn't come after either of us when all we did was look into what happened to Elysse. He wouldn't know that you had any pictures of him or proof that he was involved in what happened to Elysse. All I can do is report what was found in the postmortem. Neither of us is a danger to him."

"Well, I hope that's how he sees it," Zachary agreed. "Or that he isn't even looking at either of us." But he'd had enough cases blow up at him, with the criminal trying to take him out, that he was not convinced Jordan would leave them alone. "He killed Kristy, which means he is worried and trying to obscure his trail. He probably doesn't know whether she told me anything that would connect him to Elysse's kidnapping." He fingered his phone, thinking about it. "Where was she killed? At home?"

That was how Zachary had pictured it. Kristy had called him from home, where she was relaxing on a Sunday, taking a break from her busy life. But he wasn't sure Kenzie had actually told him that detail.

"Yes, in her house," Kenzie agreed. "Why?"

"Did her killer search through her files? Paper files or computer files? Could he have figured out that she had sent me a bunch of pictures and video without her telling him?"

"The place hadn't been ransacked, but it isn't like criminals usually turn a place over like they do on TV, with stuffing ripped out of cushions and all that. They open and close drawers, rifle through piles of papers, and leave them relatively undisturbed. So yes, he probably had the opportunity to look through whatever was in her home office and laptop. She lived alone and no one reported hearing any disturbance, so he had as much time as he wanted to search her files."

"So if he didn't already know, he found out she had sent me copies of pictures and video. He might have had reason to be concerned that I would be able to identify him. He wouldn't be able to tell what pictures and videos were copied, so he wouldn't know if it was anything to be concerned about."

"But Kristy didn't send you anything related to him. She was looking for the bushy-bearded fan that had shown up at several shoots."

"It's possible that Starr was following the tour, waiting for the right opportunity to take Elysse. In fact, he probably was. If he was following the tour, he knew who Kristy was. Kristy might have caught him in several photos, and she could have just as easily been sending me pictures of him as of Marvin."

Kenzie inclined her head. "Yeah. I guess so."

"And if she had written down anything about me being hired by Dain to investigate Elysse's disappearance…"

"Then Dain could be in trouble, too." Kenzie rubbed her forehead as if she were getting a headache. She frowned. "I can ask Cameron and the investigators if there was anything to indicate that Dain had hired you… but if there was a note in a notebook, or a sticky note, or if it was in her digital filing…"

"He could have taken it from the scene or destroyed it. So we have to assume that he *does* know."

"Even if he doesn't know that Dain hired you, it's pretty easy to figure out that you are a private investigator. So he knows that you didn't just happen to be talking to Kristy because you are a fan."

It was not hard to figure out Zachary was a private investigator. He advertised the fact. Made it as easy as possible for people looking for a private investigator to find him.

"Well, this is a pretty mess," Kenzie observed. "But it's not the first time you've been in this kind of situation, and it won't be the last…"

Zachary *hoped* it wouldn't be the last.

69

Since meeting with Detective Cameron, Zachary had been calling and texting Dain without any success. This had been making him very anxious, so he was relieved the next day to receive a text from Dain just after lunch telling him that he wanted to see Zachary and Kenzie if they could make some time for him.

Zachary wasn't sure whether it was because he wanted to get an update on the investigation into Elysse's kidnapping, or to see if they knew anything about what had happened to Kristy, or maybe to show them the progress he was making on his manuscript. Social media influencers did seem to be very self-focused, so maybe he was excited about what he had written and hoped they would celebrate it with him. There was no indication in his text what he wanted to talk about.

In the end, it all boiled down to one thing. Zachary would let him know what progress they had made. How they had discovered that Elysse had, in fact, been kidnapped by Jordan Starr in a bid to pump up his company's brand and was still being terrorized by him. But the police were now on the case and no longer believed that Elysse had just gone off on vacation as she had reported. They recognized that she had been kidnapped and everything she had said had been under duress. They would find Jordan Starr, and they would put him in jail.

Elysse would be able to leave her home in Oregon without fear. Maybe Dain would be able to join her and they could rekindle their relationship. Or not, if Elysse no longer wanted to continue their relationship. She could let Dain know that calmly instead of having a big blow-up and running away from any further contact. He could have the resolution he needed and go on with his life.

Poor sap. Zachary knew what it was like to be dumped by someone he had been with for a couple of years. Even though they'd had a tumultuous relationship, even though Bridget had been scathing and verbally abusive, Zachary had still been hurt when they broke up.

Devastated.

But maybe it wouldn't be the same for Dain. He had other women in his life, after all. They had an open relationship. Maybe it wouldn't bother him as much for him and Elysse to go in separate directions. As long as he knew what had actually happened to Elysse and knew that she was okay.

It might be best if Dain stayed in Vermont and didn't go back to Oregon to be near Elysse.

When u want us? Zachary texted Dain back. *Can we bring dinner?*

He thought that would be a nice gesture. Kenzie wouldn't be free until the end of the workday. Dain was going to need some emotional support when they explained everything to him and told Dain he might be in danger himself if Jordan Starr had figured out that he was the one who had hired Zachary to investigate what had happened to Elysse.

Sure, bring chicken, Dain texted back. *How soon are you free?*

Zachary called Kenzie at the medical examiner's office so that he wouldn't be trying to text two different conversations simultaneously and sending a response to the wrong one.

"Hey, Zachary," Kenzie answered in a calm, measured voice that meant he was testing her patience. "We're still on for couple's therapy."

Zachary looked at the clock on his laptop screen. He had forgotten the instant Dain texted, that couple's therapy was that afternoon, after which they normally went out for ice cream, and didn't plan to do anything else in the evening, since therapy could be very taxing. They might not feel up to anything else afterward.

"Zachary?" Kenzie prompted.

"Shoot. I forgot," Zachary confessed. "Dain just texted and asked if we could go over there for dinner and I said yes. But I'm not sure about doing that after therapy."

"Yeah, chances are, we aren't going to want to deal with other people," Kenzie agreed, sounding irritated.

Of course she was irritated. Why would Zachary say yes to Dain when they were supposed to have therapy that afternoon?

Some days, he needed space after therapy to think things through and recharge. Sometimes, he wanted to be close to Kenzie, to do something special with her, and to show how much he appreciated her being there for him and everything that she put into the relationship. Therapy could bring up tender feelings that he wanted to act upon.

"I'm sorry," he told Kenzie. "Now I don't know what to do. Should I cancel therapy today?"

"I already have the time off. And it's too late to cancel; you need to let Dr. Boyle know at least twenty-four hours ahead of time so she can have the chance to get someone else into that time slot."

Zachary was normally frugal, but he could give up the money for that one session if he had to.

"Can't you tell Dain you'll have to see him another day? It's inconvenient if you make changes to our schedule now."

"Uh... yeah, okay." Zachary put Kenzie's call on speaker and switched to his messaging app to renegotiate with Dain. He hated having to backtrack when he had just made the arrangements. But it wasn't like Dain had gone out of his way to accommodate Zachary. In fact, he was expecting them to accommodate him on the spur of the moment and to bring dinner. Though Zachary couldn't blame Dain for that when he was the one who had offered.

Sorry, forgot we already had an engagement, he tapped out to Dain. *Tomorrow?*

Need to see you today, Dain responded almost immediately. *Urgent.*

Zachary rolled his eyes. Now what?

"He says he can't wait," he related to Kenzie. "He needs to see us today urgently. Or me, anyway."

"Do you think it really is urgent?" Kenzie challenged.

Zachary considered. Was it? Or was Dain expecting everyone else to adapt to his schedule? Being a minor celebrity might just have gone to his head and he expected everyone to jump just because he told them to. He already had Kenzie on the phone, so it would be a pain to try to call Dain and evaluate from his voice whether it was really an urgent situation or not. As far as he knew, there wasn't anything that needed to be dealt with urgently.

"I don't know," he mumbled to Kenzie. "I'm trying to negotiate by text. Give me a few seconds."

Have previous engagements, Zachary tried again. *Maybe we could phone or video chat instead?*

No! need you HERE

"He's freaking out a bit," Zachary told Kenzie. "I think I should go see him. Maybe... you could see Dr. B individually and we could do couple's next week."

"What's going on? What is he freaking out about? I don't want to see Dr. B alone. If you think it is that important, you'll have to call Dr. Boyle to tell her to scrap it."

"Okay. I will. I'll cancel, and I'll tell Dain that we'll come out for supper tonight, like I told him initially. He said to bring chicken; are you okay with that?"

"He told you to bring chicken?"

"Well, I asked if we could bring something, and he said chicken."

Kenzie sighed loudly. "Okay. So we'll go for dinner tonight and bring chicken. You don't need me to take the afternoon off."

"No. But if you need to—"

"I'm going to stay here and finish up a few things. I could use the extra time to catch up after our road trip. I'll still leave a bit early so we can get a bucket of chicken and drive out to Dain's."

"Okay. I'll get the directions. I appreciate you—"

"Don't forget to call Dr. B to cancel. I have to go."

She terminated the call abruptly. Zachary still had his mouth open to respond to her, but she was gone.

"Okay," he muttered aloud to keep himself focused and on track as the phone vibrated in his hand with another incoming message. "Call Dr. B to cancel. Then deal with Dain."

70

Eventually, Kenzie returned from the medical examiner's office. She and Zachary went to the restaurant for take-out fried chicken and then headed out on the highway toward Dain's house. The savory smell of the chicken quickly filled the car's interior and Zachary's stomach growled several times. He hoped that the smell wouldn't stay in the car any longer than the chicken was actually there. He didn't want to get into a car that smelled like fried chicken every day for the foreseeable future.

"Dain wouldn't tell you what he wanted to talk to you about?" Kenzie asked. "Or what he wanted from you? Other than fried chicken?"

"No, he said he needed to see me face-to-face. And with all that I have to show and tell him, that's probably the best thing anyway. It's hard to explain something that complex efficiently over email or a phone call. This way, he can see the backup and exactly what we're talking about. And *who,* too. He should know what Jordan Starr looks like so that if he runs into him, he knows it. He could be going by another name or approach him on some other pretense."

"Do you think Starr would really go after any of us? Dain, or you, or me?"

"We all hold pieces to the puzzle. He can't be sure what we've told each other or how much we've figured out. He got rid of Kristy, so we know he's not going to balk at violence. If he's decided to wipe out his back trail... anyone who might know enough about him to put the story together to tie him to Elysse's abduction or Kristy's murder... then we all have to be on the lookout for him."

"How do you think Dain will take it?"

"Well... as a brash young man, he'll probably think he's indestructible. Nothing can hurt him or kill him. But we'll tell him about Kristy if he doesn't already know... I hope he'll see reason and won't do anything stupid."

Zachary stared out at the highway, listening to the thrum of the tires against the asphalt and thinking it through.

"We need to let the police get up to speed and chase down all their leads. Before they can arrest Starr, they've got to find him. I hope that if he doesn't get any chance to confront any of us in the next few days, he'll have to go back to his office in Salt Lake City if he hasn't already. He's taken a couple of weeks off for the Elysse kidnapping and now has more time off to clean things up. Who knows how many times he's run out to Oregon to check on Elysse or to confront and threaten her? He should be out of vacation days."

"Unless he isn't taking them as vacation days."

Zachary's mind went to sick days. But if he were honest, he had never worked in corporate America and didn't know how it actually worked. Could Starr take off all the time he wanted to, and it just had to be classified as vacation days, sick days, or leave without pay? Or would he be warned that he was missing too much work when he hit a certain number? Would he be fired without warning?

Or was he high enough in the organization to take whatever time he wanted? Or work remotely from wherever he wanted to?

"I mean," Kenzie said, "we don't know that he is taking vacation days off for this. It's just as possible that other people at the company are in on it. What are the chances that he would do something huge like this without any help from anyone else? Or without the approval of someone else in the company, higher up in the command structure than he is?"

"You mean they aren't days off. They're just regular workdays. Get the holiday campaign going. Run off that report. Go to Vermont and kidnap that girl, torture her, put her in Mystic Mountain togs until she is discovered…"

Kenzie shrugged. "Could he do everything he has without any assistance? What about money? Was he using his own money or an expense account or company credit card? If he's using his own money, then how is he going to be repaid? He'll just get more money as that company gets bigger and more successful? That's not the way it works. Is he relying on the profit that he'll make when his company shares increase in value? Stock options? Or is he getting cash bonuses as he completes each step?"

Kenzie was right. The plan might have started higher up in the company. Or it might have started with Starr but been approved by someone further up the chain so that he could get the money and other resources he needed to carry out the abduction and ongoing threats.

"I don't know if anyone else is in on it," he admitted. "Nothing we've heard has pointed to anyone else, but… you're right… there could be someone inside the company who knows what's going on and is making sure he gets paid for his… extracurricular activities and has the freedom to travel to take care of all of this."

"Well… I guess that's up to the police to figure out. They can get the cops in Salt Lake looking into it."

"Yeah. Some stuff you can't learn on the internet. You need boots on the ground, like we did on our road trip. Most of that stuff… we couldn't have found out through phone calls and emails. We had to be there."

They were quiet for a while; Zachary focused on his driving and Kenzie gazed out the window. It wasn't a long drive, but long enough for Zachary to get wound up about where Jordan Starr was and when they would cross paths, or whether the police would find him first. Driving was normally relaxing for him, but thinking about what Kenzie had said was not.

Following the GPS and Dain's instructions, he pulled into Dain's yard. It was a modest farmhouse, not a mansion. Isolated enough that he would not have to worry about Elysse Allan fans showing up unexpectedly. Zachary tried to marshal his thoughts and line up everything he needed to present to Dain, as he had to Detective Cameron, to show him what was going on and the care Dain needed to take to make sure he was not Starr's next victim. A step-by-step progression through the facts they had uncovered, leading to the only possible conclusion. That Jordan Starr was Elysse's captor, not just six months ago, but on an ongoing basis.

Would Dain want to go after Starr himself? To hop on a plane and fly across the country to Elysse's house to be her knight in shining armor?

Zachary grabbed the bucket of chicken from the car and tried to stay focused on that and on the information he would present to Dain to keep himself from compulsively checking whether the car was properly locked, which he tried not to do if he was with Kenzie or someone else.

Kenzie joined him on the doorstep and Zachary pressed the doorbell.

He had barely taken his finger off the bell when the door opened. Dain had obviously been watching for them, eagerly awaiting his chicken.

Only it wasn't Dain who opened the door.

71

Zachary found himself staring not into the eyes of the man he had been studying on his computer screen for the last couple of days, but into the barrel of the gun held in the man's hand.

Starr changed his aim from Zachary to Kenzie and back again, making sure they both saw that he was the one with the power. He could shoot one or both with ease.

"Let's not do anything stupid," he told them with the shortened vowels of a Utah accent. "Come on inside and bring that chicken. I've been here all day and I'm starved."

Zachary glanced at Kenzie, checking to see what she wanted to do. If she wanted to run for it, he would cover her, standing in Starr's way and not letting him out the door, to give her as much time as possible. If she wanted him to cooperate, he would, watching for a way for them to get out of the predicament. Fried chicken was really a two-handed meal, so what was Starr going to do with the gun while he ate?

Kenzie gave a slight shake of her head. She didn't tense and look back at the car. He knew without words that they would go into the house and do their best once they got the lay of the land.

So he stepped in the door with the chicken, standing between

Starr and Kenzie. Subtly, so Starr would not notice and get angry about it. Just keeping her covered. Protecting his mate the best he could.

Starr sniffed the air. "Smells darn good. Is it still warm?"

"Sure," Zachary agreed. "It wasn't that long a drive."

"Stupid idiot here doesn't have a lick of edible food in the house. It's all greens and sprouts and unprocessed crap. I'm not a rabbit. When I want food, don't give me carrots and lettuce."

"This has been driving me crazy in the car," Zachary said, taking the bucket to the dining room table and pulling the lid off. "It smells so good; my stomach has been growling the whole way." He peered into the bucket. "No sprouts here," he said with a smile.

He helped himself to a drumstick. Hopefully, not Starr's favorite piece. Though there was a second. Zachary hoped to force Starr to eat two-handedly, putting down the gun. If he was that hungry, he might do it without thinking.

Zachary looked around for Dain or any sign of what had happened to him. Had he been texting with Dain earlier in the day? Or with Starr? He supposed that the request for chicken meant that it had been Starr. Not the semi-vegetarian, healthy greens-eating Dain.

There was no obvious blood spatter anywhere. Maybe Starr had just commandeered the dwelling while Dain was out of the house or out of the state. Maybe Dain was perfectly fine and didn't even know that his house had been taken over by a murderer.

Except that Starr had been texting him on Dain's phone. Dain wouldn't go anywhere without his phone. It was like Cameron had said. It was hard to imagine anyone going anywhere without a phone now. Dain wasn't as much of a social media darling as Elysse, but he was still an influencer in his own right, with thousands of followers and the need to post several times a day to keep them satisfied.

Starr motioned Zachary back from the bucket of chicken and peered inside, grabbing the second drumstick for himself. He looked over Zachary and Kenzie while he ate the first few bites, chewing vigorously and gulping the food down greedily.

"I didn't get any coleslaw or anything," Zachary said, "I hope you don't mind. You just said chicken."

"Don't want any frickin' salads," Starr agreed. "Don't ask me why they even include that stuff on the menu. People don't go there for salad."

"Exactly," Zachary agreed, nibbling at his chicken. He looked at Kenzie. "Did you want some, Kenz? You've had a long day. You must be hungry."

She rolled her eyes at him. "I don't want to eat standing up. And unlike the *men*, I do like a bit of something green. You mind if I see what's in the fridge?" she asked Starr.

His lip curled in a sneer. "You think I don't know what you're up to? You're not going into the other room by yourself." He nodded toward the bucket. "Cell phones on the table."

Neither of them moved. Starr pointed his gun at Kenzie. "You first. Cell phone. Now."

Kenzie obeyed, pulling it from her purse and setting it on the table.

Starr turned his gun on Zachary. "Now you."

Zachary took his from his pocket and set it beside Kenzie's. He hadn't expected either of them would be able to make a covert call to the police, but that was out of the question now.

"*Now* can I go into the kitchen?" Kenzie asked.

He studied her. Trying to figure out how much freedom to give her, Zachary assumed. Anything could happen once she was out of the room.

Except she had no phone and they were practically in the middle of nowhere, so it wasn't exactly like she could call for help or make a run for it.

"If you do anything that bothers me, I'm going to shoot your boyfriend."

Kenzie swallowed. When she spoke, her voice was steady, but Zachary could see the tightening of her jaw and how she was holding her body rigid.

"I just wanted something to eat. If you don't want me to go into the kitchen…"

He considered for a few seconds, and Zachary thought he would tell her to go ahead, but he decided to err on the side of caution.

"No. You can eat in here. Have some chicken or don't, I don't care. But I'm still going to shoot him if you try anything stupid."

72

What was Starr's game plan? Why hadn't he just shot them the instant they walked in the door? What was the point in keeping them alive? In standing there having chicken with them as if they were visiting neighbors who didn't know anything about him.

Maybe that was it. Maybe Starr didn't know if they knew anything. He needed to talk to them to find out what they knew and who they had talked to. If Starr were going to contain this, to keep Operation Elysse going, he needed to know how far the information had spread. He needed to plug up the leaks.

And if he found out the police already knew and were investigating him, he might decide to cut his losses.

"Where is Dain?" Zachary asked, looking around. "I don't understand what is going on here. Exactly who are you, and why..." He made a helpless gesture. "What makes you think you need to hold us at gunpoint? We haven't done anything. We just came here to have dinner with a friend."

Kenzie shifted. Zachary darted a glance at her, then looked back at Starr.

"I just don't understand what this is about," Zachary repeated. "Is this some kind of joke? I don't think it is in very good taste."

"I never did get Dain's sense of humor," Kenzie contributed. "You really had me scared at first." She relaxed her shoulders and blew out her breath. "Whatever this is about, I don't think it is very funny."

Starr's gaze shifted between Kenzie and Zachary. Zachary didn't think he was fooled, but it was the best chance they had. Feign complete ignorance. Make him reconsider the assumptions he had made. Starr probably didn't want to believe that his operation was blown. He would prefer to think he could keep it going for a few more months. Every month brought in millions. If Starr could avoid getting caught, he could enjoy whatever portion of the money and recognition was his.

"Is Dain joining us for supper?" Zachary prompted, watching Starr's eyes.

There was a very quick glance toward the staircase. So Dain was probably upstairs. That was more reassuring than a look outside or to the garage. Dain was more likely to be okay if he were in the house.

Zachary put his chicken bone on top of the bucket lid to avoid getting grease on the table, and looked into the bucket for his next choice. "It's been a long time since I had fried chicken. It's pretty good. I like this coating. It's nice and crunchy. Not soggy."

Starr motioned with the gun. "We're not here to exchange chicken recipes," he growled. "Sit down. I don't know who you think you're fooling. I know you know."

Zachary picked out a breast and sat down on the couch where Starr pointed. At least it was a leather or vinyl couch, any grease would wipe off.

And any blood.

He pushed the thought out of his mind. No one was going to get hurt. They would make Starr believe they didn't know anything. They would make him believe he was safe and he didn't have to kill them. Whatever he had done, he still had a chance to escape.

"You think I don't know you know?" Starr demanded when they were all sitting down. Zachary felt like a child, sinking down into the butter-soft couch, looking way up at Jordan Starr with the gun.

How many times, in his years in foster care, had he been in positions where he had been at the mercy of an adult or an older child with power over him, whether because of their position or just age or size? He was good at reading people. He was good at bluffing and talking his way out of trouble. Kenzie was doing a good job projecting calm and unconcern, pretending she didn't know what was happening either. That things might change any minute with Dain coming down the stairs and ending the prank.

"Is there a hidden camera?" Zachary asked, looking around. "I really think this has gone on long enough. Why don't we put the gun away and just visit until Dain decides he's ready to come down and join us?" He tore at the chicken. It *was* good, but he had trouble chewing it properly and getting it down, his throat constricted and heart pounding in his chest so it felt like there wasn't any room for the food to squeeze by. "By the time he gets down here, the food might be all gone."

"That would serve him right," Kenzie asserted.

"What are you doing here?" Starr demanded. "Exactly what is your connection with Dain?"

Zachary didn't need Kenzie's warning look to know not to reveal that he was a private investigator and Dain had hired him to investigate Elysse's disappearance. If Starr did not already know that, Zachary wasn't going to give him any other information.

"We're friends," Zachary told Starr with a shrug. "Where did we meet Dain...?" He stared into space as if trying to remember. "Was it that fundraiser...?"

Kenzie nodded. "The kidney research fundraiser...?" she suggested. "He was doing some kind of crowdfunding campaign. I never did understand all the details. I'm okay with email and posting pictures on Facebook, but all the new stuff... I can't keep up with all the other socials and how you make money. How exactly *does* an influencer make money by posting pictures?"

Zachary shook his head as if it were all beyond him, too. A couple of weeks ago, he'd hardly known anything about social influencers, sponsorships, and all the rest of it. He never would have guessed that a person could make millions just by wearing certain clothes or subtly showcasing a product in a video.

"Yeah, you're right. I think it was the kidney fundraiser. It's funny that we just clicked. Different lives, different worlds, but…"

"Sometimes you just get along with someone right away," Kenzie agreed. "Sense of humor. A love of backwoods Vermont…" She motioned toward the big window, which showcased the snow gathered in the branches of the trees.

"Photography," Zachary said, "but I'm more old school." He reached inside his jacket with his free hand to fish out his camera.

Starr's hand jerked and for a split second, Zachary thought he was a dead man. But Starr managed to stop himself before pulling the trigger. He stared at Zachary, his face white, puffing for breath.

Zachary raised his brows, looking at Starr as if he didn't know what his problem was. He twisted his camera in the air. "It's a camera, dude. Not a Glock."

"You're an idiot!" Starr exploded. "You want to get your head blown off, pulling out hardware like that? Don't you understand what is going on here?" He sputtered, nearly losing it. "This is not a joke, an act. This is not a prop. I am going to blow your flipping head off!"

Zachary restrained a snort at Starr's strong language. He displayed the camera to Starr again, hoping that in the bright light of the room, the red LED indicator would not be obvious. "It's a camera," he repeated slowly and calmly. "I'm not armed. I don't know what you think this is all about, but we were talking about *photography*. Dain had all his fancy phone stuff and social networks, and here I am with an analog camera, going old school. But art is *art*, you know? It doesn't matter if the mediums are different."

Of course it was a lie. It was not an analog camera, which Starr was bound to know if he took a good look at it. But Zachary kept it in motion, kept talking so that Jordan Starr wouldn't focus on the lie. If Zachary could keep him distracted and make him think that they only knew Dain socially and didn't know anything about what

Starr had done, maybe they had a chance to talk their way out of the situation. Or to keep him occupied until they could get help.

"I just use my phone," Kenzie said, looking back at the table where she had put down her phone. "I never did understand all that stuff about F-stops and whatnot. The phone camera is good enough for me. And it has all the filters built in. You don't have to develop it to get special effects. It's instant."

Zachary rolled his eyes. "It's just not the same," he said. "It's like comparing digital music to vinyl." He appealed to Starr. "You *know* there's nothing like vinyl, don't you? It's a whole different experience. It has depth. It has... all the background stuff. The scratches and pops can't be replicated through digital effects. Whatever you do, I would still be able to tell whether it was the real thing."

"Just shut up," Starr ordered, leveling his gun at Zachary. "Anybody ever tell you that you talk too much? Just shut up and let me think."

Zachary held the camera casually, hoping it was properly focused on the gun in Starr's hand. Starr shook his head irritably and paced, trying to sort everything out in his head. When he turned away, Zachary hit a few buttons on the camera.

Zachary darted a glance at Kenzie. She took a deep breath in and let it out again. She wasn't sure what he was doing, but it was clear she knew he was up to something.

73

Starr turned abruptly back to them. "I *know* you know," he snapped at Zachary. "I don't know what game you're trying to play, but you're not fooling me one bit. I know who and what you are. Both of you."

Zachary shrugged, inviting Starr to elaborate.

"You are a private investigator. You think I don't know that? I know that you're following me. Investigating everything I do."

"Following you? I'm not following you. I don't know what it is you think I know…"

"And you're the medical examiner." Starr pointed at Kenzie.

She nodded. "Yes, I am. Did Dain tell you that?"

"The two of you working together," Starr muttered. "There must be laws against that. You can't be sharing autopsy information with a private investigator! PIs don't even work with the police. They're not allowed to."

"No," Zachary assured him. "If I show up on a crime scene, they run me out on a rail. They don't want me to have anything to do with police investigations. And Kenzie…" He chuckled. "Do you know how many times she's told me that she won't share information on an autopsy? Almost makes me wonder why I stay in the relationship."

"Must be my cooking," Kenzie said dryly.

"But you don't make anything like this," Zachary pointed out, waving his piece of half-consumed chicken. "This is really good."

"Are you telling me you would prefer this over garlic bread?"

"Oh…" Zachary considered. "Well…" He looked over at Starr. "I'm sort of addicted to garlic bread. What about you? What's your favorite?"

"Didn't I tell you to shut up?" Starr snapped.

"Well…"

"Good luck with that," Kenzie said.

After an endless period of Starr pacing back and forth, watching out the windows and trying to get everything straightened out in his mind, he decided on the next step in his plan. Luckily, that did not involve shooting them both and leaving their bodies there, which gave Zachary some hope that Dain might still be alive.

But Starr's plan did involve tying their wrists and ankles with zip ties and leaving them on the floor while he went outside. Zachary panted, his ribs burning with the position of his arms.

"Is that it?" Kenzie asked after a minute or two of waiting for Starr to return. "Is he done? Taking off and going home?"

"I doubt it," Zachary said. "I didn't get the feeling that he's done yet." He squirmed around to get into a sitting position, allowing him to see out the very bottom of the front window, looking out to the yard and Zachary's car. He tried to keep his head low enough that Starr would not immediately see him if he looked back at the house.

"What's he doing?" Kenzie asked. She squirmed around to get into a more comfortable position, but she did not sit up so that she could see out too. She probably didn't think it would be a good idea for them to both be sitting up when Starr came back into the house.

"Something with the car… I don't know what for sure."

He watched Starr walk around the car, crouch down to look

and feel underneath it. He tried the door handles and the alarm started whooping. Zachary grimaced. His heart raced. He was already in a dangerous situation and knew it, but his body thought it was more hazardous because of the sound of his alarm going off.

"It's okay," Kenzie told him.

"Hate people messing with my car."

"I know."

Zachary was immobilized, in dire circumstances, a killer with a deadly weapon close at hand, but it was someone touching his car that bothered him. He could see the ridiculousness of it, but could not change the direction of his thoughts. "Just imagine how you would feel if it was *your* baby," he told Kenzie, referring to her red convertible, currently consigned to the garage until the weather warmed up.

Kenzie laughed, her tone bordering on uncontrolled. "He'd be in deep trouble if he touched my baby," she admitted.

Zachary gave himself a moment to envision Kenzie furiously breaking out of her restraints like a she-hulk if someone touched her car. He strained at the zip ties. He had watched a number of videos on getting out of handcuffs or zip ties, but he had not been able to master the techniques himself. He twisted and pressed, tried snapping them with a jerking movement, but was unsuccessful.

He turned his attention back outside, but he could not see Starr. "Where did he go?"

"You can't see him anymore? Is he coming back?"

Zachary looked around, but Starr was out of sight and Zachary wasn't sure what direction he had gone.

"Maybe he's leaving?" Kenzie suggested. "How long do you think we'll have to wait until help arrives?"

"Not too much longer," Zachary assured her, hoping it was true. He was relying too much on chance, knowing that technology didn't always work the way it was supposed to and people didn't always respond the way he expected them to.

"Do you want me to see if I can get over to the table and get one of the phones?" Kenzie suggested.

It wasn't impossible. Kenzie only had to scoot herself over there, stand up, turn around, and grab it with her hands behind her back. But then she needed to be able to operate the phone behind her back, and Zachary wasn't sure she would be able to. Could she send out an emergency alert? And would it be received? While, as far as he knew, all areas of the state now had 9-1-1 services, isolated areas often did not have cell coverage. If they managed to get through, would the police be able to get a GPS lock on the phone? Would it be accurate enough to find them?

74

There was movement outside and Zachary strained to see what was happening. Starr was walking back toward Zachary's car. With a toolkit and a wheeled creeper for him to slide under the car. Zachary growled angrily at the sight.

"What is it?" Kenzie asked.

"He's sliding under my car with a box of tools."

"Uh-oh."

Zachary swore, watching Starr lie down and scoot under the car. It was one thing to suspect that someone had been messing with his vehicle. It was one thing to suspect tampering; it was another to witness it firsthand. What was Starr planning? His pacing back and forth made it clear he was working out a plan. Whatever that plan was, it apparently involved tampering with something in Zachary's car.

"You can't tell what he's doing, can you?" Kenzie asked.

"No idea. Cutting my brakes. Doing an oil change. Setting a bomb. I have no idea."

"Why would he want to do something to your car?" Kenzie mused. "I understand him wanting us out of the way because we know too much, but why mess with your car?"

"Maybe he has a thing about white compacts."

"Seriously, Zachary, let's figure this out. It's not like we have anything else to do lying here."

"Aside from trying to escape."

"We can try to escape while we talk."

Zachary twisted and tried to snap his plastic restraints. "Okay," he agreed, hoping that talking about it would keep him calm and he wouldn't have a meltdown over the thought of someone installing another bomb in his car. "You, me, and Dain. He has to get rid of us. We know too much. But he can't pick us off one at a time because every time he does that, he increases the risk that the police are going to catch on and be able to catch him. It's much better to get rid of all of us at once. One investigation instead of three."

"One-third the risk," Kenzie suggested.

"Maybe. Probably not that much. But if Starr can cut the risk by half, why wouldn't he?"

"So he gets us here using Dain's phone."

"Maybe he checked out the house and decided our security was too good. So he texts me. Says it's urgent. Lures us here."

"But he still isn't sure how much we know, so he tries to figure that out. But eventually, he decides… what? It's too late to back off and say it was just a joke or prank. We tried to give him that out, but he didn't take it. So he's committed. He has to get rid of us."

Kenzie didn't say the word *kill* but, of course, they both knew what she was talking about. Zachary tried to look at the logistics. What was Starr planning to do?

"If it looks like murder, like with Kristy, that makes the police more suspicious, they go digging into it. So he wants to make it look like an accident." Zachary nodded to himself. That was it. "He wants it to look like an accident. A car accident."

They were both silent for a few minutes. Zachary tried not to think about that accident they had been in shortly after they had met. The brakes on his car had been tampered with. The resulting wreck had left Zachary concussed, hypothermic, hanging upside down from his seatbelt. Worse still, he had sustained a spinal cord injury. He was lucky there had been no permanently injured nerves. Just swelling that had resulted in temporary paralysis.

It had been terrifying.

Kenzie, luckily, had only sustained minor injuries. She had not been hospitalized at all. But if they were to go through a repeat performance, how would she fare?

Starr would leave nothing to chance. He would make sure that they were dead or very close to it before sending them over the cliff or into whatever accident scenario he had planned.

"Do you think he is cutting the brakes?" Kenzie asked.

"I don't know."

"Or weighing down the accelerator?"

Zachary didn't answer.

"I guess it doesn't really matter what he has in mind," Kenzie said a few minutes later, coming to the same conclusion as Zachary. "He's going to make sure that we don't survive it."

"Yeah."

Zachary wiggled his hands and twisted his wrists, trying to stretch or snap the plastic ties. He didn't know how long it would take Starr to complete his preparations. It would be best if they could free themselves before his return.

"There are probably knives in the kitchen," Kenzie suggested.

But they were probably too high to reach with their hands restrained behind their backs.

"Why don't you see what you can find," he told Kenzie.

"What are you going to do?"

"I'll see if I can get anywhere with the phones."

They both started to push themselves across the floor to their destinations. Zachary suspected he would need the help of the wall to get to his feet. And then... he was hoping that he would be able to set off the emergency alert sequence on one or both phones to reach the closest emergency department.

Then he paused. He could hear an engine racing. No siren, but there was a car coming down the feeder road to Dain's property.

75

"K enz...?"

She turned to ask him what he wanted, then he saw her cock her head as she heard the engines as well.

"What is it?"

"Stay down."

"What?" Kenzie stopped in her struggle to get to her feet. She looked at Zachary and then toward the window.

"Do you think...?"

"Get as low as you can. Against a wall, if you can."

"Okay."

Zachary pushed himself to the front wall of the living room. With his back against it, he lay down as flat on the floor as he could.

Starr figured out a few seconds later that he might be in trouble. Zachary heard him cursing outside, and then he ran back to the house, blasted in through the door, and looked around for his hostages, the gun in his hand once again. Zachary was the closest to him, which was good. Starr would come after him rather than Kenzie.

"You should surrender," he told Starr.

He didn't think Starr actually would. It would be nice if he did, but Zachary wasn't counting on it. He hoped to keep Starr's attention on himself rather than on Kenzie, and to wind him up so that he panicked and made mistakes.

"Shut up!" Starr shouted, focusing on him, pointing the gun at him.

"You won't be in any danger if you surrender. If you give yourself up, they'll just take you into custody. If you resist them, someone could get hurt or killed—namely *you*."

"How did they know? How did they come here?"

"I don't know. You must have tipped them off somehow. If you give yourself up—"

"Stop saying that!"

The car engines reached a crescendo as the vehicles pulled up in front of the house. Zachary couldn't see them, but he could tell they were stopping right outside. He tried to keep Starr's focus entirely on him. Not on Kenzie, not on the cops.

"Do you have any idea what you've done to Elysse?" he demanded. "How she is suffering? All for what? To boost your company's reputation? Why couldn't you approach it like any other *sane* company? Sign an endorsement deal with her. Pay her for an appearance instead of kidnapping her and locking her away for six months. What kind of a person does that?"

Starr rushed toward him, but he did not pull the trigger. He aimed a kick at Zachary instead. Zachary managed to avoid the first one, throwing himself to the side, but doing so jolted his ribs and sent pain coursing through him just as if the kick had landed. He cried out. He heard his cry echoed by Kenzie, distressed by his pain.

He tried to tell her he was okay, but couldn't get his breath back. Starr kicked again, landing a blow this time, but thankfully on the unbroken side of Zachary's rib cage. But it still caused a blinding burst of pain. Zachary howled, trying unsuccessfully to swallow his cry. Starr tried another kick and missed.

There was a metallic clunking sound. Starr turned away from Zachary, distracted, and, for a moment, he was worried that Starr was going after Kenzie for having kicked or thrown something at him.

But smoke was billowing from a canister on the floor. Starr immediately buried his eyes and nose in the crook of his elbow and made a break for the open door. Zachary pressed his face as close to the floor as possible to avoid breathing in the smoke. He could already barely breathe because of the pain.

As the smoke spread, obscuring his vision and making his eyes and nose stream, he was ten years old again, an inferno blazing around him, lungs burning with the smoke, trying to make a pocket of breathable air around his mouth. Every cough brought a new flare of pain and tears streaming down his cheeks.

"Everybody down, on the floor," came a shout, and the pounding of boots. "Let's see your hands! Hands!"

How he expected two people who were lying on the floor, bound hand and foot, choking on the smoke, to obey his command, Zachary didn't know. He tried to focus on the cops. On everything different from that Christmas Eve fire so many years ago. But he found himself slipping away, spiraling into it.

The fire, the smoke, screaming for his family to get out of the house. Thinking he was going to burn to death and never see anyone he loved again.

Strong hands picked him up by ankles and wrists and carried him out of the house. The ambulances were not there yet. Ice and snow covered the ground. Someone laid down a blanket and Zachary was placed on it, coughing uncontrollably, the cold air a fresh irritant to his throat. His hands were freed. He reached for the firefighters, begging. "Where? My family?" He couldn't get the words out.

76

"Let me go to him," a familiar voice said. Kenzie was coughing a little, but not as much as he was. "Zachary. Zachary, it's okay. Just relax your body. You're okay. Slow down. Focus on my voice. There's no fire. You're safe."

"Family," Zachary protested again, throat raw, ribs burning.

"Everyone got out of the fire. Everyone is safe."

He found her hand in his and squeezed. "Keep talking."

Kenzie coughed again, delicately, ignoring Zachary's racking coughs and whimpers of pain.

"That was quite the show you put on there. That's your new strategy? Make the guy so mad that he wants to tear you apart with his bare hands rather than firing his weapon at you?"

Zachary would have laughed if he'd been able to, but he couldn't.

"We need a doctor!" someone shouted. Kenzie squeezed Zachary's hand and let go.

"You just breathe. That's all you need to do right now. Watch him," she instructed someone else. "Try to keep talking to him so he has something to focus on. I'm a doctor, they need me inside."

Zachary wanted to tell her not to go back into the house. You couldn't go back into a burning building. But she was gone and he couldn't call her back. Zachary swallowed, trying to get rid of the burning lump in his throat and to talk again.

With the cool, fresh air and a cop talking to him, Zachary's breathing and coughing started to slow. He could see the activity around him and the flashback was fading. He looked around, blinking, trying to bring it all back into focus.

"Where's Kenzie?" he croaked.

"Dr. Kirsch? She's helping with another patient."

Zachary coughed again and curled up on his side, trying to find a position that was easier on his ribs. "Who?"

"I'm sure they'll let everyone know when things settle down. Everything is pretty chaotic right now."

"You got... you got... Starr?"

"Yeah, we got him. How are you doing there, Mr. Goldman? Can we get you anything?"

He didn't know why he should be surprised the cop knew who he was. He knew Kenzie's name, so someone had briefed him on what was going on and who was who.

"Zachary," he corrected. "And... I'm okay. Yeah. I'm fine."

"Ambulances will be here shortly. They're still a few minutes out."

Zachary sniffled, his nose still running from the tear gas. "I'm okay."

When the ambulances did arrive, Zachary made sure they went to look after the other patient first. Whoever had needed Kenzie's attention was obviously in worse shape than Zachary was.

In a few minutes, Kenzie returned to his side. "Now, how are you doing?"

"Better. How is... Dain...?"

"He's lost a lot of blood. They'll start transfusing him at the hospital. Hopefully... he'll be okay."

"It's pretty bad?"

She nodded, very serious. "It's a good thing we didn't put off the meeting until tomorrow. It would have been too late. Has anyone taken a look at you?"

"I told them you needed help with Dain."

"Well, let's see what we can find. You're breathing better."

"Yeah."

"Flashbacks on top of tear gas on top of broken ribs. That's fun."

Zachary snorted, which brought a fresh dart of pain.

Kenzie touched his cheek, then felt his pulse, her fingers laying lightly on his throat for a few seconds.

"I've seen you worse," she said lightly.

After the package bomb, for instance. And after the car crash. Zachary groaned.

"What is it?" Kenzie asked worriedly.

"My car. What did he do to my car?"

She laughed. "We'll have to figure that out. Later. You've got a ride back to town. We'll get it towed, and Jergens can look at it and make sure that everything is in order."

"I hate when people mess with my car."

"Well, at least this time, you weren't in it. I suspect that if we'd gotten into it… we would not have gotten back out."

"He was going to drive us over a cliff somewhere, wasn't he?"

Kenzie nodded. "That would be my guess."

She settled in beside him so they were sharing the blanket and she wasn't sitting directly on the snow and ice.

"Now you have to explain to me what kind of magic you did with your camera!"

Zachary grinned. He readjusted carefully, trying to find a position that was easier on his ribs. "The camera has Wi-Fi. It has a built-in sharing app that can access the contacts list on my phone and send out photos or videos using the phone signal. As long as the phone has a cell connection. Luckily, this isn't a dead zone, or I don't know what I would have done."

"Who did you send it to? I don't see how you had time to look for a contact name and send it out. You were just waving it around and clicked a button or two."

"I had already set it up to auto-send to Mr. Peterson unless I tell it not to."

"So you sent him the video and he figured out we were in trouble."

"A video of a guy waving a gun at us and making threats… yeah, it probably didn't take him long to figure out we were in trouble and to get the police moving. I should call him." Zachary patted his pockets, but didn't have his phone.

"I'll get our phones back once they've finished going through the house. I don't want to be in the way."

"Okay." Zachary put his head down again. He was exhausted. He sniffled, wishing that his nose would stop running. "Who is here? Detective Cameron?"

"Yes, he's here. And a lot of cops I don't know well. Recognize their faces, but don't know their names or have much to do with them. But they sent out a lot of firepower. Luckily didn't need it."

"Not one shot fired."

"I thought Starr was going to shoot you! Why were you provoking him?"

"To keep him focused on me. Give the police a chance to get in safely."

And to keep Kenzie safe, but he didn't say that part. She didn't want him to think that she needed to be protected. She wanted to be strong. Indestructible.

But Zachary knew that nobody was indestructible.

EPILOGUE

There was a larger crowd at the bookstore than Zachary had expected. That was good; it meant more business for Dain. Zachary supposed that with all that had happened, the book had launched successfully. The demand for anything *Elysse* had not diminished, even when she had tentatively started posting again. If anything, her return to the public eye had fueled the fires.

Dain saw Zachary from across the room and motioned to a woman assisting him, pointing Zachary out. The woman made her way across the busy store and greeted him. "You're Zachary?"

"Yes."

"Come with me. You don't need to wait for everyone else. You're a VIP."

She took him by the arm and steered him back through everyone again to reach the table where Dain was signing books and posing for selfies.

"Zachary!" Dain stood up and insisted on giving Zachary a bro hug, thumping him vigorously on the back in a way that made Zachary very grateful that his broken ribs had healed. "I'm really glad you could make it! Thank you for coming!"

"Looks like things are going very well," Zachary observed.

"Yeah. Getting lots of attention. The publisher says I'm breaking all kinds of records for a new release. They're talking to Oprah!"

"Wow, good for you. And… how are things with Elysse?" Zachary asked delicately, not sure he wanted to hear the answer.

"It's not the same as it was… I guess you'd say we broke up, but it was more like… we just couldn't get things going again. Elysse has had a lot of problems since the abduction. Of course. Anyone would. You and Kenzie know that better than anyone. But we just weren't able to… I couldn't be there for her. She needed a lot more than I was able to give. And I was working on the book, which she *kind of* doesn't like and didn't want me to do, so there was that. But we had already broken up before everything happened… so it wasn't so much breaking up as… finally walking away."

Zachary nodded. "I'm not surprised. How is she doing? Is she in therapy?"

"Quite a bit, from what I understand. I've gone a few times myself, but I don't think I have the right personality for it. I don't want to talk about what happened. I just want to move on. And never look back."

"I can relate," Zachary acknowledged. "I avoided therapy for a lot of years."

"That sounds ominous."

He shrugged. "For me… it's better to go. And the harder it is for me to go, the more I need it. Maybe someday it will feel easy to go, and then I'll know I don't need it anymore."

Dain chuckled and patted Zachary on the arm. "Well, here's hoping that day comes… for all of us."

Did you enjoy this book? Reviews and recommendations are vital to making a book successful.

Please leave a review at your favorite book store or review site and share it with your friends.

Don't miss the following bonus material:
Sign up for mailing list to get a free ebook
Read a sneak preview chapter
Other books by P.D. Workman
Learn more about the author

DON'T MISS A THING! GET THE LATEST NEWS AND A FREE EBOOK

CURRYING DEATH

KENZIE KIRSCH MEDICAL THRILLER #11

Currying Death is Book 11 in the **Kenzie Kirsch Medical Thrillers** series, a spin-off series from Zachary Goldman Mysteries, and takes place after She Once Vanished.

PREVIEW CHAPTER 1

K enzie was bent over her computer finishing up her notes and reports on the death of an elderly man, Casey Earl, when Dr. Cook approached her desk. He walked with a sense of purpose but did not have a stack of paperwork in his hands, so Kenzie straightened up expectantly. She brushed a few dark curls away from her face.

"What's up?"

"Feel like attending a death scene?"

"Sure," Kenzie agreed. She saved and closed her documents and started to tidy her desk. "What have we got?"

"Man found dead in his apartment. Paramedics were called to the scene. Nothing they could do; he'd been lying there dead for some time."

Kenzie nodded. Probably not anything too unusual about it. Someone who had died in his sleep, maybe a heart attack or stroke.

"How long is 'for some time'?" she asked cautiously. It could be anywhere from a few hours to a few weeks, and she wanted to be prepared for what she would find.

"Sometime today," Dr. Cook told her with an understanding grin. It always threw her for a loop when he smiled like that. He had the face of a movie star, not an experienced pathologist. Most of the time, she didn't really see his good looks anymore. They had worked together for a few months while Dr. Wiltshire was on medical leave, and once she'd worked over a few dead bodies with him, her consciousness of his appearance had faded. She didn't notice it unless he did something like smile at her in that relaxed, understanding way.

Whew. Zachary was lucky she didn't believe in office romances.

"Nice and fresh," Kenzie approved. "That's good. Looks like natural causes?"

Cook pursed his lips. "I will leave that up to you to determine; I would not want to bias you in any way."

Of course not. Kenzie nodded her agreement. "I'll let Carlos know we've got a transport. He and George can stand by for when I am done."

"I already paged him. He should be there by the time you're ready for him."

"Great." Kenzie opened her mouth to ask for the address when a text arrived on her phone. When she swiped the screen to reveal it, she saw it was the information she needed. He must have sent it as he had approached her desk, but had taken a minute to arrive. She read the address and nodded. "Okay, thanks. I'll get on this."

If it was pretty clear that it was a natural death, Kenzie should have the death scene cleared and the body back at the medical examiner's office within a couple of hours.

+++

Kenzie parked her "baby," a cherry red convertible, in front of the apartment building, ignoring the tow-away zone. The parking permit hanging from her rearview mirror identifying her as being from the medical examiner's office would prevent her car from being impounded. At least, it should. She popped the trunk to retrieve her small scene-of-death kit. She would be quickly in and out. The body would not need to be autopsied immediately. It might not require an autopsy at all if the man was elderly and his doctor informed her that he had a history of heart disease or was being treated for some other potentially fatal condition.

There was an elevator to the third floor. A good size for transport. Everything looked like it would fall into place, and they would not have any difficulties. She walked down the hall to apartment 302 and found the door standing open. Peering in, she could see the paramedics standing in the living room chatting while waiting for her arrival. She nodded and stepped in. She was not familiar with the paramedics, so she introduced herself. They would not expect a stranger to walk in off the street, but sometimes, people got overly curious and stepped into death scenes without authorization.

"Dr. Kenzie Kirsch," she advised them, holding out her hand. "Assistant Medical Examiner."

"Oh, doctor." The female paramedic shook her hand. "Thank you for getting here so quickly. Sometimes we have to hang out for hours."

Roxboro was a small town, so they really shouldn't have to wait a significant amount of time at any death scene. Except that being a small town meant that there were a limited number of people who could do the job, and if there were several deaths to attend to in a day, there might be a delay in getting to one of them. But that rarely happened. Since Kenzie didn't know the paramedic, she might have moved there from the city, where it was more likely that she would have to wait for a death scene investigator to arrive.

"Great, well, if you would like me to—" Kenzie stopped herself and studied the two other people in the room. A young man and woman in their late twenties or early thirties. The man's children? Grandchildren? Maybe one of them was a nursing care provider or aide? "Hi. I'm sorry. I'm Dr. Kenzie Kirsch. Medical examiner's office. Are you the ones who discovered the body?"

They both nodded.

"I'm Rachel Evans," the young woman introduced herself. She hugged herself tightly. "This is kind of weird. I'm a nurse practitioner."

"Mr. Robertson's care worker?" Kenzie asked expectantly.

"No." She shook her head vigorously, her eyes widening. "No, I was his girlfriend."

"Oh, I'm sorry." Kenzie's cheeks heated. How much younger than Robertson was his girlfriend? She didn't like putting her foot in her mouth like that. She should know better than to make assumptions. "I just assumed when you said you were a nurse…"

"No." The pretty blonde was flushing as well. "I should have told you. I don't know why I said I was a nurse before I told you about our relationship. I just mean, that's what is so weird. I deal with sick people, deal with death all the time, but I feel like… I don't know. It was just so surprising to find him like that."

Kenzie nodded understandingly. "It's not the same when it is someone you know. If he wasn't in your care, you didn't think of him that way. Had he been ill for a long time? Actually—" Kenzie held up her hand to prevent Rachel from answering the question. "Let me examine the body and the scene before you say anything. I don't want to be influenced by anything else." She turned to face the other person in the room, the young man. "And are you…?"

She didn't want to put her foot in it again by asking him if he was Mr. Robertson's son, so she left the sentence hanging, waiting for him to complete it.

"I'm his roommate."

"Oh, okay." Kenzie felt uneasy as she looked toward the bedroom. If the girlfriend and the roommate were both in their early thirties, then she had might have been wrong in her assumption that the man who had died had been elderly like Casey Earl, whose file she had just closed, or even middled-aged. He was probably around their age. "What did you say your name was?"

"Alex Collins."

"Okay. If you would just stay out here…" Neither of them appeared to be inclined to follow her into the bedroom. "Which room is it?"

"Last one at the end of the hall."

PREVIEW CHAPTER 2

Kenzie nodded and stepped away to examine the body. She didn't want to be influenced by anything else they might have to say. One of the paramedics, the woman, trailed along behind her. Always best if there were two witnesses to corroborate each other's testimony if there were ever any questions as to what had taken place at the death scene.

Kenzie went through the door standing open at the end of the hall. The room was warm, the blinds drawn, like he had still been sleeping, maybe feeling sick. Or maybe he was a shift worker. He could be a medical professional like his girlfriend, someone she had met on the job.

Robertson was still in the bed. The paramedics had not moved the body to the floor to examine him or to do CPR. They knew a dead man when they saw one. Robertson lay as if asleep, partially on his side. He was a young man, like his girlfriend and roommate.

It was a queen-size bed that took up most of the small room. There was already a faint odor of death. He had been there most of the day, if she had to guess just by the stuffiness of the room. She moved closer to him, pulling on gloves. In the artificial lighting, his skin seemed to have a yellowish cast. He was overweight, puffy and bloated, his belly hanging out from under the t-shirt he had worn to bed. Someone who had not, at first glance, taken good care of himself.

Kenzie touched his neck to confirm death. His flesh was waxy. Rigor had set in. Nothing about the body suggested that it had been moved after death. Kenzie looked slowly around the room. There were several pill bottles on the side table, which she examined one at a time. A statin for high cholesterol. An SSRI antidepressant. Xanax for anxiety. All prescribed by the same doctor.

Kenzie pulled evidence bags out of her scene of death kit and sealed each one individually. She looked through the drawer of the side table to see if there was anything more. She found over-the-counter remedies. Antacids, allergy pills, painkillers, cold and sinus. The same as she would find in practically any bedroom or bathroom cabinet. She bagged each one.

Pulling out her phone, Kenzie looked up the prescribing physician online and called his office.

"Dr. Brandon is with a patient at the moment," the receptionist advised. "Did you want to set up an appointment?"

"This is Dr. Kirsch from the medical examiner's office. I need to talk to him about the death of one of his patients."

"Oh, dear!" the receptionist sounded concerned. "I'm sorry to hear that. I will have him call you back. Can I get your number? And the name of the patient so he can review the file before calling you?"

"Patient's name is Scott Robertson." Kenzie gave her phone number. "If I could get him to call me back as soon as possible. I am at the death scene right now, and I don't want to release it until after I have talked to Dr. Brandon."

"I'll try to have him call you before his next patient. We do have a busy practice…"

"I understand that. And hopefully, he does not have the ME's office calling him about too many of them. It is quite important that he take the time to call me back."

"I will let him know."

Kenzie sighed. "Thank you."

There wasn't much else for her to do. She would do a full examination of Robertson in the morgue, but it appeared that he had not been in good health and there were no preliminary indications that it was anything other than a natural death.

The room was not exactly neat, but there was no sign of any violence there, either. No sign of a struggle. Robertson was in bed, where he had likely been since the night before. There were no visible injuries. His laptop sat on his desk, along with his phone and a few other items that any self-respecting burglar would have taken.

As she looked around the room, there was a noise in the closet. Kenzie froze, her heart racing.

Was there someone in there? Even though she had been thinking of a burglar, there was no sign of any burglary. If it had been burgled, why would the thief have stayed in the room for hours to risk discovery by the girlfriend or roommate? Obviously, he couldn't show himself once they had shown up, and then the paramedics had come, and then Kenzie, so there hadn't been any time in which someone could sneak out from the time the body was discovered.

Kenzie had heard of cases where a burglar had fallen asleep in the middle of his burglary and been discovered at the scene. She looked at the bed, but there was no sign that anyone had been sleeping there other than Robertson. She didn't think that a burglar would have lain down next to a corpse. But then, she wouldn't have thought they would lay down at all, much less fall asleep in the midst of a burglary.

"Is somebody there?" she asked in a loud voice.

The paramedic, who had followed her to the bedroom but was stationed outside the door due to the lack of space inside the room, stuck her head in the door.

"Did you call me?"

"No, there's... I think there's someone in the closet."

The paramedic looked at the door, closed most of the way but still slightly ajar. She turned and shouted back to the others in the living room. "Is there anyone else in the apartment?"

Kenzie could hear Rachel and Alex coming down the hall

toward them, arguing about something. It sounded like an old argument, something they had hashed over many times before and barely had the energy to get mad about now.

"You know she isn't allowed in there! You're supposed to keep track of her," Rachel insisted.

"I do. Who left the door open? It wasn't me."

"You're not supposed to let her roam everywhere."

Alex marched into the bedroom, forcing Kenzie to step back so that she was squeezed against the bed. He paid no attention to her and walked over to the closet door, pulling it open with a whoosh.

"Cuddles!" He snapped. "Get out of there! You know you're not supposed to be in there!"

Kenzie couldn't help grinning as he bent over to push things around the bottom of the closet, coming out with an armful of fluff.

"This is Cuddles," Alex said unnecessarily. The fluffy tricolor cat glared at Kenzie, ears folded back. "Sorry. She's not supposed to be in here; she must have snuck in while we were calling the paramedics. We were both kind of in a panic. We weren't expecting… something like this."

Now that he had retrieved the cat, he stopped and stared at Robertson's body on the bed. His cheeks turned pink and he swore.

"I didn't mean to just barge in here like that. I kind of forgot myself… I'm sorry." He shook his head.

"If you could just step out with Cuddles, that would be great. We don't want her contaminating the scene or getting in the way."

"I told you!" Rachel was saying in the hall. "If you're going to have a cat, you need to keep it shut in your room. It can't just be wandering all over the apartment. I told you before that she aggravates Scott's allergies!"

She suddenly went quiet.

"Well, she isn't going to aggravate them anymore, is she?" Alex sighed. "I _am_ sorry. I said that. Neither of us was watching her when we went to call the ambulance and answered the door. She just snuck in. It was unintentional. Normally, she couldn't get into Scott's room; that was why she was so curious about it."

"She shouldn't have the run of the apartment. You shouldn't have even gotten the cat while he was living here. It's common courtesy. You talk to the people in the household before you bring an animal in. Scott would never have agreed to a cat. His allergies were so bad."

So Cuddles was the reason for the antihistamines in the side table. Kenzie felt sorry for Robertson, who had not been in good health, to have had this additional trial to deal with. Not just the allergy, but the ongoing fight with his roommate about it and the contention between his girlfriend and his roommate. It wouldn't have been easy for him to deal with on top of his illness.

"Why don't we go back out to the living room," she suggested. "It is going to be a while before I can transport the body. I may as well ask a few questions while I am waiting."

Currying Death is Book 11 in the *Kenzie Kirsch Medical Thrillers* series, a spin-off series from *Zachary Goldman Mysteries*, and takes place after *She Once Vanished* and can be purchased at pdworkman.com

ABOUT THE AUTHOR

P.D. Workman is a USA Today Bestselling author, winner of several awards from Library Services for Youth in Custody and the InD'tale Magazine's Crowned Heart award, and has published over 100 mystery/suspense/thriller and young adult books, including stand alones and these series: Auntie Clem's Bakery cozy mysteries, Reg Rawlins Psychic Investigator paranormal mysteries, Zachary Goldman Mysteries (PI), Kenzie Kirsch Medical Thrillers, Parks Pat Mysteries (police procedural), and YA series: Tamara's Teardrops, Between the Cracks, and Breaking the Pattern.

Workman loves writing about the underdog, who the reader may love or hate. She has been praised for her realistic details, deep characterization, and sensitive handling of the serious social issues that appear in all of her stories, from light cozy mysteries through to darker, grittier young adult and mystery/suspense books.

> P. D. Workman, does not shy from probing the deep psychological scars of childhood trauma, mental illness, and addiction. Also characteristic of this author, these extremely sensitive issues are explored with extensive empathy, described with incredible clarity, and portrayed with profound insight.
>
> — —KIM, GOODREADS REVIEWER

Some of Workman's titles have been translated into Spanish, French, Portuguese, German, and Italian.

Workman began writing at an early age and is a prolific reader as well as writer. She is also passionate about teaching and learning, expresses her creativity through art and cooking, and loves exploring the Calgary parks and green spaces where the Parks Pat Mysteries are set. She was a legal assistant for many years and has done extensive charitable work.

Workman was born and raised in Alberta, Canada, and is married with one adult son.

———

Please visit P.D. Workman at pdworkman.com to see what else she is working on, to join her mailing list, and to link to her social networks.

———

If you enjoyed this book, please take the time to recommend it to other purchasers with a review or star rating and share it with your friends!

tiktok.com/@pdworkmanauthor

facebook.com/pdworkmanauthor

x.com/pdworkmanauthor

instagram.com/pdworkmanauthor

amazon.com/author/pdworkman

bookbub.com/authors/p-d-workman

goodreads.com/pdworkman

linkedin.com/in/pdworkman

pinterest.com/pdworkmanauthor

youtube.com/pdworkman

patreon.com/pdworkmanauthor

reamstories.com/pdworkmanauthor